COMES THE AVENGER

Dev could feel the power surging around him, through him, felt the challenge and the pounding bloodlust of single combat on a scale no mere human ████ ████ ███wn. He stood i████████████████████ ▒ to the mounta███████████████████ . . . and throug███████████████████▒s, DalRiss an█████████████████ike parts of th███████████████ ██ he would stretc███ ███ ███ hand.

In a sense, Dev's mind was scattered across the entire combined fleet. He could feel the flutter of probing, targeting radar, feel the prick and stab and sting of beams and missiles, hear the steady background roar of thousands of voices speaking, ordering, acknowledging, shouting, pleading, praying at once . . .

It was like being God.

WARSTRIDER

SYMBIONTS

WILLIAM H. KEITH, JR.

AVON BOOKS • NEW YORK

WARSTRIDER: SYMBIONTS is an original publication of Avon Books. This work has never before appeared in book form. This work is a novel. Any similarity to actual persons or events is purely coincidental.

AVON BOOKS
A division of
The Hearst Corporation
1350 Avenue of the Americas
New York, New York 10019

First AvoNova Printing: April 1995

AVONOVA TRADEMARK REG. U.S. PAT. OFF. AND IN OTHER COUNTRIES, MARCA REGISTRADA, HECHO EN U.S.A.

Printed in the U.S.A.

RA   10   9   8   7   6   5   4   3   2   1

Prologue

It was early morning and the tiny, arc-brilliant disk of Alya A was just rising above the mountains to the east, setting golden clouds aflame in a silver-and-violet glare that touched the domes and upthrust commo towers of the Imperial base with white flame. A storm the night before had left puddles of highly acidic rainwater steaming on the pavement. That once-smooth surface was going to need replacement soon; the elements on the world called ShraRish were hard on structures and materials fabricated by Man.

Inside the perimeter fence that surrounded the human base, a warstrider stood watch, an Imperial KY-1001 Katana, five and a half meters tall and massing thirty tons, its jet black, armored hull bristling with articulated lasers and missile pods. Servos whined as one great, flanged foot lifted clear of the pavement, then set down again with a heavy thud, a three-meter step. External sensors were fully deployed, scanning in a complete circle around the lumbering machine.

Shosa Shigetaro Tsuyama had been on duty that morning since the end of the first watch. His number two aboard the two-slotter Katana was *Chu-i* Yoshikata Sanada, jacked into the strider's right-side pod. At the moment, Sanada had control of the Katana's main gun, the big, blunt 150-MW laser in its universal mount set beneath the strider's flattened, aircraftlike hull, while Tsuyama had reserved piloting functions and the secondary weapons to himself. Briefly, he halted the Katana's pacing and focused his main sensor array toward the sunrise.

Linked through the web of nano-grown threads riding in and over the folds of his cerebral cortex, jacked into the Katana's artificial intelligence through feeds plugged into sockets behind each ear and at the base of his neck, Tsuyama was for the moment completely unaware of his flesh-and-blood body, tucked away within its coffinlike command slot inside the warstrider's hull. As far as he was concerned, *he* was the warstrider, the big combat machine's precise and graceful movements guided directly by his brain's neural impulses, which were rerouted through his cephlink and the Katana's AI before they reached his spinal column.

The sun climbed slowly higher, clearing the mountains and brightening in his vision until the automatic filters in his optics cut in. Beyond the blasted patch of naked ground staked out by the electrified perimeter fence, the ground cover, ruffled clumps of gold and yellow, began its writhing dance.

Sugoi, he thought. The Nihongo word could mean marvelous or wonderful, but the taste he gave it now in his mind carried the connotation of weird, even ghastly. Tsuyama longed for a decent world, one where a man could breathe the air and where the plants didn't crawl, where there were colonist girls to jack with and where the native population didn't look like some horrid mixing of eyeless monstrosities best left in the blackness of the ocean depths.

With an inward sigh, he checked the time. Another two hours to go. Warstrider sentry duty here, he decided, was a complete waste of time. The security watch behind the perimeter fence could just as easily have been left to robots or to the automated laser cannons in their teleoperated turrets. The DalRiss were harmless, and everyone knew that the Xenophobe on ShraRish was dead.

Everyone.

"Shosasan?" his number two said over the strider's intercom. "Are they sure the Xenophobe here is dead?"

The sublieutenant might have been echoing Tsuyama's own thoughts.

"Certainly, *Sanadasan*. The creature is no more. Otherwise it would have eaten us in the night, *neh*?"

Things weren't quite that simple, of course. During the past half century, the life-form originally labeled "Xenophobes" had been encountered on half a dozen inhabited worlds of the Shichiju. Their seemingly irrational attacks on human colonies, the mass murders of entire populations on planets like Herakles and Lung Chi, were assumed to be the result of some xenophobic twist in their psychologies, hence their name. Contact, when it was made at last, had demonstrated that the Xenos—

renamed "Nagas" after the pacific serpent deities of Hindu mythology—had not even been aware of humans as intelligent individuals. Indeed, their introspective and strangely inverted worldview had kept each world-Naga from realizing that there was any intelligence, any *life* in its entire inside-out universe of Rock and not-Rock other than itself.

The DalRiss also had an odd way of looking at things, though their worldview didn't seem so alien to Tsuyama as did that of the Naga. They, at least, possessed a technology of sorts, and cities, and starcraft . . . though they seemed to have developed that technology along almost entirely biological lines, breeding their machines rather than manufacturing them.

"*Shosasan!*" Sanada sounded worried.

"What is it, *Sanadasan*?"

"I . . . I think something is moving out there."

"Where?"

"At zero-eight-five degrees. Just outside the fence."

Almost directly into the rising sun. Tsuyama squinted against the glare, dazzling even through his stopped-down optics. Briefly, he shifted to radar, then to ladar ranging, and finally to infrared, heavily filtered. "I see nothing but the city," he told Sanada, interpreting the radar and laser returns as DalRiss buildings. The alien city, if that was what that strange clumping of organic forms really was, lay just beyond the perimeter fence to the east.

"Something is moving there! I'm sure of it!"

"*Kuso!* Everything on this accursed planet moves!" Motion sensors here were all but useless, fooled by the peculiarly twitching plant life. Even the DalRiss buildings—if you could call them that—could move at times. Tsuyama had seen one once, slowly gliding into the nearby city like an enormous slug.

The DalRiss moving about? Possible. Even probable, though the aliens, like most of the rest of the life on this star-baked hothouse of a world, got much of their energy directly from sunlight and rarely stirred until later in the day. Certainly the Rebellion posed no threat, this far from the Shichiju. Or so he and Sanada had been repeatedly told. . . .

Still, Tsuyama was fully on his guard now. While the Rebellion that was tearing the Terran Hegemony apart was a long,

long way from ShraRish, he'd still heard plenty of rumors brought in by the shipjackers aboard freighters and escorts that continually came and went between the Shichiju and the twin Alyan suns. According to some stories, the rebels and their so-called Confederation had won a battle against Imperial forces on a planet called Eridu . . . and during the battle the Eriduan Naga had appeared from underground, attacking Imperial forces as though it had allied itself with the enemy. Even stranger things were rumored to have happened in a space battle a few months ago in the Heraklean system. The cargo jacker who'd whispered that story to Tsuyama had insisted that an Imperial Ryu-class carrier had been destroyed. Ridiculous, obviously . . . and yet the rumors, as they so often seemed to, were taking on a greater and greater life of their own.

A rebel treaty with aliens? No one seriously believed that creatures as alien as the Naga or the DalRiss could understand the intricacies of human politics . . . or care enough about them to ally themselves with one side or the other. But here, in this harshly alien setting, it was possible to imagine almost anything. . . .

An alarm shrilled in Tsuyama's mind, a harsh ululation relayed through the Base Military Command Center. Warnings scrolled down the right side of his visual field; something . . . something *big* was coming through the fence.

Tsuyama urged the Katana into a lumbering run, thumping across the uneven pavement to take the target, whatever it was, out from between the strider and the rising sun. "*Shiro Hana! Shiro Hana!*" sounded over his communications link, the code name for his patrol. "Fence breach, section two-one! What do you see?"

It *looked* like one of the bizarre, living DalRiss buildings, tangled in the fence, but Tsuyama wasn't sure enough of what he was seeing to want to report it. The fence, eight meters tall, was a crisscrossed weave of conductive ferrofilament, each line thread-slender but with a superconducting core that charged the entire structure with high-amperage current. The . . . the building, if that was what it was, had blundered into the fence forty meters from the nearest gatehouse, snapping the lower portion of the mesh in a crackling haze of sparks and lightning.

DalRiss buildings—when they were stationary, at least—had always reminded Tsuyama of enormous gourds or summer squash, shiny, smooth-surfaced, organic shapes eight or ten meters long and perhaps half that in diameter. Moving, they appeared more worm- or sluglike, crawling along with slow-motion contractions of their bellies that could propel them at a good half kilometer per hour or so across level ground.

The front end of the one on the fence gaped like a distended, open mouth; less identifiable growths, like great blisters or air sacs, were scattered randomly across its back. Ancestors! Was the thing sick?

It was still twitching as the lightning played across it, but surely it must be dead by now, the body convulsing with the arcing current. But another DalRiss construct was pressing up close by . . . and beyond that another . . . and another . . .

"Command Center!" he called. "This is *Shiro Hana*! It . . . it looks like DalRiss buildings on the move. Gods! The whole city is moving! Coming this way!"

"*Muri-yo!*" Ops Command snapped back. "That's impossible!"

"It's true! I see ten . . . twelve of those building-creatures! They're smashing through the fence!"

With a final crackle of electricity, a twenty-meter section of the fence went down. Three of the DalRiss buildings lay partway into the compound, motionless now, but the others were still coming, sliding over the dead bodies of their fellows like enormous, shell-less, cave-mouthed snails.

From his new vantage point, Tsuyama could see that hundreds of the huge, slow gourd creatures, the entire DalRiss city, were moving now, all traveling in the same direction. The place where the city had rested was almost deserted, a barren and rugged expanse of rock so pocked with holes it looked like a granite sponge.

"All units! All units!" sounded over the comlink. "Code Priority One. Weapons release!"

From behind Tsuyama and to his right, a turret rotated, tracking, then fired, the laser pulse superheating dust and air in a dazzling streak of blue light accompanied by a thunderclap. A massive, wet chunk of one of the moving gourds spun through the air, but the thing kept coming.

"Fire, *Chuisan!*" Tsuyama yelled over the strider's ICS. "Open fire!" He loosed a salvo of M-21 rockets, sending them slashing into the tangle in the perimeter breach on trails of fire. Sanada triggered the main laser an instant later, and in seconds the advancing wall of DalRiss constructs was masked by a churning cloud of smoke and steam.

Other parts of the fence were going down now, despite the barrage of laser fire and missiles from the base defenses. It was as though the entire alien city had suddenly decided to launch an unprovoked attack against the Imperials on ShraRish.

"Fire!" Tsuyama yelled, his cephlinked voice shrill with growing panic. "Fire! *Fire! . . .*"

Chapter 1

It was Dai Nihon *that exploited Man's first few, tentative steps into space from Earth's cradle,* Dai Nihon *that built the first orbital factories and Lunar mines,* Dai Nihon *that developed the first Quantum Power Taps, subsequently making possible the miracle of entering the* Kamisama no Taiyo, *the Godsea that gave Man the stars.*

How strange, then, that Dai Nihon's *children throughout the Shichiju grow restless, when Greater Japan remains the fountainhead of technological innovation. Or perhaps it is not so strange after all. Children often grow impatient with the wisdom of their elders and need to be reminded of their* on, *their moral and devotional obligations to parents and Emperor.*

—Man and the Stars: A History of Technology
Ieyasu Sutsumi
C.E. 2531

Falling through star-scattered night, the Confederation destroyer *Eagle* had already matched course with the two targets.

White plasma tinged with violet glowed in the throats of her aft thrusters, then faded. *Eagle* would be within visual range of her prey within minutes.

Dev Cameron was linked into the destroyer's tactical program. His body lay comatose within one of the ship's command link modules, but through the metallic traceries of the cephlink, his awareness was centered within the virtual reality of *Eagle*'s combat direction center. In his mind's eye, he stood with the ship's senior bridge officers, as glowing paths traced themselves in the air above a 3-D projector.

Voices murmured at the edge of awareness, spills from other channels, reminders that he was part of a network of hundreds of people working the ship. *Eagle*'s AI would see that he heard those conversations he needed to hear. Printed data scrolled past his awareness as well, words and figures overlaying the edge of his vision describing range, approach vectors and velocity, and the design and weaponry of the two ships ahead. Most of the information was being relayed to *Eagle*'s CDC from a small fleet of remotes, meter-long probes directed by ViRcom-linked pilots aboard the destroyer, fanning out ahead of the ship, and now closing to within a few hundred kilometers of the targets.

His first guess had been correct. The Imperial ships were a freighter and an escort. Though details were tough to glean at this distance, *Eagle*'s AI estimated an eighty percent chance that the freighter was a Type IV, grossing at least forty-five thousand tons, with an even higher probability that the escort was a Chitose-class corvette. They were inbound toward New America; it had been their bad luck to emerge from K-T space within half a million kilometers of where *Eagle* had been lurking, well beyond the immediate response radius of any of the Imperial ships orbiting the planet.

"They've detected us, Captain," Lieutenant Commander Kelly Grier reported. She was *Eagle*'s bridge scan officer and was receiving data feeds from twenty tech stations and several remotes. "The corvette has gone end-for-end and is decelerating, putting itself between us and the freighter."

"I see it," Dev replied, watching the symbols shift on the 3-D display. "He's going to fight. Weapons!"

"Ready to fire," Lieutenant Commander Tomid Messier,

Eagle's senior weapons officer, snapped back. "In missile range in thirty seconds."

"I want a single Starhawk," Dev told him. "Canister warhead, and I want a cripple, not a kill. Put your best operator on it."

"I'll take the bird in myself, Skipper."

"Grier? How long do we have to make a clean getaway?"

Dev glimpsed a flicker of alternate projected courses and situations in front of the sensor officer's slender, blond-headed analogue, sensed rather than heard the rustle of parallel computations through her linkage. "Twenty-eight minutes, Captain. If we're not aboard by then, there are at least two Impie destroyers at New America that would be able to intercept us on the way out, no matter what evasive action we took."

"Not very long. We're going to have to hustle, people. Engineering!"

"Yes, sir!"

"Acceleration to four Gs."

"Four Gs, aye, aye, Captain."

"That'll make docking a problem," *Eagle*'s executive officer observed. Her name was Lisa Canady, and she was a full commander only recently transferred to *Eagle* from the Confederation Yards at Rainbow. "We're going to have a hell of a time matching velocities. Especially with the corvette."

"We'll lose the corvette if we have to," Dev told her. "I want that freighter."

"We have a long-range visual from Remote Five," Lieutenant Grier reported. "Confirm the escort is Chitose-class, INS *Teshio*. And I'm picking up radar originating from New America. They'll see us in another thirty seconds."

That was how long it would take those radar signals—or the call for help that was certainly flashing toward the planet from both targets—to reach New America across nine million kilometers.

Downloading a command code from his personal RAM, Dev opened a new window-world in his linked awareness. He was still in *Eagle*'s CDC but looking into night blackness strewn with stars. Brightest was the primary, 26 Draconis A, a yellow sun slightly brighter and hotter than Sol; Draco B, a red dwarf, glowed like a sullen ember in the distance, while the dim and distant third member of the trinary system was invisible from this angle. Centered in the window, the fourth planet in A's five-world retinue was a gleaming spark with a tiny companion: New America and its moon, Columbia. The Imperial ships were invisible at this distance, of course, marked on the display by a blinking red square encompassing both world and moon and indicating unidentified but presumed hostile fleet elements.

Almost directly between New America and the *Eagle*, the images of the two ships the rebels were pursuing had been captured by one of the remote, high-speed probes launched minutes ago. They appeared toy-sized, their edges white-lit in the glare of 26 Draco A. Course and speed data glowing alongside each showed that the corvette was indeed slowing, blocking *Eagle*'s approach while allowing its larger consort to continue falling toward the planet.

A suicide's choice. A Chitose corvette massed nine hundred tons to *Eagle*'s eighty-four thousand. One salvo from *Eagle*'s forward laser batteries would leave the escort a riddled, airless hulk.

"We should smash the goking bastards."

Dev wasn't sure who'd muttered those words over the command link. He could have checked with *Eagle*'s AI, but it didn't really matter. "Steady there," he said. "Our target is the freighter. If we stop to play with that corvette, we'll be doing exactly what they want."

Downloading another command, Dev returned to the CDC. He could feel the tension building among the officers in the linkage, in the clipped exchanges, in the lack of the usual bridgelink banter. That was to be expected. Many of the officers and crew members aboard *Eagle*, including both Grier and Messier, were New Americans. It must be especially hard for them, Dev thought, to be operating within sight of their homeworld, unable to do a thing about the Imperial battlefleet holding it captive.

Well, the war had been hard on everyone, and they all knew things were going to get worse before they got better. It was a bitterly unbalanced struggle. The *Shichiju*—"The Seventy," a term that had been out of date for some time, now—numbered seventy-eight populated worlds in the seventy-two star systems governed by the Terran Hegemony, the nominal government which in turn was anchored in place by the military might of

Dai Nihon, the empire of Greater Japan. So far, just eleven of those worlds had declared their independence by signing the Confederation's Declaration of Reason, and of those, two of the most important, Eridu and New America, had promptly been occupied by Imperial forces.

Until just a few months ago, New America had been the capital of the rebel Confederation, the spiritual rallying point for all of the systems that had so far broken with Hegemony and Empire. Almost fifty light years from Sol, New America was one of the richest of the Shichiju's worlds, with no fewer than three separate colonies—North American, Cantonese, and Ukrainian—and one of the precious few planets discovered so far with a native ecology where men could live without having to terraform climate and atmosphere to human specifications.

The Empire's decision to invade New America had been a major escalation in what until that point had been little more than sparring, a contest of skirmishes, words, demands, and minor armed incidents testing willpower and resolve rather than an outright war. The invasion had marked a turning point in the war, one bearing the promise that the purchase price of Confederation independence would not be cheap.

A second escalation had occurred at the world called Herakles, a few months later. The Confederation government, fleeing the debacle at New America, had taken refuge in a system abandoned by man decades earlier. At least part of the reason for that decision had been the presence of the Xenophobe; Dev had managed to make contact with the strange being, had enlisted its aid in the war against the Empire. Almost certainly, the Naga was incapable of comprehending such human concepts as "allies" or "war," but with the Naga joined directly with Dev's nervous system, the two of them had created . . . something new, something smarter and more powerful and far more dangerous than man or Naga alone.

That symbiosis—Dev still had trouble confronting the memory of that time—had ended with the obliteration of a major Imperial battlefleet. Just three enemy ships had escaped to spread the news of a terrible and incomprehensible weapon in the rebel arsenal on Herakles. Early hopes that the Battle of Herakles might end the fighting and establish independence for the Confederation worlds had been dashed, however, when the

Imperial Staff had announced that there could be no dialogue, no peace, and no quarter for traitors. The war was going to continue for a long time, with Naga participation or without.

So far as New America was concerned, the Confederation would be returning there one day; the world, its resources, its people were too valuable to the Rebellion to simply abandon them to the Hegemony and its Imperial masters. That day was likely to be awhile in coming, however. The infant Confederation Navy mustered a fraction of the number of ships on the Imperial lists, and *Eagle*—formerly the Imperial destroyer *Tokitukaze*—was the rebels' single most powerful warship, dwarfed in size and firepower by the Empire's cruisers and kilometer-long dragonships. In the meantime, the Confederation would have to limit itself to hit-and-run strikes against lightly defended Hegemony outposts.

And commerce raiding. The glowing starpoints on the 3-D navigational graphic flashed out, replaced by a combat display, gleaming colored lights floating against blackness. *Eagle*'s weapons systems showed full readiness.

"Identity of corvette *Teshio* confirmed," *Eagle*'s communications officer reported. "They're hailing, demanding identity codes."

"No reply," Dev said. "They know we're up to no good."

"We're in range, Captain," Messier reported. "Starhawk Three is powered up and ready to accept link."

"And target is launching," Grier added. "Two . . . no, make that four missiles. Definitely remote-piloted, probable Starhawk class."

New points of light appeared on the combat display. The pace of data flow, of urgent, low-voiced exchanges between members of the bridge crew and with the enlisted personnel manning stations throughout the ship increased. It was often said, Dev remembered, that life in the military during wartime consisted mostly of sheer boredom, punctuated by rare, brief interludes of stark terror.

The terror had begun. He knew his heart rate was up, that adrenaline was flowing through his sleeping body, though he couldn't sense the changes through his analogue.

"Countermissile defenses standing by. Tracking."

"Scans show nuclear warheads in those missiles, probable one-to-three–kiloton range. They're arming."

Nukes. For centuries, *Dai Nihon* had maintained a monopoly on all nuclear weapons, part of the control they wielded over Earth's Hegemony. That had been changing lately, as the rebellious colonies scrambled to develop nuclear weapons of their own, but few warheads were available yet. *Eagle* possessed only conventional warheads in her magazines.

Dev watched the glowing lines of light curving back from the target, seeking *Eagle*. Excitement thrilled through his awareness, the pulse of battle. Combat between starships took place at ranges and speeds too great for merely human minds to comprehend; the tempo was set by the AIs, the artificial intelligences that governed each ship, and which could react to sudden threats or wield laser weaponry while the electrochemical impulses warning that action was required were still crawling slowly up human optic or aural nerves. But the *shape* of the battle was determined by humans. Dev watched the spread of Imperial missiles as they began to curve inward toward the *Eagle*.

It was time. "Launch Starhawk Three."

The weapons officer's computer-generated analogue winked out of the CDC simulation, an electronic convention reminding the others that Messier's awareness was no longer with them in CDC, but loaded aboard the Starhawk missile now boosting toward the corvette at 50 Gs. CDC weapons control was automatically transferred to Messier's number two, a New American lieutenant named Lerran Dole.

"Fire control reports PDLs coming on-line," Lieutenant Commander Charl Fletcher, *Eagle*'s combat direction officer, reported. PDLs—point defense lasers—were a warship's primary defense against remote-piloted missiles like the Starhawk.

"I'm reading *Teshio*'s PDLs on-line as well," Grier announced. "And they're rotating their ship to give their AI the best shot with the largest number of batteries. Estimate fifteen PDL batteries will have clear fields of fire at our Starhawk."

"That's okay," Dev said. "Let 'em." Starhawk Three would not be coming close enough to its target to trigger its AI-controlled antimissile defenses.

Minutes passed, the starpoints on the 3-D display slowly shifting relative positions. The red graphics marking the Starhawks drifted more quickly, swiftly bridging the narrowing gap between *Eagle* and the Japanese warship. *Teshio*'s missiles had been launched first, but they'd been launched on widely dispersed paths in order to split up the destroyer's point defense batteries. They would reach *Eagle* at almost the same moment that *Eagle*'s Starhawk reached the *Teshio*.

"I'm within canister range," Messier's voice announced suddenly, as new targeting graphics winked on in the air above the CDC projector, bracketing the *Teshio*. "Targeting aft fuel tankage spaces and maneuvering jets. Detonation in three . . . two . . . one . . . *fire!*"

Starhawk canister warheads were a new twist to an ancient idea. As the missile closed with the target, its orientation precisely controlled by laser sensors and the controller-AI link, a fifty-kilo charge of high explosive detonated, shredding the missile and propelling a cloud of marble-sized ball bearings in a titanic shotgun blast. Already traveling with a relative velocity of tens of kilometers per second, the shot received an additional kick from the explosion. Triggered by proximity alert sensors, *Teshio*'s PDLs flared in rapid-fire pulses, but where an instant before there'd been a single target, now there were hundreds . . . too many for the corvette's defenses to handle in the scant seconds remaining before impact.

"Incoming missiles entering PDL reaction zone," Fletcher announced. He might have been announcing shipboard time. "*Eagle*'s PDLs are firing."

"Watch it!" Dole added, and his voice betrayed the high-keyed pitch of his tension. "One's coming—"

A dazzling, white sphere of static engulfed the combat display, momentarily blotting out the moving symbols. There was no sound, no sensation of shock or blast, but Dev knew a nuke warhead had just detonated close enough aboard to fry some of *Eagle*'s sensors.

But they were still in the fight or they wouldn't be wondering about it. As the static from the nuclear detonation cleared, the graphics reappeared on the combat display. An instant later, the shotgun blast from *Eagle*'s Starhawk reached its target.

Every projectile massed thirty grams and was moving at a velocity of twenty-five thousand meters per second relative to the target. When they struck *Teshio*'s hull, each bore a transitional kinetic energy of 9.4 million joules, equivalent to the detonation of just under two kilograms of TNT.

That was insignificant compared to the fury that had just brushed lightly across *Eagle*'s hull, a blast equal to some one thousand tons of TNT. But this time there were dozens of solid strikes instead of one near miss, scattered across the aft half of the corvette. The image of *Teshio* transmitted from Remote Five lit up with a ragged pattern of dazzlingly bright, white pinpoints. Most of the canister in the expanding cone of shot missed the corvette completely, but those that hit gouged craters in armor, pierced cryo-H tanks like bullets hurtling through plyboard, and peeled back duralloy hull plates in a silent, deadly storm of high-energy hail. Cryo-H—slush hydrogen held at near–absolute zero temperatures—boiled as kinetic energy was transformed into heat and fuel tank walls glowed red hot. Impact, and the sudden gush of hydrogen into space, set *Teshio* tumbling slowly end over end, as a slowly expanding cloud of metallic debris glittered in the sunlight.

His link with the Starhawk broken at the instant of detonation, Messier had reappeared with the other CDC officers. "Hit," he reported.

"*Teshio* has lost maneuvering control," Kelly Grier announced. "They still have power and weapons on-line."

"CDO!" Dev snapped. "Report on those Impie missiles!"

"Our PDLs took out three of them," Fletcher replied a moment later. "The fourth detonated short, just out of effective range. That could have been due to damage from a sublethal PDL hit, or it might have been deliberate strategy, hoping to hurt us with the EMP and blast effects."

"What's the bill?"

"Damage control reports only minor damage to external hull, frame seven and forward. No breaches, no radiation, no casualties."

Dev let out a small sigh. *Eagle* might be many times larger than the little *Teshio*, but size alone meant little when the other guy had nukes. But they'd survived . . . this time.

"Communications," Dev said. "Set up that com channel now. Let's see if they'll talk to us."

Normally, of course, the Imperials would not even consider negotiating with rebels, especially with help, in the shape of an

Imperial squadron, already on the way. *Teshio* was damaged, but not yet out of the fight . . . and if the corvette's commander had any more nukes aboard, he might easily get lucky.

But now that he'd gotten the guy's attention, Dev had an idea that might make *Teshio*'s commander agree to almost anything.

The thrill of combat singing through his mind, Dev began downloading a new analogue for himself.

Though fraud in other activities is detestable, in the management of war it is laudable and glorious, and he who overcomes an enemy by fraud is as much to be praised as he who does so by force.

—*Discourses*
Niccolo Machiavelli
C.E. 1517

The crippled *Teshio* lay between *Eagle* and the fleeing freighter and had to be neutralized fast, or the Confederation destroyer risked facing another missile strike. With Imperial reinforcements already boosting clear from New American orbit, Dev had time to take the corvette or the freighter, but not both. An invisible beam of low-energy laser light tagged the Imperial ship, as Dev issued a chain of mental commands, assuming the appearance of a very special, newly programmed ViRcom analogue.

Analogues were AI-generated programs used in ViRcommunications and in workstation simulations such as *Eagle*'s CDC. Normally, an analogue resembled the person "wearing" it, though for a few extra kiloyen or with the help of someone skilled at reality programming, it could be spruced up with richer or fancier clothing, more attractive physical features, or the background trappings of wealth or power. A personal analogue's appearance, in fact, was one of the more important social markers throughout the *shakai*, the upper-class culture of Imperial society that had left its imprint on most of the cultures throughout the Shichiju.

There was nothing to stop a user from radically changing his analogue's appearance save convention and the social risks of being found out. In fact, some such changes were obligatory. Enhancing certain aspects of one's own body for virtual sex involving two or more players, for instance, was considered quite proper, at least within certain boundaries of taste, physical compatibility, and believability. In combat, however, virtual communications were generally kept more or less honest, if only because extensive data bases on both sides could be used to check on exaggerated claims, threats, personal identities, or boasts of military prowess. A lieutenant, for instance, who impersonated a captain through a reprogrammed analogue in order to impress an opponent ran the risk of being found out and ignored. Such an imposter was *sho ga nai*, literally beyond help, and if he was captured, he could be killed.

More than once in the past, though, in situations where he thought he could get away with it, Dev had deliberately used false-front analogues to deceive the enemy; in particular, he'd worn a computer-generated analogue of a Japanese naval officer to carry off a deception that allowed *Eagle*, a Japanese warship until her capture at Eridu, to masquerade as an Imperial destroyer, slipping unchallenged into the midst of an Imperial squadron.

He wouldn't be able to try that particular trick again, of course. The Imperials had figured out what he'd done soon after he'd carried it off, and they would be on the lookout for such deceptions from now on. The thing had been possible at all only because he'd managed to acquire the Imperial access codes for that particular fleet operation. Likely, too, they'd changed the IFF codes on all of their fleet units, making impersonations of Imperial officers or their ships almost impossible.

What he was trying now was similar in application to those earlier deceptions . . . but quite different in spirit. Judging from their maneuvers so far, the Imperials clearly knew the lone destroyer was a Confederation raider. But they couldn't be sure of their opponent's exact nature.

Within the shadow world of his awareness, Dev's 185-centimeter frame grew taller, approaching two full meters, while dwindling in mass to an almost skeletal lankiness. His skin turned black, his lengthening hair and thickening eyebrows an iridescent white. His outward appearance completely transformed, Dev opened the readied ViRcom channel to the Japanese corvette.

Since Dev had initiated the link, an image of *Teshio*'s bridge became the backdrop for the meeting. Though the reality aboard the damaged corvette must by this time be a confusion of zero-G, smoke, and pressure loss alarms, the scene showed no urgency. The looming bulk of the bridge link modules crowded one another beneath a low, conduit-covered overhead. Only one figure was visible, the image of a Japanese naval officer in formal dress blacks. The link program maintained the illusion of gravity.

"This is *Shosa* Ohira, of the Imperial corvette *Teshio*," the figure said stiffly, facing Dev. "I demand—"

"You will demand nothing," Dev interrupted, barking the phrase in Nihongo. He waited then, allowing Ohira to see and understand the image before him now. The Imperial's analogue would not betray its owner through any physical change in expression, of course, but Dev did see the man's eyes widen slightly and guessed that Ohira knew what was confronting him.

"*Teshio!* I am Captain Kwasa of the Confederation destroyer *Ya Kutisha*. You will release computer control to me immediately, or you will be destroyed."

"This . . . is piracy," Ohira said. The hesitation, the rasp in his words betrayed his confusion and his fear. He was a young man, in his early thirties, Dev guessed, and not practiced at hiding his emotions. "Piracy! I cannot surrender to *you*!"

There was a world within the Shichiju, innermost planet of a red dwarf flare star called UV Ceti and known to its Swahili-speaking inhabitants as Juanyekundu, Red Star. Exploited for its mineral resources with Imperial help almost three centuries before by a consortium of African nations, the world had been abandoned, its colonists left to shift for themselves, because evacuating them would have been too dangerous and too expensive an undertaking for the then brand-new Hegemony. UV Ceti was a dim-glowing coal of a sun circling another red dwarf only marginally brighter than itself nine light-years from Earth; it was also a flare star, given to periodic seizures when a tiny portion of its surface suddenly and briefly erupted in a storm of light and hard radiation, drastically increasing the star's brightness.

Very few of those first colonists had survived; the descendants of those who did lived in deep-tunneled habitats kilometers beneath their world's airless surface, but those first few generations had undergone a rather brutal selection process. Modern Juanyekundans tended to have a high tolerance for radiation, as well as the physiques and the hair and skin colorations unique now to natives of the planet. Those descendants also possessed a singular hatred for the Empire, their ancestors' betrayer, and despite its isolationist tendencies, Juanyekundu had been among the first of the Shichiju's worlds to side openly with the Confederation by signing the Declaration of Reason.

Unfortunately, Juanyekundu was a poor world that possessed no warships of its own. There was no *Ya Kutisha*—the name was Swahili for "Terrible"—and Captain Kwasa was a fiction of *Eagle*'s AI. Dev was counting, however, on whatever stories Commander Ohira had heard about the Juanyekundans' hatred for the Japanese, as well as on the physically impressive display they made over a ViRcom link. "Kwasa" towered over *Teshio*'s captain, his head brushing the low overhead.

"Turn control of your computer over to us," Dev said reasonably through his terrifying alter ego, "and we will not be forced to board your ship. As you can tell by examining our approach vector, we cannot dock with your ship and hope to capture the freighter you were escorting as well. Given a choice, we would prefer to ignore your command and take the freighter. If you would prefer, however, that we come discuss this with you *personally . . .*"

Ohira growled something unintelligible, then acquired for a moment a glazed, faraway look, an indication that the *real* Ohira was somewhere else, frantically discussing the situation with his officers.

The answer came back in seconds. "Very well, ah, Confederation destroyer." The words were harsh, angrily bitten off. "You have control."

In an earlier age of broadsides and wooden decks, a beaten ship signaled its desire to surrender by lowering its flag. In space combat, surrender was signaled by granting the victor access to key computer systems. Access codes flashed back along the lasercom linkage, to be copied by *Eagle*'s computer personnel and sent back to unlock *Teshio*'s AI. There would still be reserved files within the corvette's memory that the Confederation personnel could not read; in fact, at that moment Ohira and his people were probably busily deleting every byte of secure and classified data they could lay their figurative hands on. *Teshio*'s primary ship functions, however, including maneuvering and weapons, were now under *Eagle*'s direct control.

"Give them damage control and enough maneuvering to stop that spin," Dev told his own people. "Don't give them ViRcom access until we're clear."

"We should just tell the gokers to self-destruct," a voice said. Dev thought he recognized Grier's voice that time.

"Negative," he replied, an edge to his voice. "I want them to pass this story on to their bosses at New America. Now let's run down that freighter!"

Allowing *Teshio* to live would do more for the Confederation cause than would reducing the corvette to a glowing cloud of plasma. The entire rebel navy at this point consisted of *Eagle* and a handful of frigates, corvettes, and gunboats. They had no other destroyers of *Eagle*'s class . . . but the enemy couldn't be sure of that, not when they'd lost several similar destroyers at Herakles. It was not impossible that several of the ships thought lost had been captured instead, to be employed against their former owners. By pretending to be captain of the *Ya Kutisha*, Dev was spreading doubt within the Imperial High Command about the exact composition of the Confederation fleet . . . and its capabilities.

Eagle passed the helpless *Teshio* less than a thousand kilometers off her port beam. In another ten minutes, she was closing with the freighter, a forty-eight-thousand-ton merchantman called the *Kasuga Maru*.

"I've got a clear reading on the ships breaking New American orbit," Grier reported. "Two Amatukaze-class destroyers. Four smaller vessels—frigates, probably, judging from their mass readings." Her analogue glanced up from the 3-D navigational plot, clear blue eyes locking with Dev's. "Looks like we got their attention."

"Let's see if we have the freighter's attention," Dev said. "Communications. Patch me through."

The bridge of the *Kasuga Maru* was tiny compared to the corvette's, possessing only four link modules. *Eagle*'s data base on active commercial vessels listed her as an independent trader currently under contract to LaGrange 5 Orbital. Having once served in the merchant fleet, Dev knew that such enterprises tended to cut costs in every way they could, meaning they boosted with an absolute minimum of crew members, twelve or fifteen at the most, just enough to jack critical ship's systems, and to ride the vanes and sweeps during godsea passage. Almost certainly, *Kasuga Maru* wouldn't be carrying gun jackers or weapons officers; Class IVs devoted their hull space to cargo in any case, rather than losing precious ship mass to nonpaying systems like antiship missiles or heavy combat lasers.

Even so, a freighter possessed weapons that could cause a problem for any warship trying to capture it, especially when there were time constraints to the operation. *Kasuga Maru* would possess at least two AI-governed PDL batteries as a defense against meteoroids and orbital debris. Far more deadly to a warship as large and as well armored as an Amatukaze-class destroyer, though, were a Class IV's two Avery-Mitsubishi Sunburst fusion-plasma engines. The storm of charged particles emitted by those white-glowing venturis aft could fry any vessel coming up astern.

Which was one reason it was imperative for a commerce raider to acquire computer control of an enemy ship before trying to overtake it.

Kasuga Maru's captain was a surprise, a short, older man with a red beard going gray and an angry scowl lining his features. The Imperial High Command had recently prohibited *gaijin*—foreigners—from serving in any command capacity aboard Imperial warships, but most Hegemony and independent vessels were manned by non-Japanese. Still, Dev had assumed that a cargo ship making a run from Earth to New America would have been commandeered by the Imperials. Tensions between *Dai Nihon* and the rest of the Hegemony had been running high of late—the Confederation had been counting on that fact to win more converts to their cause— and it seemed like a breach of security for military supplies under escort by an Imperial vessel to be in the keeping of a *gaijin* crew.

The freighter's captain, standing in a hands-on-hips attitude of sheer defiance, looked Dev's image up and down. "Hah! So *you're* the goking pirates! Bring that rattletrap of yours any closer, you black divil, an' we'll melt y'down for scrap!"

Dev was still wearing the Juanyekundan analogue, of course. He had to maintain the deception if he wanted the Hegemony to believe the Confederation fleet included a destroyer with a crew from UV Ceti. That hardly seemed to account for the man's hostility, however.

"This is Captain Kwasa of the Confederation destroyer *Ya Kutisha*. Your escort has been disabled. Please release computer control of your vessel to us at once. Your cargo is being appropriated for the Frontier Confederation, but we have no desire to hurt you or your crew."

"Gok it! Do your worst! We'll see how bandit scum like you likes hot protons for breakfast!"

Dev paused, unsure of himself. He wouldn't have hesitated to fire on the *Teshio* again if he'd had to. This was war, after all. The man on the *Kasuga Maru*'s bridge, however, was a civilian, a noncombatant. To simply burn him out of existence . . .

"*Kasuga Maru,*" Dev said. "If I have to burn out your command center with a high-energy laser in order to save the lives of my crew, I will. Believe that. Why should you and your people be willing to die? Give us access to your AI and no one will be harmed. I promise you."

Dev could see the struggle going on within the man's thoughts. Surrender clearly was a bitter pill.

"No one aboard the *Teshio* was hurt," he added. "And believe me, sir, we have a lot more reason to hate them than we do you."

Kasuga Maru's captain was weighing the loss of his crew against the loss of ship and cargo. That seemed to decide him, as Dev had known it must.

"*Take* the ship, you scrawny, rad-blasted goker," he barked. "An' be damned to ya!"

"Thank you, *Kasuga Maru,*" Dev told him, flashing white teeth against skin as black as space. "We will. You may take to your boats. Those among your crew who wish to join the Confederation forces may remain aboard."

"That'll be the day, y'bastard. This crew'll have no truck wi' kaizies!"

Kaizies—Dev guessed the word was slang based on the Nihongo *kaizoku*, pirate.

"We are fighting for our independence," Dev said slowly, trying to give the phrase a dignity that he didn't quite feel. "We're not pirates."

"Independence? You're gokin' pirates and thieves an' scuttin' bastards, the lot of you! You're *wiping us out*, don't you see? This old ship might not look like much, but she's everything we own an' you're resettin' us t'zero! Gok, you 'n the Empire can squabble with each other till universal heat death, but why do you have to drag us into it, huh? All decent folks want is t'be left alone!"

"Relinquish control of your AI, please."

"*There*, gok you!"

Minutes later, a lifeboat bearing *Kasuga Maru*'s crew accelerated clear of the freighter's command and hab section. A hastily devised program hidden within the freighter's life support routines and set to trigger the main engines in an uncontained fusion ignition was spotted and deactivated by Lieutenant Simone Dagousset, Dev's chief AI programming officer, well before *Eagle* came up astern.

The encounter with the freighter's captain—his name, according to the ship records, was Alistair MacKenzie—had shaken Dev. True, the Confederation still wasn't taken seriously by most of the people on most of the worlds of the Shichiju. Imperial control of official news and information download networks was largely to blame for that, of course. The Hegemony—and behind it, the Empire—controlled all such services on the inhabited worlds, as they controlled the ships plying the vast emptiness between neighboring star systems. News of major Confederation victories at Eridu and Herakles had been easily suppressed, while rumors of rebel uprisings on over a dozen worlds during the past two years had been downplayed as banditry and hooliganism. Small wonder the rebellion had largely been dismissed by most of humanity.

But the evident hatred in MacKenzie's face and voice gnawed at Dev. According to the records in *Kasuga Maru*'s AI, the man was a native of Alba, not one of the long-settled core worlds of the Shichiju, but a frontier colony, one still officially undecided in the struggle between Hegemony and Confederation but with a powerful anti-Imperial faction. Evidently, he and his crew had been working under contract for LaGrange 5 Orbital for nearly twenty years, receiving owner's shares in the freighter instead of bonuses or performance incentives. In another five or ten years, when the company was ready to retire the aging freighter, MacKenzie would have been able to assume full title and put her into service as an independent merchantman.

No wonder MacKenzie had been furious.

Dev rarely thought of himself as a rebel . . . or as someone out to overturn the established order, which, of course, he most certainly was. When he let himself think about it at all, he was simply a warrior fighting for a cause in which he'd only recently started to believe. He identified with the people—the *majority* of people, he thought—who wanted freedom for their worlds and populations from the increasingly restrictive and suffocating central authority of a distant but too-powerful Earth.

He never thought of himself as someone who might deliberately kill civilians, or steal their property, their livelihoods, their *futures*.

Kaizoku to zoku, pirates and bandits. Was that all the Confederation's rebellion really was? The odds of successfully taking on the entire Hegemony—and behind them the military might of Imperial Japan—were too long to think about. Until the Confederation was strong enough to win victories spectacular enough to attract the attention of ordinary Hegemony citizens despite the news blackout, pirates and bandits were what the rebels would remain.

Dev tried to push the thought aside.

With *Kasuga Maru* under *Eagle*'s computer control, the freighter was rotated until her main venturis pointed at New America, and then her drive was lit. Together, the two ships decelerated at the freighter's maximum of nearly two and a half Gs, as long-range radar and sensors continued to monitor the approach of warships from New America.

Hours passed, and deceleration became acceleration, as *Eagle* and her prize slowly began building speed on a vector that would take them away from New America and the oncoming enemy squadron. At one point, both drives were silenced long enough for a ship's boat to make the passage from the destroyer to the freighter. A Confederation crew jacked into the freighter's empty control slots, and the drives were lit once more.

Not long after that, with all shipjackers aboard both vessels reporting readiness for transition, Dev gave a command over the communications link, and the two ships fell into the blue-lit strangeness of K-T space.

Each step in technology is built upon the step previous. Cephlink webs of electronic feeds, connective networks and computer chips nanotechnically grown within the sulci of the human brain, were not possible until the brain had been thoroughly mapped, right down to the molecular level of stimulus and response. And upon the cephlink rests our modern understanding of mind as distinct from brain. Modern psychology, the study of mental processes and behavior, bears no closer resemblance to its precephlink forebears than does modern cosmology to astrology, than nanotechnic materials processing to alchemy.

—*Man and the Stars: A History of Technology*
Ieyasu Sutsumi
C.E. 2531

Riding the currents of the godsea, *Eagle* and her captive fell through vistas of blue light, computer simulations of a medium that was in fact incomprehensible to unenhanced human perceptions. Two days out from New America both *Eagle* and *Kasuga Maru* dropped briefly out of K-T space, emerging in the bleak emptiness of interstellar space to carefully align their four-space vector with the distant spark that was Mu Herculis.

Against the possibility that one or the other of the vessels might not survive the coming passage, full copies of both ships' AI data stores were made and exchanged. Ever since leaving New America, Lieutenant Dagousset aboard the *Eagle* and the computer techs who'd transferred to the *Kasuga Maru* had been working with the freighter's AI records, unlocking and analyzing previously sealed or coded data.

They'd struck gold with the *Kasuga Maru*'s capture—better, terbium, that rare lanthanide vital both in K-T drive systems and in certain types of AI circuitry. The freighter, it seemed, had been en route to New America not from Earth, but from the Imperial naval facility at Athena called Daikokukichi.

Her last assignment before that had been as part of a military convoy to the Alyan system.

That discovery had startled Dev and started a whirlwind of rumor and speculation within the crew.

Alya was the ancient Arabic name for the star variously listed in the star charts as Theta Serpentis or 63 Serpentis. A double star some 130 light-years from Sol, well beyond the outer fringes of the Shichiju. Alya B-V was the original DalRiss homeworld, called GhegnuRish; there, three years ago, while serving as a Hegemony striderjack with the Imperial Expeditionary Force, Dev had first made peaceful contact with the Xenophobe infesting that world. Alya A-VI—ShraRish—was a DalRiss colony world, the location of the only large DalRiss population since GhegnuRish had been abandoned to the Xeno, millennia before.

Kasuga Maru had been carrying food and organic manufactory materials to the Imperial base on ShraRish. While in orbit there, her commo personnel had recorded a number of exchanges between the Imperial commander in orbit and the base on the surface. They'd been passed on to the Imperial station at Athena, but for some reason—the inefficiencies of the Imperial bureaucracy, perhaps—copies had remained in the freighter's AI storage. As he scanned quickly through the decoded recordings, Dev knew that the Confederation Military Command was going to have to see them.

With the new course alignments complete, *Eagle* and the *Kasuga Maru* slipped back into the blue embrace of the K-T Plenum. The return to Herakles would take another thirty days.

Eagle's original crew of 310 had left her shorthanded to begin with by a factor of nearly twenty-five percent, and during the past month, a hundred of those had been told off as crews for the five cargo ships and merchants *Eagle* had captured in three star systems. Shorthanded meant long and frequent watches in the link modules, but it also meant more downtime spent jacked into *Eagle*'s recreational system. With a month to pass in K-T space, with no way to bleed off the excess heat that day by ship's day grew more and more oppressive, recreational jacking was a necessity, not a luxury, and not mere entertainment. Without it heat, boredom, and the tedium of routine would have been intolerable.

Dev enjoyed his share of ViRdramas, of course, and lately he'd been downloading literary classics as part of a deliberate attempt to widen his own horizons. He liked ViRsex, too, though instead of solo electronic trysts with AI-generated partners or with the analogues of fellow Eagles, he had a good downloaded copy of Katya Alessandro's analogue.

Lately, though, even ViRsex with Katya's image had lost some of its original charm. The program, after all, relied to a large extent on his memories of Katya to make the analogue speak and act convincingly, and the more time he spent with the analogue instead of its flesh-and-blood original, the less spontaneous, the less *alive* the simulations seemed.

And there was something preying on his mind as well, a problem that had been growing since he'd left Herakles nearly four months earlier. Soon after *Eagle* dropped back into K-T space, then, Dev spent his off-watch downtime one ship's evening loading one of the ship's psych monitor programs.

The setting was a traditional Japanese room—tatami mats, a low table aglow in black lacquer, a viewall simulating a veranda overlooking an enclosed, Japanese garden. Fuji, snow-capped and perfect, rose gracefully above cherry trees beyond a stone wall, a print by Hokusai. *Eagle*'s monitor programs had been written for her original owners, back when she was still the *Tokitukaze*, and never been updated.

No matter. *Nihonjin* or *gaijin*, *shakai* or Frontier, people were still people.

"At last," a voice said. "I was beginning to think that no one aboard this vessel cared to speak with me anymore."

Dev turned to face the speaker, a small and gray-haired Japanese man, neatly and formally dressed in a traditional white *kariginu*. The image was that of Ieyasu Sutsumi, though that master of *Kokorodo*, the way of the mind, had had nothing to do with *Eagle*'s monitor programming. Sutsumi was a venerable figure; within *Nihonjin* culture, his age alone made him worthy of respect, and his reputation as both philosopher and teacher was widely known even among *gaijin*, especially among *gaijin* who'd had training with Hegemony military forces. Dev had particular reason to remember the man; the real Sutsumi had once sat on a military review board over him, recommending that he be assigned to the leg infantry instead of warstriders because of a bout of technophobia.

"*Konichiwa, Sensei*," Dev said, bowing formally. The program would neither care nor react if he ignored the amenities, but observing the formalities made Dev feel more at ease. "I imagine most of the crew feels uncomfortable using a monitor programmed by the enemy."

One part of himself noted that it was silly apologizing for human behavior to an AI program, as though it felt hurt, lonely, or ignored. Another part acknowledged that it was just as silly for the program to act as though it had missed having conversations with *Eagle*'s crew, since the program was self-aware, within the definition of artificial intelligence, only when it was running. Still, the value of such interactive software lay in the pretense that it, too, was a human being, as capable of emotion as Dev.

The image folded its legs beneath it in a graceful descent to a *tatami*. "And you do not?"

Dev lowered himself to a mat opposite the table. "Not really, *Sensei*. I don't hate the Japanese. I hate the government, what it's become."

" 'Hate' is a strong word, Devsan, and trivialized by misuse. I doubt that many of your compatriots aboard hate anyone in more than an abstract way. I suspect that the reason you are different from them lies in your choice of birthworlds, rather than in your choice of enemies."

That, Dev reflected, was true enough. Born and raised on Earth, in an outlying enclave of the BosWash metroplex sprawl, he'd grown up in the ever-present shadow of Japanese culture and technology. Though he'd never been part of the *shakai*, Earth's dominant, elitist culture, it had been impossible to escape the distinctive reliance on advanced technology displayed by so many of the planet's citizens. There, even members of the *Fukushi*, the Imperial welfare program that provided free housing, food, and other services to perhaps two-thirds of the population, possessed the Level One, single-socket implants that let them interact with technic society . . . and receive government-sponsored information and entertainment downloads. It was much the same on the other Core Worlds, where the populations had enjoyed the status quo of Imperial-Hegemony rule for centuries.

Among the worlds of the Frontier, however, the emphasis was on people, not machines. There was more variety within the populations, too, as well as a stubborn, independent streak that cared less for fashion than for practicality. A person was more likely to work his own problems out than to rely on the help of an AI monitor program.

"So. Why are you here?" Sutsumi's image asked.

Dev took a breath before answering. The illusion of reality was perfect in every way; the breath steadied him, stilled some part of the doubt and fear that had brought him here, exactly as though it had been a real breath drawn by his flesh-and-blood body.

"*Sensei.* I need a check on my TM rating. I . . . When we took the *Kasuga Maru*, I felt like I was close to the edge. Again." He ran one hand through his hair. Again, the illusion was perfect. He felt the ceramic slickness of his right temporal socket beneath his fingertips.

"Ah." Sutsumi's eyes narrowed, as though he were studying Dev closely. "Let me have a closer look."

Inwardly, Dev sensed the flux and tickle of circuits opening and closing, of personal RAM being sampled, of neurons firing. Within the space of two heartbeats, he felt cold, then hot, smelled cinnamon, tasted salt, heard the tinkling echo of crystal bells. For the briefest of instants he was a warstrider, two-meter duralloy legs scissoring across a landscape of battle-torn earth and shattered buildings. Power thrilled. . . .

"We would need a high-level diagnostic for a full-confidence reading, of course," Sutsumi said. "But a quick reading of your psych index gives a TM of point four. That is normal for you, Devsan, *neh*?"

"Normal for me. Yeah."

The development of cephlink technology had brought its own zoo of ills and mental conditions, from people with physiologies that simply could not tolerate chips and circuits grown within their brains, to those who rejected them on esthetic, political, or religious grounds. Dozens of psychotechnic disorders, mental problems triggered by link technology, had been identified. Three—technic depression, technophobia, and technomegalomania—were so prevalent that everyone with link hardware was given a rating on a decimal scale of zero to one indicating his or her susceptibility to PTDs.

As with a drug, the effects of TM, technomegalomania, could be obvious or subtle. It could make a linked person euphoric, or it could act like a depressant when he was not linked. For some, the feelings of godlike power when they were linked to an AI or to link-driven equipment or simply while they experienced the illusion of ViReality could be overwhelming.

For some professions—jacking a military warstrider, for instance—a high TM rating was not a handicap. For piloting a starship, however, where a lapse in judgment could wreck the vessel and kill the entire crew, feelings of godlike power were not thought of as valuable assets. Riding the currents of the K-T Plenum, a starship was balanced in a tiny, self-generated pocket universe, adrift on the interface between normal fourspace and the quantum sea. Modern cosmology viewed the entire physical universe as no more than a four-dimensional bubble floating atop a polydimensional ocean of energy, the godsea. A mistake in judgment while riding the godsea currents, and *Eagle*'s eighty-four-thousand-ton mass would be transformed instantly into energy; against such furies as those a starship rode, the mass-to-energy translation would yield not even a flicker of incandescence.

For that reason, the Hegemony Navy, as Dev had ample personal reason to remember, did not admit people with TM ratings higher than point two. They wanted calm and dispassionate jackers with sound judgment who could make reasoned decisions under pressure. The independent merchant lines—and organizations as desperate for experienced shipjackers as the Confederation Navy—were not nearly so picky, however.

Dev Cameron, son of a starship captain, had yearned to be a shipjacker himself for as long as he could remember. He'd jacked aboard a freighter for a time, but when he'd tried joining the Hegemony Navy nearly four years ago, his TM rating of point four had blocked him. He'd ended up as leg infantry, then as a warstrider.

The war and the rebel Confederation's need for ships and men who could jack them had given him another chance, though, and after leading the warstrider assault team that had captured the *Tokitukaze*, he'd found his lifelong dream of commanding a starship to have become reality.

He still had that point four TM rating, though, and every time he jacked into *Eagle*'s command link he felt that familiar-yet-new thrill coursing through his being, a kind of head-spinning glory that came with riding the godsea, with tricking the cosmos into doing his bidding. Worse, he felt the same thrill during combat, a surging, exultant, and terrifying sense of invincibility.

So far, he'd held those feelings rigidly in check, mostly by clinging to the realization of just how many lives depended on his rational assessment of things both within the K-T Plenum and in combat. But things had happened to him within the past few months that had pushed him beyond the limits he'd set for his own emotions.

There were medtechs aboard the *Eagle*, and even several human psychotechnicians, but he didn't want anyone to know what was going on within his own thoughts and perceptions and memory just now. He didn't want to look closely at them himself, either, though he knew that if he didn't, things would only get worse until he made a bad and possibly fatal mistake. That was why he'd sought out the anonymous comfort of the ship's AI psych monitor. The record of what went on here was private, accessible only by his personal RAM codes or by those authorized by a military court.

He was glad of that confidentiality. Dev didn't want anybody to know just how scared he was.

"You have had some rather strange experiences recently," the Sutsumi analogue said.

Dev started, looked up. His thoughts had been wandering. "Huh?"

"You had an unusual encounter," the analogue said. "And I have the feeling that it is at least partly responsible for this atypical lack of confidence in yourself. Perhaps you'd like to discuss what happened."

"Um. You mean the Heraklean Xenophobe." He shrugged. "The word 'like' isn't exactly applicable. But I guess I have to."

"You don't *have* to do anything, Devsan. But if it would make you feel better . . ."

Dev smiled ruefully. Once, years ago, he'd downloaded a history of the development of artificial intelligence. One of the earliest experiments in that high-tech realm had been an interactive program called "Liza" that simulated the give and take between a psychiatrist and a patient. "My father doesn't like me." "Why do you say your father doesn't like you?" The conversations, such as they were, had depended on the program's use of key words that it fed back to the patient in questions designed to elicit more statements. The program had not been self-aware, not even in the limited fashion that *Eagle*'s monitor program was self-aware, and by modern standards the psychiatric practices it had emulated were scarcely a step removed from arrant superstition.

Still, people who'd interacted with Liza had reported feeling much better after discussing their problems with it. Dev suspected that the Sutsumi analogue was pushing him in the same direction. "A problem shared," ran the old saying, "is a problem halved."

"On Herakles," Dev told the *sensei*, "I, uh, linked with a Xenophobe. With a Naga, I mean." He still wasn't used to the new name for the alien intelligences. "I'd communicated with two other Nagas before, one out in the Alyan system, one on Eridu, but this was something . . . very different."

Sutsumi waited patiently, listening, legs folded on the *tatami*.

"We still don't know what happened, really," he went on. "Not the medtechs, not Confederation Military Command. Not even me, and I was there. Somehow, that Xeno and I joined so completely that we really were a new . . . entity." *Xenolink*, the AI and medical experts were calling that blending of human and Naga.

"Symbiosis," Sutsumi suggested. "Two organisms functioning together in a way complementary to both."

"Maybe. While I was linked to the thing, I could see and feel with its senses, while it could see and hear with mine. Xenos don't have sight or hearing, you know, though they have plenty of senses that we don't. They can taste magnetism in rock. Feel electrons moving like sand trickling through your fingers. I felt all of that, though I still don't understand it any more than a blind man understands blue. And I had access to . . . its past. Its memories." He shuddered. "They're still with me, though I'm damned if I can make much of anything out of them."

"You were thoroughly checked out afterward by medtechs and somatic specialists, were you not?"

"*Sensei*, you don't know the half of it. Though I'm still not sure whether anybody believes my story. Hell, I'm not sure I do. But it doesn't matter. While I was plugged into the Naga, an Imperial squadron attacked. They surprised us, came out of K-T space so close to the planet we were caught in the open, naked, almost defenseless. They *had* us, *Sensei*. But I . . . I stopped them."

"How did you stop them, Devsan?"

"By throwing rocks. I knocked them out of orbit by throwing rocks."

Sutsumi's image blinked once at that, and Dev smiled. Long before Man had first left his homeworld there'd been speculation about using asteroids nudged out of orbit or material scooped from the surface of the moon as weapons literally unstoppable if dropped toward a world's surface from the top of its gravity well.

At Herakles, though, the fusion of Dev and Naga had reversed that equation. By generating intense, swiftly moving magnetic fields, he/they had plucked one-ton masses of iron and Rogan-Process building material from the facing of an atmosphere generator and hurled them into space at one-tenth the speed of light. Imperial warships caught by that barrage, even one of the monster Ryu-class carriers, had been vaporized, like gnats touched by the breath of a laser cutting torch.

Either the monitor program had been following his thoughts, or it had just accessed records of the battle at Herakles. "The transitional kinetic energy released by the impact of a one-ton mass moving at ten percent c," Sutsumi said, "is approximately 10^{19} joules. The equivalent of thousands of high-yield thermonuclear explosions. How did you feel, wielding such power?"

Dev closed his eyes, but in his memory he saw again the cloud-wracked sky, sensed the Imperial ships overhead. *Lightnings fork from the crest of an artificial mountain. Thunder peals.* He exerted himself *so.... Overhead, the sky turns white, an illumination more dazzling than the brassy, subgiant's glare of the Heraklean sun. Another ship dies....*

"I don't think I'll ever be free of the ... feeling," Dev said. "I think it changed me. Like I can never go back to what I was."

"But you did. You broke your link with the Naga."

"Yes." He'd had to. He'd been terrified of losing his humanity. Sometimes he wondered if he was still entirely human. There were times ...

Lightning flared. Behind ... beneath him, the Naga's mind was a murmuring sea, voices, dream-memories, and above all, the power of a storm-torn sea....

Later, when the Naga was gone, there was such ... loneliness.

"I've been worried, *Sensei*," he told the analogue. "Especially when I'm linked, in combat, or while jacking a starship. I'm afraid of taking chances that just can't be justified. Of losing ... control."

"Give me a specific example."

"Okay. At New America, when we took *Kasuga Maru*. I decided to gamble, to play the part of a Juanyekundan shipjacker to scare the enemy into surrender."

"The ploy worked."

"Yes. Yes, it did. Then I went on and bluffed the skipper of the *Kasuga Maru*."

"Bluff and deception are important aspects of successful military tactics."

"Sure, but don't you see? I wasn't even thinking about the possibility of failure. If the bluffs had failed, well, I'm afraid I was ready to push ahead anyway. Even though that could have meant *Eagle* was destroyed. It's like a storm inside my brain when I link in and I'm riding the percentages. Like the burn of a jolt addict."

There were people who used their cephlinks to commit suicide, intentionally or accidentally, by channeling electronic stimulation directly into the pleasure centers of their brains. PC stimulation—whether through hardwired implants or injections of programmed nano—could destroy a person in months, even in days if he had unlimited access to the technology and lacked the power of will to resist its siren's call. Most victims died of thirst, so powerful were the cravings for the better-than-orgasms that went on and on and on. Some tried to stop short of death and found they could no longer live without it—jolt addicts and brain burners.

"I doubt that you can imagine what such an addiction is like," Sutsumi said. "Certainly you want to experience the feeling of power again. But you control that desire."

"Maybe. So far, maybe. Sometimes I wonder if I'm losing it."

"Tell me, Devsan. Do you wish to repeat the experience with the Naga?"

Lightning! A bolt of raw light, radiating far into the ultra-violet, as mass shredded air, hurtling skyward . . .

"Huh? No way! Believe me, I thought about it and no. I didn't want to be a god, throwing mountains and knowing I could kill those people in orbit just by flexing my will, no. But I'm afraid that what I felt then is, well, spilling into what I feel when I jack a starship. Or take people into combat." He held his hands before him, then slowly flexed them into twin fists. "My God, the *power* . . ."

Sutsumi's image was silent for a long time, and Dev wondered what was going on. An AI program could "think," if that was the right word, far faster than any human, considering thousands, even millions of possibilities in fractions of a second. The delay might be meant to reassure Dev that his problem was receiving careful consideration.

But more likely, the problem had no solution. Like any other citizen of the Frontier, Dev was going to have to come to grips with it himself, without help from a programmed analogue.

"Devsan," the image said at last, "all I can tell you is that the fact that you are concerned enough to bring this to me suggests that you have not lost a proper perspective. If you insisted that there was nothing to worry about, that you had been untouched by your experiences, well . . ." The old eyes twinkled in a passable simulation of humor. "*Then* I would worry!"

"Maybe," Dev said. He was unconvinced. *Lightning against a blackening sky; peals of thunder, like battle cries of the gods.*

"I wish I could forget what happened on Herakles, though."

"Why?"

"Because I have the damnedest feeling that, well, that the only way I can become complete is to merge with one of those things again and . . ." He shuddered, trying to shut out the memories. "I don't want to do it again, to lose myself that way. At the same time, I find myself wanting it, *needing* it.

"I'm wondering, *Sensei*, if I'm addicted, somehow, to the Xenolink."

Chapter 4

4. Armor

    a. The primary mission of armor units is the attacking of infantry and artillery. The enemy's rear is the happy hunting ground for armor. Use every means to get it there. . . .

       —*Letter of Instruction*
General George S. Patton, Jr.
C.E. 3 April 1944

Tucked in beneath the overhang of the VK-141 Stormwind, Colonel Katya Alessandro could neither move nor deploy the hull sensors of her warstrider. She was linked, however, with Major Benjis Nadry, the Stormwind's pilot, and she could see, as he could, the torn and convoluted landscape blurring past the combat carrier's belly scant meters below.

The ascraft was flying NOE, nape-of-the-earth, following a path worked out hours before through careful examination of 3-D radar holographs relayed by satellite. Their assigned drop zone glowed against her view forward, marked by a green square shimmering near the crest of a shell-blasted slope designated Hill 232.

"DZ in sight," Katya said, her words relayed through the

air/spacecraft's intercom to the other three warstriders suspended from the carrier's external riderslots. "Thirty-second warning."

"Copy that, Assassin Leader," Captain Frank Kilroy replied.

"Assassin Three copies," Lieutenant Virginia Halliwell added.

"And Four copies. Let's kick ass!" That was Lieutenant Hari Sebree.

She could sense the other three warstriders, armored, multi-ton monsters cradled in their riderslots beneath the stubby, anhedral wings of the ascraft, voices and the steady pulse of data feeds over hard-jacked interfaces. Katya shifted her visual display to a view aft. A second Stormwind followed in the wake of the first, a hundred meters back and so low the wind of its passage kicked dust from the hilltops and set the scrub brush to thrashing. Each Stormwind carried one element—four warstriders; Katya was descending on what should be the enemy's main artillery reserve with eight machines, a full squad. She'd have been happier with a sixteen-strider platoon at least, but there hadn't been time to scavenge more from a hard-pressed and rapidly thinning front line. She wished, too, that she could talk with Major Vic Hagan, the CO of the second element, but the assault platoon was observing strict communications silence.

"Ready for drop, Colonel," Nadry announced. "I'm picking up heavy H-band radar. Somebody just got curious."

"I see it," Katya replied. Alerts flickered across the bottom of her visual field, warning of a weapons lock, probably for a battery of strider-mounted missiles. "Kurt? What do you make of it?"

Warrant Tech Officer Kurt Allen, one of two men crammed into her Warlord with her, was already scanning the radar traces, searching for a point source.

"I've got a dozen different transmitters, Colonel," he replied, his voice as calm and steady as always. "Probably remotes, set up so we don't get an active lock on the launch platforms."

"No problem," Sublieutenant Ryan Green, her pilot, said. "We'll spot 'em when they launch!"

A green light flashed in her display. "Five seconds!" Nadry announced. "Cutting internal feeds!"

Power and sensor feeds from the ascraft switched off, and

Katya's view of the outside world was replaced by a claustrophobic half darkness: duralloy armor and a tiny wedge of moving ground beneath her feet. Display feeds and alerts glowed balefully at the periphery of her vision. "You've got the legs, Ryan," she told the pilot.

"Rog!" His mental voice was high-pitched, taut with excitement. "Jets hot!"

Abruptly, the Stormwind went nose high, bellying toward the hill at a point just below its crest. Air roared through the ascraft's intakes; fusion-heated plasma shrieked from directional, ball-pivot venturis directed forward and down, blasting at rock and sand in swirling, superheated clouds.

Ten meters above the slope, Katya gave a mental command. Magnetic grapples released their hold on her warstrider, and she fell from the ascraft's riderslot, a clean drop. The ground rushed up at her, and then the jump pack strapped to her Warlord jolted her with the savage kick of twin jets slamming upward against almost sixty tons of falling mass.

Contact! She hit gravel and dirt with a savage jar, the flanged feet of her RS-64GC Warlord gouging into the ground before whining gyros helped her recapture a precarious balance. Since Green had the Warlord's legs—meaning control of its movement—Katya simply watched as the combat machine unfolded itself into combat mode, the sharply angled, digitigrade legs taking the weight of the fuselage with the high-pitched whine of servos. The strider lurched as the left foot slipped in soft earth, then steadied itself. Nanoflage layers on the outer hull lightened to a pale, mottled tan in response to the brightly lit surroundings. The machine's name, painted on either side of the blunt, heavily armored snout, was *Assassin's Blade*.

Katya scanned the surroundings on broadband receptors. Ten meters away, Kilroy's KR-9 Manta dropped from the sky on jets of flaring plasma, landing with a crash as better than forty tons impacted on the hill. Overhead, the ascraft continued to drift upslope, spilling two more combat machines as it moved. Halliwell's Ghostrider and Sebree's Scoutstrider fell clear, triggered their jump packs, and slammed into the hillside.

Searing hot air roared and snapped around Katya's head. The ascraft's engines spooled up, carrying it in a tight arc clear of the hilltop. The other striders were unfolding now, arms and weapons pods sliding out from beneath articulated armor panels.

Warnings flashed across *Blade*'s visuals. *Missiles incoming...*

"Kurt!" she yelled over the Warlord's ICS.

"Tracking!" the weapons tech called back. "On auto!" The Warlord's high-velocity rotary cannon, under the direction of the strider's onboard AI, whipped about in its mount faster than human nerve impulses could have guided it. White flame spat from the whirling barrels.

A trio of explosions slammed out of the sky as missiles detonated short of their target, but other missiles continued to arrow in from the south at Mach 5, too fast to dodge, too fast, in this rugged terrain, for the hivel cannon to kill them all. Their target, however, was not the grounded warstriders, but the tempting bulk of the ascraft, still meters above the slope and just beginning to accelerate clear of the drop zone. Hivel cannons on the Stormwind's hull fired in automatic response to the approaching threat; more missiles detonated, but two plunged through the expanding clouds of smoke and debris to slam into the ascraft's side. The twin concussions staggered Katya; the containment fields in the Stormwind's fusorpack collapsed, releasing microfusion blasts that shredded the air/spacecraft and sent a fireball washing across the hell-blasted hillside, a tidal wave of searing heat and light that scoured the nanoflage from *Blade*'s upper hull.

Automatic filters built into the sensors darkened the landscape for a second, then faded, restoring Katya's vision. Sublieutenant Green dropped the warstrider into a half crouch as bits of shrapnel sang off the dorsal armor. Burning chunks of wreckage were pelting like hail from the sky, but in seconds, Green had the Warlord in motion, charging up the last few meters of hillside toward the crest.

They'd been spotted too early, but maybe ... *maybe*, Katya thought, willing it to be so, the enemy forces on the other side of the hill could still be taken by surprise. If the enemy forces thought the Stormwind had been destroyed before it could drop its payload of warstriders ...

"*Assassins!*" she yelled over the squad comnet. "Deploy! Deploy! Spread wide! Move it!" The second element's

Stormwind thundered in low two hundred meters to the east, spilling its cargo of four more warstriders. Through boiling streams of smoke, she saw Hagan's Ghostrider, *Mission Link*, touching down, followed by Jacobsen's lean, long-legged Stormstrider and a pair of Scoutstriders.

Gravel sprayed from beneath the Warlord's feet as it crested the hill. Beyond, sheltered in a bowl-shaped valley, was the enemy artillery park, rank upon bristling rank of track- and leg-mounted field artillery, squat-bodied Calliopedes and Basilisks and chunky-bodied Gorgons, off-line and, for the moment, unmanned. Katya could see crew personnel in red running among their machines or clambering into open hatches. The camouflaged domes of a major encampment were clustered on the far side of the valley.

And warstriders. Damn! *Those* hadn't appeared on the satellite scans, at least a full platoon of medium to heavy warstriders, deployed in a defensive perimeter about the powered-down arties. Katya knew in that moment that she'd just bitten off a hell of a lot more than she could chew.

She could still hear Vic Hagan arguing with her, just hours ago. "Damn it, Colonel, regimental commanders do *not* go on combat drops," he'd bellowed. "And they damn sure don't go behind enemy lines in squad-strength deployments!"

She'd had reasons to make the deployment, however, reasons that she didn't particularly want to discuss with her regimental number two. She was going to pay for her stubbornness now, she knew.

But it was going to be worth it!

"Assassins, this is Assassin Leader!" she called. "Ignore the striders. We're here to cripple the arties if we can. Pour it on!"

Laser and missile fire volleyed from the long crest above the valley, slashing into the parked combat machines. Katya had decided that morning, judging from the satellite imagery, that the equipment sequestered in the shadow of Hill 232 was the enemy's primary strategic reserve. Smash that, and his forward lines would have no support when the main attack went down in another . . . make it thirty-five minutes. His front line was already desperately thin; one good push and it ought to crumble, so long as there was no rear echelon mobile artillery to plug the gaps or lay down long-range fire on the advancing strider assault groups.

As unit commander, Katya was supposed to stay off-line from her Warlord's control and weapons systems. Fighting the machine was what Kurt and Ryan were aboard for. Instead, Katya concentrated on the cascade of data and AI-generated graphics moving across her visual display. It was hard to resist the temptation to take over part of the RS-64's weaponry, though. Its main armament, massive charged particle guns mounted to left and right like blocky, thick-muscled arms, discharged in flaring blasts of raw current, punching through the dorsal armor of a Qu-19E Calliopede with a blast that hurled bits and pieces of its internal mechanism high into the air. Lightning forked and crackled from the stricken vehicle to the ground as excess charge bled away; debris rained from the sky as oily black smoke boiled overhead. The Warlord's other weapons were in action too, grenades and explosive chaingun rounds from the ventral Mark III weapons pod, 50-MW pulses of energy from the stubby, twin lasers mounted to either side of the fuselage. Striker missiles shrieked from the dorsal Y-rack, arrowing into the hellfire chaos of the valley in a pair of blindly slashing salvos.

The other striders of the Assassin strike team kept up a slamming, devastating barrage. Two more mobile artillery pieces exploded into flame. An instant later, a pile of 112-mm artillery rockets stacked for loading aboard a line of vehicles detonated in a rippling chain of blasts that swept across the valley, toppling men and warstriders alike, scattering them like ninepins.

Incoming laser fire struck the rocks five meters to Katya's left. Moisture flashed to steam and the rocks exploded; gravel shrieked and rattled off the Warlord's armored flank. The enemy warstriders, taken by surprise, were starting to move toward the Assassins' positions now, their return fire heavy, and growing heavier. Sebree's RLN-90 Scoutstrider staggered under a triplet of direct hits, 90-mm high-explosive rockets spearing squarely into its pilot's module, shearing off one arm and the upper half of the machine's fuselage and leaving the rest standing, legs frozen, upper hull peeled open like a fire-blackened tin can. Kilroy's Manta took a high-powered laser hit on the ventral surface of the flattened saucer shape of its main hull. Duralloy flared with white heat; blackened, twisted wiring and severed power conduits dangled from the gaping wound, a smoking, oil-bleeding disembowelment.

But the Assassins held their ground, lowering their fuselages to take advantage of the cover provided by height and the rugged ground, slamming round after round into the packed and unmoving targets below at a range of less than a hundred meters. As the destruction continued, the valley began filling with dense, white smoke, partly from the savage detonations of the Assassins' barrage, partly from the shrouding smoke screens generated by enemy striders both to cloak their movement and to attenuate the savage laser fire snapping down from the crest of the hill.

Katya estimated that at least half of the mobile artillery walkers and vehicles had been destroyed outright or so badly crippled they would never participate in the coming battle.

A missile detonated against her right shoulder, jolting her hard. There was no pain, but she did feel as though someone had landed a solid blow on her arm, and alerts began scrolling down the right side of her visual display, warning of a short-circuiting power couple, damaged kinesthetic relays, and a failure in *Assassin's Blade*'s right CPG targeting system. The strider was moving and firing, so both Kurt and Ryan were still on-line; Katya implemented the primary damage control sequence, then checked the lasercom link with the surviving Assassins. Two dead, so far, three badly damaged, including the *Blade*.

Radar showed a solid return less than thirty meters ahead, advancing up the slope toward Katya's right. She shifted to infrared, adjusting the wavelength reception until haze coalesced into the glowing image of a warstrider.

She recognized that machine, a KR-200 Battlewraith, a fifty-four–ton monster sporting a left-side electron cannon and a heavy assault arsenal of lasers, missiles, and short-range cannon firing explosive shells. More to the point, she recognized that specific machine, for it had a General Command module strapped to its dorsal hull, a GC modification identical to the one mounted on her own Warlord. It was moving swiftly upslope, angling toward Hagan's warstrider element to the east.

"Kurt! Ryan!" she called over the ICS circuit. "I've got control!"

A mental code switched command of the Warlord to her cephlinkage, leaving Green and Allen interested spectators.

Suddenly, Katya was occupying the warstrider's body as though it were her own; her right arm was out of action, but she could bring up her left, dragging the targeting cursor blinking on her display up and onto the Battlewraith's upper hull. The target was closer now, less than twenty meters, and apparently still unaware of the *Assassin's Blade* crouched among the boulders on the hilltop. A *push* with her mind, and the charged particle bolt lanced through smoky air, striking dead on target with a flash and a crack of thunder.

Got you, Travis Sinclair! she thought with savage satisfaction. Another push sent the last of the Warlord's M-21 rockets slamming into the Battlewraith's side. *You goking bastard . . .*

The Battlewraith staggered back a step, then turned, its electron cannon sweeping up, seeking a target. Katya was already in motion, however, sprinting those last twenty meters in an all-out charge downhill, stepping beneath the wicked-looking muzzle of the EPC, slamming against unyielding armor with the deadweight of her damaged right arm/CPG mount.

The collision loosed a savage thunder and jolted Katya so hard that her data feed momentarily winked out. When it switched on again, her right arm was on the ground, torn away by the impact, while her foe's Battlewraith, caught off-balance, was rolling back down the hill, an avalanche of black duralloy. She followed . . .

. . . and caught a 100-MW laser burst squarely on the Warlord's forward glacis, a slashing attack that peeled back armor and severed her primary actuator links. She felt her legs go numb, but she was able to shift the strider's command function back to Ryan, hoping that it was her linkage that had been damaged, not his. "C'mon, Ryan," she cried into the ICS. The Wraith was getting up again, staggering erect. Sinclair's machine was terribly damaged, but still more than a match for the smaller, lighter Warlord. "Move! Move!"

A salvo of M-21 rockets slammed into the RS-64's already battered glacis. Explosions tore through the heart of *Assassin's Blade*, and Katya felt her linkage slipping. . . .

Katya found herself blinking at the smooth, gray metal of a link module's overhead. Numb with the aftereffects of battle lust, it took her a moment to remember where she was . . . what she was doing.

Today's engagement had been a full-realism sim managed by an entire orchestra of AIs to allow thousands of striderjacks and technicians to experience the joint virtual reality of a full-scale war. Katya's new unit, the 1st Confederation Rangers, had been up against warstriders jacked by the Confederation's staff command and naval contingent.

She'd not really expected the exchange to become so . . . *personal*.

"Colonel?"

Turning her head, she saw Allen's face peering into the module's opening at her. Ryan Green stood just behind him. "Hi, Kurt, Ryan. I guess we lost, huh?"

"Something like that," Allen said. "You okay?"

Deftly, she unplugged herself from the three feeds jacked into her temporal and cervical sockets. Her hair, short on the sides and neck to keep it clear of her hardware, was longer on top and in front and had plastered itself across her head. She ran her fingers through it, dragging it off her face.

"Not bad, considering I just took a hundred megs through my belly." Unstrapping herself from the link module, she swung long legs off the padded couch, stooped to get through the opening, and stood up on the gleaming white deck outside. Dozens of other link modules surrounded her, some occupied, most empty.

"Colonel Alessandro?"

Turning, she saw the gray-uniformed figure of one of the games monitors, standing behind her with a compad in her hand. "That's me."

"You're dead, Colonel. You and both of your crew members."

"So I gathered." Her eyes narrowed. "Do you have an active link with the Rogue? How about my opponent in that last exchange?"

The technician glanced down at her pad, palming the interface to open a new feed. "According to the battlesim AI," she said, reading the screen, "you inflicted sixty percent damage on the Battlewraith you attacked. One of its crew members was killed, one more badly hurt. The third was able to return fire. His missile barrage touched off your Warlord's fusorpack."

"The one I killed. Who was he?"

The technician checked her pad again. "The *simulated* casualty was General Sinclair himself. But you must have known that, Colonel. Your initial shot was quite accurate."

"Hey, if we're dead, when's the funeral service?" Ryan wanted to know. "I'd like to attend."

"That may depend on my court-martial," Katya said. She meant it as a joke, but she couldn't help wondering what was going to come of her actions this morning. She'd broken several regulations in today's full-combat simulation, as well as showing some rather impetuous recklessness. There was bound to be some fallout.

Katya didn't care. It had been worth it, damn it. Worth it and then some.

She felt lots better now, having killed Travis Sinclair.

Chapter 5

Most of the worlds of the Shichiju have at least one sky-el, a space elevator that makes travel between the planet's surface and synchronous orbit cheap and simple, if considerably slower than ascraft passage. Grown from synchorbit by enormous factories that nanotechnically transform carbonaceous chondrite asteroids into duralloy, sky-els have proven vital in the terraforming of prebiotic worlds, an inexpensive conduit from space to ground for the nanofactories and equipment necessary to rework a planetary atmosphere.

In the two and a half centuries since the first sky-el was demonstrated on Sol IV, there have been remarkably few system failures, even including those, like the one on Herakles, that were the result of deliberate action.

—*Man and the Stars: A History of Technology*
Ieyasu Sutsumi
C.E. 2531

The hell of it was, Katya had once damn near idolized the man. General Travis Sinclair was more than the leader of the Confederation in its rebellion against Hegemony and Empire. A member of the Confederation Congress from New America, he'd been appointed commander of the rebel army at a time when a unified army as such didn't even exist. Single-handedly, he'd begun building that army . . . and a navy as well, recruiting key people like Katya and Dev Cameron and turning them loose with money, personnel, and equipment raised from God knew where.

Sinclair's genius had, at the very least, avoided a crushing defeat by the overwhelmingly powerful forces arrayed against them. More important than that, he'd been the principal author of the Declaration of Reason, a document that, like another Declaration penned over seven centuries earlier, outlined the philosophy of the revolt. By condemning the evils of the centralized state and its attempts to unite disparate worlds and cultures, it had become the focus of the entire Rebellion. In many ways Travis Sinclair *was* the Rebellion.

Somehow, though, Katya's hero worship of the man had gradually been transformed . . . not into hatred, precisely, but into a distance as cold, she thought, as the cold, political calculation that had led Sinclair a few months ago to abandon her beloved New America to the Empire. Oh, she knew the reasons, the rationale for the Confederation's retreat from her homeworld. What hurt, though, were the friends, the comrades at arms left behind while a scant, chosen few had fled here, to Herakles. She'd just begun assembling and training the 1st Confederation Rangers on New America when Sinclair had issued the order to abandon the place for a secret base on this empty world. He'd brought with him a select handful of people, including Katya and Dev and a few others with experience or key skills, but the majority, of necessity, had been left behind.

How many, she wondered, were still alive, after months of guerrilla warfare against Imperial warstriders? While she was *here* playing war games!

Katya had met Sinclair on New America, where he'd recruited her to the cause. Her experience leading a Hegemony strider company had come to his attention, and he'd suggested that her talents might be best employed helping to create a Confederation armored unit that could replace the wide-scattered and poorly trained militias that were currently carrying the brunt of the fighting against the Empire. Local militias had won impressive victories early in the war, on Eridu, on Eostre, and on Liberty, but those victories had proven temporary. Eridu was again in Imperial hands after a brief period of self-rule; at New America, Imperial Marines now maintained a harsh and bloody peace while battle squadrons kept watch from orbit.

She thought about Dev, raiding the Imperial supply lines on the outskirts of the New American system.

No. Best not to think of that. Or of him. . . .

The hell of it was, moving the rebel government to Herakles hadn't purchased much time. The Imperials had figured out where they were and sent a battle squadron in, coming *that* close to annihilating the Confederation Congress and the Rebellion in one swift strike. All that had stopped them was Dev's bizarre union with the Naga lurking in the depths of Herakles's planetary crust. Three months had passed since then, with no sign of the Imperials, but everyone on Herakles knew their return was only a matter of time.

The sacrifice of New America had been wasted . . . *wasted.*

Now, scant hours after the end of the simulated battle, Katya was aboard an air/spacecraft outbound from New Argosport. The hotbox booster engines had fallen silent, and the arrowhead shape of the ascraft fell through the night above Herakles, anticollision strobes pulsing with metronomic precision at dorsal ridge, wingtips, and belly. She'd received the message from Rogue only moments after her own simulated death, a summons to join Travis Sinclair in orbit. She'd barely had time to return to her quarters and pack, arriving at the port just fifteen minutes before the scheduled launch.

Sinclair had told her nothing during their brief conversation, but she was under no illusions about why she'd been summoned so precipitously to orbit. Vic had been right. Regimental commanders don't join squad-level deployments, and they don't mix it up in strider-to-strider combat. Having logged orders to ignore the enemy strider force and concentrate fire on the artillery, they don't then disregard those orders to chase after the enemy commander's Battlewraith.

And they certainly don't turn a training simulation into a personal vendetta.

Linked, Katya tried to concentrate on the panorama spreading out around her. Astern, Herakles was a smear of oceanic blue-violet and the white gleam of clouds and ice, a vast sphere half-illuminated by the brassy, subgiant's glare of Mu Herculis A. To the right, Mu Herculis B and C were a tightly paired, ruby-gleaming doublet. Left and below, the star Vega, only a few light-years distant from the Mu Herculis system, was a dazzling gleam in the blackness, so bright it washed other stars from the sky and touched the clouds on the nightside of Herakles with ghost-pale silver.

Katya's attention was held, however, by a tight-stretched thread of silver suspended directly ahead against blackness and the glare of Herc A. Razor's-edge crisp and straight, the line seemed unmoving, though ladar returns indicated it possessed a speed of several kilometers per second and was rotating end over end. As Katya continued to watch, a subtle shift in perspective and in the silver-gilt terminator between light and shadow demonstrated movement, and a rapidly closing range.

Herakles, Mu Herculis A-III, was unique among the worlds of the Shichiju, for its sky-el was no longer attached to the planet's equator. Instead, the structure fell around Herakles in an eccentric orbit that brought one end within two hundred kilometers of the surface each week, though most of the time its center of mass was located well beyond synchorbit. Some thirty thousand kilometers long now and only meters thick, it was held taut by centrifugal force as it spun.

Katya was jacked into the ascraft's command link. Technically, she was a passenger aboard the ground-to-orbit shuttle, but Captain Chalmer, the ship's pilot, had invited her to link in from her module aft shortly after launch from the New Argos port complex. She could see the rogue sky-el ahead with the crisply detailed, unimpeded clarity of sensor feeds direct from the ascraft's visual scanners. Numbers flickering past the right side of her awareness gave range and target vectors, angle of approach, and closing velocity. The ascraft was closing with the lower arm with a relative velocity of only fifty meters per second.

"So what brings you up to synchorbit?" Chalmer asked, his voice sounding close beside her in the dark. "We don't often get to see you infantry types here on the whirligig."

"They've been keeping me pretty busy," Katya replied, distracted. "Building an army from nothing is a job for magicians, not a brain-burned striderjack like me."

"Brain-burned? You? Nah, the way I heard it, Captain Cameron's the one who's brain-burned if anyone is."

"Why do you say that?"

"Aw, no disrespect meant, Colonel. It's just that some of the stories . . . Hey, is the who-was about him the straight hont? That he was really linked in with the Xeno down there?"

"Yes. It's true."

"And it didn't hurt him?"

Katya had been hearing who-was—*uwasu* or rumors—about Dev for months, often enough that Chalmer's question didn't hurt . . . at least not as much as it might have once. She turned the query aside with a mental shrug. "He was fine, last time I saw him."

"I just can't get over the idea of . . . of touching one of those things. Touching a *Xeno*."

"Why not? That's how we communicate with them."

"Yeah, you've done it too, haven't you, Colonel? On Eridu? I'd forgotten that."

Her reply had been less than completely honest. It was true that humans could communicate with the Naga now if they wore one of the strange DalRiss comels, but Dev's experience with the Heraklean Naga a few months ago had been . . . unique, and far more intimate than any communication Katya had ever experienced with Nagas. As far as any of the medtechs and psych people who'd examined him could tell, Dev had come out of his symbiosis with the Heraklean Naga with no ill effects, physical or mental.

Still, it was impossible not to wonder . . . and worry. Dev had always shown a propensity for a brooding moodiness ever since she'd met him as a warstrider recruit on Loki over three years ago. Since his encounter with the Heraklean Naga, though, he'd seemed . . . darker, somehow. As though the black organism that had briefly linked itself to his body and his mind had also touched his soul.

She didn't like thinking about that.

Why hasn't Dev returned? she asked herself. *What's keeping him?* Checking her internal RAM's calendar for the third time that day, she noted once again that he was at least a week overdue already. Given the vagaries of mission, of K-T space passages, of loiter times in other systems, there was no reason to worry yet; the due date was simply *Eagle*'s earliest possible ETA.

Still . . .

The cast-off sky-el was closer now, its silvery length glittering in the sunlight. A number of ships, visible at this distance only as starlike gleams of reflected light, were clustered about the thread's center of spin, but the ascraft was closing on a point some distance out from the center. As the minutes passed, the sky-el's hab center became visible, first as a shadowed thickening in the thread, then as a long, cylindrical structure attached to the el's main body catching sunlight along one edge in a dazzle of white fire. Lights winked in syncopated rhythm with the ascraft's anticollision strobes. A docking collar was illuminated by a circle of harsh spotlights.

For the time being, at least, that cylinder was the location of the Confederation's capital. It seemed a strange place to house a multiworld government.

The Heraklean sky-el's elongated orbit, its end-over-end spin through space, had never been intended by its builders. Normally, a sky-el's towerdown was secured to a suitable spot at the planet's equator; the other end was anchored and held taut well beyond synchorbit by a suitably massive asteroid hauled into place by tugs. Passenger and cargo pods rode up and down the completed tower then on lines of magnetic flux, providing cheap and easy elevator service between ground and synchronous orbit. Only a few colonies did not have one, either because the world had such a slow rotation that synchorbit was impossibly far from the planet's surface, or because—as with Katya's own homeworld of New America—the tides raised by a large, close satellite made building one impractical.

The sky-el tower on Mu Herculis A-III had been raised late in the twenty-fourth century, and terraforming had begun soon after. Within a century and a half, the hot and poisonous prebiotic atmosphere had been transformed to one breathable by humans; too, replacing the carbon dioxide with oxygen and nitrogen had caused the world's mean temperature to plummet forty degrees. The colonial capital of Argos, still partly domed, spread out from the sky-el's towerdown on the Augean Peninsula, a gleaming webwork of habitats, streets, and nanomanufactory farms.

Then, in 2515, the Xeno had appeared.

Seeking the pure metals and exotic materials it could sense from its kilometers-deep tunnels, the vast, amoebic organism had reacted identically to the Xenos of other colony worlds, dispatching pieces of itself to the surface, employing an alien nanotechnology to disassemble those materials—the buildings, domes, habs, and vehicles of a civilization of which the Xeno was completely unaware. After months of battle against the marauding Xeno scouts, the Heraklean population had escaped up the sky-el while Hegemony infantry held off the Xeno attackers for a critical two weeks in a vicious, rear-guard defense. Not long after the handful of surviving troops had been evacuated, and as Xenophobes smashed through the emptied city toward the sky-el's base, a five-hundred–megaton fusion explosion had gouged a half-kilometer-deep crater where Argos had stood; the sky-el, its lower end burned off in the blast, had been catapulted into high orbit by its space-side anchor.

The stress had fragmented much of the sky-el's original length, whipcracking much of the ends, including the anchoring planetoid, into space; what was left, some thirty thousand kilometers of gleaming duralloy weave over ten meters thick, continued to circle the planet in a six-day orbit that brushed the upper reaches of the atmosphere once on each pass. Within the next century or so, those repeated brushes would degrade its orbit enough that the artifact would impact on Herakles.

In the meantime, though, and for the foreseeable future, the free sky-el offered a haven of sorts for the Confederation government. After the sky-el's link with Herakles had been broken, the Hegemony had built a watchpost there to keep an electronic eye on the Heraklean Xeno, attaching a large, cylindrical habitat to the cable, positioning it far enough from the el's center to generate a spin-gravity of roughly half a G. After the explosion that had destroyed Argos, however, the Naga had never reappeared on the surface, and the outpost was eventually abandoned. It had remained empty until the

Confederation forces had arrived, just over four months ago.

They called the free-orbiting facility Rogue.

Nudged closer by bursts from maneuvering thrusters, the ascraft rotated smoothly ninety degrees as it matched velocity with the hab's docking collar, then slipped into place with the metallic clangs and thumps of magnetic grapples locking home.

"End of the ride," Chalmer told her. "Hey, Colonel, are you going to be up here long? I mean, maybe we could get together for dinner or some duo simming or something. . . ."

"Negative," Katya said, the word curt. The pilot's attempt at familiarity explained his earlier questions about Dev. Everyone knew that she and Dev were close; Chalmer was prospecting, wondering if she was available while Dev was out-system. Or maybe he was just probing to find out if she still had the same relationship with Dev that she'd had before his bonding with that . . . *thing*.

Abruptly, she downloaded the mental codes that severed her link with the ascraft's systems. She awoke inside her link module, a padded, partly enclosed ceramplast egg on the shuttle's passenger deck. Blinking at the change in illumination, she lifted the intricate web of gold and silver wires embedded in the base of her left palm from the module's AI interface and unfastened her harness.

The shuttle had docked with the rogue sky-el with its nose oriented toward the center of rotation; sharing the hab's spin-gravity, "down" was now toward the ascraft's tail. Carefully, she swung out of the module while the rest of the passengers were still unstrapping and started climbing the ladder embedded in the deck toward the forward lock. Katya didn't particularly want to see the pilot in person, so she hurried, knowing he was still engaged in shutting down the ascraft's systems. She was afraid that if she met him outside the virtual reality of the link, it might end with Chalmer getting hurt, and she didn't want that. The Confederation was desperately short of qualified shipjackers as it was.

The habitat had been constructed by Hegemony personnel with Imperial technology. The inner door of the hab's lock didn't open; it dissolved when air pressure on both sides had matched, as the inner bulkhead's nanotechnic components redefined themselves from an impermeable solid to an elastically bonded gas. Pushing through the barrier's slight resistance, she stepped onto the hab's entry level, and the lock's bulkhead rematerialized at her back.

"Hello, Katya. Welcome to the Rogue."

"General." She felt wary, could feel the gulf that had grown between them. "How . . . are you?"

"Pretty good for someone who's just been killed by one of his subordinates." His wry grin robbed the words of any sting. "Thanks for coming up on such short notice. Have you eaten yet?"

Both Rogue and New Argos were on the same Heraklean clock, and it was well past the midday meal. Her stomach grumbled at the mere thought of food. "No, sir, I haven't. But—"

"Then eat with me, Colonel. Please."

She allowed him to lead her from the entry deck, taking an elevator to Deck Three and the main cafeteria. The room, somewhat cramped but opened up by a viewall looking into space, was not very crowded at this hour, though Katya recognized several Confed naval officers at one of the tables. She wished she could chat with them, but after getting her tray—the meal that day was a nano-grown synthetic resembling *sashimi*—she followed Sinclair back to another table.

Japanese food, especially any involving even artificial raw fish, was not Katya's favorite. The hab environmental systems, however, had been programmed years ago by the Imperials who'd set up the Heraklean watch station, and in the months since the Confederation had moved in there'd been neither time nor personnel to reprogram the manufactories. She set her tray down opposite Sinclair, who stood for her with his hand over his heart in an almost courtly display of New American etiquette.

Katya had been dreading this meeting, and she was ashamed of the fact. Travis Ewell Sinclair was indisputably brilliant, and scarcely the monster she somehow wanted him to be. The necessities of leadership forced hard choices, she knew, choices not always popular with the people who had to carry them out. The decision to abandon New America in the face of an invasion had been such a choice, as had been the decision to leave behind so many of the men and women who'd been fighting at Katya's side. She understood the military necessity of such command decisions very well. She couldn't be a colonel in the Confederation's ground forces without that understanding.

But neither could she carry out her orders without experiencing a wrenching change in her feelings for the man who'd given them.

"I'm glad you could come, Katya," Sinclair said, taking his seat. He smiled across the table at her. "I . . . have news."

She'd been expecting an official chewing out. The unexpected words startled her and then, as their meaning sank in, Katya's hopes leaped. "Dev?"

Sinclair ran one hand through his hair, which he wore unstylishly long. His hair and beard were dark, but shot through with streaks of gray. "Yes. Captain Cameron's in-system again, and with another prize. I just got word as they were pulling me out of that simulation." He gave her a rueful smile. "You pack quite a punch, young lady. Sometime, you'll have to tell me what the CO of the 1st Rangers was doing in my rear, with eight warstriders!"

"Destroying your mobile artillery, General. Wasn't that obvious? What's Dev's ETA?"

"He should be docking with Rogue in another ten hours."

"Wonderful! How . . . how is he?"

"Seems fine," Sinclair replied. "I ViRcommed with him about an hour ago, while you were on the way up. He said to give you his love."

Katya smiled at that. "Thank you, sir. For telling me."

"That's not why I asked you to come up here."

"Of course not." *Here it comes*, she thought.

"The last prize that Captain Cameron took had some rather momentous data squirreled away in its shipboard memory."

"Yes?" That apparent swerve from the topic at hand caught her interest. The most important weapon in any war was information—intelligence, in the military lexicon—and a primary source was the data banks of enemy AIs.

"It seems that the ship, an independent trader called the *Kasuga Maru*, was part of a supply convoy to the Imperial garrison on Alya A-VI a few months ago. While they were in orbit, they recorded a number of radio transmissions between the surface and the Imperial squadron. We're not entirely sure what's happening out there, but it sounds as though the DalRiss have attacked an Imperial ground base."

"Attacked it! Why?"

"We don't know. But if the report is true, it puts a new and higher priority on Operation Farstar."

Katya paused, the chopsticks holding a bit of artificial raw fish hovering between a dish of fiery-hot mustard and her mouth. Slowly, she returned the morsel to the plate and set the chopsticks down. Her hunger was forgotten, as was her dislike for Sinclair.

"I'd say it's about goddamned time."

"You still want to be a part of it?"

"Of course. If anything's going to end this damned war, Farstar is it."

"I agree. And your feelings about Dev Cameron going along?"

She had to think about how to answer that one, though she knew what her gut feelings said. "It'll be good to have him along, of course. For a number of reasons." And not just because this would be a long, long trip, and she loved him and hated the idea of perhaps another year away from his side. "I suspect that the real question is how he feels about it, though. And how you plan to handle . . . handle *it* while he's gone. It wouldn't do to leave Herakles defenseless while we're off gallivanting with the DalRiss."

"Oh, we won't be defenseless. Dev's not the only one who can Xenolink. But there has been, ah, speculation about how well he's recovered after his experience. I was wondering how you felt about Dev linking with you on this—"

"You were sure enough of Dev to let him take *Eagle* out commerce raiding." Her reply was harsher than she'd intended. "Why should this be any different?"

"Because you'll be dealing with the DalRiss. And you may well be linking with a Naga again. With *another* Naga, the one at Alya B. The strangeness factor's going to be something awful. I want to know that you can handle it. And that you think he can."

"If Dev Cameron can't handle it," Katya said quietly, "nobody can!"

"That," Sinclair said with a small grin, "is exactly what I wanted to hear."

And maybe it'll be good to get away from here, Katya told herself. *Just me and Dev and a few thousand warstriders. Like old times!*

She wondered what Dev was going to say when he heard. Most of the final plans for Farstar had been put together after he'd left. She imagined, though, that he would be pleased. He'd not been at all happy with the possibility of Xenolinking again, not after what had happened during the Imperial assault on Herakles.

A long diplomatic mission to a people still largely incomprehensible to humans might be exactly what he needed.

Cephlink technology extends human productivity by reducing the time necessary to achieve expertise.

Cephlink technology increases personal stress levels by reducing the time necessary to acquire physical experience.

—Fielding's First and Second Laws
Man and His Works
Dr. Karl Gunther Fielding
C.E. 2448

Eagle rendezvoused with the Rogue's hub fifteen hours after dropping out of K-T space. The *Kasuga Maru*, with her lower acceleration, would not arrive in Heraklean orbit for some days yet, but the treasure trove discovered in her AI by her prize crew during the long passage home had been transferred to a high-density molecular datachip, which Dev was now hand-carrying to the Confederation AI technicians on the Rogue.

Eagle was too large to dock directly with the slow-turning fragment of sky-el. Instead, she took up a parking orbit with the rest of the tiny Confederation fleet a few hundred kilometers clear of the segment's rotational hub. There were perhaps thirty vessels in orbit now, mostly freighters, transports, and small escort vessels, frigates and corvettes. Standing out among the others was the sleek, planoform liner *Transluxus*, formerly a Star Lines passenger ship, now the rather luxuriously appointed transportation for the Confederation Congress. She hung ten kilometers off, agleam in the golden light of Mu Herculis, with only a small service and maintenance crew aboard her.

After seeing to *Eagle* and the establishment of orbital routine—and consulting with Lieutenant Canady about watch schedules and liberty aboard the Rogue—Dev ferried across in a work shuttle. Docking at the hub, he transferred to a rider pod, a small capsule that tapped the centrifugal force created by the sky-el's spin and slid "down" a magnetic rail to the hab modules at the half-G level.

The hab's travel concourse was a large and comfortably furnished compartment, but one made crowded by people waiting for pods to or from other parts of the sky-el, or who, like Dev, were newly arrived. The far bulkhead created the illusion of roominess, with its curved viewall set to display a panorama of space dominated by the half sphere of Herakles.

Sinclair and part of his personal staff were waiting for Dev as he broke free of the crowd by the travel pod locks. The New American general and political philosopher was the only man present in civilian clothes, including a formal, white half-cape. The rest wore military uniforms, two-toned gray like Dev's own bodysuit for navy, two-toned brown for army. Within both the military and the government of the young Confederation, such niceties as details of dress uniforms were still in a state of flux. Even something as basic as ranks were still confused, with the rebels still in the process of switching from the *Nihongo* system favored by the Hegemony to one based on the old, pre-Hegemony systems. Though designs could easily be changed simply by reprogramming the nano that manufactured such articles as bodysuits and rank insignia, it was actually difficult to standardize such things, given the sheer size and dispersion of the forces involved, especially under the press of more urgent business. Dev noted with mild amusement that despite the impressive show of ceremony, most of the uniforms and the rank and service insignia at their collars didn't match, and one navy captain in Sinclair's entourage wore the dress whites of Hegemony service, with a *taisa*'s three chrysanthemum pips at his collar. That was understandable, of course. Most of the Confederation's naval personnel had once served with the Hegemony navy.

The display tended to reinforce the image of the Confederation military as something of a patchwork of cultures and organizations and rugged individualists. That anything was ever decided on, Dev thought, was nothing less than miraculous.

"Permission to come aboard," Dev said, rendering the crisp Hegemony naval salute.

"Granted," General Darwin Smith, the senior man in uniform, replied.

"Welcome back, Captain," Sinclair added.

"Good to be back, sir. Here's the baby." He handed the datachip, swaddled carefully within its transport case, to Sinclair, who passed it on to one of his officers. Frozen within the chip's crystalline lattice was a tiny galaxy of charges representing some trillions of bytes of data lifted from *Kasuga Maru*'s data banks. Dev hadn't had the time to go through more than a tiny fraction of that information yet—but he knew that much of it was AI encoding for several ViRcom exchanges accidentally intercepted by the *Kasuga Maru*'s communications suite and routinely filed. If the TJK—the *Taikokuno Johokyoku,* or Imperial Intelligence Bureau—had learned that an independent merchant ship had acquired such singular intelligence . . .

"Thank you, Captain," Sinclair said. "If what you've already told me about this data is true, you may well have given us the ammunition we need to shake Farstar loose in Congress."

"I hope so, sir. If there's any way at all to get the DalRiss on our side, we've got to explore it. No matter what."

"The Congress," General Smith muttered, "is as incompetent now as it was before we left New America. I still think we should do what's right, not sit around waiting for idiot delegates to get off their asses. Uh, present company excepted, of course." Sinclair still held his position as a congressional delegate from New America.

"Military rule, Darwin?" Sinclair asked the man mildly.

Smith considered the question, then curtly nodded. "If we have to, sir, yes. Desperate times require desperate measures."

"That 'desperate times' line has been used before in history, General," Dev suggested quietly. "Usually to justify dictatorship."

"We will not win this war by becoming the very monster we're fighting against," Sinclair said. "We will observe the forms of democracy, even if the substance is meaningless as yet. Congress, even an ad hoc one such as this, is the only thing that gives us legitimacy with the people we want to join us. Those 'idiot delegates,' as you put it, are the future of this Confederation."

"Well, at least," Admiral Sigismun Halleck said, laughing, "we don't have as many of the sons of bitches to contend with now."

The Confederation Congress was considerably reduced in numbers now, over a year since it had first assembled in Jefferson, the capital of New America. When Congress had fled New America just ahead of the Imperial landings, most of the delegates who'd opposed independence for the Confederation had stayed behind. Those who'd escaped to Herakles had, for the most part, been those dedicated to a complete political break with the Terran Hegemony.

But that didn't mean that all was harmonious among the remaining five-hundred–odd delegates to the Confederation Congress. Serious differences between several of the worlds continued to threaten the young government, the issue of freedom for gene-tailored people being among the most serious. The "genies" so vital to the economic strength of Rainbow were being championed by the abolitionist parties on Liberty, and the feud had spread to other worlds as well. The divisions had created enemies; battles for or against newly proposed plans had become political struggles that had little to do with whether or not those plans would help or hinder the Confederation, and everything to do with the foundations of personal power.

Of particular concern to the Congress lately had been the deployment of the Confederation's tiny fleet of warships. Too small to stand up to an Imperial battle group, it had proven good so far for little more than commerce raiding . . . and then only if it didn't run up against serious opposition. *Eagle* was still the single largest warship in the Confederation's arsenal, and even a small Imperial squadron generally included two or three ships of *Eagle*'s class as escorts for the larger cruisers and Ryu-carriers.

While Travis Sinclair had been elected by Congress to the command of the Confederation military, he still had to answer to Congress for his decisions . . . and accept its recommendations when they were put to a vote. The rebel government was as divided over what to do with its fleet now as it was over the question of freedom for the genies. Some supported the idea of using it in the long-planned, long-argued Operation Farstar; others insisted that the fleet should be kept close to the Confederation capital. Many of the delegates were still undecided, and it was their vote that Sinclair hoped to win with the news from Alya A.

"Is your crew taken care of, Captain?" Sinclair asked him.

"Yes, sir. Commander Canady, my XO, is securing the ship. She'll be letting the first liberty section come across to the Rogue starting tonight."

"That's fine. I'm afraid we still don't have much in the way of the amenities, either here or on the surface of Herakles. Things are still damned crowded up here, and a bit primitive down on the surface."

"I think more than anything else, General, they just need to see something other than the inside of *Eagle*'s bulkheads. And maybe eat something other than Nihon chow. I don't suppose? . . ."

"Ah, I'm afraid the food prep programs are still serving up the finest in Japanese cuisine," Sinclair said. "The techs have been too busy keeping the power plant up and running and getting the weapons and deep space scanners on line to worry much about the menu."

"In other words, Dev," a familiar voice said, "it's rice, vegetables, and fish for dinner again tonight."

Turning, Dev saw the slender, dark-haired woman in military browns just entering the concourse lobby. "Katya!"

"So you finally decided to come back, eh?" she said with a twinkle.

"The colonel, here," Sinclair said gravely, "has been threatening to use her Rangers as a search party if you didn't come

back to us soon. We're all relieved that you made it back."
He paused, consulting an inner voice. "Well, we have about
twelve hours before Congress is scheduled to reconvene, and
I, for one, have to review this new information that the captain
has brought us." He glanced from Dev to Katya and back
again. "Will you two be able to attend the staff briefing
afterward?"

"Of course."

"Yes, sir."

"Good. I'll see you then. In the meantime, perhaps Katya
will be good enough to show you to your quarters and get
you settled in." He grinned at them. "I imagine you have some
catching up to do."

"Thank you, sir." With military personnel coming and going
on extended missions from the Rogue, quarters were assigned
on a short-term and rotational basis, while personal effects
were stored in a cargo module near the sky-el's hub.

Dev turned to Katya as Sinclair and his entourage walked
away. "Hello, stranger."

"Hello, Dev. Welcome back. It's . . . awfully good to see
you."

"It's wonderful to see you." He glanced around the crowded concourse. "So . . . it looks like privacy is still at a
premium."

"It's worse than ever, Dev. The port and hab facilities
down at New Argos are growing fast, but not fast enough
to keep up with our growth. We've had almost eight thousand
more people arrive in the past four months, from all across
the Shichiju. The word's spreading, Dev. The whole Frontier
wants independence."

"Which leaves us looking for a place to get reacquainted."
He glanced around the concourse. The sky-el hab had originally been designed as a roomy outpost for a staff of, at
most, a hundred Imperial observers and *Sekkodan* scouts. Now,
with the facility serving both as government center for the
Confederation and as headquarters for the CONMILCOM,
the Confederation Military Command, it had a permanent
population of over seven hundred and a transient population
of perhaps a thousand more. Many people lived aboard the
various transports in orbit, but they had to rotate between
shipboard assignments and the spin-gravity habs of the sky-el

in order to stay fit and healthy. Too long a stretch of zero G made the strongest man a helpless cripple.

Most of the growing population, of course, lived on the surface. "No time to go down to Herakles, I suppose," Dev said, a little wistfully.

"Not with us as short on ascraft transport as we've been. We wouldn't make it back for at least a day or two. I think we'd better settle for a couple of com modules."

"Well, lovely lady, you provide the modules," Dev said, smiling. He tapped the side of his head with his forefinger. "And I'll provide the place. Lead on!"

Later, Dev and Katya shared a virtual reality, their bodies unfelt within separate ViRcom modules, their minds linked by software. Waves crashed along a sandy beach; the sun, westering, touched the ocean with gold and sparkling white, as sea gulls wheeled in an afternoon sky. Nearby, white foam chased skittering clusters of sandpipers up and down the sand. Dev wasn't even sure if the reality behind the scene existed anymore, so polluted had most of Earth's inshore waters been for at least the past five centuries.

But it stirred memories of home in him, and for Katya as well. Her New America had no sea gulls, but she remembered its oceans with their slow but vast, moon-driven tides, quite well.

"That's better," Dev said, turning to face her. "Alone at last!"

"Welcome home, fella," she said. "It's been awhile."

"Way too long." He reached out, took her in his arms. Their analogues in this simulation wore casual clothing, shorts and pullovers, and they were barefoot in the sand. She felt wonderful inside the circle of his arms. The simulation was exact enough that it even reproduced the smell of her hair, plucking it from his memory. "You don't know how I've been missing you!"

"Oh, I wouldn't say that. What makes you think I don't?"

They kissed. Long minutes later, Dev pulled back. "Okay. Maybe you do know." Gently, he pulled her down to the sand with him, then slid one hand up beneath her shirt, caressing bare skin.

She reached up and caught his hand, pinning it against her breast. "Dev, I'm sorry . . ."

"Oh, yeah." Gently, he pulled his hand out from under her shirt. "Sorry."

"Can we wait until we can do it . . . for real?"

"Of course."

Katya had disliked virtual sex as long as Dev had known her, even though the sensations were indistinguishable from the real thing. Sex, like any other activity and sensation, was perceived in the brain and it mattered not at all whether the stimulation came from the body's nerve endings or from an interactive data feed from an AI link. Dev never had learned why Katya felt the way she did about recjacking, but he was usually more than happy to go along.

The only problem was his aching need for her *now*. It had been four months since he'd seen her last, and the one-sided recreational simulations of Katya he'd taken along during *Eagle*'s mission no longer seemed as fresh or as real as they once had. No AI, after all, could perfectly duplicate a real person's speech and mannerisms closely enough to make them seem fresh indefinitely, not with only the linker's own memories to draw on. Halfway through *Eagle*'s passage back to Herakles, Dev had decided that it was the *unexpected* in a relationship that kept a relationship alive.

Maybe, he thought, that was why two-person recjacking linkages were so much more interesting than solos.

Since Katya didn't like virtual sex, though, they were going to have to find times and places to tryst in person, and that was likely to be impossible until they could get down to Argosport together. The "quarters" that Sinclair had mentioned was one of a number of open barracks at the quarter-G level, where as many as twenty men and women might be spending their downtime at any given hour, asleep or using the small, adjoining rec room. In a multiworld metaculture that viewed virtual sex as casually as it did downloading ViRdrama, public physical sex was tolerated, even accepted. Dev, from Earth and thoroughly familiar with the *shakai*, or Imperial overculture, was used to the idea of sex in public, though he'd never done it himself. Specific cultures within the metaculture, however, especially on the Frontier, required privacy for that most personal of personal experiences. Katya, Dev knew, was more likely to enjoy ViRsex with him than she was to engage in physical sex in one of the hab's open dorms.

Well, he told himself, he'd gone four months without the reality of Katya in his arms. He could go a few days more. It was enough just to be able to see her, to talk with her . . . at least for the moment.

"So," Dev said, trying to cover his racing thoughts, "while we were out-system, was there any sign of . . . of the Naga?"

"Nothing," Katya said cheerfully. "Not so much as a single black puddle. It seems to have retired pretty far down into the crust after it linked with you. Some of us have been speculating as to whether or not you scared it off."

"Maybe I did. It sure as hell scared me."

He shivered, and Katya reached out, putting his head in the crook of her arm and pulling him close against her side. They stared up at the slowly reddening sky.

"What do you think?" Katya said after a time. "Are they going to go with Farstar?"

"I guess that's up to Congress and to CONMILCOM," Dev replied. "I still think it's the only logical option for us. And this, this news from Alya A, gives us a chance of making it work."

"There are still people on the command staff who think the whole thing is a bad idea. In Congress, too. Sinclair has been fighting them on this idea since we got here."

"I can imagine." Dev shook his head. "I guess what continues nagging at me is, why *us*?"

"Well, our experience with the Nagas makes that part of it obvious enough."

"Why? We're supposed to make some sort of alliance with the DalRiss. The Naga don't have a thing to do with it."

"It's our experience," Katya said. "With nonhuman logic. With nonhumans, whatever they look like. Anyway, the Naga at GhegnuRish *is* helping the DalRiss reclaim their homeworld. It's part of the political picture out there." Katya was silent for a long moment. "You know, General Sinclair probably wants you at ShraRish because you're a hero to the DalRiss. If it hadn't been for you . . ."

"What hero . . . me? *Kuso*, we don't know that, Katya. We don't know enough about how the DalRiss think! Maybe they don't have heroes." He snorted. "Hell, maybe they kill and eat their heroes, or sacrifice them to the Great Boojum."

"Sorry. Great Boojum?"

"Sure. The Snark was a Boojum, you see." When Katya gave him a blank expression, he shrugged. "Sorry. Lewis Carroll. I did a lot of literary downloading while we were in K-T space. Lots of the old classics. Carroll. Hemingway. Spielberg."

"Sounds more like Lea Leanne," Katya said, naming a popular ViRdrama actress known throughout the Shichiju for her performances blending virtual sex, suspense, and danger, and usually involving monsters, both alien and human.

"Katya, I'm not a hero. Hell, I shouldn't even be a ship captain. I'm twenty-eight standard years old. Three years ago I was a legger, an enlisted grunt in the army. Now they have me commanding commerce raiders and serving as liaison to the only nonhuman civilization we know."

"You're not counting the Naga?"

"With only one Naga to a world and no knowledge of their fellows, I don't see how you can apply the word civilization to them."

"That's true. Well, I know the feeling, Dev. I'm not that much older than you, and they have me jacking a regiment. Fielding's Laws, I guess."

Dr. Karl Gunther Fielding had been a twenty-fifth–century philosopher-scientist who'd programmed a classic study called *Man and His Works*. He'd been the first to state as a law what had already been obvious for some time: *Cephlink technology extends human productivity by reducing the time necessary to achieve expertise.* The second law followed from the first. *Cephlink technology increases personal stress levels by reducing the time necessary to acquire physical experience.*

In other words, the ability to download memories, knowledge, and even certain skills into people with the right implant hardware had transformed human culture in countless ways throughout the past five centuries, but perhaps the most important was the end of the notion that "adulthood" began at a certain chronological age. A formal, career-oriented education that had required eight or ten years of advanced schooling during the twenty-first century could now be downloaded over a period of months. At the same time, however, confidence, maturity, and seasoning were still products of experience. While there was no objective difference between events experienced physically and events experienced through downloads, the fact remained that someone forty standard years old had still endured, roughly, twice as much life as someone who was twenty standard.

Within the modern, cephlink-dominated military, rank was not nearly so closely linked to age as it once had been. Dev's navy rank of captain and Katya's equivalent army rank of colonel were not unusual for people in their late twenties. His understanding of formal space navy tactics, of leadership techniques, even of political theory was as complete as that of any of his peers . . . more so, in fact, than some, because he'd had the opportunity to apply his downloaded training in combat.

The downside, though, was the uncertainty that a given course of action, a given decision, a given order was *right*. That came with a life experience that Dev was beginning to realize he lacked. Linked to a starship's AI, or—worse— caught up in the god-glory of a Xenolink, he felt invulnerable, superhuman.

But now, with no electronic enhancement save the program tricking his brain into accepting the reality of sunset, waves, sand, and the warmth of the girl in his arms, he felt very small indeed.

"Maybe," Dev said, "Congress will vote the notion down."

Chapter 7

Few technological advances have so changed the way we learn as cephlinkage. Why describe a place to students when a simple link and data download can transport them there in a fully interactive ViRsimulation?

Of course, while ViRsims can shape our thinking by providing an ideal forum for the exchange of ideas, they can do nothing about the ways *in which we think.*

—*Man and His Works*
Dr. Karl Gunther Fielding
C.E. 2488

The measure passed, 351 to 148, with 19 abstaining.

Currently, there were within the orbiting Heraklean sky-el called the Rogue 518 delegates representing various Frontier colonies in the Confederation Congress. The majority were by now dedicated to independence from the Terran Hegemony and the empire of *Dai Nihon* and had demonstrated that dedication by signing Sinclair's Declaration of Reason; a minority, about two hundred or so, either remained undecided or still hoped to achieve an eventual reconciliation with *Dai Nihon*, perhaps within the framework of some sort of commonwealth of worlds. Those delegates who'd opposed any change at all in the Frontier worlds' colonial status had been left behind on New America when Congress had fled that world ahead of the Imperial invasion force. Whether or not they could still be considered to be delegates of the Confederation Congress, albeit nonvoting ones, was still a matter for frequent debate.

As currently interpreted, however, the rules for passing major, policy-level measures or legislation required a two-thirds majority of those delegates present, so Operation Farstar had needed 346 yes votes to be approved. Obviously, many of the delegates who did not yet agree on the need for a complete break with the Terran government had voted yes on Farstar. Dev wondered why they'd supported the measure.

"I'd have thought," Dev told Sinclair, "that they'd be afraid we'd really screw things up by getting involved in whatever's going on out at Alya A-VI."

They were in the conference room set up as part of CONMILCOM's Headquarters suite aboard the Rogue. There were no chairs present, but at the sky-el's half-G level that was little more than a minor annoyance, and it did allow more men and women to crowd in next to the round, central desk with its holographic projector and AI interface pads. The low, gray-surfaced egg shapes of link modules lined the compartment's bulkheads. Most were empty now, but a few were occupied by duty officers maintaining a communications watch with Argosport and with picket ships scattered across the Mu Herculis system.

Eighteen CONMILCOM staff officers were gathered in the room for the briefing, not counting Dev, Katya, and Sinclair himself. One civilian was present as well. Her name was Professor Brenda Ortiz, and she was a xenosophontologist, the closest thing to an expert on the DalRiss that the Confederation had. An attractive woman of perhaps forty-five standard years, she wore her dark hair long at the top and braided down her back but had shaved the sides of her head to give free access to the T-sockets behind her ears. Dev felt a sense of kinship with her; like him, she was from Earth.

"They are afraid of exactly that, Captain," Sinclair replied. "That we'll screw things up. But they're more afraid of doing nothing, which is what will happen if we can't break this deadlock of personnel, weapons, and supplies. Right now, Congress feels—and for once our intelligence sources tend to support the feeling—that we have five months, possibly six, before the Empire moves against our base here at Herakles. Our fleet is still no match for theirs, so if we first move against the Imperial forces at any of the other colony worlds we're going to get slapped down, hard. If we stay here and wait, sooner or later we get slapped once and for all."

"Damned if we move," a short, dark-skinned man with silver hair and a major general's rank tabs on his collar said, "and damned if we stay."

"That's about where we stand, General Chabra."

"Well, there's a problem then, sir," Dev pointed out. "The Alyan system is one hundred thirty light-years from Sol, so that's . . ." He consulted his personal RAM files, performing a quick calculation based on Mu Herculis's distance from Sol and the angular separation between Alya and Mu Herc in Earth's skies. "Make it one hundred five lights from here to Alya," he said a second later, as the figure appeared in his mind. "That's a three-and-a-half–month trip, minimum. I don't care how glad the DalRiss are to see us, we're not going to be able to travel there, kick the Imperials out and get solid DalRissan help, then make the voyage back here before that five- or six-month deadline. It's impossible."

Sinclair nodded. "Actually, we've had a thought on that, but it's such a long shot we can't realistically count on it. But the one DalRiss starship we've seen in action demonstrated instantaneous travel, all the way from Alya A to Altair in literally no time at all. If you succeed in your mission, you may find your trip back to Mu Herculis takes less time than you imagine. In fact, the single most important reason for establishing close ties with these people is the possibility that we can learn how to duplicate that."

"Surely that's what the Japanese have had in mind all along, Travis," General Darwin Smith said. "They've had a presence at Alya A-VI since 2540, now, and they still haven't found out how the DalRiss manage that trick. How is our expeditionary force supposed to do in weeks or days what the best Imperial scientists haven't been able to accomplish in three years?"

Sinclair glanced across at the civilian. "Professor? You had some thoughts on that."

"Actually," Brenda Ortiz said, "we think the Imperials may be asking the DalRiss the wrong questions. They want to know how to duplicate DalRiss technology through machines, especially that remarkable space drive of theirs. The idea, of course, is to learn how to build our own version, to install it on our ships, though some of us doubt that it can be done that way. We know the DalRiss use a biologically tailored organism, something they call an Achiever, in order to bend space. The thing might not be possible at all unless we use DalRiss technologies."

"In other words, we'll have to grow our starships the way they do," a woman, a brigadier general, suggested, "and crew them with Achievers?"

"Exactly," Ortiz said. "We don't know how to do it yet, and it might take years to figure it out. But before we can even begin we have to be able to talk with the DalRiss. As long as the Imperials are there, we won't have that chance."

"I bring all of this up," Sinclair said, "to stress again the importance of Operation Farstar, to the Rebellion, to the future of the human species. We'll be dealing with a technic culture that has evolved—in its social systems, its logic, and its technology—along a completely different path than we did. No, Dev, you probably won't be able to zip home in the blink of an eye, but even the faintest possibility that you'll learn how makes the gamble worthwhile."

"It won't help if we make it back," Katya said, "and find out that the Imperium invaded Herakles the month before."

"We'd kind of like to know that we'll have a Confederation to come back to," Dev added.

"Of course." Sinclair nodded. "The truth is, we, the Confederation government, I mean, won't be able to stay here much longer in any case. As I said, intelligence thinks another five months or so before the blow lands. Me, I'll be surprised if it takes that long."

"They could have scouts snooping around the edge of the system now," one of Sinclair's aides pointed out. "If they dropped out of K-T space far enough out, then came in slow, low-powered, and in stealth mode, we'd never know they were there."

"My point exactly, Paul. For the time being they're being cautious, but they can't just let us squat here and thumb our noses at them. They'll be back, and with numbers enough to overwhelm even your rock-throwing trick, Dev."

Dev nodded. "They might also try coming in on the other side of the planet, where a rock thrower wouldn't see them and couldn't get at them. If they sent fighters in low and fast, coming in over the horizon . . ."

"Or they could bombard the surface from a distance," Sinclair said. "Or try to board the Rogue with marines while it was on the other side of Herakles from New Argos. One way or another, they'll get us. They must be devoting considerable AI program time right now to the problem of which way to try it."

"So what can we do?" Katya asked. "What will *you* do, I mean, since we're obviously not going to be here."

"Leave," Sinclair said. He gave Katya a hard glance, as though he expected her to say something. When she didn't, he went on. "Right now, the Confederation delegates who make up our Congress number some five hundred people from various Frontier worlds, and there are as many more staff personnel, aides, programming technicians, and the like. With some crowding, they could fit aboard the *Transluxus* and a few of our merchantmen, if they were converted to handle passengers. I intend to give the Confederation a migratory capital, one always on the move from system to system."

"Nomads," Ortiz said, surprised.

"Well, there's no law that says your capital has to stay in one place, is there? We'll avoid Imperial fleet concentrations, try to move to wherever they're not."

"Even the Imperium can't be everywhere at once," Dev said thoughtfully. He was impressed by this idea, a new twist to an old, old problem. "Not with seventy-some star systems scattered across a hundred–light-year volume of space."

"And in each system we visit," Sinclair continued, "we can counter Hegemony propaganda, recruit new personnel, arrange for maintenance for our ships, buy supplies . . . and in general let the people know what we're fighting for."

"Well, sooner or later you will run into the enemy," Katya pointed out. "The Imperials pose the most serious threat, but every system has Hegemony system defense craft, orbital monitors, that sort of thing. And sooner or later you're going to drop out of K-T space and find an Imperial Ryu there waiting for you."

"In which case," General Chabra said, "we drop back into K-T space as quickly as we can and go someplace else. As you say, they *can't* be everywhere."

Sinclair spread his hands. "I'm damned if I can see another way to manage this. We came to Herakles in the first place hoping we could find a place to set up shop that the Empire would overlook. Unfortunately, they found us despite our precautions, so they know we're here and they know we're a threat. They *will* come after us because they can't afford to let us grow strong, and they can't afford to have the Hegemony see them acting with weakness.

"If we stay put on any one world, whether it's Herakles or New America or some world far outside the Shichiju, the Empire's going to find us and they're going to squash us like a bug. If we stay on the move, well, we have a chance, at least, of staying ahead of the Empire, hidden by the sheer enormity of space . . . and we keep the Rebellion alive."

"I still wonder how you'll be able to carry on the business of running a government," Katya said. "I mean, how eager will a world be to see this migratory fleet suddenly appear on its doorstep. 'Hi, there. We need to tank up on slush hydrogen, and, by the way, how would your young men and women like to join the Confederation army?' I'd imagine the local populations would be reluctant to help us, especially if they know that helping the Confederation fleet is going to bring an Imperial squadron in to exact some kind of retribution. The Imperials will have observers everywhere, remember, taking notes."

"A very good point, and one we've given considerable thought to," Sinclair said. "For the most part, I doubt that we'll be that obvious about it. The fleet could take up a distant orbit, for example, out in the fringes of the star system and send ascraft and fuel shuttles in to the planet itself. Every world that has sent us delegates has a local Network, an anti-Imperial underground. We'll be able to make the necessary arrangements secretly, maybe set up a trade deal with the corporations for what we need, have them handle recruiting covertly. We could be in and out before the Empire knew we were there. In some systems—Liberty, for instance—we could be more open in our activities, simply because the Imperials seem to have given up trying to control the locals. We'll have to rely on those worlds for ship maintenance and overhauls, of course."

"Payment?" General Smith said.

"We could keep using the yen, like we have been. More likely, though, we'll end up forming an independent monetary standard before this is over. Maybe terbium, to get away from Tokyo's control of platinum stocks."

And that, Dev reflected, would lead to a whole, jam-packed cluster of problems he was glad he didn't have to deal with. Nearly all transactions were handled electronically, but some sort of standard was necessary to back the symbolic yen that held commerce throughout the Shichiju together. The Imperial yen was currently backed by platinum.

"You know," Dev said, "it occurs to me that we still have a problem so far as Farstar is concerned. When we get back, eight or ten months from now, where should we go? The government could be hiding out anywhere in the Frontier, and it might be kind of dangerous for us to keep jumping from system to system looking for you. Especially since the Imperials are likely to be a bit upset over what we were doing at Alya."

"We'll have to work out the details, of course," Sinclair said. "But that shouldn't pose any real difficulty. We'll arrange a communications protocol through each system's Network. We'll leave word at certain key systems, with code words or blind message drops so we don't leave clues to Imperial Intelligence."

"You'll need something of the sort just to operate on an interstellar scale," Dev said. "You'll need ways for delegates from member worlds to find you, ways for our agents to pass intelligence back to CONMILCOM in the shortest possible time, ways to agree on rendezvous points for our naval squadrons."

"Exactly. There'll be a certain vulnerability in the system, just because so many people will have to be trusted with the information, but we can keep a handle on things by moving often and by compartmentalizing our activities. The Networks already utilize the classic revolutionary cell structure, and we'll continue to build on that. Don't worry, Captain. We'll make sure there's a way for you to find us when you get back!

"In any case," Sinclair continued, "the important question's been settled now, and Farstar is a go. The only real problem remaining is how to actually carry it off."

Sinclair brought the palm of his left hand down on the interface screen in front of him. The desktop projector switched on in response, and a holograph glowed to life in the air just above it.

Dev studied the display with keen interest. It showed a base, a fairly standard one as Imperial bases went, with six small domes surrounding a single large structure like a truncated pyramid in the center. Communications towers rose from the main facility's corners, while ascraft rested on its flat upper surface, which was as broad as a football field and ringed by walkways, barricades, and the stubby turrets of high-power laser batteries. The entire facility was surrounded by a ten-meter electrified fence, complete with gate houses, guard stations, and overwatch towers. The base squatted on a circle of ground blasted of all plant life, then scraped level by constructor tracks and striders bearing shovel blades. Inside the fence, the ground had been covered over by RoPro ferrocrete, an artificial material nanotechnically grown in and spread by mobile vats.

"Professor Ortiz?" Sinclair prompted.

"This," the woman said, "is Dojinko. So far as we know, it's the only Imperial base on the surface of ShraRish. It's located on the largest of the three southern continents, directly adjacent to one of the biggest DalRiss cities. Some four months ago, according to the data from the *Kasuga Maru*'s AI memory, the base was attacked, for reasons unknown. The Imperial records are unclear about the exact nature of the attack. . . ." She hesitated.

"Professor?" Sinclair said. "If I may?"

"Of course."

Sinclair's hand was still on the interface. He closed his eyes, concentrating, and a moment later a three-dimensional image of a Japanese officer appeared in the air next to the display of the base. He looked scared, and his face was blackened with smoke.

"They came through the perimeter fence twenty minutes ago!" he was shouting in panic-ragged *Nihongo*. "Our defenses killed hundreds of them, but they kept coming . . . they're *still* coming, and we can't stop them! We need immediate assistance! Hello . . . are you there? Does anyone—"

The image winked out.

"We think a laser communications tower was knocked over at that point," Ortiz said a moment later, speaking in the death-still silence of the briefing room. "Other fragments of communications we've found in the *Kasuga Maru* files talk about the city attacking the base. We don't really know what that means. The DalRiss have a fairly well-defined military structure. They were forced to create one when they were fighting the Naga. Are these communications saying the local civilians rioted and overran the base? Or that the military forces camped there launched an attack? Why did they attack? Was there some incident that angered the DalRiss, maybe a violation of some taboo or custom? We really don't know. From the sound of things, the Imperials don't know what happened either."

"Sounds like they don't know what hit them," an aide said.

Dev glanced at Ortiz. "Professor? You called the place . . . Dojinko?" *Ko* was the Japanese suffix that meant "port," but the only *dojin* he knew was a harsh, derogatory term.

"On Earth a few centuries ago," Ortiz explained, "on the Japanese island of Hokkaido, there was an aboriginal people called the Ainu. A couple of thousand years ago they occupied most of the home islands, but the Japanese emigrations from the mainland gradually wiped them out, pressing them farther and farther back into a corner of Hokkaido, forbidding them by law to hunt or fish or even use their native language. By, oh, I guess the middle of the twenty-first century, the Ainu were extinct as a culture, as a people."

"Genocide," Katya said. The word was hard and cold.

"I suppose it was, though I doubt that genocide was ever the conscious purpose of the *Nihonjin*. In any case, the ethnic Japanese called the Ainu *Dojin*. Later they applied the word to any primitive aborigines. It's . . . not a very nice word. The connotation is of something dirty, slow-witted, and morally repugnant. I'm not sure, but it may be related to the Nihongo word for a kind of mudfish. I gather they use the term now to describe the DalRiss."

"That figures," Dev said. "They have trouble with anyone who thinks too differently from the way they do."

"The Japanese aren't alone in that, Dev," Sinclair said. "I'd have to say that intolerance is a human trait."

"Some cultures incorporate it more than others," Katya said. "Just by seeing *different* as *wrong*."

"I'm wondering if that might be what caused the problems out there," Dev said. "The Imperials can be a bit heavy-handed, sometimes. If the DalRiss took offense . . ."

"That," Sinclair said, "will be one of the first things you'll have to determine. Why did the DalRiss attack?"

"And are they mad at all humans, or just the Imperials?" Smith suggested. "Can we use their anger as an opening to get them on our side?"

"The biggest problem," Ortiz pointed out, "will be to find out if concepts like anger mean the same to the DalRiss as they do to us."

"Is the base even still standing?" Dev wondered. "Maybe the Imperials don't have anything left on the ground."

"That could be good for us, or bad," Katya said thoughtfully. "If the Imperials have abandoned the surface, it might be harder to approach the DalRiss. They could have some sort of quarantine up, something that would make getting in difficult."

"I didn't claim this mission was going to be *easy*," Sinclair said. The others laughed.

"Can we get a closer look at that base?" Dev asked.

"No problem," Sinclair told him. "Hang on."

The domes swelled in the observers' perceptions, rotating in space as their walls became transparent. The display now showed the interior structure, color-coded to indicate sleeping and living facilities, storage areas, power plants, environmental systems, control centers, and the other minutiae of a self-contained base in an alien environment.

The largest structure, the topless pyramid in the center, included a hangar with elevators for shuttling air- and space-craft up to the top-level flight deck, where three Kamome-class ascraft rested in holding areas separated by protective revetments. Inside the hangar, another four shuttles rested in maintenance cradles. The building's lower level housed thirty-two warstriders, a full company standing in motionless ranks, their torsos encased in wirework service gantries. The schematics showed them as scarcely more than outlines. KY-1180 Tachis, Dev thought.

"I take it the Kamomes and the Tachis are educated guess-work," he said.

"Guesswork," Sinclair added, "and at least four months out of date. Still, it should give you an idea of what they could have in a base that size. And there are heavier machines there. The intelligence data that you brought back mentions at least one Katana."

"And any word on what they have in orbit?"

"Nothing positive, and again, by the time you get to Alya the intelligence will be almost eight months out of date. However, we can assume that they will have the equivalent of an escort squadron there, at least, plus transports and stores ships."

"I'm more concerned with how we're going to convince them that we're different from the Japanese," Katya said. "They can't be all that aware of the differences between individual humans, and they probably won't understand our motives."

"This sounds familiar," Dev said. Contact with the Naga had encountered similar difficulties. How does one communicate in any meaningful way with a being that possesses an entirely alien structure of logic and thought?

Sinclair laughed. "Well, Dev, why else do you think that we've given this assignment to the two of you? We have complete faith in your ability to communicate with these . . . people."

"Have you considered the possibility of trying to commu-nicate with the Japanese instead?" he suggested. "It would be a hell of a lot easier."

But then they began discussing the details of the mission.

Chapter 8

First contact was made with the DalRiss in 2540, when one of their living starships materialized near Altair, a star chosen by their Perceivers because of its similarity to their own sun. Communications, facilitated by the DalRiss constructs known as comels, led Hegemony authorities to the conclusion that the DalRiss had been fighting for some time against their own Xenophobe invasion. Friendly relations were soon established, primarily as a direct result of human intervention in the Alyans' struggle against a common foe.

Despite this alliance, however, to date human and DalRiss remain strangers to one another. Mutually alien to a degree not easily grasped even by xenosophontologists, the two civilizations seem to have remarkably little in common save for their respective drives for survival.

> —*Alien Perspectives*
> Dr. Hector Ferrar
> C.E. 2542

They walked together in strangeness, Dev and Katya, Sinclair and Brenda Ortiz. The light was harsh, blue-tinged and heavily laced with ultraviolet, the sun shrunken but so dazzling that it seemed to fill the sky. The plants—could they be classified as plants?—the red and purple growths around them, then, were flat sheets of flexible, spongy material, continually twisting and writhing in a slow-motion dance designed to keep a maximum of surface area in direct sunlight, and animating the landscape with an unsettling life of their own.

Despite the fact that Dev had been in an environment like this one before, he was having trouble understanding what he was seeing. The setting was one where even comfortable and easily grasped referents like scale and the sense of perspective generated by a gentler sun had been altered. A sulfur haze in the air made things look more distant than they actually were, and in all that landscape there was nothing as recognizable as a tree or a building against which he could compare the stranger aspects of his surroundings.

None of them wore protective suits, which would have been necessary had they actually been standing on the surface of one of the two DalRiss worlds. This was a ViRsimulation, run through the Rogue's AI and downloaded to the four as they lay in com modules in Sinclair's office suite.

"So you're coming along, Professor?" Dev asked Brenda Ortiz, who was serving as their guide.

"Do you think I'd miss an opportunity like this, Captain?" she replied. "I've been working for this for three years now, and I may never have a chance like this again."

Originally an AI metalogician from the Universidad de México on Earth, Professor Ortiz had first visited the Alyan system with the Imperial Expeditionary Force three years before as an expert on alternative logic. Since the IEF's return to the Shichiju, however, she'd been attached to the newly founded Xenosophontology Department of Jefferson University on New America.

The outbreak of open civil war had stranded her on New America until the Confederation government decided to abandon that world. From what Dev had heard, Ortiz was completely apolitical, uninterested in taking sides in the worsening rebellion that was flaming across the Frontier. She'd reasoned, however, that the Imperials would be unlikely to allow anyone on New America access to the Alyans. If she wanted to continue her studies of them, she would have to do so through projects sponsored by the Confederation.

And as far as the Confederation was concerned, they couldn't afford to lose her expertise. Not now, with Farstar at last about to bear fruit.

"Is this sim supposed to be set on ShraRish or GhegnuRish?" Sinclair wondered aloud.

The fifth world of Alya B was GhegnuRish, the original DalRiss homeworld; the sixth planet of Alya A was ShraRish, a once-lifeless world altered some twenty thousand years before to support a DalRiss-engineered ecology.

"This is A-VI, General Sinclair," Ortiz replied, looking around with something like a proprietorial pride in her eyes. "According to our most up-to-date information, the DalRiss are back on Ghegnu again, but not in large numbers. The tame Naga there is helping them rebuild the place, but I gather it's still not much like what they think of as home."

"Hell of a note," Dev said. "Having to terraform your own homeworld. Or maybe 'DalRissaform' would be a better word."

The others laughed.

DalRiss civilization on GhegnuRish had been destroyed long before by the Naga occupying that world's crust. Dev had haunting memories of that silent, tortured landscape, of strangely grown buildings and less identifiable structures consumed and reworked by the alien Naga. By the time the Imperial Expeditionary Force had arrived, a second Xenophobe had nearly wiped the DalRiss out on their colony world of ShraRish as well. The IEF had used deep-penetrator nuclear weapons to destroy the Xenophobe manifestation on ShraRish, but on GhegnuRish, Dev had managed to make contact with the Naga, the first time such a thing had ever been tried.

"What we're seeing here was programmed by the Imperial mission at Dojinko," Ortiz continued as the group picked its way past a sponge-covered outcropping. Overhead, sulfur clouds bulked huge, violet-silver where they faced the sun, golden brown to red-black in their shadowed bellies. "I gather some of your intelligence people copied it from a research station and smuggled it out to New America. It's about two years old."

"Are we sure the data's solid?" Sinclair wondered. "Some of this looks so strange. Like some Imperial intelligence officer's nightmare."

"It looks like I remember it, sir," Dev told him. "Pretty much, anyway. I don't remember seeing a lot of these plants when we were at ShraRish before, but from what I understand there's a lot more variety to the life there than on most human worlds." He nudged a writhing clump of purple vegetation with the toe of his boot. "That's why there are so many different shapes and colors."

"*Deliberate* variety," Ortiz agreed. "The DalRiss genengineer everything, remember, including themselves. Natural evolution is faster, too. The ecosystem is driven by very high levels of ambient radiation."

That much was obvious simply from the activity displayed by the ground cover. The Alyan suns, circling one another at a mean distance of nine hundred astronomical units, were a type A5 and a type A7, respectively nineteen and thirteen times brighter than Earth's sun. Energy spendthrifts, such stars squandered their hydrogen capital in a fraction of the time taken by older, cooler suns like Sol. Where life on Earth had taken the better part of four billion years to evolve from self-replicating molecules to intelligence, the same process had taken a few hundred million years on Alya B-V, in a high-energy environment where all of the processes that made life what it was, from biochemical reactions to metabolisms to random mutations, seemed speeded up from a human perspective.

"All chemical processes are faster?" Katya asked. "I wonder, do the DalRiss think faster than we do?"

"Almost certainly," Ortiz replied. "In our discussions with them, we get the definite impression that they spend a lot of time—from their points of view, anyway—just standing and waiting for our replies. Fortunately, they seem to possess more patience than do most humans. Otherwise we might never have been able to talk with them at all."

Drops of rain began falling, though Dev felt nothing in the simulation. That was just as well, he thought, for rain on the DalRiss worlds contained high concentrations of sulfuric acid. "This is why we'd need suits in the actual environment," Ortiz said cheerfully. "It's actually possible to walk around with no special gear at all save a breathing mask, for short times, at least, but this rain could burn you."

"The ultraviolet's pretty harsh for unprotected skin," Dev added. "That would burn you too."

"The predominant gas in the mix is nitrogen, as I recall," Sinclair said. "But less than nine percent oxygen."

"Depending on who you talk to," Ortiz said. "For a while, the Imperials were confusing the issue with data that suggested the DalRiss worlds were just like Venus, except for low surface pressure. Impossible to visit without very special gear."

"They wanted to discourage unofficial exploration," Katya said. "And casual visitors."

"Are those buildings?" Dev asked, pointing at some low, slick-surfaced shapes of various dark colors a hundred meters off. Actually, they looked more like trees than artificial structures . . . though Alyan trees little resembled their Earth-grown namesakes. They were squat and rounded, growing out of the ground rather than sitting on it, more similar to large gourds or oddly carved lumps of sponge than anything else.

"Dwellings, yes," Ortiz replied. "Of course, while they're normally sessile, they *can* move, and they're more attached to their owners than to the landscape. We've found that DalRiss family groups tend to shift and change around a lot. When an individual leaves the current grouping, his part of the group's communal dwelling goes with him."

The DalRiss had followed a cultural and technological evolution quite different from that pursued by Man, developing the biological sciences almost to the exclusion of the others. They grew homes and workplaces and entire cities rather than building them, using genetic engineering to develop a bewildering array of organisms, from manufactured viruses to vast organisms of obscure purpose hundreds of kilometers across. For the DalRiss, chemistry had been a product of biological research, rather than the other way around. Mining, refining, and smelting were relatively new processes carried out by organisms that extracted elements and compounds from rock or the sea, and the products were generally incorporated into new life-forms, rather than being assembled as the inorganic components of lifeless structures.

Even the physical appearance of the DalRiss could vary tremendously, for individuals seemed to have less interest in outward form and appearance than did humans. DalRiss were composite creatures, a relatively small and physically weak *Riss*, or master, symbiotically riding the nervous system of a gene-tailored *Dal* that provided it with legs and strength. Most common were massive creatures like spiny, six-legged starfish that bore their riders in a mouthlike orifice atop their bodies, but Dev had seen organic combat vehicles, living warstriders, mounting weaponry based on explosives and complex acids. As a human might plug himself into an AI-directed vehicle or other piece of equipment, a Riss could plug itself into its Dal, into its dwelling, or into some other creature designed to eat or manufacture things or procreate. Even their spacecraft were enormous, deliberately bred organisms that used hydrogen combustion to make orbit and an as yet unidentified means of bending space to cross from star system to star system.

Raindrops splattered about them, then dwindled away. The sky was as active as the vegetation, with clouds gathering, then breaking up in surreal patterns of silver, violet, and brown.

The group was walking toward the crest of a low ridge nearby. As they started climbing, movement caught Dev's eye. "There's one," Sinclair said, pointing. "A DalRiss, I mean. What's it doing?"

The DalRiss was standing on the crest of the ridge about twenty meters away, a bristling of spines and tentacles growing erect atop its ponderous, six-limbed organic transport. Its head—at least, Dev thought of that ragged crescent shape with the odd, eyeless protuberances to either side as a head—was cocked back at an angle, and the tentacles were telescoping in and out with a flickering, bewildering rapidity that had no obvious purpose. The leathery swelling at the back of the crescent, which Dev had been told housed the creature's braincase, was glistening wet, perhaps from some internal secretion, though it could have been the rain. A trilling sound, wavering at the very edge of human hearing, fluted in and out of Dev's perception.

To Dev, it looked as though the thing was singing in the rain.

"Unknown," Ortiz said, answering Sinclair's question after a brief pause. "Art form? Religious observance? Singing? Eliminating body wastes?"

"They see with active sonar," Dev said. The crescent-shaped "head," he'd been told, was a fluid-filled organ used to focus sound waves, while the widely spaced stalks to either side picked up the echoed returns. "Maybe it's looking for something."

"A lost compatch," Katya suggested. "I'm always losing *mine*."

"In the sky?" Ortiz asked. She sighed. "Three years of research and we still know almost nothing about them."

"You know, I thought we had their language down pretty well," Sinclair said. "If it wasn't for their comels, we'd never have been able to communicate with the Naga. They must understand interspecies communication in ways we can't even guess at yet."

"Oh, we can talk with them, if that's what you mean, thanks to their comels, and thanks to that patience I mentioned. We can share impressions and some sensory data and, with a computer's help, we can translate the sounds they make as articulate speech. The comels go a step further and actually translate certain nerve impulses into recognizable analogues, allowing, well, not telepathy, exactly, but a way of sharing feelings, emotions, even some memories, though we still don't know how they do that.

"But the cultural and physical framework behind their language is different from ours, obviously. A *lot* different. We ask a question and we get what sounds like a rational answer. The only problem is, we often don't know if either the question or the answer means the same to the DalRiss as it does to us."

"Well, have you asked about what it's doing now?" Katya wanted to know. "What's its 'rational answer'?"

"It depends," Ortiz said, smiling. "Sometimes they say communing, though they won't say with what. Our translation programs also render it as easing, or sometimes as draining. You see, their spoken language is quite complex, with multiple layers of meaning. Um, imagine having three mouths, and being able to carry on a conversation with one voice, while adding a running commentary with another and providing thesaurus elaborations or dictionary definitions with the third, all at the same time."

"They have three mouths?" Sinclair asked.

"No. They use what we call a mouth for eating, not for speaking. Their speech is generated by a series of bladders inside their sonic organ, that big crescent on top of the body."

"Okay, so what does this communing you mentioned mean?" Dev asked. "I don't care how complex the word is, it's got to have meaning, right? What do the experts say?"

Ortiz shook her head. "There are no experts in this business, Captain. Only guessers, and sometimes one guess is as good as another, especially when the, the elaborations by the different voices are contradictory. Or *seem* contradictory to us.

"Look, the modern approach to human psychology is, what? Three or four centuries old. If you count the half-superstitious speculation that passed for a science before that—and there were some important insights to come out of precephlink research, of course—then it's a lot older than that. Yet we *still* have trouble understanding why people do what they do, why they think the way they do, today. We've been studying these people for three years, now. How much progress do you suppose we could make in that short a time, given that we knew almost nothing about their ecology, their evolution, their moral and ethical standards, their motivations to begin with. Hell, it took us awhile just to figure out that what we thought of as a DalRiss was really made up of two more or less separate organisms. We're not going to really understand these folks for a long, long time to come!"

The solitary DalRiss was joined by a second being apparently identical to the first, its six-limbed Dal moving with a peculiar grace for such a large creature. A third arrived moments later, joining the first two in a rapid-fire flickering of their tentacles and a piping cacophony of peculiar, fluting sounds. Dev could detect no difference among them as individuals, and even their gestures appeared eerily coordinated. Their movements, lightning quick, possessed a fluidity that belied the ponderous mass of their mounts.

"Are they aware of us?" Dev asked.

"The sim's been set to show them without interaction," Ortiz replied. "So they'll act as though we weren't here. But we can reset if you want to question one. This sim has a fairly extensive data base. Their replies will be pretty close to what the real ones might say."

"I don't think that'll be necessary," Katya said.

"Yeah," Dev added. "I'm not sure at this point if I'd even know what questions to ask."

"The fact that they're blind must make their perception of the world quite different from ours," Sinclair said.

"They're not blind," Ortiz said. "They don't have eyes, but they're not blind. They use sonar, like bats or dolphins, though it seems to provide them with a genuine image of some kind, rather than just an echo. They have other imaging senses, too, apparently overlapping their sonar. They can sense motion, for instance . . . and, at least according to them, they can sense something they call *ri*, which they equate with some kind of life force. In fact, they visualize their surroundings more in terms of a three-dimensional sea of life through which they move than as empty space that happens to be occupied here and there by other creatures. They, well, they do perceive the world quite differently from the way we do."

"Like the Naga," Dev suggested.

Ortiz laughed. "Maybe not *that* differently. At least these folks don't see the universe inside out! But a DalRiss can scan you and tell what you ate for lunch, see what you're hiding inside your closed fist, and just by 'looking' at you, can trace your cephlink circuits from your palm implant to the feeds running up your arm to the sockets, cephware, and internal RAM nodes hidden inside your skull. They have trouble discerning human facial features and they don't know what color is, but they have senses that we don't. They see nonliving things— rock, for instance—as a kind of empty void with a definite shape. That difference in the way they perceive things makes aspects of their logic quite different from ours."

"How?" Dev asked.

"Um, well, one of their nonhuman senses is a little like the lateral line in fish. It detects extremely minute variations in air pressure and seems to help them sense the positions of objects around them. See those three on the ridge? Do you see how their heads are all held at the same angle, and how their limb movements are coordinated? It's almost as though they're performing a dance, but with a very precise awareness of each others' attitudes and gestures."

"Group mind?" Sinclair asked.

"We wondered about that for a time, but no. They're still individuals. But they do have much more of a sense of, call it *community*, than we do. With us, there's a certain amount of social pressure to blend in, to be just like everybody else, right? But that only extends so far. There've always been people who disliked the herd mentality, who struck off and did things on their own and in their own way. We think, *think*, mind you, that the DalRiss find it easier to come to a group consensus because they're so attuned to one another's attitudes—both physical and mental. There's almost certainly less of a sense of self, compared with more of a sense of the group as a whole. Not a group mind, General Sinclair, but a feeling that the needs of the group come before the needs of the individual."

Dev felt an inner stirring of worry, almost of fear. "You know, Professor, what you've just described is a large part of the difference between Japanese culture and most Frontier societies. The Japanese feel they have a social obligation that should be placed ahead of the needs of any one person."

"Captain, I think even the Japanese would be uncomfortable with what the DalRiss consider to be social obligation."

"Arranged marriages," Katya said, grinning.

"That's one. Mating among the DalRiss is done strictly according to genetic considerations, and mates are frequently changed to ensure the widest possible distribution of certain characteristics within the gene pool. Genetic defectives are killed at birth, that's another. And the old, I gather, are eaten, with great ceremony."

"Arranged marriages, infanticide, and cannibalism have all been practiced by various human cultures, Professor," Sinclair pointed out. "And the acceptance of those practices by the community reflects what the group at large believes in."

"Sure. But human cultures have always had rebels," Dev said. "People who bucked the system because they saw a better way, or because they didn't fit in, or because they wanted to marry for love, or whatever."

"Any of which would be unthinkable among the DalRiss," Ortiz put in. "As near as we can tell, there is no rebellion against the DalRiss group consensus, none, and there has been none for some tens of thousands of years of unbroken cultural history."

"Odd," Katya said. "As fast as the pace of life and metabolism and evolution seems to be, you'd think there'd be social evolution as well."

"Maybe," Dev suggested, "their society is the one stable thing they have to rely on. Unlike us."

They continued climbing the slope, until they came to the sponge-covered crest overlooking the valley beyond. The vegetation in that valley was, if anything, more curiously shaped than anything they'd seen so far on the tour. Spires, domes, and arches of pastel-colored growth crowded one another around tar-black, rippling pools. Hundreds of massive, squashlike structures covered the ground in a complex and interconnected maze of living structures. All of those shapes, the pools included, rippled and throbbed, obviously alive. The tallest spire was topped by something like a jet black rose, slowly twisting open in the harsh sunlight. Most of the growths pulsed in unison, like interconnected hearts. Though the first impression was of a forest moving with the wind, Dev had seen areas like this on both ShraRish and on the dead DalRiss homeworld. It was a DalRiss city.

Beyond the edge of that organic metropolis, a cluster of silvery domes and an unmoving patch of nano-grown pavement grabbed Dev's attention, the first structures he'd seen since entering this simulation that felt like the product of human engineering. That bit of familiarity in the midst of so much strangeness quickly made itself the measure for everything else. A large ascraft on the landing field, a lasercom tower above one of the domes, provided the scale that had been missing before; the city, the valley itself was not so large as he'd thought at first glance, and the air was hazy with a light, golden mist that fooled the eye.

Ortiz seemed to sense Dev's interest in the human-built facility. "That, Captain," she said, "is Dojinko."

"If it's still standing when you get there," Sinclair pointed out, "that will be your principal target on the planet."

"I wonder," Katya said softly, her gaze still fixed on the alien city, "what they did that made the DalRiss attack them?"

"That," Dev replied, "may be the most important question we have to answer."

Chapter 9

No one who, like me, conjures up the most evil of those half-tamed demons that inhabit the human breast, and seeks to wrestle with them, can expect to come through the struggle unscathed.

—Complete Psychological Works
Sigmund Freud
C.E. 1905

They'd found time at last to be alone together, and a place as well—inside the cargo bay of an ascraft slung from *Eagle*'s belly. Technicians and crew members were still swarming through the *Eagle*, getting her ready for her long flight, but the air/spacecraft, already packed with provisions and secured for the voyage, was deserted. There was room enough, just barely, for the two of them to float together in weightless ecstasy, moving gently to rhythms old long before man had left his homeworld, urged on by drives ancient before life had left the sea.

The cargo bay was crowded, packed with kiloliter canisters of water, for the most part. The Farstar mission was expected to last the better part of a year, and, since there was no guarantee of their welcome in the Alya system, consumables enough for some twelve hundred people for that long a time had to be carried along. Every spare cubic meter of space aboard each of the starships was packed with supplies, especially with Organic Precursors, or OPs, stores of carbon, nitrogen, oxygen, hydrogen, phosphorous, and all of the other elements that would be nanotechnically assembled into food during the voyage. It was often jokingly said that starship crews on long missions had to literally eat their way into their own living spaces. That was exaggeration, perhaps, but there was very little free space left anywhere in the fleet, and the ascraft, which would not be used until they reached their destination, made ideal stores carriers.

Still, a passageway leading aft from the cargo bay's dorsal entryway had been left clear for the loading robots and cargo handlers to come and go, and there was space enough there for the two of them to shed their uniforms and stress and all save that which made them human for a few precious hours. Now, the air around them was aglitter with a few tiny, stray, drifting spheres of perspiration, and it was musky with the mingled odors of their lovemaking. Dev had one hand out grasping a handrail on the bulkhead, bracing the two of them to keep them from bumping randomly into a wall of stacked stores containers.

"That," he said with a deep and long-anticipated contentment, "was wonderful."

"Better than sex-in-a-can?"

"Than what?"

She snuggled closer. "Than mental masturbation in a couple of comm modules."

"Much." It was a small lie. Dev still couldn't tell the difference between real and virtual sex, and sex with a person's analogue didn't leave you so obviously in need of a shower. But as Katya clung to his sweat-slick body, he thought that he might now have at least a small understanding of what it was she sought.

Mostly, he wanted Katya to be happy. He loved her, and he wanted to understand.

"How are you feeling, Dev?" Katya asked him after a long period of comfortable, drifting silence.

"Silly question. . . ."

"About what happened with you and the Naga, I mean. I've been wanting to ask, and others are wondering too."

How did he feel? For a time, while floating in Katya's warm embrace, he'd all but forgotten the sense of otherness that still lay coiled somewhere within the deeps of his own mind.

"Others? You mean Sinclair?"

"And some of the staff people here. Farstar is awfully important to the Confederation—"

"And they wouldn't want a schiz-out or a burn-brain to be dictating policy with the DalRiss. I can understand that." He sighed, then pushed back slightly away from Katya's body. They were joined together at the hips by a *tsunagi nawa*, a lightweight, elastic tether that allowed them to move together in microgravity without becoming uncoupled. He touched the connector and the harness unsnapped. They drifted apart, and Dev reached for his bodysuit, hanging in the air close by the bulkhead.

"Dev? . . ."

"We really ought to get back. I've got so much admin garbage downloaded onto my sched it's going to take me a year just to—"

"Dev, talk to me." She bumped up against his back, her long legs circling his hips from behind. The movement sent both of them drifting, and Dev had to let go of his clothing to keep from hitting the bulkhead.

"Katya—"

"The last time we talked about it you were still half in shock. Sinclair's giving you command of this squadron. I'd kind of like to know if we've got a psychotechnic problem in our senior staff."

"I've run the diagnostics on myself," he said quietly, disentangling himself and turning in the air to face her. "Several times. Believe me, I wanted to know too."

"And?"

"I'll download them to you if you want. There's been no change. Same TM rating . . . high, higher than the Hegemony Navy would accept, but okay for the likes of us."

"Point four?"

He nodded.

"And no TP or TD?"

"Insignificant. Believe me, I'm *not* afraid of AIs and they don't depress me."

"Dev, there's something wrong. I can feel it in you."

"Nonsense—"

"*Kuso*, don't lie to me!"

He frowned. "Katya, I'm not lying. Okay, I wonder about myself sometimes. About my own stability. But the monitor programs check out. I . . . it's hard to put into words. Best I can do is say that there's a, a *craving* for what I felt when I was Xenolinked. A need for more." He swallowed. "You know, coming in-system, before we dropped into fourspace, I was afraid I was going to have to meet you and Sinclair down in Argosport. I was worried about that, afraid of having to get that close to . . . to . . ."

"To the Naga?"

He nodded. "When I volunteered to take *Eagle* out raiding, I thought that enough time would pass that I could forget what it was like, linked into the Naga. But I haven't. If anything, the memories have been getting worse. Stronger. And there are dreams . . ." He saw the alarmed look in her eyes and smiled. "No, I'm okay. I can handle it. It's not like I'm a PCS addict or anything like that."

When Katya didn't immediately reply, he went on.

"I do feel . . . changed, Katya. I'm not sure how. It's like, well, it's as though my perceptions of myself were completely rewired while I was Xenolinked. Even now, I can examine my memories of those few moments, and it's like reading about a stranger. I don't recognize myself in what I see." He took a long breath. "If an ant could become a man . . . would it later be able to accept becoming an ant again?"

"Is that the way you feel? A man's mind, trapped in an ant's body?"

"I feel trapped. I'm not sure I can put it into clearer words than that."

"Ever since you were Xenolinked, you've seemed, I don't know. Distant. Isolated, somehow. You were that way right after you broke your link with the Xeno. I was hoping four months would have fixed it, but I, I sense it, that isolation, still in you now." She hugged him closer. "I want to help, Dev."

He clung to her for a long time. He was remembering. . . .

"Katya, can you imagine what it was like, being some kind of super genius, having a sensory network that stretched across half a planet, knowing things, *thinking* things, that even now I can just dimly recall? It's like having had the most wonderful and lavish meal imaginable . . . then not being able to remember the individual dishes or the people present or the reason for the banquet in the first place, but still being able to savor the memory of the food's smell . . . just the smell. I find myself wanting that, that sense of connectedness, of *belonging* again. Without it, I feel very . . . lonely."

Katya moved closer, took him again in her arms. "Oh, Dev. It must be awful."

"It isn't, really," he said. "It's not like some pain that won't go away, or anything like that. It's just a very deep sense of, of sadness, I suppose. A sadness that I don't have what I once had. And believe me, despite that, I don't want to go through a Xenolink again. I think that's what has me confused the most. I've lost something, something that I miss very much and that I'd love to have again . . . but I'm terrified that I might find it. That's why I didn't want to go back to the surface of Herakles. I was afraid that I might find it again, and that the temptation there would be too strong."

"You know, Dev, there's a Naga out at Alya."

"Yes. On, or rather, *in* GhegnuRish. But we're going to ShraRish, the colony world, and the Naga there is dead. We'll be five light-days away from the other one."

"That's not so very far."

"It's a hell of a lot farther than we are from the Heraklean Naga right now," Dev said. "Believe me, Katya. I'll be fine. I just need some time . . . and maybe some human companionship. Some closeness."

She dimpled. "You had plenty of companionship aboard *Eagle* these past four months. From what I hear, Lisa Canady is quite skilled in such things, and I doubt that she minds sex-in-a-can."

"*Kuso*. You know what I mean." He reached out and pulled her close. Again, her legs entwined about him and they kissed.

Dev tried hard not to think about the fact that this would be their last time alone together for quite a while. During the long voyage to Alya, Katya would be with her troops aboard one of the transports, while he remained on the *Eagle*. He would see her again when they reached Alya, but time alone together then would be desperately hard to find.

This time they made love without the tether. It took skill and concentration not to slide apart, and their movements were, of necessity, restrained. If anything, the limits set on their motions by zero-G drove their mutual sensations to an even higher pitch than before. Afterward, adrift together in the warm, narrow volume of the compartment, they slept.

The being that had once been Dev Cameron reared higher on its mountain ledge, scanning sky and horizon with a complex amalgam of senses—human sight and hearing, combined with eighteen external Naga senses ranging from the perception of magnetic fields to the rippling feel of flowing electrons to the dimly sensed mass of bulky objects bending space....

It was the dream again. After the first few terrifying moments, Dev knew he was dreaming, though despite the lucidity imparted by his cephlink control he could not will himself awake. Part of him did not want to wake. The sensation of surging, triumphant power was overwhelming; at the same time, he could sense the Naga supracell embedded within his body, distributing itself throughout his nervous system in a fuzzy cloud of alien nanotechnics and molecule-slender threads, a blending, a *union* so complete it would have been difficult for any outside observer to tell where Dev's body had stopped and that of the Naga had begun.

Externally, he wore the shimmering black-silver serpent-form of a Naga traveler, rearing high atop the man-made mountain of the pyramidal atmosphere generator on the plains north of New Argos; his mind, while it included all that Dev Cameron once had been, was now far more than human, with a scope and a depth and an unhumanly cold precision that felt more machinelike than anything alive. Effortlessly, he traced the threadlike lines of radio communications webbing the battlefield spread out below him like a cluttered playroom floor, penetrated the artificial intelligences of the Imperial warstriders moving across that floor, reprogramming them, ordering them to shut down.

And in synchronous orbit thirty-two-thousand kilometers overhead, the Imperial fleet hovered like carrion crows. His mind reached . . . stretched . . . focused . . . and found linkage with an Imperial cruiser. Another reprogramming, and the magnetic fields containing the furiously orbiting pair of power-generating microsingularities within the quantum power tap of the cruiser Mogami *shut down.*

One of the microscopic black holes evaporated in a flood of radiation; the other, loosed like a pebble from a slingshot, tunneled through the ship's length, devouring everything in its path in a frenzy of gravitational feeding. To Dev, it was as though he'd reached out a hand and squeezed . . . *feeling the bulk of* Mogami *crumpling within his grasp. . . .*

The Imperial ships shut down their radio communications circuits, cutting his link with them like the snapping of a thread. Around him, meanwhile, the bulk of the Naga was spilling from the mountain, its tar-black surface alive with newly shaped eyeballs . . . a trick learned, he knew, from its first encounter with a human—him.

The thrill of vision was as heady as the sense of uncoiling, unstoppable power. Thrilling, too, was the thundering gallop of thought. Creativity and intuition both were a function of the interconnectivity between the two hemispheres of the human cerebrum, the left and right halves of the brain. Part of the change in himself, Dev could sense, lay in the myriad nanotechnic connections still growing through the corpus callosum that bound the two together. He was thinking faster, and more clearly, despite the bewildering flood of alien thoughts and perceptions.

* I/we see. . .
** You/we can generate powerful magnetic fields.
* Yes. For movement, for . . .
** . . . navigation, for . . .
* . . . for launching the Will-be-Selves into . . .

** *. . . the Void, yes. That is what we will do.*
* *The Will-be-Selves are not . . .*
** *. . . ready, of course. I have other missiles.*
* *What?*
** *These. . . .*
* *Rock . . .*

With a shriek of tortured steel, a chunk of iron and ferrocrete, part of the outer shell of the artificial mountain on which he stood, shuddered, then wrenched free from the framework beneath as the human/Naga symbiont generated a magnetic flux. Lightning flared, as storm winds swirled about Dev's being. Clouds blackened the sky, but Dev could still sense the Imperial ships, fleeing now on searing cones of fusion fire.

With a thought, the chunk of iron and rock flickered into the sky, accelerated in a blink to ten percent of the speed of light. In space, the cruiser Zintu vanished in a flare momentarily brighter than the sun, and over a thousand men died. . . .

He did it again . . . and again . . . and yet again. Ship after ship flared and died.

* *Is this what you/we call war?*

The godlike feeling of power vanished, wiped away by that single thought. In an instant, Dev—the human part of Dev— became aware of those motes of light in the sky as frail shells enclosing thousands of human beings, and he had been hunting them down, swatting them with a ruthless and appallingly precisionist efficiency.

My God, what am I doing? What have I become?

"Dev! . . ."
** *No. This is not war.*
"Dev, please! . . ."
** *It's slaughter. Useless slaughter.*
"Dev, wake up! You're hurting me!"

His eyes snapped open. Katya's eyes stared back into his from centimeters away, wide and terrified, her wide-mouthed scream dwindling to a gurgle as Dev's fingers tightened about her throat, his thumbs pressing home beneath the soft-skinned angle of her jaw. He gasped and released her, and the sudden motion sent the two of them drifting apart. The back of his head impacted sharply on a store's canister, a ringing crack that blurred his vision.

"Oh, *kuso*! Katya. . . ." Reaching out, he snagged a hand-hold, arresting his motion.

She braced herself against the canisters at her back with one hand and massaged her throat with the other. "I guess you were dreaming. . . ."

"Kat, I'm so sorry. I . . . I . . ."

"S'okay." She moved her head back and forth experimentally, then managed a smile. "I'm okay, Dev, really. I was just . . . scared. I was afraid if I hit you or anything, you might just fight harder. So I went limp and screamed to wake you up."

"That . . . that was good thinking. Katya, I didn't want to hurt you. . . ." He was trembling now, partly from the fast-evaporating emotions of the nightmare, partly with the terror of what he'd almost done. "God, Kat, I could have *killed* you! . . ."

"It was just a dream. Really, Dev, it's okay. You told me you'd been having bad dreams. Was it the Xenolink again?"

Jerkily, he nodded. "I've been consulting a monitor, but—"

"Dev, after what you went through, I'm astonished your head's still in one piece. It's going to take you some time, that's all."

"I've had four months. I'm terrified that I'm, I'm changed, somehow. That my mind has changed."

"You're still Dev, the Dev I know. *Believe* me. It'll just take a little more time."

But it seemed to him that she looked away after that, as though unwilling to meet his gaze. Hastily, she reached out and snagged her uniform slacks out of the air nearby and let them mold themselves to her legs.

For Dev, the nightmare had left him numb with shock. God, what was *wrong* with him? The encounter with the Heraklean Naga had transformed him into something inhuman. He'd thought, *hoped* that when the Naga had withdrawn from his body, it had left him as it had found him. No matter how he tried to deny it, though, the experience had altered him in ways that he still couldn't wholly define or measure.

Suppressing a shudder, he reached for his own clothing and began to dress.

Chapter 10

The genius of the ideal subordinate officer in war lies in his ability to receive orders from his superiors and execute them according to his own interpretation of the actual situation and his understanding of his superior's intent and purpose—in short, to read his mind.

The genius of the ideal superior officer lies in his ability to choose those subordinates who read his mind most clearly.

—*Kokorodo: Discipline of Warriors*
Ieyasu Sutsumi
C.E. 2529

Hours later, Dev was jacked into *Eagle*'s psych monitor program when Commander Lisa Canady's voice reached him through the ship's ICS. "Sir? General Sinclair is coming aboard."

"Eh? Why wasn't I told he was coming? I should have met him at the lock!"

"Sorry, sir, but no one knew. His ascraft was listed as a scheduled cargo run from Rogue to *Eagle*, all very mysterious and secret. I had no idea."

"Never mind, Lisa. I'm coming." He began downloading the commands to terminate his link with the ship's AI. "Have him escorted to the main lounge."

In preparation for their departure, *Eagle*'s spin-grav habs had been deployed and set rotating. Most of the living areas—crew quarters, recreation decks, crew's and officers' mess—were located in these pods that had unfolded from *Eagle*'s central core and were now turning with speed enough to create a half G of out-is-down simulated gravity on their outer decks. The main lounge was actually part of *Eagle*'s recreation suite, a place for crew and officers to mingle, with plenty of AI interface screens for access to the ship's library and comm modules lining the bulkheads for those who needed a complete linkage.

Dev was delayed by a junior ship's staff officer who needed a list of consumables checked and palmed for. Dev used the implant in his left hand to download the data, checked it against a master list stored in his RAM, then fed his electronic approval to the lieutenant's compad. By the time he reached the ship's lounge, Sinclair had already arrived. There was an unusual touch in evidence, however—four Confederation soldiers in full armor and carrying PCR-28 high-velocity rifles at port arms standing guard in the passageway outside. The entryway dissolved and the guards ushered him through.

It was not roomy inside; large as a destroyer was, there were few places aboard the ship accessible by humans that were, especially now that she was fully loaded with provisions for the long voyage to Alya. Still, the compartment had comfortable couches and a large viewall set to show a nonrotating scene gazing aft from *Eagle* at the now-full gold, white, and violet disk of Herakles. The deck was carpeted, and soundproofing panels on bulkheads and overhead muffled the steady throb and murmur of noise from the rest of the ship.

Sinclair was waiting for them, along with Brenda Ortiz. Katya was also present, the accidental attack in the ascraft apparently forgotten, though the memory made Dev inwardly cringe. To his considerable surprise, another man was waiting there as well, the slim, dapper, and silver-haired Grant Morton, the current President of Congress.

Like Sinclair, Morton was one of the original delegates to the Confederation Congress, and like both Sinclair and Katya, he was a native of New America. From what Dev had heard about the man, he was as politically conservative as Sinclair, but more willing to compromise than his more famous compatriot. It was largely due to Morton's influence that the genie slavery issue had not already fragmented the delicate coalition of colony worlds after initially being polarized by Liberty and Rainbow.

"Well, don't stand there like a damned newbie recruit," Sinclair said, rising from the couch he was sharing with Morton. "Come in and drag up a seat for yourself."

"Thank you, sir," Dev said. "Sorry I'm late. I wasn't told *either* of you was coming."

"You weren't supposed to know, Dev," Sinclair said with a wink. "In fact, as far as you're concerned, neither of us is here."

"If you say so." He turned to face President Morton. "Mr. President, this is an unexpected honor."

"Hardly that," Morton told him. "An honor, that is, though I'll allow you that it's unexpected. Actually, I came over to download some more problems on you."

Dev blinked at that. If the President of Congress had made a special trip across from the Rogue to the *Eagle*, it could only be because he feared that a ViRcom module communication might be somehow monitored.

"What can we do for you, sir?"

"Palm me."

Puzzled, Dev held out his left hand, palm up, the intricate network of gold and silver wires embedded in the skin winking in the compartment's overhead lighting. The president stepped forward and laid his own palm implant across Dev's, and he felt the tiny thrill of incoming data.

"What's . . . this?" Dev blinked, trying to read the file as it loaded itself into his personal RAM.

"A promotion, of course. We've created a whole new rank for you. Dug it up out of the archives, actually. You're a commodore, now. Basically, that means you're still a *taisa*, a captain, I mean, but with the authority of a flag officer to command a squadron." He glanced at Katya, then back at Dev. "This expedition needs a single, clear-cut leader. We've decided you're it. You'll notice that the packet I just gave you includes a promotion for your ship's XO. We're giving the *Eagle* to *Captain* Canady, to free you up for your duties as commander of this squadron."

"I . . . see." In the flurry of preparations for Farstar, Dev had given little thought to the expedition's command structure. Both he and Katya had held ranks corresponding to the *taisa* of both Hegemony and Empire. In the Confederation's new rank structure, which had been drawn from that of the Frontier militias, he was a captain, she a colonel, which meant basically that he was in charge of the spacecraft involved, while Katya ran the regiment-sized ground contingent. Morton's promotion took things a step farther, placing him in definite command of the entire expedition. "Sir, I'm not so sure this is a good—"

"Can it. Sinclair and I decided this last night. We don't have time to change things now, especially over an attack of modesty."

Dev could hear the worry in Morton's voice, could read the sense of urgency.

"You're moving the schedule up," Dev said bluntly. "There's a problem. What is it?"

Morton and Sinclair exchanged glances. "Told you he was quick," Sinclair said dryly.

"Commodore, Colonel Alessandro . . . you're not supposed to know this and you didn't hear it from me, but Lauer and his clique have forced a new vote on the agenda tomorrow. That he did so can only mean he thinks he has a chance of winning a two-thirds majority."

"A vote? On what?" Dev was confused. Ronal Lauer, he knew, was a delegate from Rainbow, and a representative of the population of one of the largest of that world's genie farms. As such, he was among the most outspoken of those in Congress supporting the institution of genie slavery. Dev had heard more than one of the man's speeches . . . undeniably brilliant, but how could anyone reasonably claim that gene-tailored workers had any less right to life or liberty than the full humans already fighting for independence from Imperial tyranny?

"About whether or not you, Commodore, should be permitted to go with this expedition."

"Dev not go?" Katya asked. "That's crazy! Why not?"

"It's the Xenolink," Sinclair told her. "There's considerable concern around here that Dev here is the only one with the, ah, experience necessary for linking with the Heraklean Xenophobe. And the Xenophobe . . . or rather, Dev *and* the Xenophobe together, are all that's keeping the Imperials from moving in and grabbing us all."

"That doesn't make sense," Dev said. "I was just gone for four months. Why didn't they oppose that?"

"Some of them did, at least privately," Sinclair said. "I felt you needed some time away, so I arranged for your raiding expedition without, um, consulting with some members of the War Council. Could be they remember that and are trying to steal a march on me this time."

"And now you're getting ready to go again," Morton added. "When it's almost a sure bet that the Imperials will be attacking soon. Lauer's faction wants to keep you here to link with the Naga again, if it becomes necessary."

"But the Naga hasn't even been seen," Katya protested. "Even if Dev stayed, there's no guarantee that he could link with it again."

"Agreed," Sinclair said. "And we do have volunteers ready to try linking with the Naga again if the Imperials return. *When* they return, I should say. Dev's description of what happened during his debriefing strongly suggests that it will know how to initiate a full link with a human, even if we don't."

"It must," Dev said. "I sure as hell don't know how to do it. I was unconscious when it happened to me last time."

"Logic doesn't necessarily work with some people," Morton said. "Sometimes I suspect that my distinguished colleague from Rainbow is less susceptible to its lures than others. Even so, I can understand their reluctance to lose you, young man. You saved us, all of us, in your one-man stand atop that terraforming pyramid. Another man might not have done so well."

Dev tried to suppress an inner shudder, and failed. For the briefest of instants, the nightmare was back. He had reached out with his mind, and lightnings had stabbed and crackled in the sky about him, fiery gestures in a cascade of raw, searing power. He caught Katya's hard gaze, and the memory crumbled. He felt embarrassed, even ashamed.

"Sir, I really don't think I'm the one for this job."

"Eh?" Morton snapped. "Nonsense."

"What's the problem, Dev?"

"I . . . I have reason to doubt my, my mental stability. . . ."

"He's had some nightmares," Katya said, quietly interrupting. "Bad ones, just since the Xenolink four months ago. We've talked about it, and he's been using *Eagle*'s psych monitor program. In my opinion, sir, he's fully able to carry out this mission. In fact, I can't think of anyone else in the whole Confederation fleet who could carry it out better than him."

Dev blinked at Katya, trying to see behind the calm of her eyes.

"All the more reason not to stay here and link with the damned Naga," Morton said, trying to make it sound like a joke.

"Dev, I've known you since Eridu," Sinclair said. "I have complete faith in you, in your tactical grasp of things, in your ability to handle yourself and your people. Now, has anything measurable changed in your psych profiles, anything that should disqualify you as a military officer?"

"Nothing . . . measurable. The monitor says I need rest."

Sinclair gave a wry grin. "Unfortunately, I can't let you go on vacation. I need you too much."

"I . . . I kind of assumed that was the case, sir."

"You'll have another three- or four-month trip en route to Alya. Think that'll take care of your problem?"

Dev frowned. The more he thought about it, the sillier disqualifying himself for a tendency to have nightmares seemed. Of course he was fit to command . . . and forcing Sinclair and Morton to rearrange their planning now would prove nothing, would do nothing, for him or for the expedition.

Besides, if he stayed, he would be expected to join with the monster again if the Imperials attacked. To become the monster.

He couldn't face that.

"General Sinclair," Dev said, drawing himself up straighter. "Mr. President. I'm fully ready and able to accept command. Under whatever command structure you care to name."

"That's settled then," Sinclair said. He smiled. "So. How quickly can you leave?"

Dev turned inward for a moment, consulting records stored within his RAM. "We could leave in twenty hours," he said. "*Eagle* is about ready for boost now except for loading the last of her OP stores. But none of the other ships have reported readiness for boost yet. As of six hours ago, they had anywhere from ten to another fifty hours' work remaining."

The squadron readying for the Alyan mission was an odd patchwork of a fleet. *Eagle* would be flagship, of course, while the two twenty-five-thousand–ton Commerce-class freighters *Vindemiatrix* and *Mirach* carried the bulk of Katya's 1st Confederation Rangers, complete with warstriders and other heavy equipment. *Tarazed* had started off as a New American cryo-H tanker, but she'd been converted into a carrier; packed into the hangar deck in what had been the forwardmost of five huge containment spheres were eighty-two warflyers, the equivalent of an entire Imperial dragonship fighter wing. There were also several unarmed merchantmen devoted to carrying military stores and equipment.

Escorting these larger vessels were the light destroyer *Constellation*, two frigates, the *Rebel* and the *Valiant*, and three corvettes. These were six of the eighteen warships Dev had captured in a lightning raid against the Imperial shipyards at Athena months earlier, just before the rebel evacuation from New America. The rest would stay behind to protect the Confederation's government . . . whether here at Herakles, or while moving from system to system as part of Sinclair's plan to avoid confrontation with the Empire.

"That'll be damned tight, Dev," Sinclair told him. "The vote is scheduled in Congress in another twenty-two hours. Make arrangements with your ship captains. If they're not ready to boost at the same time as you, they'll have to follow later and rendezvous with you at Alya."

Dev nodded. "We already have the navigational arrangements and protocols set up," he said, "since we can't keep track of one another in K-T space. If some of us make the K-T transition before others, it won't matter."

"Good."

"Our biggest problem, sir, is the CT. The last I heard they wouldn't be coming aboard until late tomorrow. I was told they were still working on some contact scenarios through the Rogue's AI."

Sinclair looked at Ortiz, who'd been sitting quietly throughout the discussion so far. "Professor?"

Arguably the most important contingent on the expedition was the Contact Team, fifteen men and women with experience dealing with the DalRiss, or who'd extensively studied various aspects of DalRiss culture, science, and language since the return of the Imperial Expeditionary Force three years earlier. Professor Ortiz was the senior contact officer. Technically, Dev and Katya were both members of the Contact Team as well, since both of them had dealt with the DalRiss during that earlier expedition, but since they were likely to be busy dealing with Imperials once planetfall was made, they would join the team only for negotiations with the DalRiss government, or if their particular expertise was needed.

"I'll talk to my people, sir," Ortiz said. "We ought to be able to keep working on those sims aboard *Eagle*. The less complex ones, anyway."

"That sounds satisfactory," Sinclair said. "See if you can move up the timetable. But don't discuss the change in boost time, please. I'd rather my compatriots in Congress didn't know you'd gone until after the fact."

"Won't this get you into some kind of trouble?" Katya wanted to know.

"I doubt it. Lauer already hates both Grant here and me. He'd love to see supreme command given to someone else . . . preferably a Rainbowman. He'll bluster and fume if he finds out you've already left, but there won't be much he can do about it. The danger is if he gets word you're bolting early and takes it into his head to order troops to stop you from leaving. That could split CONMILCOM and the government wide open. I'd rather not risk that, not now."

"You *could* keep me here, General," Dev said slowly. "I'm not absolutely necessary to the expedition."

"Maybe. I think you are. Of all the ship captains in the fleet, even those with experience with squadron-level tactics, you're the best we have. You've proved it, at Eridu, at Athena, and at New America." He shrugged. "You know, we have no idea how large the Imperial squadron at Alya is. You might get out there and find a couple of frigates. We *hope* that's the case, and Intelligence suggests that the Imperial fleet assets at Alya are, in fact, quite small. With the Rebellion spreading through the Frontier, they can't afford to tie down too many ships that far from home.

"But you just might break out of K-T space out there and find a major squadron waiting for you. Cruisers. Even one of their Ryus, though Milliken has personally assured me that all of their dragonships are accounted for." Charles Milliken was the Confederation's head of Military Intelligence.

"Charming thought," Katya said. Dev remained silent, wondering where Sinclair was going.

"Dev, this mission is a long shot. We all know that. Even if the Imperials prove to be no problem at all out there, there's no guarantee that the DalRiss will be willing to cooperate, and we *must* have their help, or we're going to lose this war."

Dev blinked. "Sir, you *can't* believe that. Or you wouldn't have brought us to where we are. The whole war can't depend on whether or not a handful of us are able to establish communication with—"

"It can, and I'm afraid it does, son. You know, when this thing started, I wasn't looking for a clean break with the Imperium. I thought maybe we could reach some sort of accommodation, a compromise, but it's gone too far for that, too far by half. When it turned into a military struggle, with the fighting at Eridu, a lot of us thought that simply demonstrating that we were willing to stand up against the Empire would be enough to force them to back down, to say, 'all right, this is getting expensive, let them go.' "

"It didn't happen that way."

"No. It didn't. Because we underestimated just how far some elements of the Imperial and Hegemony governments were willing to go to hang on to the power they had. Or to save face. We also underestimated—*I* underestimated—the willingness of the Frontier worlds to take a stand. Some of them, Liberty and Rainbow, for instance, are in the thick of it, but a lot more are sitting on the fence, sending delegates to Congress but unwilling to send men, ships, equipment. Our revolution is going to die, Dev, unless we can turn it around with something big.

"That's why I'm investing so much on this mission. You, Katya, with most of your regiment. You, Dev, with a fair-sized percentage of our entire fleet. If anyone can exploit this, this rift between the DalRiss and the Empire, it's the two of you."

"You're leaving a terrible hole in the defenses here, sir," Dev said quietly.

"Not really. Here, *Eagle* and *Tarazed* and the other ships in your squadron might delay the inevitable . . . how much? A month? A year, perhaps? But the end would be the same, sooner or later. Mostly, our survival depends on whether or not I can avoid large-scale contact with the enemy, because when that happens, the Confederation Navy is finished, and *Eagle*'s presence won't make that big a difference, one way or the other.

"Out there, though, well, who can say? We have a chance, a small but clean chance, of winning friends powerful enough that we just might end the war. Of convincing the Imperials that it would be cheaper to let us have our freedom than to keep fighting.

"But the key is not going to be how many troops or ships I send to Alya. It's going to be the genius of the people leading them, because, thank God, people still make better decisions than machines, and some people perform far better than others. You two are such people, and the fate of the Rebellion, of this Confederation, might well be riding with the two of you."

"My God," Katya said, her voice so low that Dev barely caught it. "You sure don't believe in putting any pressure on your people, do you?"

If Sinclair heard her words, he ignored them. Dev said nothing, his mind was racing. He ought, he told himself, to tell Morton and Sinclair that he was not the man to lead the Confederation squadron, that it would be better—*safer*— to assign him to one of the ships remaining at Herakles. There were other senior officers better qualified than he—Admiral Herren, for instance, or Captain Jase Curtis of the *Tarazed*— people who did not question their own sanity.

As Dev had recently begun questioning his.

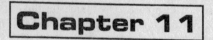

Chapter 11

Individuality is alien to Naga thought. With only a sin-gle organism occupying a given world, that organism believes itself to be the sole intelligence in its entire universe; indeed, for the Naga, intelligence and self are indistinguishable concepts. In the course of its explora-tions of its universe, a Naga will "bud" pieces of itself as scouts capable of independent action and thought, scouts that return to the parent body the memory of the scout's wanderings. By building on this experience, planetary Nagas can form conceptual analogue-pictures of sepa-

rate entities, each with a unique viewpoint and history. This requires considerable flexibility on the Naga's part, however, far more than that required, say, by a member of one human culture attempting to understand the point of view of someone raised with a different cultural world view.

—*Intelligent Expectations*
Dr. James Phillip Kantor
C.E. 2542

Thirty-two thousand kilometers above Herakles, the Imperial fleet decelerated into synchronous orbit. The planet, half-full, gleamed in the warm yellow light of Mu Herculis, its seas blue and violet, its clouds and polar ice caps gleaming white with golden highlights.

The fleet, designated Ohka Squadron, consisted of nineteen warships ranging in size from eight-hundred–ton Hari-class corvettes to the flagship, a Ryu-class carrier, massing two million tons and just short of one thousand meters in length. Nudged by brief flashes from maneuvering jets, the armada deployed, the ships spreading out across six thousand kilometers of empty space. Blocks of data flickered and shifted next to the images of the various ships, information telling of vectors, relative velocities, and combat readiness.

The scene, portrayed through virtual reality, was being experienced by a number of observers, an invisible gallery of onlookers whose vantage point shifted back and forth among three of those orbiting Imperial warships. They included captains and department heads from several vessels; senior was *Chujo* Takeshi Miyagi, commander in chief of Otori Squadron. Among the watchers was the bright and tactically innovative *Shosho* Tomiji Kima, commanding officer of the flagship *Karyu*, the *Fire Dragon*. Kima had been *Karyu's* Executive Officer under Miyagi until eight months ago, when Miyagi had been promoted to full admiral and given command of Otori Squadron.

"At this point," a voice was telling the watchers in *Nihongo*, "the Ryu-class carrier and two of the cruisers have already begun their bombardment of the rebel position on the planet's surface. So far, there is no response from the enemy on the ground."

Kima studied the data displays carefully, encoding ship positions and deployments within his personal RAM for future study on his own. Later, too, he would examine in detail the disposition of the squadron's marine warstriders and infantry on the surface. This ViRsimulation would be restricted to the battle, if such it could be called, fought in orbit over Herakles some four months earlier.

One of the ships, he noticed, one of the four big Kako-class cruisers, was in trouble.

"It was at this point that something went badly wrong," the voice continued. The speaker, Kima knew, was *Shosa* Chokugen Takaji, the fleet's senior military intelligence specialist. "We believe that the rebels were able somehow to take over *Mogami*'s engineering AIs and instigate a quantum power tap start-up."

"I don't understand, *Shosasan*," another voice said. "How could turning on a QPT be considered a weapon?"

"Obviously, *Imadasan*," Admiral Miyagi said, replying for the *shosa*, "you xenosophontologists are taught nothing about starship engineering or power core operation." A ripple of polite laughter sounded from the other unseen watchers.

"Quite so," the intelligence officer said. "The QPT uses paired, artificially generated microsingularities to extract energy from the quantum plenum. These are molecule-sized black holes orbiting one another at speeds approaching that of light, and with mutual, finely tuned harmonic resonances. They are rarely used in close proximity to a planet, since local gravity fields distort the shape of space and can affect that harmonic tuning. Somehow, we presume through one of our own communications bands, someone on the surface linked with *Mogami*'s AI, started up the power tap, and then ordered the computer to shut down. Without the computer to tune the singularities' harmonics from microsecond to microsecond within a gravitational well, they went random and initiated an uncontrolled power cascade. One evaporated in a burst of energy. Note the readings there on the right. Intense X rays and gamma radiation are flooding *Mogami*'s engineering spaces."

Indeed, the readings taken from a nearby ship had gone off the scale. A schematic diagram drew itself in an empty patch of space nearby, sketching in the interior spaces of the six-hundred–meter cigar that was *Mogami*. The observers watched as the cruiser's engineering decks began crumpling inward, the pace of the vessel's destruction slowed to a fraction of its realtime pace.

Implacably, the voice continued, describing the cruiser's death. "With the evaporation of one microsingularity, of course, the second was flung clear in a gravitational slingshot effect at relativistic speeds. It was moving more slowly by the time it left the ship. Repeated interactions with *Mogami*'s interior structure slowed it significantly as it passed along the cruiser's length, devouring armor, hull metal, bulkheads, circuitry, crew members, and anything else that happened to lie in its path before emerging . . . *there*."

Mogami and its transparent cutaway view both were crumpling as the observers watched, the one a mirror to the other. A dazzling point of light emerged from just behind the ship's bow, streaking outward. An instant later it, too, evaporated and vanished into the depths of space in a nova's glare of visible light and hard radiation that silently washed across the hulls of every ship in the Imperial squadron.

"Many of the ships sustained lethal damage at this point," the admiral's voice went on, emotionless. "The micro black hole's explosive evaporation must have been equivalent to the simultaneous detonation of some thousands of nuclear warheads. EMP and radiation damage crippled at least half the ships and inflicted thousands of casualties.

"Admiral Kawashima recognized what was happening, of course, and shut down all external communications links. The rebels were unable to directly influence any more of our shipboard AIs. As a result, they almost immediately changed tactics. Please keep your attention focused on the planet."

The face of the world, half-full, was changing.

The transformation was so rapid that Kima was not at first sure what he was seeing. At a point not far from the equator, clouds were gathering in a great, spiraling whorl, moving so quickly that even from synchorbit their movement could be seen by the naked eye as a slow, writhing crawl. Under extreme magnification and image enhancement, they took on a distinctly three-dimensional aspect, each tiny thunderhead edged by its own shadow. Where seconds before perhaps half of the planet's seas and barren stretches of land and ice cap were visible, new clouds were appearing, puffing up out of nothing, crowding together, deepening, quickening, building a hurricane that spanned a quarter of the planet's visible disk as Kima watched.

At the heart of that eerie, titanic storm, lightnings pulsed and throbbed, like a heartbeat cast in light to make it visible, each silent flicker muffled and diffused by the masking clouds. Near Herakles's north pole, a thin smear of pale, wavering light just visible against that portion of the polar zone in darkness faded, then winked out almost magically. Data flickered and shifted in the overlaid information displays.

Abruptly, *something* happened . . . a flicker of motion, a flash of light. Those in the audience could not be sure exactly what, if anything, they'd just seen. New blocks of data wrote themselves across parts of the display, registering events invisible to human senses.

"That first shot missed," the admiral said. "I'll have the simulation AI play the next one at a reduced speed. Time factor five to one."

It happened again, but this time slowly enough that the watchers could perceive a thread of intensely brilliant, blue-white light streaking up from the precise center of that whirl-pool of clouds, a point marked by a tiny hole, the storm's eye. The thread drew itself skyward, razor crisp, laser-beam straight, detaching itself from the planet slowly at first, then spearing into the midst of the Imperial fleet with an apparent acceleration, an illusion created by perspective.

"Time factor one thousand to one."

The movement slowed again, sharply. The thread became a tiny, fiercely radiating star drifting rapidly upward through empty space, targeted precisely on the heavy cruiser *Zintu*, sister to *Mogami*.

The imagery obviously had been captured at the extreme limit of those sensors recording the event, but the resolving power was good enough to record in detail the explosion unfolding like a blossoming flower, a blinding dazzle of actinic violence that briefly outshone the glare of Mu Herculis itself. *Zintu* simply vanished, her enormous, cylindrical bulk converted in an instant into that glare of raw energy . . . plus a few hurtling scraps of twisted and half-molten debris flung clear by that rapidly expanding wave front. Other ships nearby, a frigate and a small destroyer, were lightly brushed by *Zintu*'s flowering, a caress that boiled away hull metal and armor, turrets and fairings, and left both vessels lifeless, blast-tortured wrecks.

"*Kuso*," someone in the audience said quietly, almost reverently.

"The missile," the admiral continued as though he'd not heard, "was analyzed spectroscopically. It was nothing more than a block of nanofactured fabricrete and iron massing approximately one metric ton, accelerated to a velocity of over ten percent of the speed of light and glowing partly from the friction of its passage through the Heraklean atmosphere, and partly from the play of incredible energies across its surface. We believe it was part of the outer shell of one of the atmosphere generating units on Herakles's surface. After traversing the thirty thousand kilometers between the ground and *Zintu* in nine-tenths of one second, it struck the cruiser amidships. We calculate that the transitional kinetic energy liberated by that impact was somewhere between 10^{19} and 10^{20} joules, or some one thousand times the yield of a twenty-megaton thermonuclear warhead. It appears, gentlemen, that the rebels have found a dramatic means of overcoming their lack of nuclear weaponry."

There was an uncomfortable stir among the watchers, and Kima heard the murmur of urgent, low-voiced exchanges among them. The Imperium had long maintained its military superiority over the Shichiju through the simple expedient of being the only one of the Hegemony's member states permitted through the government's charter to possess nuclear weapons. There were rumors that the rebels were working on developing such weapons for themselves. With this demonstration at Herakles, perhaps they no longer needed them.

The physics of that demonstration bothered Kima, however.

"The energy required to accelerate a one-ton mass to thirty-some thousand kilometers per second," Kima pointed out, "must be nothing less than astronomical. . . ."

"Nothing less, *Shoshosan*," Miyagi replied, the words dry.

"But where could they get such power? Or . . . have they found a means of creating a quantum power tap on the planet's surface?"

"Unlikely, *Shoshosan*. Such installations are extremely large and require enormous technical staffs, assets that we do not believe the rebels possess." The admiral gave a command, restoring the normal one-to-one time factor of the scene.

Once again, there was a flicker of motion, a flash of light. This time the target was one of the squadron's outrider ships, a destroyer positioned to intercept fleeing rebel ships some half a million kilometers farther out.

At that distance, the hurtling missile took an agony of time, more than fifteen seconds, to reach the target. The destroyer *Urakaze*, suddenly aware of its danger, engaged its main drives in a desperate attempt to step aside. Unfortunately, the huge ship was moving tail-first toward the planet, having just completed its deceleration from the outer system; it took precious seconds to bring its fusion drives on line, precious seconds more simply to kill the last of its planetward velocity . . . and whoever was aiming those rocks had clearly anticipated the Imperial warship's attempt at escape.

The missile struck *Urakaze*'s stern directly between its paired, glowing venturis, and the destroyer vanished in a silent nova's flare of light.

"Note the fact," the admiral continued, "that Herakles's magnetic field has vanished. The event registered on our sensors, of course, and in the disappearance of the planet's aurorae. Our scientists are unable to explain the mechanism, though it strongly suggests that the Heraklean Xenophobe is behind the phenomenon. We know Xenophobes make extensive use of magnetic fields. They generate an intense, highly localized field, for example, that actually changes the structure of rock by rearranging its constituent atoms. That's how they're able to tunnel through solid rock at relatively high speeds. Presumably, the Heraklean Xenophobe somehow tapped the planetary magnetic field and used the energy to launch those boulders. Since Xenophobes are thermovores, it undoubtedly also directly utilized the heat of the planet's core, though we had no way of measuring that."

The next shot to come streaking up out of the eye of the storm struck Ohka Squadron's flagship, *Donryu*. Its kilometer-long, gun-bristling length resisted the inconceivable energies of the high-speed missile no better than had the hull of the far smaller *Urakaze*.

"Such power," someone in the audience said.

"Such power can be countered," Miyagi said curtly. "Ideally, it can be turned against itself, in the best traditions of the martial arts."

"But how can such a weapon be resisted?" one of the watchers asked. Kima thought that the voice was that of the xenosophontologist who'd asked about QPTs earlier. His name was Imada, and he was a civilian, a scientist attached to the Imperial *Sekkodan*, or scout service.

"In this case, by making a preemptive strike with irresistible weapons of our own," Miyagi said. "That, however, is not our primary problem. The Emperor, gentlemen, is troubled by reports that the rebels have managed to ally themselves with the Xenophobe. Clearly, the control these creatures have over the physical environment gives them awesome power and makes them a threat wherever they may be encountered. It is the Imperial Staff Command's belief that they will pose a threat only on worlds already occupied by a Xenophobe, worlds such as Mu Herculis, and these, fortunately, are rare.

"Still, the possibility remains that this rebel Confederation will learn how to seed other worlds with Xenophobes, with Xenophobe 'buds,' rather, from organisms that they have communicated with. They might learn how to employ Xenophobe fragments aboard their ships or use them as a kind of infestation introduced onto worlds that we control. At Herakles, we've all seen how deadly this alliance of Man and Xenophobe can be."

"Sir . . ."

"Yes, *Taisa* Urabe."

Urabe was captain of the cruiser *Kuma*, a dour and phlegmatic man. "Sir, if the rebels have achieved some sort of alliance with the Xenophobe, isn't, I mean, wouldn't it be better to let the rebels go their way?"

"*Neboken-ja nayo?*" Miyagi snapped. Literally, the phrase meant "Aren't you half-asleep?" and, depending on the tone, could be humorous or harsh. The admiral used the words like a whiplash, chastising. "Our new Emperor has determined that the rebels must be brought back into the fold," Miyagi continued. "If we fail—and I must stress that the responsibility is upon us, upon the men and ships of this squadron—if we fail, we invite the rule of Earth and the Empire by the half-civilized *shiro* of the Frontier."

A deathly silence hung among the virtual presences gathered within the electronic conference space. The word *shiro* meant "white" but could be construed as "white boy," as much an epithet as "nigger" was to a black. Miyagi, Kima knew, was part of the inner circle of high-ranking military officers within the Imperial Staff Command who were determined to eliminate *gaijin* influence from all levels of the Imperial government and military . . . and from the subsidiary government of the Terran Hegemony as well, if possible. He hated *gaijin* with a passion, and Kima was pretty sure that that was why the man had been chosen to command this mission.

"I apologize," Urabe said. "It was certainly not my intent to question the Imperial will."

"Of course not," Miyagi said, the words softer now. "And I understand that you all have been under considerable strain, preparing for this mission. Remember, however, that the Emperor and his senior people, including *Gensui* Munimori and the entire Imperial Staff Command, are watching us with the most exacting scrutiny. We cannot fail. To do so could encourage the rebellion's supporters on fifty worlds and fan the flames of insurrection to a blaze that we could never contain or extinguish. The rebel weapon is a fearsome one, yes, but the mission planners and our colleagues with Imperial Intelligence are certain that this operation, if carried out precisely according to plan, will allow us to avoid the destruction suffered by Ohka Squadron. Instead, the Heraklean Xenophobe will be destroyed, together with the so-called rebel government and whatever scraps of disaffected Hegemony deserters they may have assembled there. We will strike without warning and without mercy. The Rebellion, gentlemen, will be crushed with this single blow, once and for all."

From the way he launched into the speech, Kima wondered if Miyagi might not actually have been waiting for Urabe's statement, and the chance to demonstrate, with his outburst, the importance of victory.

Whether the outburst had been arranged or not, Kima agreed with the reasoning behind it. The rebel challenge to the order and stability of the Hegemony—and behind the Hegemony, of *Dai Nihon*'s Imperium—could not be permitted to stand, not without crippling the government's effectiveness forever. If the rebels won, the future promised to be a howling darkness, as the barbarians assaulted the rational order of the Empire.

As commanding officer of the *Karyu*, he'd been personally involved in the drafting of the squadron's operational orders, and knew the plan was a good one, with a good chance of success. Still, Kima's military experience had taught him to be cautious about confidence in any venture with as many unknowns as this one, however. No plan survives contact with the enemy. Who had said that? A Western strategist, he was sure. And the Western-descended inhabitants of the Frontier had more than once demonstrated the truth of that axiom.

He would not feel truly confident until the Imperial fleet's first blow had fallen. That blow would be irresistible, deadly . . . and inescapable, no matter how close their alliance with the world's damnable black Xenophobe.

After that blow had fallen, the rebels would have no chance for survival whatsoever.

Chapter 12

The true test of man lies in space travel . . . not in the mastery of the technology that makes it physically possible, but in the mastery of self and mind and imagination that bridges the psychological gulf that for so long isolated Man on the world of his birth. It was this mastery of self that gave us the stars, far more than the mastery of such purely physical systems as the Power Tap and the K-T drive.

—*Man and His Works*
Karl Gunther Fielding
C.E. 2488

If I'm not careful, Dev thought, late one shipboard evening as he climbed out of a comm module on *Eagle*'s recreation deck after another session with the AI monitor, *I'll be interfacing with AI software more than I am with human beings.*

Despite the intense crowding aboard any military warship, it was actually difficult to do otherwise. It had always required an effort of will for Dev to communicate with other people on any level deeper than polite greeting or shipboard routine. In fact, *Eagle*'s close quarters tended to increase Dev's isolation, as week followed week in the unending monotony of the K-T Plenum. Most military personnel, through both their Hegemony training and experience, tended to adopt an almost *Nihonjin* sense of personal space, a privacy of the mind in a place where physical privacy was hard to come by, and Dev was no exception. Imperials referred to it as *naibuno sekai*, the inner world, and the walls it raised were seemingly as impenetrable as duralloy sheathing. A man and woman could be furiously coupling against a bulkhead in the main passageway and others would pass them by, not staring, not even seeing, a selective blindness that allowed crew personnel to maintain their sanity as day followed day in unending and unchanging routine.

Starships were by their nature crowded. *Eagle* was a giant, 395 meters long and massing eighty-four thousand tons, but the vast majority of her bulk was taken up by power plant, drives, and reaction mass tankage; four hundred men and women lived in her two rotating habs, in quarters that might have comfortably accommodated fifty.

The best therapy for the pressures induced by a long K-T passage, of course, was the time rationed to each person for access to a ViRcom module. There, for an hour or two every other day, dreams became reality, and the stinking, overheated, overcrowded monotony of shipboard life could be forgotten for a time within the virtual reality of the dreamer's choosing. Dev spent much of his time in multiple linkages with members of his staff, of course, just in pursuit of his day-to-day routine of conferences and planning sessions, but interaction there was impersonal and professional. He could count most of *Eagle*'s officers as friends, including both Lara Anders, her senior pilot, and Lisa Canady, her new skipper, but in an unwritten law extending back to an era when wooden ships sailed liquid seas, no commanding officer could afford friendships, platonic or otherwise, that might hamper his ability to command.

So despite the crowding, Dev felt alone . . . and lonely. His sense of isolation had steadily increased since his hasty departure from Herakles. He was having trouble reading those he talked to, he often missed the undercurrent of emotion and body language that was the foundation for any communication deeper than "hello." Virtual reality linkages made things so easy—remote, detached, and sanitary—that they were infinitely preferable to meetings face-to-face.

He missed Katya, of course, missed her more, if possible, than he had during their last separation, but she was where a regimental commander was supposed to be during a transit, with her troops aboard their ship. She was making the passage aboard the transport *Vindemiatrix* and would not be shifting to *Eagle* until after they arrived at their destination.

In any case, after the disastrous nightmare in the cargo bay of the docked shuttle, he scarcely dared to open himself to anyone. Command granted him a privacy that he appreciated now.

The AI continued to give him a technomegalomania rating of point four. He was convinced now that there was something else wrong with him, something stemming from the Xenolink. He felt torn—dreading the power that had been his during the Xenolink on one hand, craving the sense of power and completion and wholeness that was his while linked with a ship's AI on the other. At first, he couldn't relate those two seemingly opposite drives in his mind, not until he began questioning whether or not the comforting embrace of a ship's AI might not be, in some small way, at least, a substitute for the far vaster and more sweeping transformation of mind and body that had been his, briefly, on Herakles.

Was he going mad? Could he *know* if he was going mad? There were no answers, no promises of answers. All he had was the growing desire, the need to link again with *Eagle*'s AI and take the ship into combat.

Linked, he felt complete. When unjacked, an ordinary man, he tended to avoid the other members of *Eagle*'s crew, withdrawing into the *naibuno sekai* if he could not withdraw from them in the real world. His status as the commodore in command of Farstar helped maintain that separation, a certain measure of personal isolation that he found he now welcomed.

He did remain available to those who needed to talk, of course. Many of the people aboard *Eagle* had wives, sweethearts, and family members still living on New America or on other worlds threatened by the Empire, and the enforced separations added to the pressure cooker atmosphere of shipboard life. Occasionally, when the pressure got too much, there would be a fight or some other infraction of the tightly woven web of rules and regulations by which every ship lived and died, and then he would officiate over a punishment mast. Sometimes, punishment consisted of forfeiture of recjacking time in the modules, but as time went on, forcing members of the crew to endure shipboard life without the temporary reprieve of virtual reality became counterproductive. Most often, fights between crew members were themselves resolved through ViRsimulation, with the combatants assuming fighter analogues for themselves or engaging in battle through simulated warstriders or flyers. Therapy, Dev found, could double as training, a means of keeping his people jacked in and hard, ready to meet whatever was waiting for them at Alya.

Through all of this, Dev remained as aloof and as uninvolved as possible. He could not risk showing even a hint of favoritism, needing to be seen by all in the crew as both fair and impartial. At the same time, he found himself erecting higher and higher barriers against the other officers aboard, until by the end of the passage he was taking most of his meals alone in his quarters and talking to others only in the strict line of duty.

Fifteen weeks after their departure from Mu Herculis, *Eagle* emerged into normal fourspace on the fringes of the Alya A system. *Constellation, Rebel*, and the corvettes *Intrepid* and *Audacious* were already there, having arrived on station several hours earlier. Passive scanning had detected the neutrino emissions of fifteen ships already in-system, twelve of them tucked in tight around Alya A-VI, the other three in transit to or from the planet. So far, there was no sign that the newcomers' arrival had been detected.

The sun Alya A was a tiny, intensely brilliant disk set in a milky glow of zodiacal light, while its distant twin glowed more brightly than Venus seen from Earth. The Alyan suns were young as stars go; less than a billion years had passed since they'd emerged together from the nebula that had given them birth, and both nestled at the centers of vast accretion disks of planetoids, dust, and meteoric debris. Comets, too, were more common in these younger systems, and several glowed with pale, wispy delicacy, their tails aimed outward away from the sun.

Dev, linked into *Eagle*'s sensor suite, considered the vista of light-scattering dust and debris ringing Alya A. The speed with which life had attained intelligence here was astonishing; more astonishing still was the tenacious grip with which life clung to existence in a system where meteor and comet impacts were commonplace. Dev remembered watching the meteors visible as golden flashes against ShraRish's nightside during his previous visit three years before. Brenda Ortiz had told him during the voyage out that dinosaur-killer impacts—strikes as devastating as the one that had driven so many Terran species to extinction sixty-five million years earlier—probably occurred on ShraRish every few tens of thousands of years. Somehow, life on the DalRiss worlds had learned to survive the cosmic bombardment. Current theory suggested that the frequent impacts were partially responsible for the diversity and toughness of Alyan life; if radiation from those young, hot stars drove evolution in the system, the weeding-out of existing life by infalling planetoids and comets contributed to the cold discrimination of natural selection.

The dust had also suggested a strategy, one that Dev had been working on in simulations throughout most of the long passage from Herakles. They had deliberately emerged within the outer fringes of the star's accretion disk, far enough out from ShraRish that the burst of energy released from the K-T plenum by their arrival should have gone unnoticed, as had the steady flux of neutrinos from their fusion power plants. The debris fields sheltered them from radar and ladar detection from the planet, of course, and shielded their own infrared emissions.

There, the tiny fleet waited for the arrival of the rest of the squadron. While fifth-generation K-T drives allowed ships to cross space at the rate of roughly a light year per day, the skill of the jackers, the unpredictable effects of currents within the godsea, or the pure, random bad luck of a malfunction could affect a ship's expected arrival time by days one way or the other—more if a power plant or drive breakdown left the ship helplessly adrift in the deeps between the stars.

They could not afford to wait longer, however, even hidden within the outer edge of Alya A's accretion disk. The neutrinos released by a ship's fusion plant were not masked by interplanetary dust. The fact that the Confederation ships could detect the neutrino emissions of the Imperial ships meant that the Imperials could in turn detect them. Each passing hour increased the chance that the sensor suite aboard one of the Imperial ships in orbit would spot the Confederation vessels . . . or that mistake or bad luck would in some other way reveal their presence.

Dev had wished he could try deception to get close enough to launch an attack but knew that would not be possible here. There was too much chance that the enemy commander had heard of similar deceptions, at Athena and at New America. Besides, the rebels would have to use reconnaissance probes during the approach just to find out what they were up against, and no incoming Imperial squadron would ever do that.

An operational plan for direct attack, then, had been worked out before they'd left Herakles, and polished in sim during the voyage. The squadron would wait, lurking in the dust and maintaining communications silence for fifty hours past the arrival of the *Rebel*, by chance the first Confederation ship to reach Alya. During that time, all but three of the other vessels arrived—*Constellation*, the frigate *Valiant*, the corvettes *Intrepid* and *Audacious*, the big ex-tanker *Tarazed*, four of the five unarmed merchantmen, and, much to Dev's relief, the *Vindemiatrix*. Still missing were one of the merchants, the corvette *Daring*, and the armed transport *Mirach*.

That last absence could mean trouble. *Mirach* was carrying half of the 1st Confederation Rangers' troops and equipment, and he didn't want to commence the attack without her, but to wait longer exposed the squadron to discovery and attack. Briefly, *Vindemiatrix* docked directly with *Eagle*'s ventral access hatch, allowing personnel to cross from one ship to the other.

Eagerly, then, Dev waited for Katya in *Eagle*'s lounge.

Katya, too, had been lonely throughout the long passage out from Herakles. *Vindemiatrix* was roomy as starships went. Less maneuverable and with a lower acceleration than any warship, she required far smaller reserves of reaction mass and could devote a much larger percentage of her onboard space to passengers than could *Eagle*. But even with half of her huge, rotating cargo bays equipped for passenger accommodations, *Trixie* was carrying nearly eight hundred troops and maintenance personnel in addition to her crew of forty-five, twice *Eagle*'s complement crammed into vast, open dormitories that allowed no privacy at all save that of the inner world. The transport did have one hundred link modules installed in one of the zero-G bays, which meant that the passengers could enjoy a positively luxurious three hours of recjacking out of every twenty-four. The rest of the time was spent in training, shoulder-to-shoulder calisthenics in the dormitories, and classes in tactics, maintenance, field ops, and planetology delivered the old-fashioned way, by lecture instead of by cephlinkage . . . anything to keep the troops busy.

By the time they'd emerged from K-T space, though, her unit had been ready to face any odds, any enemy, if just to escape the gray-walled prison of the transport.

And Katya, too, for that matter. She was mildly claustrophobic, a hangover from an accident suffered while she'd been jacking a merchantman years before, an AI link failure that had left her awake but blind for long hours before her rescue. Normally, she was able to keep the feelings of dread when faced by small enclosures or pitch-blackness under control, but enduring fifteen weeks locked up in the hot, people-stinking closeness of the transport had taxed her self-control to what she was certain was her limit.

When Katya boarded *Eagle*, along with her battle ops staff, she half expected herself to fall into Dev's arms in a most unmilitary display the moment she saw him. The incident aboard the ascraft months before was all but forgotten; what remained was her worry for him, and her need. But when the lounge door dissolved and she stepped into the compartment and actually saw him standing before the viewall, she found herself behind that long-held wall of her inner world, unable to bridge the gap between them.

"Welcome aboard, Katya," he said. He was smiling, but Katya could sense the distance in him as well as in herself. Behind him, the viewall showed the *Trixie* backing off from the *Eagle*, taking up station a safe distance from the destroyer in preparation for the final jump into the inner system of Alya A. In the passageway outside, booted feet rattled across ferroplas deck plating; battle stations had been sounded, and *Eagle*'s crew was still responding.

"Thank you, Dev," she said, almost shyly. "It's . . . good to see you again."

"We seem to be spending most of our time apart these days. I'm beginning to think we should see about getting ourselves assigned to the same ship . . . preferably a two-man scout."

"I've had the same thoughts myself. Only if we did that, we might not get much work done."

"True. And speaking of work, how would you like to link with me for the final approach?"

She nodded. "That would be good. I'll especially want to see what you pick up on the Imperial dispositions on ShraRish when you get close enough to send in the probes."

"Right. We don't have anything yet, of course, but we'll be launching the RD-40s as soon as we emerge from the next K-T hop. That ought to give us a pretty good look at what we're up against."

More than anything else, the Farstar squadron needed up-to-date intelligence. Exactly what kinds of Imperial ships were in orbit, and what was their operational status? How many troops were still on the surface? What kind of orbital defenses had they built? Had their defensive status changed since the DalRiss attack?

To find the answers to these and other, related questions, they'd planned to launch over one hundred RD-40 remote-linked scouts, a small cloud of teleoperated eyes and other senses that would provide a detailed, composite view of everything on and near ShraRish. Each scout was a small spacecraft, a thick-bodied saucer shape five meters across with almost all of its interior space devoted to reaction mass tankage. Its flattened ventral surface and stubby wings allowed the craft to operate within a planetary atmosphere. A compact Mitsubishi PV-1220 fusor unit provided thrust and shipboard power; a rather small-brained AI allowed the vehicle to be remote-jacked from one of the fleet's larger ships. Capable of pulling 50 Gs of acceleration—Gs unfelt by their pilots, who remained safe aboard the ship that launched and directed them—the RD-40s were far faster and more maneuverable than any human-occupied fighter or warflyer, and since they were expendable, they did not need to reserve reaction mass for a return trip. They were unarmed, but a command from the craft's pilot could switch off the fusorpack's containment field, causing a plasma detonation almost as powerful as a small, low-yield thermonuclear explosion. The single major disadvantage of remote scouts lay in the difficulties of teleoperating such craft over distances of more than a small fraction of a light second. Time delays while radio or lasercom signals crawled back and forth at the sluggardly speed of light made any maneuvers at long range dangerous and rendered atmospheric maneuvering all but impossible.

As part of going to battle stations, *Eagle* was shifting from normal flight mode to combat mode. The rotation of her hab modules was slowed, then stopped, and the modules slowly hauled back into recesses within the ship's armored hull. In zero-G, then, Katya and her ops staff followed Dev down a connector corridor from *Eagle*'s Number Two Hab to the main ship's access passageway running along her spine. An enclosed transport pod whisked them aft to *Eagle*'s bridge, a chamber buried deep within the destroyer's hull. There, crew members waiting in the disorienting bob and drift of zero-G helped Katya and Dev slide into the padded embrace of the ViRcom modules that lined the ship's bridge and jack connectors into their C- and T-sockets. The module's hatch became solid, and Katya nervously braced herself against a darkness relieved only by the wink of system status lights. Her left palm searched for the interface panel. When she found it, she downloaded the necessary link codes . . .

. . . and she was in space, staring into a light-frosted blackness given depth and volume by scattered stars, the glare of Alya A, and the soft-haired wisps of comets.

"Linked in?" Dev asked her, a voice in the emptiness beside her.

"All set."

"Hey, Katya," Lara Anders said over the pilot's linkage. "Saw you come aboard but didn't get to say howdy. How's it feel to be aboard a real ship again?"

"As opposed to a cattle transport? Pretty good, Lara."

"Here's the feed on the Impie ships in-system," Dev told her.

Data scrolled past her awareness, partly overlaying her view of space as graphic symbols marked targets and projected courses. Except for one far-distant reading that was probably a supply ship of some kind, all of the fusion-driven targets in the system save those of the Farstar squadron itself were still tightly clustered about Alya A-VI. Cross hairs were now centered over the pinpoint of light representing the planet. There was still no sign that Farstar had been detected, but she reminded herself that the radiations she was sensing now had begun their journey from the target world hours before.

In the background, Katya heard the commanders of other ships in the squadron reporting readiness for K-T space. Only the eight warships would be making this final translation; the four merchantmen would stay behind, to stay clear of the battle and to await the arrival of the three missing ships.

"Hang on, then," Dev said. She heard the excitement building in his voice. "Things are going to be happening fast."

"That's affirmative," Lara said. "K-T translation in five . . . four . . . three . . . two . . . one . . . *mark!*"

Around her, space blazed into blue-white glory.

Eagle leaped toward ShraRish at over three hundred times the speed of light.

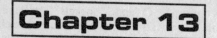

Chapter 13

. . . Axial tilt: 3° 05' 12"; Temperature range (equatorial): 40°C to 50°C; Atmospheric pressure (arbitrary sea level): .75 bar; Atmospheric composition: N_2 83.7%, O_2 8.7%, O_3 3.6%, SO_2 2.4%, Ar 1.2%, H_2O (mean) .2%, H_2SO_4 (mean) 850 ppm, CO_2 540 ppm . . .

—Shipboard ephemeris data
Extract on Alya A-VI
C.S. *Eagle*
C.E. 2544

Their final immersion in the godsea lasted for less than one second, a burst of blue-white light exploding past *Eagle* in a shuddering surge of cold flame. The light faded again to black and the more familiar scatterings of the stars of normal fourspace as they emerged, close enough to Alya A-VI now that the planet showed a perceptible disk, close enough that there was no longer any question of masking their arrival from the enemy's sensors. All eight Confederation warships emerged together, six hundred thousand kilometers out from the planet and still tightly clustered. With so short a jump, there was little difficulty keeping the squadron in close formation.

Dev rode the cascade of raw data surging through his mind and exulted. Targets that had been indistinguishable point sources of neutrinos a moment before could be resolved now in detail. Two of the ships in close planetary orbit were light destroyers, almost certainly Yari-class like the *Constellation*, and they were the heaviest ships the Imperials had on station. Most of the rest were transports and supply ships, guarded by two frigates and a pair of corvettes.

"Release probes!" Dev snapped over the squadron's tactical frequency, and from each of the warships tumbled sticks of jet black projectiles, the layer of programmed nano coating their hulls drinking light and rendering them nearly invisible.

One after another, then in twos and threes and fives, the remotes accelerated, the drive venturis tucked into the stern of each scout silently flaring as brightly as the surface of a sun. Balancing on slender cones of star-hot plasma, each scout saucer arrowed toward ShraRish, accelerating at 50 Gs until it was traveling at better than two hundred kilometers per second.

"Looks like we're in luck," Dev told Katya as they watched the constellation of drive flares dwindling into the distance. "For a change we actually outnumber and out-mass the bad guys, and that's with three of our ships still missing."

"For how long?" Katya wondered. "Their relief fleet can't be very far behind us, can it?"

They'd discussed that aspect of the problem at considerable length before leaving Herakles. No matter how weak or strong the enemy's strength in the Alyan system, it was a sure bet that the Imperials would be sending reinforcements, and soon. By acting immediately, as soon as they'd heard about the DalRiss attack on the Imperial base, Farstar had bought itself a small bit of time . . . but only as much as the Imperial Staff Command allowed them as it considered the problem at ShraRish. Imperial military reactions tended to be a long time in coming, slowed by their sheer size and ponderousness. CONMILCOM felt that this time the Imperials would move with particular deliberation, for they would be reluctant to get involved in a full-scale war with the enigmatic DalRiss, especially when the DalRiss motives for their original attack were still unclear.

Still, *some* response must already be en route from Sol, one powerful enough to meet any threat—including that presented by the Confederation force. CONMILCOM had ViRsimmed the possibilities endlessly and felt that the relief force would at the very least include four or more Amatukaze-class destroyers, like *Eagle*, and might very well include one of the big Ryu carriers, together with a suitable escort. Once a force that large and powerful dropped out of K-T space, the only course of action left open to the rebels would be headlong flight.

There was a moral dilemma inherent in the situation, one that had been nagging at Katya throughout the weeks since they'd left Herakles. If the DalRiss had attacked the Imperial forces on ShraRish, logically it could only be because they felt they were strong enough to throw the Imperials out and keep them out, no matter what they sent as reinforcements. The question was, however, whether the DalRiss had a realistic understanding of just how powerful the Imperial Navy actually was. They'd seen only those Imperial vessels that had come and gone in the Alyan system over the past three years, and no one knew how good their information on Hegemony and Imperial strengths might be, or how much of that information they might understand. Chances were, they understood humans about as well as humans understood them . . . which meant not very well at all.

Now the Confederation Expeditionary Force had arrived, hoping to establish a military alliance with the DalRiss, encouraging the Alyans to join in the fight against the Imperials.

And the moment a major Imperial flight entered fourspace near Alya, the rebels would be forced to flee or be destroyed.

The DalRiss, however, would have to stay and take whatever punishment the Empire decided to deliver against their worlds. The situation was damned near intolerable for Katya, who still chafed at Sinclair's decision to abandon New America to the enemy. When Farstar had first been proposed, when Sinclair had first suggested that she might serve as liaison to the DalRiss, in fact, she'd thought alliance with the DalRiss might well be the one hope the Confederation had for survival.

Now, though, she wasn't so sure. What good would alliance with the Alyans be if all it served to do was bring them under the Emperor's guns too? Their biologically based combat technology had lost the fight against the Xenophobe on GhegnuRish and had been losing the one on ShraRish; a relatively brief campaign by the Imperial Expeditionary Force in 2541 had destroyed the ShraRish Xeno in short order, and the IEF would have taken on the one occupying the DalRiss homeworld as well had Dev not managed to establish contact with it. Clearly, human military technology was far tougher—faster, meaner, and lugging heavier firepower—than the equivalent DalRiss biotech.

How long could the DalRiss possibly hope to survive a full-scale war with the Empire?

"Damn it, Dev," Katya said, her mental voice low. "The Confederation is going to carry the guilt of their destruction for a long time to come."

"Sorry?" She could hear his puzzlement and knew he'd misunderstood her. "Kat, this is war. *Civil* war, and those are the bloodiest of all."

"No, I mean the DalRiss. It'll be our fault if the Imperials come back in and raze their whole planet. They won't have a chance."

"Well, I might point out that we're here because *they* started shooting at the Imperials, so if they're in a war now, it's because they started it. That's part of what we're going to have to talk with them about, isn't it?" He sounded casual, almost uncaring. "The DalRiss strike me as bright folks. Whatever their reasons for hitting the Impies, they must've been good ones."

"*Kuso*, Dev. How can you be so cold about it?"

"Not cold at all. Just practical. Besides, we're talking about an entire planetary population. If they do help us, it'll be with . . . what? The secret of their magic space drive. Maybe some of their living warstriders if they really want an active part in this war, though I wouldn't recommend putting one of those things up against a KY-1001 Katana. The Empire'll take note, sure, and they might hit back, but they're not going to destroy the whole DalRiss planet, any more than they'd destroy New America just to take out the few thousand people there who happen to be New Constitutionalist rebels. Hell, Katya, they couldn't. They know Herakles is one hundred percent rebel, and the worst they might try would be saturation bombing from orbit with nukes. They can't destroy an entire planet."

"A saturation nuclear bombardment could render the place uninhabitable," Katya pointed out, "and that's the same thing. I damn sure wouldn't put it past them, some of them, at any rate."

"The *Kansei*," Dev said. "Yeah. Some of them would at least give the idea serious thought. If it meant a quick, cheap end to the rebellion, well . . ."

The *Kansei no Otoko*, the self-styled "Men of Completion," were a faction within the highest levels of the Imperial military and government. Confederation intelligence knew little about them, save that they were dedicated to cleansing the upper ranks of both the military and civilian Imperial governments of all *gaijin* influence. It was strongly suspected that the previous emperor, a man known for his desire to integrate Japanese and non-Japanese leadership at all levels throughout both the Hegemony and the Empire, had been assassinated by the Kansei faction. The new Tenrai Emperor—his *nengo*, or era-name, meant Heavenly Thunder—was a weakling propped up on his throne by Kansei officers.

"I don't know about you," Katya continued, "but I wouldn't put anything past Munimori."

She meant, of course, *Gensui* Yasuhiro Munimori, commander of the First Fleet and a senior admiral on the Imperial Military Staff. It was he who'd issued the notorious Edict of 2543, expelling all *gaijin* from senior line naval posts.

"Maybe not," Dev agreed, somewhat grudgingly. "Still, even Munimori's not crazy. Human-habitable planets are rare. That's why we invest so much in terraforming the prebiotics. Even he won't turn a world like Herakles into a radioactive desert just for the thrill of killing a few thousand rebels, right? And he wouldn't risk genocide because a few DalRiss decided to side with us. *If* they side with us. We still don't know that they will, or can."

"I wish," Katya said quietly, "that I could feel as sure of that as you are."

It was the nature of space combat that events either dragged across vast distances, or passed so swiftly that they were beyond the reach of purely human intervention. Even accelerating at 50 Gs, it would take the teleoperated drones over eighteen minutes to cross six hundred thousand kilometers.

Rather than wait impatiently in the primary tactical linkage, Dev chose instead to enter the computer-generated alternate reality being grown from the data transmitted back from the probes and correlated through *Eagle*'s AI. When he linked with the new sim, the display field was black emptiness occupied solely by the bare globe of ShraRish, so far an empty, translucent sphere.

"Commodore Cameron," the simulation's director said in greeting. Commander Paul Duryea was *Eagle*'s senior sensor imaging specialist. "It's too early to tell much as yet."

"That's okay, Commander," Dev replied. "I want to be here as it starts coming in."

"Help yourself, then. There won't be much to look at until we're considerably closer."

A close inspection of the blank globe revealed the faint outlines of known planetary landmarks. ShraRish had no oceans or separate continents; instead, its single, globe-spanning land mass was broken here and there by large, landlocked seas, enormous bodies of water first mapped by the Imperial Expeditionary Force three years before. Still, Dev was unwilling to rely too heavily on data about the world that had come through Imperial sources. More than once, he'd seen clear evidence of Imperial attempts to alter or suppress information about the Alyan systems.

The local atmosphere, for instance. There was no denying the fact that the ShraRish atmosphere was poisonous to humans, partly because the CO_2 level of about five hundredths of one percent was dangerously high, partly because the partial pressure of oxygen was far too low. There were also significant levels of sulfuric acid on the planet, both as a vapor in the air and as a liquid component of both rain and the seas.

Frequently in the last three years, however, information about the Alyan worlds disseminated by the Imperials had made their surface environments seem far worse than they were. The atmosphere favored by the DalRiss was described as being like that of Venus, albeit without the crushing pressures and molten metal temperatures; during one of Dev's first ViRsimulations of a DalRiss environment, in fact, the atmospheric CO_2 had been described to him as "over eighty-three percent," which was actually the percentage of *nitrogen* in the planet's air. As for the sulfuric acid, it was usually described as "dangerously corrosive." That was true enough perhaps for unprotected metal or fabricated building materials left to face the elements for weeks at a time, and *prolonged* exposure by unprotected human skin was certainly not advised . . . but the truth of the matter was that humans could survive on the surface of either Shra- or GhegnuRish wearing nothing more than ordinary clothing, goggles to protect their eyes from the acid in the air and the ultraviolet in the sunlight, and a breathing mask to concentrate the oxygen to breathable levels and filter out about half of the CO_2.

Dev knew; he'd *been* there, as had Katya and Brenda Ortiz and quite a few of the other scientists, troops, and shipjackers with Farstar. It was damned hot on the surface, uncomfortably so, but he'd needed to have one arm bare at least to accept a translator comel; and during his final confrontation with the Naga beneath the surface of GhegnuRish, he'd actually left the environmentally controlled safety of his warstrider in order to be able to touch the alien creature directly, wearing nothing more than a shipsuit and a mask.

He was pretty sure that the data was being deliberately manipulated by the Imperial and Hegemony authorities to make communication with the DalRiss seem even more difficult and dangerous than it actually was. That was one reason why he'd insisted on such a large complement of teleoperated scouts. He wanted to enter the Alyan system with the assumption that he knew nothing, taking nothing for granted, and build up a data base independent of anything that had reached the Confederation by way of Imperial data bases, simulations, or scientists.

He was beginning to suspect that the most devastating weapon either side could wield in war was not thermonuclear warheads or kilometer-long dragonships or new and more powerful warstriders. No, the key weapon in any war was *in-*

formation, and Dev intended to gather as much of the precious commodity as he could before the shifting tactical situation forced him into combat.

Time passed, and the RD-40 scouts closed the dwindling gap between themselves and the alien world, fanning out from a straight-line course to make their final approach from several directions. Halfway to the target they separated into two groups, one of which continued accelerating all the way while the other flipped end over end and began coasting, ready to decelerate at the same rate. After pushing 50 Gs for over eighteen minutes, the first group was hurtling in at nearly six hundred kilometers per second, flashing through and past the Imperial squadron so quickly that only weapons directed by high-speed machines could have any chance of hitting them.

Even at that speed, however, the probes' AI-directed sensors gathered enormous volumes of data in flickering instants of time, relaying it all back down the lasercom links to the Confederation ships. Soon, the Imperial vessels were known in enough detail to assign them names from *Eagle*'s warbook. The two Yari-class destroyers were the *Asagiri* and the *Naginata*; the frigates were *Hayate* and *Reppu*, both of the big, twenty-four-thousand–ton Arashi-class. The two smallest were twelve-hundred–ton Tidori-class corvettes, *Sagi* and *Hatukari*.

Rippling flashes marked missile launches from the Imperial warships. By absorbing all light and radar energies that struck their nano-camouflaged hulls, the probes were nearly invisible both optically and to radar and ladar detectors. Such invisibility was never purchased without a price, however. Energy absorbed had to be balanced by energy given off; the remote probes were fairly bright infrared targets, and the plasma trails from their drives were easily tracked when the craft were under full thrust.

The Imperial missiles were set for IR homing, and they had accelerations at least as high as those of the RD-40s, or better. And the problem was complicated now by time lag. At a range of six hundred thousand kilometers, the speed-of-light gap between the Confederation squadron and the scouts was four seconds; it took two seconds for imagery and sensory data gathered by one of the scouts to travel by comm laser back to the linked brain of the man piloting it, and two seconds more for his steering and thrust commands to return to the craft's tiny onboard AI ... by which time the high-velocity probe had moved almost twenty-four hundred kilometers.

Four seconds matters little when dealing with tens of thousands of kilometers of empty space; in close combat with enemy warships, however, four seconds becomes an eternity, a fatal eternity when fractions of a single second measure the difference between a successful maneuver and the impact of an IR-homing missile. As the RD-40s neared ShraRish, the Imperial forces in orbit began responding, sluggishly at first, then with a fast-growing firestorm of missiles and energy beams.

In rapid succession, the teleoperated probes began dying in flares of dazzling light, as IR-homing missiles slammed into their targets in direct, head-on impact, or detonated at a distance in shotgun sprays of pellets that shredded the scouts' thin hulls and transformed them into hurtling clouds of white-hot scrap.

The battle for Alyan space had begun. So far, the exchange was bloodless, the only casualties creatures of plastic, duralloy, and electronic circuits.

But with such energies involved, and so many people, it could not remain bloodless for long.

Chapter 14

"Necessity," runs the old proverb, "is the mother of invention." Nowhere is this more evident than in the history of modern warfare. From the very first use of the tank in warfare, developed as a means of breaching the barriers of barbed wire, trenches, and interlocking fields of machine-gun fire on the Western Front in the First World War, to the introduction of beam and missile weaponry on orbital constructors and tugs,

*humans have used remarkable ingenuity both to kill and
to survive.*

> —*Juggernaut: A Brief History of Armored Combat*
> *Chujo* Aiko Hayashiya
> C.E. 2525

Dev remained linked with the data simulation from the probes,
listening in as Commander Duryea coordinated the far-flung
network of teleoperated scout craft and operators. The voices
of the linked operators formed a soft background murmur to
the scene, punctuated by Duryea's terse and number-heavy
orders and demands for more data.

"Seven-two, Seven-five, Eight-one, this is Thunderhead,"
Duryea's voice said. "Divert to three-one-five at plus zero-
one-one. Give us a close-up on target Tango-one-niner."

"Roger that, Thunderhead. Seven-two breaking left and high.
I've got Tango-one-niner locked in and on approach."

"Nest, this is Eight-one. I copy. Locked in and on approach."

"Probe Seven-five, Seven-five, this is Thunderhead. Do you
copy?"

"Nest, Seven-five! I've got three India-Romeos vectoring
in! Don't know if I can dodge 'em!"

"Seven-five, Thunderhead, we copy. Maintain full Gs and
pitch right to zero-five-one at plus zero-seven-three."

"Nest, Seven-five! I can't get clear! They're on me! I
can't! . . ."

"Probe Seven-five destroyed," the sonorous and unhurried
voice of *Eagle*'s AI announced. Two light seconds away, one
of the probes had just been smashed from the sky, while
somewhere aboard one of the Confederation ships, a probe
jacker, severed from his mount, was blinking awake inside
a ViRcom module. Dev checked the tally list and saw that
twenty-eight of the remote probes had already been lost.

But the Battle Ops rundown on the Imperial fleet was complete. In another fifteen minutes, the second group of probes,
decelerating now to velocities of only a few kilometers per
second, would reach ShraRish and begin mapping that world
in exacting detail. The rest had either sailed past ShraRish
and the Imperial squadron and were already out of the battle,
or they were attempting to change their combat roles, from
surveillance drones to antiship missiles.

*   *   *

The chances of one of the remote drones scoring a hit were slender. At the RD-40s' incredible closing velocities, their pilots could do little more than point their steeds in the general direction of an enemy target and hope for the best. They had little in the way of lateral maneuverability, and the four-second reaction time between the moment a probe's scanners detected something in its path and the instant its pilot's commands reached it made fine course adjustments or complex maneuvers useless. After boosting across over half a million kilometers at 50 Gs they were low on reaction mass as well, which meant that when their containment fields collapsed, the resultant plasma detonation delivered little more than the kick of a fair-sized warhead of conventional high explosives.

Despite all of that, Probe Three-three managed to close with the *Asagiri*, coming in on the light destroyer nearly broadside-on. Listening to the symphony of mathematics and intercept plots singing in his brain, the jacker waited until the probe was some twelve hundred kilometers from the target before triggering the craft's drive; two seconds later and six hundred thousand kilometers away, Probe Three-three flashed into plasma as hot as the core of a small sun.

The strike was, as it turned out, a near miss, the explosion flaring briefly against the blackness of space twelve kilometers short of the destroyer's hull. Considering the distances and speeds involved, that was pinpoint accuracy indeed. The expanding plasma cloud and a clutter of molten debris slammed into *Asagiri*'s ventral side starboard a fraction of a second later.

Any kind of debris moving at a relative velocity of better than six hundred kilometers per second is a terrifying weapon in space. Fortunately for *Asagiri*, the debris cloud was expanding; much of it missed entirely, most of the surviving bits were wiped from existence by the flash of automated point defense lasers, and only a few grams of solid material actually struck home. Still, the kinetic energy of those flecks of debris was great enough that the destroyer's hull was breached. Atmosphere spilled into space, along with some furniture and several charred bodies from her crew's mess, but the leak was swiftly sealed off by automatics, and, in any case, the shipjackers aboard were securely enclosed within their pressurized link modules, safe from all but a direct hit on *Asagiri*'s heavily armored core stations. The damage was not severe enough to cripple her. A power conduit was broken, a control circuit melted, but redundant backup systems kicked in and, for the moment at least, no serious damage registered within the damage control subroutine of *Asagiri*'s onboard AI.

Lagging behind the faster ships of the Confederation squadron, the converted hydrogen tanker *Tarazed* could only manage 2 Gs, and so she maintained station with the equally slow transport *Vindemiatrix*, well astern of *Eagle* and the more powerful, more maneuverable warships.

Tarazed was constructed as five huge spheres strung together like pearls in a necklace between a tiny command module and the boxlike complexity of her fusion drive. The lead sphere had been remodeled to carry cargo and passengers; specifically, it housed the hangar decks and maintenance bays of the 1st Confederation Air/Space Wing, recently nicknamed the Bluestars.

Though acceleration dragged at him, making his lean, seventy kilos' mass feel like a leaden one-sixty, Sublieutenant Nevin Vandis—Van to his friends—took a final walk-around, giving his warflyer a final exterior inspection. He wasn't entirely sure what he would do if he found something that would warrant a downgrudge on the ugly little ship; he *was* sure he wouldn't report it. A story popular with members of his squadron was that of Lieutenant Ben Skarbeck, an ascraft fighter pilot who, during the defense of New America, had found his number one cryo-H tank holed by a bit of shrapnel just as the alert sounded for another incoming wave of Imperial fighters. According to the story, which had already assumed mythic proportions, Skarbeck had plugged the hole with the wad of chewing gum that always seemed to be working its way around between his cheek and his gums, fueled up his ship, and launched in time to down two Imperial Ko-125 *Akuma* attack craft and one Se-280 interceptor.

Van chewed gum as well—it seemed to be part of the persona of front line fighterjacks when they weren't linked to their steeds—but he wasn't convinced that the Skarbeck story was true and didn't really want to test the idea in combat. Most substances became uncompromisingly brittle when subjected to the temperatures and pressures required to store cryogenic slush hydrogen, and he frankly doubted that a mix of chewing gum and saliva had the chemical or physical properties of, say, the nanolayered polyduraplas sheathing the inside of his flyer's cryo-H tanks.

Vandis was typical of the fleet's small contingent of fighter pilots, which meant he knew he was the best of the best, the top of the link-jacked military hierarchy that ran from space fighterjacks like himself down to the mud-slogging leggers at the bottom. He'd started out five years earlier as a warstrider with the Newamie militia; his skill with finely detailed linking had qualified him as an ascraft fighter pilot, and he'd flown both I-20 Shorishahs and I-32 Sensokanazuchis for New America's Hegemony government until the rebellion had forced him to choose between the rule of distant Earth or the more immediate and representative government of rebel New America. In point of fact, he cared little about politics one way or the other, though he was well aware that the war had already had one profound impact on his life. More than anything else he loved to fly, and since he'd been assigned to the Bluestars' 3rd Squadron, he'd done very little else. Even during the long periods when *Tarazed* was isolated in K-T space, Van and his yujos in the squadron flew endlessly in simulations, jacked into their fighters and living the fantasies fed to their brains by the ship's combat AI.

"Hey, Lieutenant!" a voice called from behind. "You really gonna wire that piece of hardware to your brain?"

Van turned, grinning. "You know a better way to get a fast jackin'jolt, Chief?" Van replied, grinning. "Anyway, she would never do anything to hurt me."

Julio Cordova was Van's crew chief, a short, stocky man with a heavy mustache and ebony skin who thought of the ugly little fighter as his personal property, something to be loaned out to Van with some concern about whether or not it would be returned in one piece.

"Wasn't worried about *you*." He reached up and laid a proprietary hand on the vehicle's starboard weapons sponson. "I'm more concerned about what your impure thoughts'll do to her once you launch."

"Ah, you never see the parties I take her to soon as we clear the chute." He shook his head in mock dismay. "Dancing naked on the bar . . . it's shocking, Chief. You wouldn't recognize her. How was the diagnostic?"

"Well, we had her guts out all day yesterday, Lieutenant, tryin' to find a short in her nav system interlock."

"You find it?"

"Nope, but the diagnostics stopped showing a downgrudge when we swapped out the EL-30 module. Could've been a programming glitch. Then again, maybe we bumped a loose wire back into place when we slammed the access shut."

"Yeah, well, if I lose track of *Tarazed* while I'm out there, Chief," Van said slowly, "I'll be sure to let you know the thing's not fixed."

"Just so you bring her back, Lieu. Otherwise, she comes out of your pay. *And* your bar tab."

"Confederation credit?"

"*Gok*, Lieu! That scuttin' *kuso*'s not worth a nullhead's download. Make it Hegemony yen."

"Christ, Chief, just whose side are you on, anyway?" Van continued his walk-around beneath the hanging bulk of the ship, scanning the cryo-H tanks carefully for any ice, for any telltale wisp of vapor that might indicate a containment breach. The craft's belly checked, he grabbed hold of a levitator strap, slipped his left boot into the stirrup, and rode up the support gantry. Careful where he placed hands and feet—a two-point-five-meter drop under two Gs killed you as dead as a five-meter fall under one—he stepped off onto the catwalk that gave access to the vehicle's dorsal side.

At least it looked as though he wasn't going to have to put the chewing gum idea to the test. His warflyer, an aging DR-80, was battered and chipped and scoured, with mismatched patches showing a long history of past field-expedient repairs, but its pressure hull was tight, its circuits checked out operational—with the possible exception of that glitchy nav interlock—and the RM tanks were holding pressure. *Van'sGuard* was ready for launch.

Warflyers were themselves the product of field expediency. Though they'd been designed originally as tugs and high-mass manipulators for construction jobs in orbit, local planetary militias had found them useful as space-maneuverable weapons platforms . . . a fancy term for *cheap* space fighters. The young Rebellion, with access to few modern air/space fighter craft, had seized on warflyers as a means of addressing the Imperium's superiority in both technology and numbers. They were slow, they could neither operate within a planetary atmosphere nor achieve escape velocity, and many were so old that their pilots proudly claimed that stranger things than chewing gum maintained pressure and hull integrity.

Van'sGuard was a prime example of the type. She was a Mitsubishi DR-80, originally an orbital constructor modified for a military role under the name *Tenrai*, the "Heavenly Thunder." With the new Emperor taking *Tenrai* as his Nengo era-name, however, Confederation pilots had taken to calling the DR-80 other things, few of them complimentary.

"Warhawk" was perhaps the most consistent name out of many, though, one without obscene or scatological implications and bearing a long tradition in the history of military aviation. A propeller-driven fighter called the Warhawk had fought with distinction in the Second World War; a nuclear-powered transatmospheric craft had been dubbed Warhawk during the Third American Civil War.

This Warhawk was an inelegant contraption, a squat cylinder three meters long stacked atop a pair of cryo-H storage tanks and a massive fusorpack and thruster. Bulky, round-ended sponsons mounted port and starboard housed weapons systems, maneuvering jets, and manipulators. The ungainly craft was, in fact, little more than a conventional warstrider with the leg assembly replaced by a thruster and six tons of reaction mass. Nose art graced the craft's stubby and debris-scarred prow, a naked woman flying above the script-written name *Van'sGuard*, her back arched and her head back, her arms outstretched like wings and her prominent breasts thrust forward in blatant mimicry of the Warhawk's paired weapons sponsons.

The warflyer, massing eighteen tons fully fueled and loaded, was suspended from an overhead rack in Bay Seven of Hangar Deck One aboard the Confederation carrier *Tarazed*. The former hydrogen tanker had been converted years before into a carrier; her complement of eighty-two warflyers—six squadrons of twelve plus ten in reserve—was roughly equivalent to an Imperial air-space wing aboard one of the big dragon-carriers. Most were converted constructors like the DR-80. A few were genuine ascraft fighters, sleek darts that were all wing surface and streamlining, but even the best of those were obsolete compared to the Imperium's faster and more maneuverable Se-280s. Van had been flying the Warhawk exclusively now for over a year, and with good-natured scorn grudgingly preferred it to anything else in the rebels' flight-capable inventory.

The hangar deck was a clashing, clattering, deafening place, a steel-walled cavern in which several hundred men were hard at work on dozens of warflyers of different types. Battle stations had sounded before *Tarazed* had come out of K-T space the first time, but the activity in the fighter bays, though chaotically loud, was smooth and purposeful. A tractor growled past below the catwalk, towing a DY-64 on a wheeled cart. Julio called something to him just then, but the words were lost in the shrilling of the tractor's horn.

He leaned against the catwalk's railing, taking some of the weight off his aching feet. "What'd you say?" he shouted back.

"I said, have you heard the who-was about Deadly Dev?"

"I make it a point never to listen to gossip about my superior officers. What'd you hear?"

"Word is he's already made contact with the Alyans through that mess of RD-40s." He pronounced the name "aliens," as did most of the Confederation's Inglic-speaking rank and file. "The whole gokin' Alyan fleet's comin' out to take the Impies in the rear."

"I'll believe that one when I've got 'em pegged and IDed in my primary scan," Van called back. Who-was and rumor defined military shipboard life as much as overcrowded quarters and monotonous food. There were always a dozen prime bits of who-was floating around, and both the number and what Van liked to call the disbelief factor tended to shoot up astronomically just before an action.

Julio rode a levitator strap up to the catwalk. "Maybe you're right, Lieu," he said cheerfully. "Just the same, be damned sure of what you're shootin' at out there. I'd hate you to take out one of our new allies by mistake!"

A touch of his palm to an interface panel opened the Warhawk's command slot, a padded, coffin-shaped recess buried within the warflyer's main hull. With Julio's help, Van lowered himself in, careful not to let himself drop and injure a tailbone or an elbow. He was already wearing a shipsuit, a gray, skintight garment that covered everything but his hands and his head. Gloves and helmet were waiting for him inside the command slot. The gloves sealed over his cuffs, and the left one possessed circuitry that matched the cross hatching of gold and silver threads embedded at the base of his thumb, allowing him to touch an AI interface panel even with his shipsuit sealed.

The helmet possessed three internal jacks on short leads. Again with Julio's help, he snicked the jacks into his cervical and temporal sockets, then carefully seated the helmet on his suit's self-sealing collar. Life-support feeds snapped home in connectors on his right chest and side. Data feedback from the suit's intelligent circuitry projected a status report against the upper left corner of his vision. Air . . . pressure . . . gas mix . . . physiology . . . all within normal parameters.

Carefully, Van lay down in the slot, stretched out full length on the padding. He could hear Julio's harsh breathing as the crew chief leaned over him, jacking the datafeed cables inside the slot home in the receptacles in Van's helmet.

"Luck, sir!" Julio shouted, raising his voice unnecessarily. Despite the racket in the hangar bay, the pickups in Van's suit were working fine, but even people familiar with the technology tended to assume that someone swaddled head to toe in a sealed shipsuit was cut off from the rest of the world. "You bring my baby home, y'hear?"

Van touched his right forefinger to his visor in ironic salute, as Julio gave him a cocky thumbs-up, then thumbed the control that closed the Warhawk's pilot slot. There was nothing so fancy—or as expensively complex—as a nanotechnic dissolving accessway. The hatch slid shut with a squeak and a bang, sealing Van in a stifling, close-in darkness.

He brought his left palm down against the interface panel positioned close by his hip. There was a flash of static . . .

. . . and suddenly, again, Van remembered just how cut off from the rest of the world he *had* been. Walking around in your skin you tended to forget how sharp your senses could be, how clear your vision, how complete the array of data available through a full-socket feed in your cephlink. From his point of view, Van now was the DR-80, hanging from its cradle above *Tarazed*'s hangar deck. He could see now in a three-sixty arc all the way around and top and bottom as well, though he tended to focus in one direction at a time, just as if he were still seeing with human eyes. His view in one direction—directly aft—was blocked by the slush hydrogen tanks and fusion thruster, but he could see the other warflyers of his squadron—Third Squadron, the Gold Eagles—resting in their cradles around him, could see the vehicles and individual maintenance personnel and pilots by their ships, could see Julio riding a strap back down toward the deck.

"Gold Eagle Lead, this is Three-five," he announced over the tactical circuit. "Logging on."

"Copy, Three-five," a woman's voice replied. Lieutenant Commander Jena Cole was the Gold Eagle squadron CO. "Welcome aboard. Ready for tacfeed?"

"Hit me."

Data sluiced through the cephlinkage as a new window snapped open, covering half of Van's view of the hangar bay. Readouts showed the readiness of each of the ascraft and warflyers of the wing, four squadrons readying for launch, with the other two as backup on a five-minute hold. A 3-D, over all tactical view showed *Tarazed* and the transport *Vindemiatrix* running side by side, with *Eagle* and the smaller ships of the squadron spreading out in a broad, arrowhead shape ahead. The Imperial squadron, each ship neatly tagged with an identifying code and block of data, was coming to meet them, accelerating out from ShraRish at 3 Gs.

"Looks like the welcoming committee's on its way to meet us," Van said. He looked, but he saw nothing that might have been Alyan starships maneuvering behind the enemy ships.

"You've got that right, Three-five," Cole replied. "Current plan calls for a four-squadron release in . . . one hundred thirty-two minutes. In the meantime—"

"We're gonna run sims," he interrupted.

"How'd you guess?" That was Sublieutenant Gerard Marlo, Three-seven.

"Hey, if we have time to kill, let's do some *flying*."

"Yeah, we're hot," Sublieutenant Lynn Kosta, Van's wingman, chimed in. "Let's burn some mass!!"

"Here comes the feed," Cole told them. "We'll start with polishing our close-assault SCM."

And he was in space, bearing down on an Imperial light destroyer.

Chapter 15

Though the term "military intelligence" has been considered an oxymoron ever since it was first coined, the fact remains that the gathering of intelligence— about terrain, climate, enemy strengths and dispositions, and anything else of either strategic or tactical value— remains the most important facet of military planning. Without solid intelligence, the best general's keenest evaluations remain guesswork, his shrewdest guesses little more than wishful thinking.

—*Juggernaut: A Brief History of Armored Combat*
Chujo Aiko Hayashiya
C.E. 2525

Still linked with Commander Duryea and the probes' data simulation, Dev watched as the globe of ShraRish expanded in his vision, as complete and as gloriously complex in the details of cloud patterns and mountains and rugged, island-edged coastline as it would have been had *Eagle* already entered low orbit. The tracks of a number of probes showed as green lines curving in toward the cloud-wreathed sphere. Special targets were known DalRiss cities, as well as any clusters of buildings, nuclear power plants, grounded ascraft, or other anomalous structures that would indicate the presence of humans on the planet's surface.

The lead group of probes, the ones that had slammed through the Imperial fleet, were all destroyed now, or else they'd long since passed the Imperial squadron and were headed now into deep space, out of fuel and beyond the range of their jacker links. The second group, however, had been decelerating for some time now, until their speed was measured in only kilometers per second . . . instead of *hundreds* of kilometers per second.

As the second wave of RD-40s neared ShraRish, the almost featureless globe in the data simulation began to take on more and more detail—a rugged band of upthrusting mountains stretching along the equator between two golden seas, a vast expanse of red-ocher desert near the south pole, gleaming pinpoints that might be DalRiss cities, the precise positions—and, moments later, as their movements were assessed, the precise orbits—of all of the Imperial ships. The remote probes were programmed to assimilate a wide range of data, including scans of every available electromagnetic wavelength, of neutrino flux, and of mass and gravitational anomalies such as those linked to QPT plants. RF leakage from communications systems and computers gave hints regarding the Imperial commander's tactical frequencies, his weapons status as lasers powered up and missile batteries were readied for firing, and his ships' engineering status as fusion power plants were brought to full output. Both of the Yari-class destroyers were tracked as they broke orbit, and the telltale gravitational ripples emanating from them indicated that they were bringing their power taps on line.

Faster and faster, the probe data rippled through the simulation's framework, expanding, adding detail, revealing new targets of opportunity. The globe representing ShraRish grew from empty translucence to a globe as clear and as detailed and as beautiful as any visual image of the real thing seen from orbit, complete with swirling clouds and the eye-aching glare of sunglint off the surface of a gold-brown sea.

"We're starting to get some good feeds from inside the atmosphere, Commodore," Duryea told Dev.

"How many do you have targeted on the main Imperial base?"

"We had three, but only one's made it through. Five-nine."

"We're going to need that download, top priority."

"Yes, sir. Ah! Looks like the Dojinko feed's coming through now. Pull down a window and enjoy the show."

Dojinko . . . the DalRiss city where the primary Imperial surface base had been attacked. The scurrilous name grated at him, but he uplinked the appropriate codes, then watched as a secondary ViRsim display opened inside his mind, overlaying his view of ShraRish. This new scene was a feed from Probe Five-nine, now at an altitude of less than fifty kilometers and angling steeply down toward Dojinko.

The image was trembling violently despite the system's valiant attempts to hold it steady. Warning discretes flashed and scrolled at the edges of Dev's vision. Despite the deceleration, the probe still had tremendous velocity, was still traveling so fast that the outer layers of its duralloy hull were vaporizing, creating an ionization trail that made holding even a lasercom lock with the craft difficult.

Too, the high speed of approach guaranteed that its initial transmissions would mean little to human viewers. To Dev, the probe's motion rendered the view little more than a confused and vibrating blur of color, the white of clouds, the gold and russet and ocher of what might have been vegetation or simply desert sand . . . and then the picture tilted wildly and vanished in a burst of static.

"Probe Five-nine destroyed," *Eagle*'s AI reported. "Probe Seven-eight destroyed. Probe One-two destroyed. . . ." The list was growing longer, the reports of destruction coming in now faster and faster. According to the tally board, fewer than two dozen of the RD-40s were still transmitting.

"That went by too fast for me to make anything of it," Dev admitted. "Can I have a playback?"

"Absolutely. Set time factor at fifty to one."

This time, Dev could see the clouds and the wrinkled expanse of golden ground clearly, surrounded by the glowing haze of the probe's reentry trail. As the probe plummeted toward the ground, he became aware of terrain features spread out below him like a map, while the horizon curved gently away beneath a gold-and-violet haze. The AI added graphics to orient him. *There* was the Imperial base, a tiny, quadrangular gray scar against the golds and browns of the surrounding landscape. A pair of brackets winking just to one side of the quadrangle marked where the DalRiss city ought to be.

"Enhance," Dev said, staring hard at the brackets to tell the AI what he was interested in seeing. "Max resolution." The quadrangle seemed to rush toward him, expanding to fill half the display, edges blurred by distance and atmosphere suddenly sharpening into computer-drawn crispness of line and detail.

The terrain within the brackets was pockmarked and broken, but otherwise empty. Abruptly, the scene rolled away to port, was replaced by a brief flash of sky, and then the display filled with static. According to the transmission data, Five-nine had not been hit by enemy fire but had simply broken up in the atmosphere during the final, fiery instant of reentry.

"Odd," Dev said. The DalRiss city wasn't there anymore. He ordered a repeat of the imaging sequence, shifting his attention this time to the Imperial base.

The facility looked fairly typical and had probably been grown on the site from standard nanofabrication programs. The pavement had most likely been laid down with Rogan molds, while the gun turrets perched on their ten-meter towers looked like ordinary ship weapons installed in standardized hardpoint mounts. Two big transport ascraft were parked on the black surface of the landing field that roofed over the large, central structure. A perimeter fence—a high-voltage, high-amp barrier fence to judge from the design of the support struts—surrounded the entire facility.

No . . . that wasn't quite accurate. The fence encircled the base perhaps halfway, but as Dev froze the display in place and again enhanced the resolution, he could see that the entire eastern and southern sides of that barrier had been knocked down. Checking the data readouts, he noted that the probe had detected no power flow through the barrier; the thing was dead. Mixed in with the wreckage were a number of bulky, gray-white, and wrinkled objects that he couldn't resolve well enough to identify. DalRiss buildings? Plant life of some kind? Vehicles?

Interesting. Some of those objects had obviously broken through into the perimeter, and they'd brought some of the gold-brown-ocher ground cover with them. The vegetation had spilled through the wreckage and taken root on the pavement inside, giving the facility the look of age-old ruins abandoned by its builders long before. Some of those buildings, he saw now, showed extensive damage. A lasercom mast leaned at a drunken angle, and a gun tower had been snapped off near its base and now lay full length on the pavement where it had fallen, the quad barrels of its 80mm lasers pointed uselessly at the sky. Nearby, an outlying dome had been torn open and its contents scattered. Dev couldn't get resolution enough out of the system to make out what those contents might be, but they looked like crumpled paper or rags. Bodies? He couldn't tell. Probably not . . . unless fighting had been going on recently. He had to remind himself that the original reports of fighting on this world were now eight months old.

Eight months, and the Imperials had not rebuilt the fence or repaired the damage to the outlying buildings. Dev searched the image for signs of recent repairs or building but found nothing obvious.

He did see four warstriders, two Katanas and two smaller Tachis standing in what might be guard positions close by the central structure's surface access lock. He saw no other sign of life, no workers in E-suits repairing exterior damage, no legger infantry on patrol, nothing but gray buildings, gray pavement, and the four jet black combat machines standing guard.

Dev emerged from the secondary imaging window. "I'll want everything you have on that base," he told Duryea. "I'm probably not picking up on more than a fraction of what there is to see here, and I'll need time to study it in detail. Have you picked up any other Imperial facilities on the planet?"

"No, sir," Duryea replied. "Not operational, anyway. There are some structures about five thousand kilometers to the northwest that were erected three years ago by the Imperial Expeditionary Force, but they definitely look abandoned."

"And the base they call Dojinko? It looks pretty badly used."

"It's still operational, though. No power to the perimeter fence, but we've got power usage inside the main building and the weapons are charged and ready. IR plumes from their heat vents show their air conditioning is running full blast, and their nuclear reactor is at about fifty percent of max output. Two of their lasercomm towers at least are operational, and there was a fair amount of radio traffic. No, sir, I'd say that, whatever happened down there, Dojinko is still very much alive and operational."

Dev was going to need to go over the scene with Katya. If there were intact Imperial units on the ground, her people would have to go down and root them out. He wished, though, that Probe Five-nine had revealed more of the current status between the Imperials and the DalRiss. Except for those enigmatic gray lumps scattered about the base perimeter, which might or might not be DalRiss vehicles or structures of some kind, there was no sign of the aliens. Hell, their entire city was simply missing. He knew individual DalRiss buildings could move . . . but a whole city? Or had the Imperials destroyed the city, or tried to, and thereby instigated the attack?

"Commodore?" a woman's voice through the link interrupted his thoughts. "This is Canady."

"I'm here, Commander. Go ahead."

"The Impie fleet is definitely deploying to meet us. Looks like they want a fight. If we hold to four Gs' acceleration, our projected intercept will bring us within maximum missile range in another forty minutes. Thought you'd want to know."

"Thank you, Commander. I'll shift over to Battle Ops in a minute."

"Yes, sir."

"Have your people start analyzing the data in ViRsim," he told Duryea. "If you find anything more of tactical significance, patch through to me in Ops and download it, fast."

"Absolutely, sir." He sensed the man's grin. "That includes any DalRiss stuff we find?"

"Especially any DalRiss stuff," Dev replied. That, he realized, was partly what was nagging at him. The DalRiss had enormous cities, vast living structures of unknown purpose . . . hell, they had *starships*, weirdly shaped hulks a kilometer or more long. Where were they?

So far, there was nothing to indicate that there were any DalRiss left on the planet at all.

The Imperial squadron was clearly in serious trouble from the start, if only because the Confederation's *Eagle* was half again larger and carried more than twice the mass of either *Asagiri* or *Naginata*. *Eagle*'s laser and particle accelerator batteries were more powerful and had greater range, and the big Confederation destroyer's fire control systems allowed her to remote link with many more teleoperated missiles at a time. Since space combat was basically a matter of overwhelming the enemy's defenses with sheer, raw firepower, the Confederation force possessed an enormous initial advantage.

On the other hand, advantage in space combat could be fleeting. *Eagle* was certain to be identified as the most dangerous of the Confederation warships approaching ShraRish, and she would be targeted accordingly. The Imperials could afford to ignore the frigates, corvettes, and converted freighters for a time in an all-or-nothing attempt to knock *Eagle* out of the fight. *Constellation* would be targeted next, but if the *Asagiri* and the *Naginata* could destroy or cripple *Eagle* without suffering critical damage themselves, they would have the Confederation light destroyer at a two-to-one advantage in mass and firepower; the rest of the rebel fleet could be mopped up more or less at the Japanese squadron commander's leisure.

He was *Shosho* Kenji Hattori, a thirty-eight–year Imperial Navy veteran in command of His Majesty's Alyan Contingent. He was *kokkyojin*, a "Frontier-person," meaning he was Japanese, but born and raised off Earth. Originally from the *Nihonjin* colony world of Ebisu, he tended to be direct and less than subtle, with a bluntness that frequently bordered on rudeness. His Frontier manners had won him few friends within the Imperial nobility, and he was proud that he'd earned his present rank—the equivalent of rear admiral—through merit and sheer bullheaded tenacity. His family had been ocean nomads; Ebisu, named for the ancient Japanese god of fisherfolk, was largely ocean, with scatterings of islands and island continents and the floating city-ships of its colonists. When, at age twenty, Hattori had been sent to Japan to complete his education, it was only natural that the seafaring tradition in his blood find outlet with the Imperial Navy, navigating the seas of space and the K-T Plenum instead of the immense, hurricane-scoured oceans of Ebisu.

From his vantage point within the Battle Ops simulation aboard the light destroyer *Naginata*, Hattori had watched the rebels' approach with interest. Some of those ships matched the description of vessels reported to have attacked the Imperial shipyards at Daikoku; if they were the same, that one that looked like a tanker would actually be a carrier, with several squadrons of warflyers loaded aboard. The armed transport would be carrying the rebel ground troops.

The transport. Kill it, and the whole point of the rebel attack would collapse.

The rebels could have no reason for being here other than a landing. Presumably, they'd somehow learned of the trouble at ShraRish and had come hoping to exploit it. Hattori smiled to himself at the thought. Knowing what the enemy wanted in a battle was more than half of his defeat. It gave the planning of this battle a Zen-like simplicity and economy of purpose. That big Amatukaze-class destroyer—he thought it must be the *Tokitukaze*, the ship captured by the rebels at the Battle of Eridu. She was the key to the rebel formation. The light destroyer, corvettes, and frigates were no match for the Imperial squadron without the Amatukaze destroyer backing them up; the space wing aboard that converted carrier would be warflyers for the most part, and no match for the advanced interceptors carried by *Naginata* and *Asagiri*.

So, destroy the large rebel destroyer while using fighters to fend off harrying attacks by enemy warflyers, and then go for the transport.

That was Hattori's preferred approach in all things . . . simple, blunt, and brutally direct.

"All ships!" he commanded, speaking over the Japanese squadron's primary tactical channel. "This is Hattori. Take formation One! Target on the big Amatukaze. *Susume!*"

The two battlefleets closed rapidly.

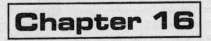

Chapter 16

Modern space combat can be broken into three major phases, the approach, the long-range battle, and the close-range battle.

The approach: the two respective forces are too dis-

tant to affect one another save by extremely long-ranged teleoperated missiles. The time is spent arranging the formation for maximum effect, to circumvent expected enemy strategies through tactical deployment, cloudscreens, and last-minute maneuver.

The long-range battle: at ranges of between one hundred thousand and one thousand kilometers, high-G missiles are the only effective weapon, though these can be countered by the point defense lasers (PDL) of target ships. The emphasis here is to overwhelm the targets' defenses with saturation bombardment. . . .

> —*Strategy and Tactics of Space Warfare*
> Imperial Naval War College
> Kyoto, Nihon
> C.E. 2530

Dev knew that the Imperial commander would have to take out *Eagle* before attempting anything else. She was too big to ignore, too powerful to pin or block with anything less than his entire squadron. Once *Eagle* was crippled, he would almost certainly attack *Vindemiatrix*. Since *Mirach* hadn't yet arrived in-system, the *Trixie* would be the only ship capable of carrying large numbers of troops. Her destruction wouldn't necessarily protect Imperial troops on the surface of ShraRish—a prolonged and pinpoint bombardment from orbit would wipe them out sooner or later without ever needing to land troops—but if the rebels wanted anything in this system more than simply annihilating the Imperial forces, they would need troops.

He'd strongly considered leaving the *Trixie* at the outer fringes of the system with the unarmed freighters. His decision to bring her along had been almost instinctive, born partly of the knowledge that he would need every ship-mounted weapon available in this fight, but more of the knowledge that her presence would give a shape and a form to the coming battle that it wouldn't otherwise have had. Including her in his line of battle was equivalent to a warstrider commander choosing the ground for a battle; it gave him the considerable advantage of knowing where the enemy *had* to attack and how he would have to maneuver to get there. For the opening few moves of the contest, Dev would know what his opponent was thinking.

With the familiar gallop of combat linkage drumming through his awareness, Dev felt nothing for the men and women waiting out the battle, helpless within the *Trixie*'s thin-skinned hull.

The tactics needed to crush the Imperial force spread themselves out in his mind with crystalline clarity. To counter the expected Japanese strategy, the Confederation squadron would go in head-on in a spear-shaped formation. The first shock would be taken by the point, a three-sided pyramid, with *Constellation* at the apex and *Valiant, Audacious,* and *Rebel* at the three corners of the base. A thousand kilometers behind them would be four of *Tarazed*'s six warflyer squadrons, followed by *Tarazed* herself. *Eagle* would be the spear's shaft, hanging well back, using her longer-ranged weapons to strike the enemy at a distance, while *Vindemiatrix* took up station even farther astern, but positioned so that she could move up and tuck herself in close to *Eagle* for protection if any Imperial leakers broke through.

And they *would* break through. The key to this type of space naval battle, with the opposing forces on opposing courses and closing head-on was to do as much damage when the two forces interpenetrated as possible.

With six ships in his command, the Imperial CO had chosen an octahedral formation, placing his two destroyers in line ahead, positioning the four smaller ships at the remaining four corners halfway between them. It was, Dev had to admit as he studied the approaching formation through the tactical sim, a good choice, probably the best possible given the Imperials' disadvantage in numbers. It concentrated his strongest units along the axis of the Confederation squadron and ensured that the smaller ships were well placed for maximum mutual support.

And after that there was nothing to do but wait.

It was a fact of modern combat that the troops—whether fighter pilots like Vandis, or striderjacks, or even legger infantry in combat armor—had at their command far more information about what was actually going on around them than had their predecessors throughout history. Direct data feeds and downloads gave them up-to-the-second information on the positions of friendly and hostile forces, gave them superbly detailed views of the fighting, allowed officers to see what their troops were seeing, permitted frontline troops to request artillery or air support and have it delivered with an accuracy that would have seemed magical to soldiers of even just a few centuries before.

The problem—one that had plagued all of humankind since the beginnings of the Information Age five centuries before— was that often there was simply too much available information. A general in command of an army, or an admiral commanding a fleet, was expected to see the big picture without becoming entangled in the fussy detail of managing the battle at the level of individual squads, platoons, or ships. A single striderjack, on the other hand, or the pilot jacked into a warflyer or the legger crouched in a trench, didn't need to know how his decisions and actions fit into an entire, sprawling battle involving tens or hundreds of thousands of other people; indeed, it was usually desirable that he not be aware of more than his immediate responsibilities. More than once in the past, democratically run armies had faced disaster when the soldiers decided to vote on whether or not a suicide attack or a last-ditch defense or even participation in a war was really necessary.

How much to tell the troops about a given tactical or strategic situation was one of the great ethical dilemmas of modern warfare. The technology was such that individuals like Sublieutenant Vandis could watch the entire battle unfold within their cephlinked reality. In general, and within the limits imposed by the need for security, the Confederation military was more liberal with the information it allowed its troops to have than was the Imperium, which preferred to ration battle management information to its troops with rigid and miserly precision. Often, this had worked to the Confederation's advantage—as when Dev Cameron had for purposes of propaganda and disinformation bluffed a Japanese escort captain into believing that he was a UV Cetan.

For the moment, at least, Sublieutenant Vandis had access to very nearly as much information as had Commodore Cameron. He lay within the padded coffin of his Warhawk's slot, watching the battle unfold with the superbly sharp and crisp detail of a full cephlinked download in his mind. Acceleration had ceased some time ago and *Tarazed* was in free-fall, but Van felt the weightlessness no more than he'd noticed the 2 Gs after jacking in.

Van'sGuard had been lowered into a launch tube and locked in, chambered like an eighteen-ton shell in the breech of some gigantic cannon. Though he could have maintained the feed from the probe data simulation, he'd chosen to switch that channel off in order to concentrate on more immediate problems. He was surrounded by pitch-blackness now, but he wasn't aware of the monotony of the view. He concentrated instead on the squadron's prelaunch checklist, which flickered through his mind as Commander Cole ran through the entries, a litany of ship systems answered by "go" or "no go."

"Power systems," Commander Cole's voice announced.

"Go," Van replied, his attention focused on the constellation of tiny green lights aglow in his mind next to scrolling blocks of data.

"Port attitude thrusters."

"Go."

"Starboard thrusters."

"Go."

"Dorsal thrusters."

"Go."

"Ventral thrusters."

"Go."

"Thruster interlock and system program."

"Go. And go."

"Navigational systems."

He checked that readout with particular care, searching for signs of the short that had been plaguing the maintenance crew, switching it on and off several times through his link. "Zeroed," he said at last. "Set and go."

"Weapons."

"Lasers charged to one hundred percent. Missiles loaded and safed."

Some part of his awareness, though, was still focused on the unfolding battle ahead. Both fleets had ceased acceleration; if no further burns were made by either side, their respective lead elements would pass through one another in thirty-five minutes. The waiting, Van decided, was going to kill him long before any Imperial missile even had the chance.

It was always this way before a launch, whether he was

doing it in sim or for real. The pressure built, he felt impatient, even angry, willing the time to pass and the action to start. Later, he knew from experience, he would go iceworld, cold and hard as water ice on an outer system world at fifty Kelvin. For now, it was all he could do to focus on the simple checklist.

"Targeting systems."

"Checking . . . go."

"Life support."

"Go."

"Communications. Switch off ship internal circuits. Go to squadron tactical."

"Switching to squadron taccom, and testing: alfa, bravo, charlie, delta . . ."

"Read you on taccom, Three-five. Comtest go." There was a pause as Commander Cole checked the communications frequencies of each of the other warflyers in the squadron one by one.

"Okay, children," Cole finally announced. "That's twelve for twelve, checked and go. The Gold Eagles are ready to fly."

Chatter from the various members of the squadron cut across Van's comm channel. "So what the hell is an eagle, anyway?"

"A mean-ass aviform, Carey. Like a grimmoth, but bigger."

"And extinct."

"If they were so mean, why are they extinct?" Van wanted to know.

"Hey, mean isn't all there is to survival, Van," Sublieutenant Carey Graham told him. "Ask T-rex or the slashertooth grynx."

"That's right," Lynn Kosta added. "Takes smarts, too."

"Okay, okay, listen up, people," Commander Cole announced, breaking in. "We're getting a feed from the Fleet CO."

"Whoa, there," Gerard Marlo said. "Deadly Dev on line, folks."

"Here it comes."

An instant later, it seemed to Van as though he were standing in the large compartment aboard *Tarazed* that served as the wing's lounge. The place wasn't large enough for the entire wing to gather at once; to Van, it looked as though only the members of his own squadron—twelve pilots plus perhaps thirty maintenance personnel and technical staff— were present, though Cameron's audience must in fact include everyone in the 1st Wing, nearly five hundred men and women all together. The viewall on one bulkhead showed space and graphic simulations both of the deployed squadron and of the approaching Japanese formation. Dev Cameron, wearing the two-tone grays of the new Confederation Navy and with a captain's insignia gleaming at his throat, stood before the 3-D display. He looked, Van thought, terribly young. What was he . . . twenty-eight, twenty-nine standard, maybe?

But then they were *all* young.

"Within the next fifteen minutes," Cameron said, starting off without preamble, "we are going to pull a type-one fleet encounter with six Imperial ships. The first shots have already been fired, the first maneuvers already implemented. I don't expect that the other fellow has any nasty surprises waiting for us, not when you remember that *we* are the nasty surprise for *him*. After all, he hasn't had time to organize anything special for us." A polite ripple of laughter ran through the lounge. Van felt a surge of impatience, though. He was ready to *go, go*. . . and he damn sure didn't need the pep talk that the high command always felt obligated to deliver.

"You people don't need a speech from me," Cameron went on, almost as though he'd read Van's mind. "You know your jobs and you're the best there are at what you do. Your squadron COs'll already have downloaded the basic op orders to you, so you know as much as I do about what we're trying to accomplish.

"What I do want to say, though, is that this one has to be one hundred percent. We must achieve total control of near-Alyan space so that we can land the Rangers and protect them. And if we don't destroy, cripple, or drive off all six Imperial ships, then they're going to be between us and our freighters back at our first entry point. If they want to, they could defeat us simply by slipping one corvette past us, heading out there and knocking off our stores ships. We'd be stuck, then, with nothing to do but turn around and go back to where we started. With rationing, we just might have enough stores left on board to make it back to Herakles, if we left right away.

"But I'm not going back to Herakles, not until I've carried out the orders General Sinclair gave us. We came here to enlist the help of the DalRiss in the cause we're fighting for. I don't intend to go back until we have it."

The other pilots and technicians in the simulated lounge were cheering now, and Van joined in, yelling as loud as he could. The excitement was contagious. On some quieter, deeper level, he was able to analyze Cameron's words and see them for what they were—*just* words, delivered without flourish or even emotion.

But the warflyer pilots were ready to die for the man. Van wasn't sure he understood the phenomenon; all he knew was that there was something in Cameron's openness and directness, in his trust of the people under his command, that Van would have followed anywhere, even to *jigoku*, the icy Japanese hell.

"We'll do our best to cripple those ships for you," Cameron continued, reaching out to point at the graphic display of the Imperial squadron on the viewall. "But we won't have the time to carve them up or deliver a killing blow. That will be your job, and I'm counting on you, on *all* of you, to make sure those people don't get through!

"Good luck! Let's show the DalRiss what Confederation warflyers can do!"

The lounge scene faded, replaced by the darkness of the warflyer launch tube. Green lights showed readiness for launch. Julio's voice called softly over a private channel. "Luck to you, Lieu. Take out one of them destroyers for me, eh?"

"You got it, Julio."

"And bring my girl back in one piece, or you 'n' me'll have words!"

Van laughed. "Yes, *sir*!"

"Gold Eagle clear for launch," Cole announced on the primary tac channel. "Primary sequence. Thrusters to stand by."

And then *Tarazed*'s launch officer was counting down the final seconds in Van's ear. "And *four* and *three* and *two* and *one* and *launch*!"

There was a blur of motion, and *Van'sGuard* was flung outward by a powerful, surging magnetic flux. Stars, and the dazzling glare of Alya A, exploded against Van's awareness, with Alya A-VI a brilliant star almost dead ahead.

An ice-cold calm descended on Van, clamping down over his emotions, over his impatience and the surging exultation of being in free flight once again. He gave the mental command to fire his primary thruster, and white light exploded behind his head, driving his ship forward. Astern, the five-pearls-on-a-string bulk of the *Tarazed* dwindled rapidly until it was nothing more than a bright star. Van countered a slight roll to starboard, then fired his ventral and port thrusters to align himself on the rest of the squadron, arrowing now straight down the axis of the Confederation fleet's course. His Warhawk's AI painted new stars of red and green on his view of space, showing the positions of the other ships ahead. A silent flare of light there marked the detonation of an Imperial missile.

The battle proper for Alyan space had begun.

Dev relaxed into the tactical command sim, watching the battle unfold. He'd done all that he could at this point, from double-checking the position of each ship in the deployment to that final pep talk to the pilots of the 1st Wing. He hoped the speech had not been too transparent, too obvious in its inspirational flag-waving psychology. More than anything else, he felt that he'd had to say *something*, to acknowledge the bravery and loyalty of those people who were about to take eighteen-ton singleships up against Yari-class destroyers.

Much was riding on them, and on what they would be able to accomplish against very long odds indeed.

Flashes of light were flaring across his tactical display now. *Eagle*'s AI identified the flashes as a barrage of EWC-167 nanomunitions, each detonation expanding rapidly into merging, mirror silver clouds composed of trillions of microscopic flecks of crystal.

Cloudscreens, designed to reflect or scatter laser light. The Imperial fleet had ceased acceleration some time ago, so they remained behind the drifting clouds, which would render laser fire useless until they dispersed, or until the combatants were much closer than they were now.

More time passed, the range closed. The Imperials were first to fire, loosing a cloud of teleoperated missiles. At Dev's command, countermissile fire began picking off the incoming warheads. Then the surviving missiles were close enough that point defense lasers could lock on and fire, vaporizing the swiftly accelerating missiles in soundless blossoms of light.

Computer graphics continued to update the formations arrayed beneath his gaze. *Constellation* was nearing the closest of the vast, shimmering cloudscreens, traveling stern-first.

"Now!" he ordered, and *Constellation*'s drive venturis flared white-hot. Seconds later, their invisible exhaust of high-energy plasma seared into the approaching cloudscreen. The frigate and the two corvettes, meanwhile, accelerated sharply, rapidly overtaking the destroyer. Portions of the screen blackened or wisped away into transparency as *Constellation* plunged through the cloud, closely followed by *Rebel, Valiant,* and *Audacious.*

Dev suspected that the Imperials planned to hit *Constellation* as soon as she emerged from the cloudscreen; he'd timed it so that all four of the ships in the Confederation vanguard would emerge at once, and at different speeds, a maneuver designed to confound the Japanese fire control AIs.

"Dev?"

Lasers fired, a crisscross of invisible beams of energy made tangible by *Eagle*'s AI, threads of green and red that instantly identified shooter and target.

"Dev, are you there?"

That was Katya, seeking a conference channel, but Dev ignored her. His worry about how his speech had been received was gone. In its place thundered the familiar, surging exultation of raw power, a victorious affirmation of triumph. He had brought this entire fleet to this, a frenzied few moments of largely automated maneuver and countermaneuver that would in scant seconds decide the winner.

He watched, emotion shaking him like a storm, as Katya continued to try to break in.

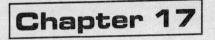

*The close-range battle: takes place at ranges less than
one thousand kilometers, the maximum effective reach
of beam weapons—lasers, charged particle guns (CPG),
and similar exotic weaponry. Also effective at short
range are high-speed gunfire, "dumb" rocket barrage,
and various forms of nano weaponry.*

*Due to the typical high velocities of approach, this
final phase of battle will last for only a few seconds
at most.*

—*Strategy and Tactics of Space Warfare*
Imperial Naval War College
Kyoto, Nihon
C.E. 2530

"Dev! Do you copy?" Still there was no response, and Katya
drew back. She could sense Dev above her in the tactical
net, a massive, dark, and self-confident presence within the
complex web of communications and data feeds channeling
through his link.

Bad timing, she thought. She knew he could hear her, but
he was obviously focused so completely on the battle that he
couldn't break away. No, *wouldn't* break away. It wasn't as
though a squadron commander was so busy he had no time
to spare at a moment like this. It was more like . . . like he
didn't care.

That couldn't be the case, not if Dev truly hadn't changed.
In all the time she'd known Dev, she'd not known another
man who cared more, who worried more about the men and
women under his command.

She decided to back off. A battle was no time to discuss
personal frettings. Her news—that *Mirach* had just been picked

157

up coming out of K-T space at the edge of the system—was available to him from other sources, and there was no reason for her to force an on-link interrupt.

Katya was pretty sure that the change she'd perceived in Dev since his encounter with the Xenolink was deepening, an isolation and a remoteness that enclosed him like a wall. *What can I do?* she wondered. *What should I do? Has he just grown so much that we no longer have anything in common? Or is the change something worse, something dangerous?*

And how do I tell the difference?

With black concern, she slipped out of the tactical simulation and into a new display of her own, one through which she could watch the head-on clash of the squadrons.

Things were happening very quickly now, and she tried to tell herself that Dev's indifference had simply been his need to follow the quickening pace of the battle.

The close-range portion of the exchange, when it came, was so brief that only later, through replayed simulations at reduced time factors, could the humans who survived it perceive exactly what had happened. With a high relative closing velocity, the two squadrons were within range of one another's lasers and other beam weapons for scant seconds. *Asagiri*, at the head of the Japanese formation, fired first, targeting the *Constellation*. *Constellation* replied an instant later and, to the Imperials' surprise, her first salvo was augmented by a barrage from *Valiant, Audacious,* and *Rebel* as they emerged unexpectedly from the tattering remnants of the Japanese cloudscreen. Concentrating their fire inward, they bathed *Asagiri* in burning, coherent light. Portions of *Asagiri* turned a brilliant silver as the programmed nano coating most of her outer hull flashed over to reflective mode, scattering laser light like the rainbow glint from a faceted diamond.

High-velocity rotary cannons in snubbed, dome turrets fired streams of depleted uranium slugs, ten or twelve per second. The massive deplur rounds gave an action-reaction deceleration to the firing ships that slowed them somewhat; the projectiles' speed, combined with the high velocity of approach, sent them slamming into the target with an explosive, buzz-sawing effect, tearing out huge sections of hull plate, gouging and cratering armor, snapping off antennas and PDL turrets, crumpling sponsons and wheel habitat mechanisms in a firestorm of destructive fury. Silvered nano could not resist that sleeting assault, and lasers seared and burned where the protective film had been scraped away. *Asagiri* staggered beneath the combined assault; her return fire concentrated first on *Constellation*, then shifted to the nearer *Valiant*. The Confederation frigate yawed suddenly to port, her primary cryo-H storage tank slit open from fore to aft, spilling reaction mass in a gleaming, frost-silvered cloud.

Then the Confederation ships were well past the damaged *Asagiri* and they shifted aim, targeting the four smaller ships at the corners of the Imperial octahedron. *Reppu* and *Audacious* exchanged repeated salvos; a lucky burst of deplur rounds slashed through *Reppu*'s ventral hull, savaging her fusion plant and knocking both her primary and secondary power systems off-line. Instantly, *Audacious* shifted her targeting to the much smaller corvette *Sagi*. A volley of rockets—so-called "dumb rockets" because they had no AI guidance—caught the Imperial corvette along her starboard side, badly cratering her lateral weapons sponson. A particle beam from the *Constellation* detonated her number two hydrogen tank a half second later; the glare of the explosion illuminated the warring ships like a searchlight, casting sharp-edged shadows through a volume of space grown misty from the intermingling clouds of debris, scoured-off flecks of nano, and crystallized droplets of cryo-H and freezing atmosphere.

Sagi's sister ship *Hatukari* exploded two seconds later, a victim to concentrated fire from the *Rebel* and from the surviving laser and cannon turrets aboard the shattered *Valiant*. The Imperial frigate *Hayate* concentrated her fire on *Constellation*, scoring several critical hits.

Then the first fighter wave burst from behind the cloudscreen, descending on the Imperial squadron like a swarm of angry wasps.

"Targeting!" Sublieutenant Vandis yelled into his link. The lead Imperial destroyer was still only a tiny graphic symbol in his display as he focused on it, bringing together the two halves of the targeting cursor and giving the download command to lock on. Other targets appeared, sleek, delta-winged Se-280 interceptors spilled from the destroyer's cargo bays, but he ignored them, knowing that at this speed of approach, they

might hit him or not but that there was precious little he could do to affect their aim, one way or the other. Instead, he concentrated on the much larger and richer target ahead, a Yari-class destroyer IDed by his warbook as the *Asagiri*.

Then the target was swelling huge in his vision. There was no time for anything fancy, no time for anything but the near-automatic response of intuition and training. His Warhawk mounted four MDA-74 infrared-homing missiles; a thought sent all four slashing into the target at a range of scant kilometers. Laser fire slashed at his warflyer in the same moment, the destroyer's PDLs. He felt the jolt as hull metal boiled off into space.

Then he was past, hurtling into darkness before the detonating warheads registered in his optics. An old, old aphorism of space fighter combat held that a fighter really required a minimum crew of three: one to see the target's approach, one to watch it pass, the third to see it vanish astern. An AI worked better; for now, Van had to content himself with the words TARGET HIT that flashed four times in his vision.

"Hit!" he called over the squadron tactical channel. "I nailed the goker!"

Then his threat alarm went off, an insistent bleeping cutting through the background chatter of the squadron. Data on the new contact scrolled across his vision. It was a small missile, probably loosed by one of the interceptors moments earlier, but fired *aft* as the bad guy passed to counteract its speed. With an acceleration of 50 Gs, it had quickly killed its velocity in one direction and begun accumulating speed in the other. Now it was gaining slowly on Van's warflyer from behind.

Van cut acceleration, then spun his warflyer end over end, seeking the oncoming missile. With a cold prickle at the back of his thoughts, he realized that his targeting system was dead. That PDL strike by the destroyer must have wiped his targeting optics . . . that or it had bored through and killed his tracking processor. He'd need to run a diagnostic . . . but he didn't have time and, more to the point, knowing what was wrong was not going to get him out of this one.

"This is Three-five!" he yelled over the tac channel. "This is Three-five! I need assistance here!" At the same time, he spun the Warhawk again and kicked in the thruster. Perhaps he could outrun the goker. . . .

No, that wouldn't work. The missile was gaining, and damned fast.

"This is Three-five! Three-five! I've got an India-Romeo on my tail and I can't shake it! I need some help, somebody!"

"Hang on, Van!" Gerard Marlo's voice rang across the taclink. "I'm on it!"

His wingman had been following a thousand kilometers astern; when the Imperial missile locked on, he'd cut in his port thrusters and slipped neatly into its plasma wake. In his mind, Van twisted, peering back over his shoulder. Though no physical movement was involved in the linkage, the thought let him peer aft, past the plasma flare of his own thruster. He saw the missile, a graphic point of light ten kilometers astern. Then he saw Marlo's warflyer and the pulsing gleam of his laser, followed instantly by a silent flash that wiped the warhead away in a shower of molten fragments. Tiny shards of metal pinged off *Van'sGuard*'s aft hull, but none was traveling more than a few hundred meters per second or so faster than the Warhawk and no damage was done. Van directed a relieved thought at Marlo. "Thanks, Ger! That was gokin' close!"

"Easy feed, yujo! Where next?"

Van returned his focus forward again. In the several seconds since the missile had picked him up, both he and Gerard had hurtled past the rest of the Imperial squadron. ShraRish hung before them, a golden sphere three-quarters full.

"It's going to take us awhile to reverse course," he told Marlo. "And more reaction mass than I have left in my tanks right now. How 'bout we check out that planet?"

"I'm reading ships in orbit, Van. Big ones."

"Freighters," Van agreed. "Probably the Impie logistics ships. Let's take 'em!"

"My mouth's watering already, yujo. Lead on!"

Van did a quick series of calculations through the AI link. "Okay. A one-eighty flip and decelerate at five Gs for twelve minutes, with a midpoint course correction. That'll drop us behind ShraRish with just a little more than orbital velocity. Enough that we can come up over the horizon and nail those freighters from below."

"Got it. Let's hit it!"

Together, the two fighters flipped end over end, then cut in their thrusters.

They would be the first Confederation ships to reach ShraRish.

When *Asagiri* was damaged by the exploding probe, some time earlier, her captain had ordered that the ship be oriented in space to turn the damaged portion of its hull away from the oncoming Confederation light destroyer. Unfortunately, that meant that when the Warhawk had broken through the cloudscreen, dead on course for the *Asagiri*, the plasma-scorched breach in her hull happened to be facing the oncoming fighter.

Point defenses had killed two of the four missiles scant meters from the hull, so close that the fighter's AI registered their detonations as hits. The remaining two missiles struck the light destroyer squarely, gouging deep holes in her armor, severing the main power leads, cutting primary weapons control. As power failed to the forward half of the ship, *Asagiri*'s AI rerouted the feed through the secondary backup.

A circuit board damaged by the earlier near miss of the detonated probe overloaded, then failed in a spectacular eruption of molten plastic and nanofilament. A relay failed to close, current arced to a fusion initiator, and the entire alfa sequencing chain went off-line and took the primary fusion containment field with it.

For the briefest of instants, a tiny sun blossomed where an instant before there'd been a three-hundred–meter starship.

Shosho Kenji Hattori watched a glowing number dwindle in his linked mind and knew that the battle was lost. The Imperial Navy had long taught its leaders to honor the cold, hard logic of numbers, which so often described life and death against the unyielding harshness of space. If there were six hours of air left for four men aboard an escape pod, say, then there was air for twelve hours if the number of men was reduced to two, and twenty-four if the number was only one. A radiation count of six-hundred rads in the habitat module of a stricken ship meant that nine out of ten of the unprotected crewmen there were going to die, with no right of appeal against the grim mathematics of death.

The number Hattori was watching was the probability of success as calculated by *Naginata*'s AI, a complex percentage drawn from such varied factors as the mass of the surviving combatants, the number of weapons remaining in action, and the amount of reaction mass necessary for the maneuvers the various ships would have to employ in order to keep fighting. At the moment, the number read twenty-three percent—less than one chance in four that the Emperor's Alyan contingent would be able to stop the rebels from achieving local space superiority.

The situation wasn't good. Two Confederation fighters had already slipped past the battle zone and appeared to be making for ShraRish; other fighters were following, a ragged cloud of warflyers too fast and too scattered to stop. The Imperial squadron itself had lost four out of six ships; the spectacular destruction of the *Asagiri* alone had dropped the success probability from forty-five percent to its present level. Not counting some fourteen warflyers slapped down by the Imperials' antimissile defenses, the Confederation had lost only two ships in exchange, plus the damage wreaked against the Yari-class destroyer. The Imperial squadron had not done well this day . . . not done well at all.

"*Chikusho!*" he snapped, the curse hard and violent. Savagely, he opened a tactical link to the Imperial freighters still in orbit around ShraRish. "Blue Peacocks! Blue Peacocks. This is Red Sword. The battle here is lost. Save yourselves, any way you can. I suggest you break orbit at once, get to a safe distance, then return to Earth orbit and rendezvous with the First Fleet. Hattori out!"

He didn't bother waiting for a reply. Instead, he shifted channels to *Naginata*'s internal communications and ordered the destroyer's captain to engage full acceleration.

Naginata's drive plumes exploded astern, dazzling suns driving the destroyer forward under a full 6 Gs. Bits and pieces of debris—fragments of exploded missiles or the blast-shredded remnants of hull armor torn from starships—thumped and clattered along her slender, heavily armored prow. The Confederation carrier flashed past fifteen thousand kilometers to starboard, but Hattori ordered the *Naginata*'s weapons officer to ignore it. The destroyer had already expended over three quarters of the missiles aboard, and he wanted to preserve them against the possibility of ambush later. *Eagle* passed seconds later, close by the Confederation transport.

Then they were safely out of range, heading for deep space. At Hattori's command, the ship's quantum power tap was engaged, then the ship was translated into the blue flame of K-T space.

He would decide just where it was they were fleeing to later.

Within the victorious Confederation squadron, damage control measures were under way as personnel fought to save the damaged ships. *Constellation* had taken some serious hits but was not in immediate danger. *Valiant* was in a much more serious way; her exchange with the *Asagiri* had savaged her RM storage tanks and forced an automatic scram on both her fusion plants and her QPT, leaving her powerless, a drifting hulk.

Corvettes and frigates, the low end of the mass-ordered hierarchy of starfaring warships, were hybrids. Originally designed as small, in-system escorts and patrol craft, they massed from one to five thousand tons and were powered solely by the compact fusion plants that converted slush hydrogen to plasma—simple fusion rockets incapable of traveling from one star system to another in anything less than decades.

As Hegemony and Empire had spread through the nearer stars, however, it had been discovered that small warships, massing a thousand tons or so and with crews of 150 or less, were far more efficient at patrol duties than the light destroyers, the smallest of which were 250 meters long and massed over forty thousand tons. The reason for their enormous size, of course, was the quantum power tap arrays necessary both for channeling energy from the Quantum Sea and for prying open the fabric of normal fourspace that let the starship slip into the *Kamisama no Taiyo*, the "Ocean of God" where jacker-oriented maneuvers allowed the ship to bypass space, effectively traveling three to four hundred times faster than light. The smallest power tap, complete with the field generators and shielding needed to call two mutually orbiting microsingularities into existence, hold them in finely focused harmonic tuning, and channel the cascade of energy they released across the quantum barrier, required a structure the size of a skyscraper and massing forty thousand tons or more.

The answer was to build drive modules—more popularly called skip riders—forty- to fifty-thousand–ton constructs that housed QPT and drive arrays, fusion plants, plasma thrusters, and reaction mass tankage enough to fuel the thing. The relatively tiny corvette or frigate rode perched atop the whole assembly like the upper stage of one of the clumsy, multistage rockets of the pre–fusion era of spaceflight. Using the skip rider, a frigate could make the K-T passage to another star. Once there, it could park its drive module in some convenient orbit and carry out its assigned deployment, a shark instead of a whale.

Asagiri's barrage had gutted *Valiant*'s drive module, leaving it a twisted tower of wreckage, half-melted and dangerously radioactive. Her crew was now hard at work attempting to release the frigate from the deadweight of its skip rider. Unfortunately, the magnetic clamps that secured the ship to the drive module had been frozen shut by the module's power failure. *Rebel*, braving the radiation leaking from *Valiant*'s dangerously hot carcass, was rendering assistance, but it was too early yet to tell whether *Valiant* could be freed from the deadly embrace.

The rest of the Confederation ships had begun decelerating toward ShraRish orbit.

Slowly, slowly, Dev came down from the high-tide storm of emotion that had burst through him during the battle. God . . . he was *shaking*, or he would be, as soon as he broke his linkage and stepped out of the ViRcom module. He could feel that telltale tremulousness, the weakness that made him wonder whether he would even be able to stand once he was out of linkage.

The battle was over. One of the Imperial destroyers, by accelerating right through the Confederation deployment, had put itself out of reach and minutes later had translated into K-T space. At ShraRish, the freighters were scattering like sheep as the warflyer wolves descended on them. Most would probably escape; with luck, the fighters might cripple one or two. Their cargoes would be welcome additions to *Farstar*'s inventory of expendables.

Carefully, Dev downloaded the command that would break him out of linkage, then executed the withdrawal.

Nothing happened.

Startled, Dev stared at his surroundings . . . still the tactical simulation showing the Confederation fleet and, ahead, the tiny gold orb of ShraRish. Something had gone wrong; he'd tried to disconnect and failed. There was no way that could have happened. The AI feed, his own cephlink, and the programs that ran the simulation, all were designed to boot him clear of the hookup should there be a major failure in any system.

What had gone wrong?

Again, with an almost exaggerated deliberation, he downloaded the disconnect codes, then initiated the withdrawal sequence. There was a terrifying moment of emptiness . . .

. . . and then he was back in his physical body, lying inside the ViRcom module. Quickly, he slapped the release that freed the life-support tubes from his shipsuit and thumbed the control that dissolved an accessway through the module's side. Light spilled in from outside and he blinked; tears blurred his eyes.

Oh, God! What happened there? He took a moment to pull a diagnostic log on his cephlink's processor. Yes . . . the correct command had been issued. A fault in *Eagle's* AI, or in the module hardware? The gleaming constellation of green lights on the module's panel said all was well on that end. He reran the diagnostic, tracing the scrolling lines of data flickering through his awareness farther. There! A subroutine in his own link hardware had blocked the link termination protocol before transmission to the module. He froze the mental display and stared at the data accusingly. That should not, *could* not have happened. He had, in effect, unconsciously stopped his own coded order to *Eagle's* AI to disconnect.

Clearing the display from his mind, he opened his eyes, unjacked his helmet feeds, then slipped off his helmet and stowed it in its recess. Stepping out of the module, he found the deck with his feet. He felt . . . strange, light-headed, a little dizzy.

Nausea rose up unexpectedly, gagging him, taking him by surprise. He vomited onto the deck, then nearly fell as the weakness swept through his body.

Unaccountably, he found himself wanting to crawl back inside the module, to jack in and lose himself again in the glorious emptiness of space. He hurt . . . and he felt so weak he could scarcely stand.

Supporting himself with one hand against the module, he looked up. Katya was there, looking at him with mingled fear and concern. He remembered her trying to get through to him, remembered ignoring her. There'd been nothing deliberate in that, he recalled. She simply hadn't mattered.

He swallowed, the taste acid-hot and bitter.

Something was very seriously wrong with him, and he had to find out what it was.

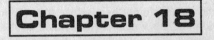

Chapter 18

*Where earlier advances in communications and elec-
tronics represented obvious progress in Man's technical evolution, the development of cephlink technology
represented a leap greater than those earlier developments by many orders of magnitude. Where earlier
advances might be compared to the biological evolution
of the eye, say, or of chordate anatomy, the cephlink
could be compared to one of those unforeseen shifts in
evolutionary direction that created whole new universes
for life to exploit—comparable, say, to the colonization
of the land, or the invention of sex. Many today accept
human-cephlink cyborgs as an entirely new order of
creature, as distinct from homo sapiens as the amphibian
is from the fish and with the same, greater evolutionary
promise.*

—The Rise of Technic Man
Fujiwara Naramoro
C.E. 2535

Seen from orbit, ShraRish was exactly as Katya remembered it. Like Dev, she'd last orbited the world aboard the transport *Yuduki*, one of the armada of Hegemony and Imperial ships that had visited the twin Alyan system back in 2541. Its small oceans and landlocked seas gleamed purple beneath the blaze of Alya A, while the land was covered in vegetation that overall looked gold, but which when examined closely showed a beautiful mottling of orange, brown, ocher, yellow, red, and pink.

And the mountains. She'd forgotten the mountains. Three billion years younger than Earth, ShraRish was more tectonically active by far than that relatively placid and middle-aged world. From orbit, the largest ranges looked like wrinklings in the skin of overripe fruit; active volcanos were marked by thousand-kilometer plumes of gray-brown smoke and ash, while on the planet's night hemisphere the eruptions showed as sullen red pinpoints wreathed in the silent throb and pulse of lightning storms. The nightside, too, was brought alive by the planet's auroral displays and meteor falls. With a more active, energetic sun than Earth, the darkness-shrouded portions of the polar areas of this world were always crowned by pale, shifting circlets of light, while a sharp eye could discern the steady flicker and streak of meteors vaporizing as they struck atmosphere.

Two hours earlier, *Eagle* had entered low orbit around ShraRish and her hab modules had been set to rotating, providing a half G of spin-gravity. *Valiant* and *Rebel* were still en route; the frigate had finally been freed from the wreckage of her drive module by surgically directed laser bursts from the corvette and was now being brought in under tow. The rest of the squadron was with *Eagle* in orbit, as the widely scattered fighters of the 1st Wing continued to straggle in. *Mirach* and the Confederation freighters were inbound from their vantage point at the frontiers of the Alyan system.

The entire squadron was still on full alert, but unless the enemy had more ships hidden somewhere with reactors scrammed and power sources shut down, it looked as though the Confederation now controlled near-ShraRish space. Two Imperial freighters had been caught by *Tarazed*'s warflyers before they could break orbit. The others, together with the lone surviving Imperial destroyer, had made the translation to K-T space and were long gone, almost certainly on their way back to the Shichiju.

There'd been no response, so far, from the Imperial forces on the surface of ShraRish.

*   *   *

Katya had joined Dev in *Eagle*'s lounge, where he'd taken a seat on a low sofa bordering a sunken area in the middle of the room, while she stood before him, hands on hips. She was furious at him, more angry, if that was possible, than she'd been when Sinclair had given her the order to leave New America.

"Just what the hell is the matter with you, Dev?" she demanded, ignoring the white, gold, and violet panorama on the lounge viewall behind the sofa. Set to display the planet's surface as seen from a camera mounted on *Eagle*'s bow, the screen revealed no movement save the steady, silent glide of clouds, seas and mountains over the curve of the planet.

"Nothing," Dev replied. "I told you, nothing! I'm fine!"

"You get sick all over the deck coming out of link, you can hardly stand up, and you tell me you're *fine*?"

He looked a little better now than when she'd met him by the link module. She'd slap-injected him with medical nano, then helped him back into the module, jacked him in, and summoned a med-psych monitor on the link.

"It's okay, Kat. I'm okay. Don't make more of it than it is."

"That, Dev, sounds like a classic case of denial. I don't want to hear what *you* think. What did the monitor program say? Or do I have to haul you down and let the nanosomatic engineers take you apart?"

"My physiodiagnostics still check okay," he told her. "I'm a little . . . depressed, is all."

"Depressed? Depressed? Depression doesn't make people vomit. And it doesn't turn people as close as we've been into strangers."

He sighed. "Hate to tell you, Kat, but you're wrong. It does all that, and more."

"Did the monitor suggest treatment?"

He nodded. "It prescribed a series of sex and relaxation ViRsims, and a daily, five-minute series of in-link alpha modulations. Tranquilizers, in other words."

"Okay. Fine. Are you doing it?"

He gave a half smile. "I've hardly had time to, have I? Anyway, I . . . I don't think I really want to."

"Why the hell not?"

"Because I'm more than halfway convinced that linking is my problem."

Katya felt herself go cold. "What, you think you're going null? That's ridiculous, Dev, and you know it."

Nulls were those people who, for physiological, psychological, religious, or ethical reasons could not accept the nano-grown cephlink hardware that allowed them to interact with technic society. They formed a substantial, if largely invisible, minority throughout both the Core and Frontier of the Shichiju.

"No, I'm not going null. Quite the opposite, in fact. I . . . think I'm in some kind of withdrawal."

Katya looked for the right words to say, then failed. Withdrawal? She knew whatever Dev was going through had to be wrapped up in his experience with the Xenolink, since he'd never had any real trouble with linkage one way or the other before. He'd always shown a slight tendency toward technomegalomania, enough, she remembered, to get him disqualified for the Hegemony Navy, but except for an occasional touch of recklessness, it had never seemed to affect him.

What had changed?

At that moment, several off-duty engineers entered the lounge. Katya didn't want to discuss something so personal as this in public, especially something that could erode the confidence the squadron's personnel felt in their military CO if it got around.

Dev was obviously thinking the same thing. "Well, Katya," he said rising from the sofa, "I'd better get back to work. Want to be linked in when *Rebel* hauls the *Valiant* into orbit. I'll talk to you more about it later, if you want. I assure you, though, that there's nothing wrong. Later?"

"At dinner," she told him. "Officers' mess."

"At dinner." He walked out, leaving her alone by the viewall.

But he wasn't at dinner. When she inquired through *Eagle*'s AI network, she learned he was in a tactical sim, overseeing the beginnings of the repair work to both *Constellation* and *Valiant*. She left word for Dev that she would be in the lounge, then returned there to find a seat in front of the viewall.

The compartment was fairly crowded when she got there. Brenda Ortiz was there, along with several of the scientists and programmer techs from the expedition's contact team.

She stood before the viewall for a time, watching the drift of ShraRish's seas and clouds. In the distance, an odd assembly of bulky, angular shapes gleamed in the sunlight. Frigates were, by ship-class definition, larger than corvettes, but *Rebel* was still wearing her skip rider, and the dismounted *Valiant* looked like a toy clutched tightly against the other ship's belly.

Was Dev really addicted to linkage? She'd heard of such things happening, of course, though usually it involved some poor guy—or gal—wiring into a continuous orgasm loop and burning out the pleasure centers. Such people weren't good for much after that, not without a massive neural rewrite, a reprogramming of memory and personality that amounted to wiping the brain clean and starting over.

She shuddered, preferring not to think about that. Whatever was haunting Dev was nothing so obvious as sex addiction. He'd mentioned being depressed, but this was more subtle than TDS, or technodepressive syndrome. He could still function and didn't seem impaired in any way.

But how would it affect his performance as the squadron's commanding officer? If he had to be relieved, Lisa Canady would replace him, and while Katya had nothing specific against her, the woman was still something of an unknown quantity.

Maybe, she told herself, *it's none of your business. Go back to the* Trixie, *see to your troops, and get ready for the landings. You're going to have enough to worry about without wondering what's going on in Dev's scrambled brains.*

But she couldn't just walk away from him. She had to help. But how?

"It's beautiful, isn't it?"

Katya started. Brenda Ortiz stood at her side, a glass of caff in her hand. She was staring at the viewall display, where the curved horizon of ShraRish bowed against the tiny, blazing disk of Alya A. *Eagle* was past the planet's terminator and falling into night.

"It makes you wonder," Brenda continued, "just how accurate our notions of our own planet's history really are."

"What do you mean?"

Brenda nodded toward the planet below. "Everything we've learned about that ecosystem has been teaching us more about our own. And about life in general. It turns out that the evolution of life isn't quite so unlikely as we always thought."

"Oh, I don't know," Katya said. She welcomed the distraction, needing to think about something else for a while, before her software burned itself into a loop. "Living ecologies are still scattered pretty thinly. Otherwise, we wouldn't have to do as much terraforming as we do, right?"

"Oh, ecologies where we can live comfortably are rare enough, all right. But everything we learn about life, about how it works as a system, how it spreads, how it evolves, *everything* demonstrates that life is a part of the natural order of things. It's as though the universe was designed specifically to produce life. It's not an accident."

"You're starting to sound like a Determinist," Katya said, grinning to disarm what could have sounded like a challenge of Brenda's intelligence. Determinism was one of the host of more or less fuzzy-minded religions that had appeared among the worlds of the Shichiju, a tenet that, like predestination before it, held that everything that happened in the universe was preordained and beyond the reach of human will.

"The first great revolution of biology," Ortiz said, with the air of a classroom lecturer, "was the theory of evolution. The second was genetics, and the understanding that life was an elaborate means of preserving and transmitting DNA.

"The third began when we realized that the beginnings of life on Earth stretched back a lot farther into the past than we'd imagined at first. Fossil evidence showed that there was life on the planet within half a billion years after a solid crust formed. Right?"

"I'm linked."

"Okay. That early appearance of life on Earth demonstrates that wherever you have CHON—carbon, hydrogen, oxygen, and nitrogen—plus assorted seasonings and a mean temperature range between zero and one hundred Celsius, sooner or later—and probably sooner—life is going to appear."

"Wait, that's what I don't understand. Most of the worlds of the Shichiju were prebiotics. No life . . . just the building blocks life needed to get started. I thought the idea was that life was limited to worlds that had something like a large, close moon to stir things up on a regular cycle."

Brenda nodded. "Ah, yes. The old Tidal Theory."

"Right. Worlds that had their own native ecologies before humans showed up are rare. Earth. New America and New Earth. Eridu. Maia. Six or eight others in a volume of space a hundred light years across. And the Alyan worlds, of course, and even there ShraRish started off lifeless."

"Exactly. Out of the eighty-some worlds we know with the prerequisite conditions for life, fifteen developed their own ecosystems. Almost twenty percent. And life was deliberately introduced on the rest."

"Well, yes, but those others were terraformed. Humans deliberately creating a new ecosystem where there was none before. It wasn't . . ."

"Natural?"

"Right. It wasn't natural."

"How do you distinguish natural from artificial?"

"Easy. We planted life on places like Liberty and Herakles by using technology, and lots of it. Sky-els and atmosphere generators as big as mountains, just for a start. Now *that's* artificial."

"How life does what it does is beside the point, Katya. Look at the Nagas. They spread from world to world too, but not by what we would call intelligent volition. They're undeniably intelligent, yes, but their world view and their version of technology are so different from what we know that the actual process, blindly firing capsules containing nanotechnic matter programmed with the template of a new Naga, really isn't any more reasoned than when two people have sex and conceive a child. The mechanics of the process aren't conscious and they aren't planned, at least not by us. Another way of looking at it is that *life* planned it that way, through biodiversity and natural selection. I've heard it said that we are DNA's way of making more DNA."

Katya laughed. "I see your point. Still, it's hard to see life as an automatic process when eighty percent of the worlds we've found that *could* have had life, didn't."

"Ah, but how many of those worlds might have developed their own ecosystems, given another billion years or two?"

"Well, as I understand it," Katya said, "that Tidal Theory you mentioned a minute ago says that strong tides are necessary for the appearance of life. That the constant mixing of CHON soup in the twice-daily rise and fall of the tides, coupled with the appropriate thermal and ultraviolet input, gives a regularity to hot and cold, light and dark, wet and dry that encourages the appearance of long-chain molecules that are both strong enough to survive the cycles and complex enough to self-replicate. That sure seems to explain the native life on New America, at any rate." Katya's homeworld possessed a single huge, close satellite, Columbia, that raised gentle but enormous tides across the world's oceans twice in each long day.

"Maybe the moonless worlds are just slow," Brenda said with a smile. "They still have the tides generated by the local sun, those that rotate, anyway. And maybe there are other ways of doing things that we don't understand yet."

"Like the way life got started originally on GhegnuRish?"

"*Especially* how it got started on GhegnuRish so early in the planet's history, and how it developed so quickly. It's almost as though life knows it doesn't have much time before a star like Alya leaves the main sequence and makes the planet uninhabitable.

"That's why I was wondering about whether we know all there is to know about our own planet's history." She gestured at the golden globe of ShraRish, a glorious splash of color hiding sulfurous volcanoes and sulfuric acid rain. "Looking at that, it makes me wonder. Those earliest fossils we've found on Earth, the ones going back to the first billion years or so of Earth's evolution, they're obviously simple things, but they don't tell us much about the actual conditions, save that there was liquid water present. We can guess about the actual composition of the atmosphere, of course. CO_2. Sulfur compounds in the air."

"You're saying conditions on the early Earth were like those on the DalRiss worlds." Katya wondered where she was going with this.

"Not really," Brenda said. "The modern Alyan atmosphere isn't any more similar to what it evolved from than Earth's atmosphere today is to its atmosphere three billion years ago. Environmental conditions are changed and regulated by life. But conditions on the early Earth and on the early GhegnuRish must have been similar. A *lot* more similar than they are today. Probably the main difference was in how much energy the system received from its sun.

"It got me wondering if maybe there'd been a time, early in our planet's history, when life was basically, uh, DalRissan. Breathing CO_2 and giving off oxygen, utilizing sulfur compounds for energy-transfer molecules, the way we use phosphates. Maybe there was a whole, entire alternate biology on Earth that we don't know about today, one that was wiped out when too much oxygen was dumped into the atmosphere or that couldn't compete with our kind of life when it wiggled along or, well, whatever. You've heard of the Burgess Shale?"

Katya shook her head.

"One of the great paleontological discoveries of history. A group of fossils from five hundred fifty million years ago that included types of animal completely unrelated to modern life. Things so bizarre that, well, the name given to one species was *Hallucigenia*."

Katya laughed. "Evidence of an alien invasion of Earth?"

"Not quite. Evidence that the course life takes as it evolves is subject to abrupt and unexpected twists and changes. But for an accident that we can't even guess at today, intelligence on Earth could have evolved from one of those Burgess monsters, maybe something like *Opabina*, with five stalked, compound eyes and a long, flexible trunk equipped with pincers on the end."

"Are you saying those Burgess creatures had a DalRissan chemistry?"

"Not at all. They didn't. But, well, look at it this way. There's life on Earth today living in the deep ocean next to volcanic vents, called 'smokers.' Life based on photosynthesis—and that includes us, of course—can't exploit those hot, mineral-rich, energy-rich resources next to deep thermal vents, because there's no light down there at all. Instead, life next to the smokers is chemosynthetic, with an ecology based on bacteria that metabolize sulfur released by the vents. Maybe once, during Earth's first billion years or so, a sulfur-based, DalRissan type of life evolved, only to be replaced later. Maybe sulfur-based life requires a lot more incident energy than is available anywhere on Earth except near those volcanic vents, which is why it thrives on worlds like ShraRish.

"I'm not really saying anything except that, given half a chance, life will appear, sooner or later, and it will adapt and evolve and diversify to fill every available niche, including some that staid and boring, carbon-based, oxygen-metabolizing, phosphate-transferring, old stick-in-the-muds like us can't even imagine. Life has a will to *be* that just can't be stopped."

Katya was silent for a long time, staring at the panorama of ShraRish. Alya A had vanished behind the planet's curved horizon in a final flash of blue-gold fire. They were in night now, though the world's horizon still showed a curved smear of clouds, bloodstained red and scarlet. Below, the mysterious fires of lightning storms and volcanoes silently glared and pulsed, together with the intermittent flash of meteors. Aurorae illuminated the poles with ghost-pale blue-and-green radiance.

"I hope you're right, Brenda," Katya said after awhile. "Sometimes it feels as though the end purpose of evolution is us . . . and all we're good for is killing one another. It would be kind of ironic if the final scene of a five-billion–year play was nothing but ruined cities and radioactive deserts and the dead hulks of derelict starships."

Brenda shook her head. "Well, I suppose we might possibly exterminate ourselves . . . but life will continue, one way or another. A billion years from now Earth will be populated by *somebody*, maybe descended from us, and maybe not. Whatever it is, it'll probably be something that makes *Hallucigenia* look like a close relative. I guarantee that it won't look like us, though, because change is one of the foundations of all living systems. It might not even be that old standby, 'life as we know it.' "

Katya reached up and tapped the side of her head, indicating the hardware nesting within her brain. "Maybe the machine component will get the upper hand. Lots of us are already hybrids of human and machine. Maybe someday the machine part of ourselves will just decide to discard whatever fragments of the animal are left."

"That's been suggested before. But saying that we're going to change into machines is missing the point. Whether life is based on carbon and subunits called cells, or on silicon and subunits called switches is immaterial. Cells are small machines. Nanomachines act like cells. Where's the difference? It's *all* life, of one kind or another, and it will ultimately fill the universe."

"I wonder," Katya said after a long silence, "if when it reaches that point, it will think the journey was worthwhile?"

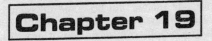

Chapter 19

Our contacts with alien species thus far, with the Xeno-phobes and with the DalRiss, strongly suggest that the logic of nonhuman intelligence does not necessarily con-form to human logic. This bit of tautology masks a deeper truth: if we have difficulty accepting the logic— the worldview, the point of view, the view of self—of other human cultures, then we may never be able to communicate on any but the most fundamental level with those other minds that we must someday meet among the stars. Somehow, somehow, we must transcend our ego-delineated limitations, must give ourselves a godlike view that incorporates the human sense of independence, the Xeno concept of Self, and the DalRiss view of life.

—*Alien Minds: A Human Perspective*
Dr. Paul Hernandez
C.E. 2543

The Imperial forces on the surface of ShraRish continued to ignore the presence of the Confederation ships in orbit, despite repeated attempts to raise them on all space-to-ground laser, radio, and ViRcommunications channels. Scans both from orbit and by ascraft dipping into the upper levels of the atmosphere detected only the one Imperial facility at Dojinko.

The close-range survey also began to positively identify concentrations of DalRiss, which had gone unnoticed for the most part during the initial probe flybys. DalRiss cities were hard to pick out from orbit in any case, for their buildings and other structures were themselves living organisms, seem-ingly designed to blend into the background of ordinary forest growth. It was, one New American computer technician informed Dev, unnervingly like searching not for a needle in a haystack, but for one particular strand of hay.

Dev, raised on Earth instead of an agricultural world like New America, wasn't sure what a haystack was . . . or a needle either, for that matter, but he could appreciate the tech's frustration. Life of one sort or another blanketed the surface of ShraRish in a bewildering profusion of growths, most with metabolic processes more energetic than those of typical plant life Dev was familiar with. The only areas on the surface not covered with living material were the most rugged portions of the highest mountains and the surfaces of the seas, and even there *Eagle*'s scanners detected tangled mats of growth thousands of kilometers square, floating on the waves and soaking up the high-energy sunlight.

Despite the background noise, as the scanner techs charged with searching for signs of intelligent life called the planet's living blanket, DalRiss cities were spotted. By far the largest concentration of DalRiss-related organisms, meaning their buildings and the various gene-tailored creatures they used as mounts or for other purposes, appeared to be in a single area perhaps a thousand kilometers southwest of Dojinko, close by the shore of a large, landlocked sea.

An interesting point observed by the orbital scanning teams was made evident through contrast photography and computer enhancement. Most of the mobile dwelling-creatures concentrated at that site, soon dubbed "the Migrant Camp" by human observers, had recently arrived there from elsewhere on the planet's surface. The marks and trails left by the passage of tens of thousands of huge, slow-crawling creatures remained visible in the bruised ground vegetation and in the barren stretches of rock, soil, or gravel scoured clean by their passage. The vanished DalRiss city that had existed just to the east of the Imperial base had apparently taken a straight-line trek across one thousand kilometers of low, rolling hills, a prairie, and a major river . . . not to mention one corner of the human base facility. Other city groups had evidently crossed much vaster distances, circumnavigating seas and crossing or bypassing entire mountain ranges to reach the new site.

The Migrant Camp was enormous. Conservative estimates suggested that twenty million DalRiss might be living there, an enormous number by their standards, at least as humans understood them. Most of their buildings were relatively small, a few tens of meters long, perhaps, and half that in height. Some retained their sluglike traveling shape; many more had adopted the more characteristic mushroom shape of most personal DalRiss structures.

There were plenty of other structures as well, though, including huge domes, spires, towers, and structures for which there was simply no apt and easy description. What, for example, was to be made of the single largest structure in the entire city, one that appeared to be the focal point of all DalRiss activity in the area? Shaped like a huge, seven-armed starfish, it sprawled near the shores of the sea. So thick at its center that it rose like a hill in the middle of the city, and with a diameter of over two kilometers from arm to opposite arm, it rested on the ground surrounded by living DalRiss structures pressing so close to one another that there was scarcely room at all between any one building and its neighbor. The starfish shape appeared to be connected to the water by a vast tangle of what might have been pipes or tubes, or possibly they were clumps of roots each as thick as the trunk of a good-size tree. Like all DalRiss structures, it was obviously alive, grown in place, but what its purpose might be was unguessable.

Adding to the mystery were indications that numerous other DalRiss concentrations had abruptly decided to pack up and move elsewhere. Dozens of sites were identified and catalogued that were identical to the barren area near Dojinko, areas several hectares in extent possessing little or no vegetation, with craters and scars showing in the bare earth or rock, and with pathways trampled through the surrounding forest suggesting that the town's buildings had simply decided to walk away. Many of those trails led to the Migrant Camp. Others led to other villages, or else dwindled away and were lost in the forest. There were even a few sites, relatively fresh-looking ones, that showed starfish-shaped markings in the ground reminiscent of the big, central creature at the Migrant Camp. Smaller versions of that creature, with numbers of arms ranging from four to nine, had rested in those towns for considerable periods of time, then vanished, complete with the DalRiss that had tended them. Why? And where had they gone?

In a simulation compiled from hundreds of accumulated

hours of orbital observation and unmanned probes, Dev studied the three-dimensional image of the Migrant Camp and its mysterious center, hoping to stumble across some clue to DalRiss behavior. With him were his battle staff, including Captain Canady, and Katya and her senior staff, flown over from the *Mirach* and the *Trixie*. Also present were Brenda Ortiz and her Contact Team people, experts on the DalRiss who more and more frequently were answering questions with frank we-don't-knows.

"Might it have a military function?" Vic Hagan asked, referring to the creature that by now was known as "the giant starfish." Hagan, an old comrade of Katya's who'd only recently received his new rank of lieutenant colonel in the Confederation ground forces, was her current number two in the 1st Confederation Rangers. During the trip from Herakles, he'd been CO of the 3rd Battalion troops aboard *Mirach*, while Katya had remained with the 1st and 2nd Battalions on *Vindemiatrix*.

"What . . . like a fortress?" Katya asked.

"Maybe it's mobile," Lisa suggested. "The Dal part of the DalRiss symbionts, they're kind of starfish-shaped, aren't they? Maybe this is just a very large Dal."

"I doubt that," Brenda said. "It's two kilometers across and must weigh a hundred million tons at least. I don't care what kind of metabolism it has, it wouldn't be able to generate enough energy to move. My guess is that it's some kind of large building."

"Yes? How do we tell?" Sergei Androyev replied, clearly frustrated. The bushy-haired linguist from New America's Ukrainian colony was one of Ortiz's best people. "If it has weapons, we can't see them. It's clearly hollow because the DalRiss appear to be moving inside, but there is quite frankly no way of determining its function."

"Not from up here, at any rate," Brenda said. "It's a strange idea for a bunch of xenolinguists, I know, but we *could* go down and ask them."

"Do they know we're here, do you think?" Dev asked.

"Almost certainly," Androyev replied. "We know the DalRiss have radio. In fact, they appear to be quite sensitive to radio emissions, the way we are to light."

"That's right. They have some kind of radio-sensitive organs, don't they?" Lieutenant Commander Fletcher said.

"According to our interviews with them," Brenda said, "going back to First Contact, they first became aware of Hegemony civilization through our radio emissions. We know they can understand our language now, and we've been beaming messages at them over several radio frequencies, both in Inglic and in *Nihongo*. They know we're here and they know we're fighting against the Empire. They just haven't answered us as yet."

"Maybe broadcasting radio at them isn't such a good idea," Lisa Canady suggested. "For them it might be like a bright light in the eyes would be for us."

"Anything's possible," Ortiz admitted. "But they seemed to respond well to radio dialogues beamed at them by 1-IEF three years ago. And presumably, that's how the Imperials have been talking with them lately. The Japanese don't much enjoy communication through the comels, I gather."

"The ones in the Expeditionary Force certainly didn't like getting their hands dirty," a senior programmer tech pointed out. "It had to do with actually wearing a living creature, I think. They tended to be pretty fastidious about sticking bare skin into anything that looks as nasty as a comel."

Several people in the linkage chuckled at that, including Dev, who'd worn the DalRiss translators on numerous occasions. Comels, the living creatures designed by the DalRiss to facilitate direct emotional communication between wildly divergent species, were disconcerting to people who hadn't used them before. Many refused point-blank to touch the things, which resembled nothing so much as soft, black or gray pools of tar or thick jelly imbued with a quivering, greasy-slick life of their own.

No one was sure where the name "comel" had come from originally. Some thought it sounded like the DalRiss word for them, though the DalRiss spoken language was so complex, involving parallel sounds and voices, that it was difficult to isolate individual chains of sounds from any single spoken phrase. Others preferred the more mundane suggestion that the genegineered organisms had originally been designated "Communicators, Living" by Imperial military scientists who studied them, a term that in Inglic readily shortened to "com-L." Whatever the origin of the name, however, they'd proven invaluable, not so much for bridging the language gap between humans and the DalRiss, which the DalRiss themselves didn't seem to regard as much of a problem, but for allowing communication between humans and the utterly inhuman Nagas.

"I certainly think our best chances lie with using the comel," Ortiz said. "It was their invention, after all."

"And if the Imperials haven't been using them," Katya pointed out, "that's an important distinction between us and them. It might make the DalRiss more sympathetic to us."

"Okay," Dev said. "Face-to-face contact is always best, I'd agree to that. Whatever we decide to do, though, whatever approach we use to make contact, I suggest we do it fast. We only have a limited amount of time to try to communicate with these people, remember."

"How long?" Ortiz asked.

Dev shrugged, then remembered that his analogue was not visible in the simulation, that the others could hear but not see him.

"At the very best, six to eight months," he told her. "That's how long it will take that destroyer and the freighters that escaped after the battle to get back to Shichiju space and tell the Imperial Staff Command that we're out here. The Imperials can't afford to let us have exclusive communications with the DalRiss. Even if we haven't figured out how to go about doing it yet.

"At the worst, well, they could be breaking out of K-T space at the edge of the ShraRish system right this moment. The Imperials in the Shichiju would've learned about Dojinko, about the problems with the DalRiss, before we did. They'll have been taking their time about assembling a relief fleet, but that fleet *will* be here, and I'd be willing to bet it'll be here damned soon. We'll have to be ready to up stakes and clear out just as quick as it takes to load our people aboard an ascraft and get them up to orbit."

"And abandon the DalRiss?" Katya said, anger flaring. "When are we going to stand and fight for a change?"

"When we have a chance of winning," Dev told her bluntly. He'd heard the pain of the unhealed wound in her voice but ignored it. This wasn't the time or place to discuss the ethics of war.

"We should probably go straight for comel communications," Hagan suggested, verbally insinuating himself between Dev and Katya. "At least that will show them that we *want* to communicate. They might not recognize our current radio broadcasts as anything more than 'hello, how are you.' "

"Commander Hagan has a good point," Androyev said. "We know that the DalRiss understand our language, the actual words, but we're still not sure how much of the meaning *they* attach to those words corresponds with the meaning *we* attach to them."

"You're saying 'Hello, how are you' could be a ritual death threat for them?" Katya asked.

"Maybe not that, exactly, but that's the idea. Most human greetings convey certain social postures and attitudes. 'I am friendly. I have no weapon in my hand. I care about your well-being.' Such sentiments tend to lose their meaning over a long period of time and become little more than a social ritual. But we have no idea what they would mean to a DalRiss."

"Ah," Dev said. "Maybe for them 'I have no weapon' means 'Hi there, I'm your breakfast.' Or, 'I care about your welfare' means 'Hey, how would you like to mate?' "

Most of the others laughed. "That," Androyev said, a little stuffily, "is perhaps the general idea."

"The next question we have," Dev said, "is where do we make contact?

"We seem to have a choice there," Katya pointed out. "The original plan called for going in and taking down the Imperials at their surface base first, then talking to the DalRiss who were on the site. That might not be practical at this point, though, since all the DalRiss at Dojinko appear to have uprooted, literally, and moved elsewhere. Alternatively, we could ignore the Imperials—they don't seem to be much of a threat now— and try a landing close to Migrant Camp. At least we know we'll find the DalRiss *there*."

"I think," Dev said slowly, "that our best course of action will be to stick to the plan as written. We could be violating some taboo or law by showing up uninvited at Migrant Camp, and if that starfish in the middle of town *is* some sort of military structure, our arrival could be seen as a threat. We'd be better off, I think, grounding near the Impie base. If the DalRiss are feuding with the Japanese, it won't hurt to show the natives that we are too. And I think it'll be important to try talking to them at the same place where the Imperials have been working with them. We still don't know how unified DalRiss society is, or if it even corresponds well to what humans think of as a social structure. If we land at Migrant Camp, we might discover that none of the locals know about humans."

"Unlikely, that last," Ortiz said. "Considering the fact that humans are responsible for ending the long DalRiss war with the Nagas, I doubt very much that there's a Riss on the whole planet who doesn't know about us in one way or another. Still, I think you're right about the need to take up communications with the DalRiss at the same place the Imperials evidently left off. There could be symbolic value in that . . . and we'll be facing fewer unknowns."

"Then we're agreed," Dev said. "Katya? The sooner we get your people down there, the better. How soon can you go?"

"We just need as long as it takes to file One-slash-one aboard an ascraft and deorbit," she said, referring to the 1st Rangers' First Company. "Say two hours."

"We're coming up on ship's night," Dev said. "Why don't we give your people a last, good night's sleep? God knows how long it'll be before they have someplace to rack out besides the link modules of their warstriders. Muster aboard your ascraft at 0800 hours tomorrow."

"Zero-eight hundred it will be, Commodore."

"You'll be pretty much under your own discretion, Katya, though I'll want to maintain full linkage with you all the way. Your overall directives will be first to assess and eliminate the Imperial threat—and I'll rely on your judgment as to just how you carry that out—and then to attempt to make contact with the DalRiss. Again, your judgment."

"Wait," Ortiz said. "Shouldn't the Contact Team be along for that, Commodore?"

"Negative, Professor. Not this time, not with this many unknowns. We'll have you packed aboard an ascraft though and ready to deorbit just as soon as Colonel Alessandro gives the word. Once the Impies are cleaned up, once we have at least some acknowledgment that the DalRiss are willing to talk to us, then we'll send you down."

"I think you're making a mistake there," Ortiz said, the frown showing in her voice.

"Maybe. But until we've sized up the political situation down there, this is still a military mission, with military objectives and prerogatives. I promise you, the colonel won't go in shooting. Not at the DalRiss, anyway."

The discussion turned next to the mechanics of contact and to what the Confederation Expeditionary Force hoped to accomplish, assuming, of course, that the Empire gave them time.

Dev was feeling noticeably better now that the mission was properly under way. He'd given in to the monitor's suggested regime of recreational linking and alpha wave control, and possibly that was helping as well. He'd noticed in any case that he felt worst when he wasn't jacked in, best when he was enjoying a full, three-jack download. He no longer dreamed as much about what had happened on Herakles. His earlier depression was largely gone, too, though there was a lurking nostalgia for the far vaster sweep of experience and knowledge and being that had been his during the Xenolink. The longing for that vaster, inner world was controllable when he was linked, with immediate access to literally any knowledge and experience he wished to have. Only when he was out of link, with nothing to rely on but his own native abilities and the few gigs of implanted RAM in his brain, did he really feel the impact of his loss.

If only he could just somehow manage to stay linked all the time. . . .

Chapter 20

Warstriders found their first military application in the Manchurio-Japanese War of 2207. It was that conflict, incidentally, that demonstrated once and for all Imperial Nihon's technological lead over the other nations of Earth, a clear result of her having seized the high ground of space during the previous two hundred years.

Significantly, though, there were relatively few new developments in warstrider technology during the next three centuries. There were experiments, of course, with changes in size, in numbers and types of weapons, in control systems, sensor packages, and armor, but the basic idea—an armored combat machine controlled by the directly channeled neural impulses of a cephlinked pilot has remained virtually unchanged since its inception.

—*Modern Military Hardware*
HEMILCOM Military Documentary
C.E. 2537

The ascraft, a VK-141 Stormwind, slanted in from the southwest nose high, kicking up a swirl of dust and fragments of vegetation as the ventral thrusters cut in. Four bulky, roughly egg-shaped packages disengaged two at a time from slots beneath the ascraft's down-canted wings, tumbled free, then steadied in bursts of hot plasma. As each touched down on howling, twin jets, side and bottom panels swung open, articulated joints unfolded, legs and arms and weapons pods deployed in smooth-moving parodies of the motions of a living creature. One after another, the machines went into full combat mode, rising on jointed digitigrade legs, weapons and sensors alike extended and scanning their surroundings. Their armored hulls shimmered as the nanoflage coating them adjusted to the new surroundings, taking on the mottled, gold-orange hues of the vegetation in the area. They didn't vanish—quite— but when the machines froze in place, their outlines all but disappeared, making a firm ID difficult. When they moved, their outlines blurred, while the color patterns twisted and moved as though the strider's entire outer surface was paneled with mirrors.

The first four warstriders were down unopposed. As the Stormwind's thrusters shrieked and the bulky craft pivoted in place, then rose once more into the sky, a second ascraft drifted in out of the southwest, followed by a third and a fourth, each stooping to disgorge its own complement of warstriders in a ragged line to either side of the first team. There were sixteen in all, a full platoon consisting of a mix of light and medium machines: RLN-90 Scoutstriders, Ares-12 Swiftstriders, and LaG-42 Ghostriders.

The largest was an RS-64GC Warlord, with the legend *Assassin's Blade* picked out in white script on its armored prow, and as the machine swung about, the warm, background colors reflected by its nanoflage surged and rippled behind the letters. Tucked away within its three jackerslots, Katya, Sublieutenant Ryan Green, and Warrant Tech Kurt Allen were linked to the Warlord's systems. Green was piloting, Allen was jacked to the primary weapons, while Katya concentrated on running the platoon.

"Skyfall, Skyfall," she announced over the ground-to-orbit frequency. "Dagger is down."

"Dagger, Skyfall, we copy that," the voice of *Eagle*'s Battle Ops officer replied in her head. "We've got you pegged at the primary LZ, with no hostiles or unknowns in your immediate area. Your objective is at zero-three-five, range five point two kilometers. You should have Point Alfa in sight to your northeast."

Checkpoint Alfa was a low, bare-topped ridge three kilometers from the landing zone, easily recognizable from the simulated runs Katya had worked on aboard the *Eagle*. "Roger that. I see it."

"Your objective should be in sight from there. How's the weather down there?"

"Hot," she replied, glancing at her met readouts. "And muggy. With a chance of acid rain. But no bandits. None that've shown themselves, anyway. Plenty of background noise, though. There could be an army out there, and if they weren't powered up, we'd never see them."

They'd landed in a broad clearing extending west from the ridge and almost encircled by forest. Their surroundings felt distinctly alive, with rustlings and subtle shiftings among the vegetation. The tallest were slender with fernlike or spearlike tips thirty meters or more above the ground, and some had a feathery look almost reminiscent of the virgin native forests back on New America. Most were rounder and squatter, though, like huge mushrooms or bloated puffballs or stacked layers of shelf fungus, while others possessed surreal clumps of light-gathering foliage that resembled huge, ragged natural sponges, all holes and pits and tatters with lots of interconnecting branches like jackstraws. Some of the vegetation exuded a thick orange or pink foam that dripped from the canopy and covered the ground, soaking up sunlight and somehow transferring it to the parent organism.

There was no sign of animal life on any of Katya's scanners, though many of the plants, including the spongy, sheetlike growths the striders were trampling underfoot, were in constant rippling or pulsing motion. Overhead, the sky was violet-blue, with scattered clouds tinged with sulfurous yellow.

"That way," she told her pilot, indicating the ridge to the northeast. "Low and fast."

"Right, Skipper."

"Dagger, Dagger One. Deploy and move out!"

The Warlord lurched forward, then shifted into a sprint, the easy, scissoring movements of its birdlike legs providing a relatively smooth ride, though each long step caused the fuselage to swoop in what a newbie could find to be a disorienting fashion. It was an old machine, one handed down from unit to unit with patches and replacement parts to show its checkered history. *Blade*'s main fuselage, Katya knew, had been cast in 2489, and it had seen service with a Hegemony line unit for eighteen years before it was sold to a New American militia unit. The body of her warstrider was damn near twice Katya's age, older by nine years than the Xenophobe War.

Older machines like this one had been the mainstay of the various Hegemony and local militia units fighting the Xenos, and they'd given a good account of themselves. This time, though, the enemy wasn't Xenophobes. The black hull armor of those Tachis and the Katana glimpsed by the remote probe earlier suggested that the Dojinko defenders were Imperial Marines, with few exceptions the best troops and machines *Dai Nihon* possessed.

They reached the base of the ridge without incident and started to climb, the other warstriders of the platoon stretching out in a line to either side, each close enough to its neighbors to keep them in sight. Katya didn't need to give more than an absolute minimum of orders. The veterans in her team knew what they were doing and knew what she expected of them; the newbies had had plenty of training and drill back on New America, and the majority of them were veteran warstriders from various Hegemony units. The true test of any military formation was how well it stood up under battle, of course, and that had yet to be tested, but Katya had been careful to select her best people for this mission. She was confident that they'd be able to face anything the Imperials threw at them, and win.

But it would help a lot if she knew just what the Imperials had prepared for her. They *couldn't* be unaware of the Confederation landings. Imperial sensors would have picked up the heat signatures and radar traces of the Stormwinds coming in; there would have been plenty of time to deploy an ambush.

The question was . . . where?

The warstrider line neared the top of the ridge labeled Point Alfa but remained in body-down position behind the crest. Extending a sensor arm above the rise, Katya could see the Imperial base, a cluster of gray towers and domes huddled against the yellows and ochers of the encroaching forest. It looked much as it had when she'd seen it last as a simulation compiled from flyby data, save that the four Japanese warstriders parked in front of the central structure were not in evidence. Four gun towers were very much in evidence, however, with heat signatures that suggested they were powered up and operational.

The absence of enemy warstriders was disturbing. Not that she'd been expecting them to make this *easy*, but Katya much preferred the enemy you could see to the one you couldn't.

"Skyfall, this is Dagger One," Katya called over the ground-to-orbit channel. "How about patching through an orbital feed? Let's see where the bad guys are hiding."

"Dagger One, Skyfall. We copy. We don't see anything from up here, but here's the feed."

A window opened against her awareness, small enough not to obscure her view forward, large enough to give considerable detail to an elaborate, three-dimensional map of the Dojinko region. Compiled from data picked up both in orbit and from high-flying, teleoperated drones, the image gave her an eye-in-the-sky false-color view of the landscape that included land forms and vegetation, artificial structures, and the heat and neutrino sources that might be enemy vehicles. She could clearly see the eight Confederation warstriders like tiny, glowing toys spread out along the crest of the ridge, could see the individual buildings of the base nestled into the valley two kilometers away. There was no sign, however, of hidden or camouflaged warstriders in the forest nearby.

"Maybe they all went inside," Captain Kilroy suggested. "Their neutrino emissions would be masked by the reactor leakage."

"That's a thought, Frank," Katya said. As she shifted her attention back and forth between the map and the actual layout of the terrain around her, she began to think that turning the base into a fortress might have been the Imperials' best tactical choice after all. In the same situation, she would have much preferred leaving a back door for herself, an escape route through difficult terrain, rather than letting herself get shut in within a wall-encircled trap. But if the Imperials were suspicious of the forest, possibly afraid of DalRiss that might still be in the area, and knowing that there was no escape for them into orbit until a relief force showed up . . . yes, they might very well be prepared to hold out for as long as possible inside their base.

"Kilroy's right," she told the others. "Unless they've pulled out and headed for the hills in the last few hours, which I doubt, they're waiting for us inside."

"The base is surrounded by a kill zone," Virginia Halliwell pointed out. "We won't get halfway across before they drop us."

"What do you think, Skipper?" Captain Ward asked. "Maybe we call in a bombardment from orbit?"

"No," Katya said after considering the thought for a moment. "Not when we don't know what's going on in there, or with the DalRiss."

Arguably, that was the worst aspect of this mission. Any combat deployment becomes more and more difficult—and risky—as additional requirements, objectives, and restrictions are added onto the original operational orders. Farstar had the dual objective of neutralizing the Imperial presence on ShraRish and of making peaceful contact with the locals. Since they had no way of knowing how the DalRiss were going to react to a pitched battle right in their own backyard, they would have to proceed carefully, and that would put some fairly serious constraints on what they could and could not do. An assault by warstriders represented one level of threat, while laser bombardment from space represented quite another.

"Well, the first thing to try is to tell them to surrender," Katya said. "Who knows? Maybe we'll get lucky."

"Colonel," Captain Kilroy said. "I'm picking up an accelerated power flow through that nearest gun tower. I think—"

There was a flash on Katya's tactical display as her AI painted the laser pulse in brilliant green light, and vegetation on the hillside thirty meters to Katya's left erupted in a geyser of smoke, steam, and organic debris. Lieutenant Halliwell's Ghostrider, caught at the fringe of the blast, staggered on the uneven ground, desperately attempting to remain standing.

No luck today. "Skyfall, Dagger, we're taking fire from the gun towers!" Shift to tactical. "Dagger, Dagger One, commence fire!"

The thin, white contrails of antiarmor missiles scratched their way into the sky above the base. All along the ridgetop, Confederation warstriders opened fire, loosing volleys of laser and particle beam fire, missiles, and unguided flights of rockets. Within seconds, the entire base was masked behind a thundering, flashing wall of high-flung dirt and smoke. A one-hundred–meter length of the fence disintegrated under that onslaught, as the nearest gun tower took half a dozen direct hits within the space of two seconds. Chunks of fabricrete rained across half a square kilometer; part of the turret, with the twisted barrel of a 103-mm laser still extending from its mount glacis, spun end over end, trailing a long streamer of black smoke. Smoke and nanoaerosol shells burst between the base and the ridge, adding to the impenetrable murk.

The missiles already launched from the base began arching over, seeking targets. Katya sensed the dome of the hivel cannon mounted on her Warlord's back swivel, then fire with a buzz saw rasp of sound, but she kept her attention focused on her tactical deployment display, where the warstriders of First Platoon were picked out in clean, graphic symbols representing the various types of machines in her command. A game . . . a low-res vidsim empty of the emotion of blood and death.

"Laser fire on target sighting only," she ordered. At the moment, there were no ground targets visible, and random laser bursts would be swallowed in the black pall of dirt and smoke screening the base.

But that screening effect worked two ways, which had been part of Katya's plan from the start.

"Section Two, cover us," she ordered. "Section One, with me!"

Breaking from cover, the big command Warlord crested the ridge, then crashed through the ground cover on the opposite slope. Dirt slid and crumbled from beneath the Warlord's broad, duralloy-flanged feet, and Katya could feel Ryan Green struggling to maintain the machine's balance on the uncertain ground. Warheads from the base exploded blindly around her; rockets and missiles that her AI decided were on an intercept course were clawed from the sky by the Warlord's hivel cannon or by bursts of laser fire precisely aimed by Warrant Tech Allen. She felt the Warlord stagger as it hit the bottom of the slope, then recover. More explosions, softer ones, this time, bumped and thudded in front of her, erupting in clouds of dense, low-lying smoke.

"Nano-D!" Green snapped. "Point three-oh and rising!"

"Push through! Kurt! Stand by with the AND dispensers!"

Nano-D, short for nanotech disassemblers, was a relatively new weapon, one suggested by combat with the Xenophobes. Shells and rocket warheads were loaded with nanotech molecules that, when activated by the breaching of the container, were programmed to seek out certain materials, such as the layered duralloy or nanoflage coatings of a warstrider's outer hull, and begin taking it apart, literally atom by atom. As with radiation, exposure was cumulative; concentrations of nano-D higher than .85 or so could strip the outer armor from an undamaged warstrider in five minutes or less.

Anti–nano-D was the logical counterweapon, nanotechnic particles dispensed as a fog over the surface of the warstrider or from shells or battlefield area sprays, programmed to hunt down and neutralize free-floating nano-D.

"AND units charged and ready to go," Allen told her. "I don't want to use it while we're moving."

"Agreed."

"Nano-D at point five-five," Green announced.

Radar showed the buildings of the Imperial base looming close ahead, still masked by the smoke and dust. Allen triggered a salvo of M-21 rockets, firing blindly at the largest radar shadows. Imperial radar painted the Confederation striders in return, then dissolved in the hissing static of broad-band jamming. Visibility on any wavelength was virtually nonexistent.

Explosions mingled with the shouts of Katya's striderjacks over the tactical channel and the shrill blasts of radio noise generated by the fringe effect of particle beams. Lieutenant Hari Sebree's Scoutstrider took a missile hit on its right side, which spun the machine back and gouged a spray of hot shrapnel from its side. Katya's Warlord halted once, swinging out the big left and right arms mounting their ponderous proton accelerators, charged particle guns that could call down a devastating lightning on targets regardless of screening smoke.

The CPGs fired, twin bolts of man-made lightning searing into the smoky gloom. Then the Warlord was advancing again. In another moment the ground beneath Katya's feet was suddenly empty of vegetation . . . and she was smashing her way past a fallen tangle of fence. Dirt and tangled conductor filament gave way to fabricrete pavement, once smooth, now pitted and cratered both by years of acid rain and by the bombardment. They were on the base now; the main building rose three stories tall less than fifty meters ahead.

"Dagger, this is Dagger One! I'm on the objective! Cease fire!"

Did the bombardment slacken a bit? She couldn't tell, and savage detonations continued to slam at her through the boiling murk, most of it friendly fire from Section Two back at Point Alfa. Unfortunately, here inside the smoke, laser communications were useless, save for talking to warstriders a few meters away, and the electromagnetic spectrum was a shrill hiss of static as each side aggressively jammed the other's EM emissions.

Then the bombardment dwindled away to almost nothing. Good. Captain Manton Crane, heading up Section Two, must have called off the bombardment when he'd seen the First Section striders vanishing into the smoke.

"Nano-D's up to point seven-one," Green called.

"Bring her to full stop. Kurt! Let's hose down the outer hull!"

"You got it, Colonel!"

White fog gushed across the warstrider's hull from nozzles embedded in the armor. The nano count fell swiftly.

Peering as far into the screening smoke as her sensors could reach, she recognized where she was . . . just opposite the main entrance to the Imperial base's vehicle bays. The enemy striders might—

Yes! The outer door of the vehicle air lock was sliding open. Black shadows, long-legged and ominous, moved against the blaze of light inside.

"I've got targets!" Katya yelled over the general frequency. A shrill rasp drowned out her voice as Allen discharged the Warlord's two proton cannons. Lightning flared behind the opening door. "Main building! Two . . . make that three Impie striders, coming out now!"

Cannon shells slammed against the hull, and Katya heard metal tearing beneath the crash of the explosions. The Warlord was going down. . . .

Chapter 21

Ten thousand highly trained fighting men are but a milling mob when they're not organized. Proper organization should result in the transmission of the commander's will to each and every person in his command, both by indoctrination and by communication. So organized, a thousand men can conquer the unorganized ten thousand.

—General Holland "Howling Mad" Smith, USMC
During the American landings on Kiska
C.E. 1943

The Kawasaki KY-1001 Katana was one of the best Imperial warstrider designs. Trading speed and maneuverability for armor and firepower, it was a two-slotter massing thirty tons and possessing multiple arms, hull turrets, and hardpoints, deploying a bristling array of rapid-fire cannon, lasers, and missile pods. Though it only weighed half what the RS-64 Warlord did, it was somewhat slower but packed a more impressive punch. As it strutted out of the Imperial base garage, the 50-mm hivel cannon mounted atop its hull continued to slam high-explosive rounds into Katya's warstrider even as the Warlord crashed into the pavement in showering sparks.

Warning discretes flashed across her visual display, and a small, 3-D, wireframe model of the RS-64 showed a brightly winking chain of lights marking primary and secondary damage. More cannon shells tore into the Warlord, exploding along the left arm in a hail of near–point-blank impacts. The big accelerator coils for the left-arm proton gun shredded; then the ball joint for the entire assembly exploded and the arm was torn away. Katya felt it as a hard jolt on her left side.

"Kurt! Hit him, Kurt!"

No response . . . and one of the warning discretes showed a pressure loss to the weapons tech's module. *Kuso!*

Downloading a rapid-fire sequence of commands, Katya shifted full fire control to her own system, then struggled to bring weapons to bear. The Warlord was on its right side, its remaining particle cannon trapped beneath the hull. One of the paired 50-MW lasers extending from the strider's prow like the pincers of some huge insect would bear, however, and she triggered a pulse of coherent light that scraped across the Katana's fuselage in a dazzling sunburst.

The Katana was definitely Imperial Marine; Katya recognized the hull markings and the overall layer of nanoflage that normally showed jet black rather than reflect the surroundings, but which flashed to mirror-bright silver at the touch of a laser. As Katya's beam struck it, it paused in midstride, dipping slightly on its back-canted legs, and pivoted with the suppleness of a living animal to deliver another salvo into her machine. Smoke steamed from a ragged scar across its hull; Katya's laser shot had at least seared some of the nano from its armor, leaving a charred furrow in its wake.

The Katana's primary weapon was a monster 150-MW laser jutting from beneath its hull in a deliberately suggestive mockery of sexual aggressiveness, while two 88-MW lasers were mounted to either side of its hull. All three guns would be ponderously difficult to aim at such close range, but a hit by any of them from ten meters would punch through Katya's armor like a knife through cardboard. The Warlord lurched to the left just as the big laser winked on. Her vision blanked out for a second as secondary sensors went dead and a filter overloaded, but Ryan had the Warlord moving before the enemy gunner could achieve a solid target lock. Katya compensated for the movement of her machine with intuitive grace, then triggered both bow lasers a second time, aiming for the damaged patch. Metal flared a dazzling white, then boiled away, leaving a gaping crater and an exposed tangle of dripping, sparking wires and power cables.

The Katana staggered and nearly fell, the main laser comically drooping as its hydraulics failed. A triplet of laser beams from Halliwell's Scoutstrider flashed across the Japanese machine, adding to the destruction. As the Warlord rose to its feet, the aim point of the Mark III weapons pod slung from its belly dropped across the target. Katya adjusted the aim, targeting the smoldering scar on the Katana's hull, then triggered a full, rapid-fire salvo of M-21 rockets.

At a range of less than ten meters, the rockets hammered into the Katana, one on the fiery tail of the next. The chain of detonations tore out the Imperial strider's exposed electronics, disemboweling the machine, then opening the fuselage from front to rear like the action of an enormous zipper. A lesser explosion barked, followed by the flutter of a hull panel blown away. One of the Katana's two crewmen had just ejected—the pilot, she thought—an instant ahead of a triple pulse of savage, internal explosions that blew the machine's fuselage apart.

There wasn't enough oxygen in the ShraRish atmosphere to support more than a smoldering fire, but the blast-savaged hull slumped between the still-upright legs, smoking furiously. Katya pulled a swift check of her Warlord's systems. Power was down by thirty-one percent, all left-arm systems were out—no surprises there—and one of her three pairs of gyros was threatening failure. ICS with Kurt Allen was down and she couldn't tell whether the weapons tech was alive or dead. Her ICS linkage with Ryan Green was also out, but the pilot appeared to be alive still, his life support intact. To simplify controlling the Warlord, Katya switched all command and control functions to her own system. That would isolate Allen, now a helpless observer, but she couldn't afford the confusion that would be raised with trying to move and fight the big Warlord without full internal communications.

Assassin's Blade was hurt, but things weren't as bad as they could easily have been; the Warlord had been hit hard but was still in action. The same, apparently, could be said of both Halliwell's and Sebree's machines.

Other warstriders from Katya's section were passing her now to left and right. She'd been so focused on the immediate threat of the advancing Katana, she'd lost track of the other Imperial machines, but one of them, a KY-1180 Tachi, had been caught in a cross fire from Kilroy's Manta and Sub-lieutenant Jesse Callahan's little Ares-12 Swiftstrider. The Tachi's low, dorsal turret mounting twin 88-MW lasers was carried away in a storm of high explosives; one of the Mark III weapons packs mounted above its shoulders rapped out a stutter of machine-gun fire before it, too, was shredded in the high-intensity fire.

A second Tachi tested the waters outside the protective shelter of the base garage, then ducked back as a storm of shells and laser fire snapped and crackled through the air. It looked to Katya as though the Imperials had deliberately opened the large, interior maintenance bay to the outside air. The main doors were doubled, providing an air lock large enough to pass one or two warstriders through to the outside at a time without contaminating the bay area, but someone had thrown open both sets of doors at once, either by mistake or because they'd wanted to get more striders through the door at once. Possibly her CPG shot had taken down a smaller strider. The lights were out inside now, and smoke was boiling out of the darkened entrance.

Outside, laser fire burned and hissed across the pavement from the remaining gun towers, but the rush by the Confederation warstriders had carried them inside the reach of most of the base defenses. Scanning a full three-sixty, Katya could see battle-armored troops scattering this way and that, some carrying weapons, others apparently unarmed. A third Tachi sprinted across the pavement, heading away from the battle in what looked like a blind attempt at escape . . . only to be hit repeatedly by fire from one of the laser towers.

At that moment, Katya knew that there was no carefully prepared Imperial trap, that the enemy was in fact little more than an armed mob. That mob was still dangerous— the damage to her own Warlord certainly attested to that—

but the defense was poorly organized and weak enough that one hard push had all but toppled it completely.

The fleeing Tachi exploded; seconds later, a pair of Confederation missiles slammed into the laser tower, setting off a cascade of savage explosions that burned through the swirling smoke like minor suns in darkness. Another explosion shook the ground, and a communications tower toppled and fell. Abruptly, the hissing static on half of the radio channels cleared, and Katya heard a babble of voices, all in Inglic.

"One-five, One-eight! I got three runners, at two-one-five. Hit 'em!"

"They're down, One-eight."

"Hey, commo's open!"

"Where's Dagger One? I saw her go down!"

"This is Dagger One-one, on the air," Katya announced.

"Colonel! You all right?"

"I'm okay. Listen, people, I think the opposition's going down. If they want to surrender, let them." She shifted frequencies, searching for an unjammed Imperial channel. There was nothing . . . no! There, a voice was barking in *Nihongo*, the words too shrill and quick for Katya to follow but apparently delivered in the clear, without the usual encryption algorithms.

"One-one, this is One-three," Halliwell said on the team's tac channel. "I'm inside the main building. There are some downgrudged Impie striders here, Katanas, Tachis, and Tantos. Some guards and tech types lit out when I came through the wall, but I'm not getting any resistance here."

"Confirmed, One-one," another voice added. "This is Kilroy, One-two, and I'm inside too. I've got people surrendering in here."

"Roger that. Round 'em up and keep 'em quiet. One-five and One-six, get in there and give them support."

"Copy, One-one. We're on our way."

Shifting back to the Japanese channel, Katya downloaded a command to the Warlord's AI to engage a *Nihongo* translation program. The sharp, barking orders in Japanese shifted to Inglic. ". . . fall back and hold your positions!"

"Imperial Commander," Katya snapped, "your position here is hopeless. Cease fire, and have your armed units lay down their weapons."

There was a harsh clatter of noise, and then the channel was again jammed tight. Whoever she'd been eavesdropping on wasn't ready to give up yet, it seemed . . . but it was clear that he was losing control of the battle. A Tanto, a light, nimble Imperial strider, moved into the open and froze in place, its weapons directed at the sky, its hull nanoflage paling to the mottled grays and browns of the metal's natural finish in a gesture of surrender. Half a dozen troops in black combat armor gathered nearby, gloved hands in the air.

"Hey, Colonel? This is Kilroy. Sounds like there's fighting inside the main building. I think we may have a mutiny under way in there."

"Hold position until we have some backup. Dagger Two-one, this is One-one. Do you copy?"

"Two-one copies," Captain Manton Crane, CO of Section Two, said. "Go ahead."

"Bring your people on down, Manny. Watch for leakers and stragglers."

"Roger that. On our way."

With the high-intensity shelling and missile attacks over, the pall of smoke over the Dojinko base began lifting. As Katya stood there on the debris-littered pavement, shafts of dazzling white light slanted through the overcast, lifting the gloom. In seconds, the patches of sunlit ground expanded, and the base stood revealed in a harsh morning light intermittently dimmed by the moving shadows from billowing clouds of smoke. Here and there across the base compound, more and more troops in Imperial armor or light environmental suits were standing up, hands raised in surrender. Occasionally, she caught the crack and hiss of a laser, or the dull thud of an explosive shell or grenade. A few in the Imperial compound, no doubt, would turn out to be fanatical holdouts, willing to die to the last man.

"Hey, Colonel? Sebree here."

"Go ahead, Hari."

"I got a prisoner here. Claims he's head of the base civilian staff, and he wants to talk to you."

"Bring him on through."

Sebree's Scoutstrider emerged from the base vehicle entryway a moment later. A somewhat more humanoid construct than most other warstriders, the RLN-90 Scoutstrider vaguely resembled a squat and headless suit of medieval armor standing three and a half meters tall, save that the right arm usually mounted either a high-speed cannon or a 100-MW laser, and KV-48 weapons packs were set into the blocky, squared-off shoulders. Sebree's battered Scoutstrider had the autocannon option, and as he walked toward Katya he kept the flame-blackened muzzle of that weapon centered on the back of the head of his prisoner.

The man wore a bright yellow environmental suit, a close-fitting garment that offered no armor protection at all, and a goldfish bowl helmet with an attached PLSS, a Portable Life Support System, slung from his shoulder. He kept his gloved hands carefully palm down atop the helmet.

Katya checked the local nano-D contamination and saw that it was down to about .2, low enough that unarmored humans would be in no danger in the area, at least not without an exposure time of several hours at least.

"You are the commander of the Confederation force?" the man asked, speaking passable Inglic. His helmet electronics broadcast his voice through external speakers in his suit, and Katya's hull sensors carried the words to her. "Please, help us! They've gone crazy in there!"

"Help you how? Who's gone crazy?"

"*Chusa* Kosaka, the marine commander. He's been shooting those of us who were trying to surrender!"

"And you are? . . ."

"Dr. Mitsukuni Ozaki. I am chief of . . . how would you say? Department of *Gengo-gaku* . . ."

Katya repeated the phrase through the language program. "Linguistics?"

"Exactly. Linguistic Department, Imperial Alyan Mission. Ozaki has ordered his marines to kill all the civilians! . . ."

"You have a link interface in that suit you're wearing?"

Ozaki held up his left hand, showing the cross-hatching of contact circuitry embedded in the palm of his glove. Katya focused her thoughts, and a panel set into the left leg of the Warlord a meter and a half off the ground slid open. It was one of several interface access ports on the machine, used for downloading new programs through direct interface with maintenance AIs, but it could also be used to pass data directly from cephlink-equipped personnel to the warstrider's systems.

"Show me," she said, advancing one step.

The man started and took a quick step back, nearly colliding with the muzzle of Sebree's gun, and Katya realized her movement had scared him. The Warlord stood over five meters tall, towering above the lone man, and even with the left arm missing it must present a terrifying aspect. The damage, in fact, might well enhance its nightmarish look; Katya had momentarily forgotten what she must look like from the linguist's point of view.

"It'll be okay, Dr. Ozaki," she said. "Interface with me."

"*Arigato gozaimasu,*" the man said, lapsing into *Nihongo*. "Thank you!" He moved forward and placed his hand against the interface.

"Colonel," Sebree said uncertainly. "Do you think that's a good idea?"

There was a danger of sabotage, that Ozaki had been primed with an AI-killing virus with or without his knowledge, but there was no time for less direct measures. Katya opened her own link and felt the trickle of data coming through from the man's cephlink RAM.

A three-dimensional map of the Imperial base floated in her mind, rotating as she examined it. The layout was identical to that provided by Dev after his capture of the *Kasuga Maru*, though some of the rooms appeared to have different functions now. One room, a barracks or dormitory area on the second level, was highlighted.

"That's where they had most of the civilians locked up," Ozaki explained. "A few of us were in ops and were able to escape. But they're going to kill the others!"

"We'll see what we can do, Doctor," she said. It wouldn't be easy. Warstriders were designed for combat in the open, not inside buildings, however large or elaborate. "Hari? Put him someplace safe." Turning her attention to the outside of the main building, she compared the structure with the diagram. That barracks area should be about *there*. . . .

"Callahan! Langley!" Katya rasped, directing the call to a pair of nearby Swiftstriders. "With me!"

She plunged ahead into the main building's open equipment bay. The brilliant lights were off now, the building's main power feeds cut, and the interior was cave-dark, illuminated only by the shifting patterns of light and shadow thrown by the high-intensity lamps mounted on the striders' hulls. Her own lights illuminated tangled pipes and cables on walls and overhead, the crisscross steelwork of maintenance gantries, the menacing but unmoving forms of Imperial warstriders laid up for repair or service. The smoking wreckage of a Tachi lay in one corner; nearby, a dozen man-sized shapes in black combat armor sprawled on the duralloy-mesh deck, scythed down by a hivel cannon burst.

A steel stairway rose to a landing halfway up the far wall; a second set of stairs ran along the wall to a second-level doorway on the right. Katya passed the updated map to the Swiftstriders. "Up those stairs," she told them. "Down the corridor at the top, then to the left. Provide cover for the civilian scientists who want to surrender, and take down anyone who tries to stop you. Move it!"

"Right, Colonel."

"Yes, *sir!*"

The two Ares-12 striders mounted the stairs, the steps bending and chirping ominously beneath their weight.

Swiftstriders were lightweight single-slotters, massing less than twelve tons apiece and standing only about three meters tall. Their 18-mm autocannon would be more suitable for the close-up mayhem of warstrider combat inside the confines of a building than, say, Katya's CPG.

In any case, the floors and stairways of this building would never support the Warlord's sixty-ton tread. Dropping her strider into standby mode, she broke linkage.

Lying in the near-darkness of her link slot, she felt a warning shudder of claustrophobia as she shifted this way and that, disconnecting her suit from the strider's life support and donning gloves, facemask, and PLSS pack. With a heady rush of relief, she palmed open the hatch, then scrambled out onto the Warlord's dorsal hull.

Using exterior access jacks, she discovered that both Green and Allen were alive. Kurt Allen emerged from his slot wearing his mask but physically unharmed. He'd been knocked off-line when his linkage systems had failed, and a hit close by his module had depressurized it. His emergency life support gear had saved him, though Katya shuddered at the thought of what he'd gone through, penned up in his black coffin, feeling the strider's movements and unable to tell what was going on outside. As for Ryan Green, his system had been fully operational, though a power failure had killed both his ICS and his comlink circuits, leaving him unable to talk to anyone.

"You two feel like stretching a bit?" she asked, jerking a thumb at the stairs. "Grab weapons. We're going up there."

Kilroy's LaG-42 Ghostrider advanced on her, its lights glaring eerily through the smoky cavern. "Colonel?" Kilroy's voice boomed from an external speaker. "What the hell are you doing?"

"Leading my unit," she snapped back. She wasn't about to wait around out here while her people finished up the fighting inside the building. "Captain Crane will be here in a minute—"

"He just arrived at the perimeter, Colonel."

"Okay, good. Tell him he's got command until I go back online."

"But sir—"

"Move, damn it!" She grabbed three combat rifles from a hull storage locker and passed two of them to Green and Allen, then checked her own weapon and slapped a full magazine home in the stock receiver. The weapons were Interdynamics PCR-28s, high-velocity rifles firing 4-mm armor-piercing rounds. One mag held two hundred caseless rounds, more, she hoped, than they were likely to need.

She also grabbed hand lights for the three of them. Out here, without a linkage to the Warlord's night- and fog-piercing senses, it was dark. She made her way down the footrails set into the side of the Warlord's leg, dropped the final meter to the ground, then waved to Green and Allen when they landed next to her. "Let's odie, guys."

Turning, Katya led the way toward the stairs.

There are three types of leader: Those who make things happen; those who watch things happen; and those who wonder what happened.

—American military saying
Mid–twentieth century

The two Swiftstriders had left the stairway all but impassable to humans on foot, and the door at the top looked like it had been smashed in by a battering ram. Air was still escaping through the opening; with an internal pressure a third higher than that of the native ShraRish atmosphere, air inside the building was now blasting into the maintenance bay with a gale-force wind. Katya and the others leaned into the howling storm and pushed their way in, taking care not to tear their suits on the jagged edges of the door.

Once inside and on the second level, it was easy enough to follow the trail left by the two Swiftstriders. One wall of the corridor had been chewed open by a burst of automatic cannon fire; several Imperial Marines in full *do* armor had been standing in front of that wall, but it was impossible now to tell how many there'd been. The sound of high-speed cannon fire, a deep-throated *bam-bam-bam*, echoed through the dark corridors. The three striderjacks, now temporarily demoted to the status of legger infantry, picked their way past steaming pools of blood and less-identifiable body fragments, then broke into a run.

The battle was over by the time they got there . . . which was probably fortunate for the three of them, Katya thought later. Wearing nothing but skin-tight survival suits, masks, and goggles, they would not have lasted long in a stand-up fight with armored marines. Still, Katya was glad they'd come, for when they burst into the barracks, they were confronted with a churning mob of terrified men.

The two Swiftstriders were there, their legs folded almost double in the close confines, their dorsal hulls brushing against the ceiling. Several marines lay dead outside the smashed-in door, and several more lay on the floor inside. Others stood with their hands raised, automatic weapons and lasers scattered about at their feet. The civilians, though, were on the verge of panic. Someone was shrieking in agony. It was pitch black inside the barracks, save for the warstriders' lights, and somewhere in the distance an alarm was shrilling, warning of pressure-wall breach and air loss.

"*Hidoi koto wa shi masen!*" Katya yelled, her voice muffled by her face mask, but still intelligible. "You will not be hurt!" Her spoken *Nihongo* was limited, rusty, and carried an atrocious accent, but she had enough of the language loaded in her personal RAM to make herself understood. "Listen to me! There are masks and air tanks in emergency equipment lockers in the passageway. File out of the room one at a time, get breathing gear, and proceed to the building's maintenance bay. Do not run. There is plenty of time. . . ."

Somehow, order was restored. The sight of the two warstriders looming through the shattered door had been, if anything, more terrifying to the civilian scientists and technicians than the appearance of the marines with orders to kill them. Having someone in human shape there, shouting orders and pointing the way with hand lights, was enough to stop the panic before it overwhelmed reason. There was plenty of time. It would take some hours for the air pressure inside the base to equalize with the pressure outside, and only then would enough of the native ShraRish atmosphere, with its sulfurous gases and dangerously high levels of CO_2, mingle with the air inside in quantities enough to pose a threat to people without masks.

Within an hour, the entire base was secure. *Chusa* Kosaka was found in the control center, dead by his own hand, and the last of the surviving holdouts among the marines inside the main building had thrown down their weapons and emerged with upraised hands. Twelve more of Katya's people had disembarked from their striders and, armed with hand lasers or PCRs, made their way through the various base structures on foot. They found a total of twenty-one of the civilian personnel dead, five of them in Ops, the rest in the barracks, but another sixty-five were still alive. Those survivors greeted the Confederation troops with that wild and somewhat embarrassing enthusiasm normally reserved for saviors and liberators. A total of over two hundred military officers and enlisted personnel had been captured as well. These were disarmed and locked inside an empty storage dome until more troops could arrive to help handle them.

The Confederation striders reported in one by one. Only three—hers, Halliwell's, and Sebree's—had been damaged, and there'd been not a single casualty in her team. Not bad, considering they'd just violated one of the oldest precepts of warfare by carrying out a frontal assault on a prepared enemy position.

Katya was convinced there'd been no other way to do it, given the limitations of the situation. She'd gone into this fearing a casualty rate of forty percent or more, though, and it could have been *lots* worse had the enemy been organized enough to put up a real fight.

She was pretty sure that the battle with the Imperials had been the easy part of the mission. Disciplined and well-organized troops nearly always won against rabble, and the Imperials had been rabble, fighting among themselves, lacking morale, and almost totally without leadership. The question they should be asking themselves, she thought, was what had gone so wrong that Imperial Marines had become rabble?

It was entirely possible, even probable, that establishing peaceful contact with the DalRiss would prove to be more challenging by far.

Hours later, power had been restored, the air leaks stopped, and the environmental systems set to full capacity, purging the buildings of every lingering trace of the local atmosphere. Soon, personnel could remove their masks and breathing gear or park their striders inside the maintenance bay and at last unjack and unseal from their duralloy mounts.

Katya, however, was within a virtual reality created by the base AI. "As near as we can tell," she told Dev as she wrapped up her after-action report, "all Imperial personnel on the planet have been accounted for. So far, we've been receiving nothing but cooperation from the civilians. I gather they've been more or less prisoners here ever since the DalRiss attack."

The ViRcom simulation had placed the two of them together in a richly furnished room with oriental decor and a view of a Zen temple's rock garden through an open door. Birds were singing outside . . . at least, Katya thought they were birds, though she'd never seen one alive. The war, the savagery of that short, sharp fight, seemed a million light-years distant.

"But why were the marines killing the techies?" Dev wanted to know.

"I think it was an abortive mutiny. I gather that most of the scientists and other civilians wanted to surrender as soon as they heard Confederation striders were on the surface. Kosaka wouldn't let them, and so some of the techs grabbed weapons and tried to take over Ops. Five civilians were killed there, and Kosaka gave orders to the marines to go ahead and shoot the rest. That's what they were doing when Lieutenants Langley and Callahan smashed through the door."

"They weren't part of some kind of secret program, then? Something Kosaka didn't want them to tell us?"

"I don't think so. Anything having to do with DalRiss contact is probably classified secret, of course, but there's not really that much to know. In fact, according to Dr. Ozaki, the Imperials haven't had any direct contact with the DalRiss since the attack, and that was over eight months ago."

"What, none at all? In eight months?"

"The Imperials have pretty much stayed indoors, trying to keep out of sight until they got some kind of definitive word from Earth. I have the feeling that they've been terrified of the DalRiss. They still don't know why the locals attacked them in the first place."

"They have no idea?"

"None at all. One day, everything was fine. The next, an entire DalRiss city was smashing through the fence. Damage was pretty bad, as we surmised from the orbital scans, though the main building wasn't touched. Kosaka didn't do a thing afterward. He just hunkered down to wait."

"I'd feel happier knowing just what it was they did to make the locals mad enough to attack them."

"Believe me," Katya said, "so would I. But Ozaki told me they haven't seen even one DalRiss since the attack eight months ago."

Dev considered this for a moment. "Okay," he said. "Sit tight and stay alert. Ground troops and more warstriders will be down soon."

"Dev, I'd like to at least put some patrols out. Nothing aggressive. I just want to know if the DalRiss are close by. I . . . I have a feeling that they are."

"You saw something?"

"No. It may just be intuition." She smiled. "Or nerves. But I'm pretty sure that nothing happens in these forests that the DalRiss don't learn about sooner or later."

"Um. Good point. We don't now how far their symbiosis goes, do we? It might extend to every life-form on the planet. Watch yourself, Kat, and don't go picking any flowers."

"There aren't any flowers to pick. I'm not sure how plants reproduce here, but apparently it's not by pollination." She frowned. "When we landed, we did trample quite a few plants . . . or whatever the ground cover here is. There's no way to avoid it, really."

"Come to think of it, I doubt that will upset the DalRiss," Dev said. "Their buildings trample ten-meter-wide swaths when they move. My read on it is that they don't have any particular taboo against killing lower life forms. They *use* them, in very direct and pragmatic ways. That would fit with the notion that all or most of the life down there was originally created, or at least heavily reworked, by them."

"Good. I was half-afraid we were up against radical Greenies, here. Even if the plant life is pink and orange instead of green."

"So far as your idea about putting out patrols—your people can be trusted?"

"They're good people, Dev. The best."

"I'll leave it to your judgment. Just don't shoot a DalRiss— or one of their damned walking buildings—by accident." He paused. "Oh, and Katya?"

"Yes?"

"That was a good job you pulled down there today."

She shrugged. "Like I said, I have good people. And the opposition was pretty disorganized."

"You carried out a well-coordinated and decisive assault in the face of heavy numbers against a fortified position. Your fast action probably saved the lives of a lot of civilians. That was great work, Katya. Real hero stuff, especially the way you charged in there to stop the massacre of the civilians, and I'll see to it that you get full credit for it."

His praise was warming. "I . . . don't feel very heroic." In fact, she felt quite the opposite. Her wild charge on the Imperial defenses could so easily have gone wrong. Now that the battle was over, she felt weak, drained of strength and of emotion. It was often this way for her after combat, and she knew the best way through it was to keep herself busy. There was certainly enough to do.

"I shouldn't have to remind you, though," Dev continued, "that a colonel's place is not running around in a firefight wearing nothing but a skinsuit and mask."

"I couldn't very well sit there in a crippled warstrider and just do nothing," she replied, a little stiffly. "And the two Ares-12s might have turned out to be too clumsy to use inside the building." She shrugged. "It worked out okay."

"Maybe. In future, Colonel, you will stay where you belong, buttoned up inside your command strider directing the overall battle. Understand?"

"Yes," she said evenly, holding her temper. "I do."

"Good. That's all I have to say right now. I'll talk to you later."

He dropped out of the linkage, leaving Katya alone. She disengaged and a moment later stepped out of the ViRcom module in Kasuko's office. The air still held a trace of the rotten-egg stink of hydrogen sulfide, lingering despite the best efforts of the building's environmental system.

She found herself teetering between conflicting emotions. It wasn't the rather mild ass-chewing she'd just received. Dev's criticism had been right on target. She'd bitten down hard on the ass of more than one cocky young striderjack who'd wandered off-line from where a strict assessment of his military duties said he ought to be; more than once, that cocky young striderjack had been Dev Cameron, back when he'd been a newbie in her platoon.

No, her growing fear had more to do with the subtle change in Dev's manner toward her. Years ago, she'd been the senior officer, he the junior. Later, especially when he had returned to almost exclusively naval service while she'd continued jacking warstriders, the two of them had been more or less equal in rank and in command responsibility, but in widely differing spheres.

Technically, the two of them shared command of Operation Farstar, with him responsible for the space-naval aspect of the expedition while she bossed the ground forces. Technically, too, his rank of commodore gave him the final say if they disagreed on some point of strategy or diplomacy; no military unit could afford the luxury of a democracy in its command structure, and some one individual had to be clearly and definitely in command.

But she was feeling more and more the growing distance between them. It was hard to put her finger on any one thing that was wrong. Oh, there'd been the nightmare back at Herakles, of course, and all that he'd told her about his battles with his own, private demons, but he'd done nothing wrong enough to warrant mention in an official report. Still, her worry for him had steadily progressed to a gnawing, trapped-animal fear. Why, Dev had actually called her *colonel* during a private ViRcom exchange, and both his praise and his reprimand had been delivered with the sure and detached formality of a senior officer addressing a junior. She was still hoping for a chance to continue the discussion they'd begun in space, but for the foreseeable future, he would be in orbit while she was on ShraRish. For now, at least, it was better to try to ignore the change she saw in the man and concentrate on the business of contacting the DalRiss.

She made her way down from Ops to the maintenance bay, which, like the rest of the building, had been sealed off and cleared of contaminated air, flushed with nitrogen from the base's reserves, then brought to standard temperature and pressure with the rest of the facility. Both sets of main doors had been closed, restoring their air lock function. Inside the bay, any lingering traces of ShraRishan atmosphere were masked by the sharper stink of smoldering wreckage—rubber and plastic, steel and duralloy.

Assassin's Blade rested in one of the service gantries, the gaping wound in its left shoulder where the arm had been torn away spilling a tangle of half-melted wires, cables, and control circuitry. It would be awhile before the big RS-64 was fit for service again.

Carefully picking her way down the strider-warped steps of the stairway, she dropped onto the metal grating of the deck and strode toward a group of eight or ten striderjacks standing near the *Blade*. One of them saw her approaching and nudged one of the others. A second later, and they all were cheering, thrusting clenched fists in the air and calling her name. "*Ka*tya! *Ka*tya!" Others in the maintenance bay took up the chant. For a moment, embarrassment warmed Katya's face and she wanted to turn and leave. Then a surge of pride kicked in . . . pride not in herself so much as in these people.

Her people.

"C'mon, c'mon," she called, yelling to make herself heard. "As you were!" She caught one of the striderjacks with her eyes. "Callahan! I need a strider. What's available?"

Sublieutenant Jesse Callahan pointed toward a pair of machines standing empty and powered-down to either side of the maintenance bay door, a LaG-42 Ghostrider and an Ares-12 Swiftstrider. "Those two are free, Colonel." He looked eager. "Where you goin', sir? Need a number two?"

"No, take me!" another called.

"I'll go!"

"Negative," Katya told them. "I'm just going out on a circuit of the base. You all carry on here. That your Swiftie, Callahan?"

"Yessir."

"I'm going to borrow it for a bit, if you don't mind."

"*Kuso*, no prob—I mean, sure, Colonel!" His face lit with pleasure. "Help yourself!"

Callahan's Swiftstrider was nicknamed *Longlegs*, and its nose art—surprisingly chaste for the art form—portrayed a woman with long, bare legs but otherwise fully clothed. It took Katya about fifteen minutes to set the Ares-12's AI to her cephlink and brain activity, with the computer asking questions or telling her to visualize certain images while it calibrated the linkage to her specs. At last, though, the full linkage engaged. Katya brought the power up full, took an experimental step forward, then swung to face the air lock doors. "Ops, this is Dagger One," she said over the tactical channel. "I'm going out."

"Anything wrong, Colonel?" Crane's voice shot back.

"Not a thing, Captain. I just want to run a quick visual check on the perimeter."

"How's your ammo?"

She'd already checked. "About half, and full power on the lasers. All systems read tight and hot."

"Opening up. Keep your channel open, Colonel, and don't get too far out."

"Will do, Captain. Thanks."

Moments later, she was outside again. Several Confederation striders were already outside, keeping watch. She ignored them, setting the Ares-12 in motion toward the tumbled-down eastern fence.

She was not going to sit and brood about Dev Cameron. Impulsively, she wanted to *do* something, and this was the one thing that came to mind.

Picking her way with birdlike agility past the fallen fence, Katya stepped into the midst of the ShraRish flora reclaiming the land that once had been the site of a DalRiss city. Beyond the clearing, the forest beckoned.

Katya set her course due east and kept moving.

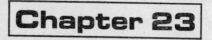

Chapter 23

One key indicator of intelligence must be the ability— and willingness—of A to communicate with B, both in B's language, and within B's cultural and perceptual framework. The converse, expecting B to speak A's language . . . or to understand it as A continues to speak A's language with greater volume and slower speed, is certainly an indicator not of intelligence, but of abject stupidity.

—*Cultures in Conflict*
Sidney Francesco Dawes
C.E. 2449

"The dead things have never ventured so far from the emptiness, Lifemaster." The Watcher tightened its grip on the projecting branch and leaned out farther past the gently twisting trunk of the tree, attempting to follow the progress of the strange shape moving into the forest. The sound combination it used for "dead things" and "emptiness" were virtually identical, and given difference only by the creature's inflection. In its perception, the forest was a sparkling, dancing three-dimensional sea of what humans might have seen as light; the "dead thing" was an empty shape, a hollow vaguely outlined by the ri-glow of life. Beyond, the emptiness was a far vaster void where life had once been, but which now had the shape and flavor of barren rock, a hole in the fabric of life.

"Keep tasting the dead thing," the Lifemaster replied, its voice relayed to the Watcher through a small organ, a living radio growing at the base of its brain. "Tasting," for the DalRiss, meant active sampling through sonar, a high-frequency, sonic probing that yielded volumes of information about the composition and workings of soft-skinned objects but told next to nothing about rocks and other dead things.

"I am tasting, Lifemaster," the Watcher said. *"The dead thing moves but has no taste at all. Do you expect it to change?"*

"We expect nothing. Keep it under observation until we arrive."

"Who comes?"

"A Decider."

"A decision is to be made, then?"

"Only if necessary. But the dead thing's movements suggest that it will be."

The forest was hauntingly beautiful despite the strangeness of the shapes, a shaded place out of the direct blaze of Alya A's light, where the trees, if they could be called that, wove interlacing tendrils overhead in a canopy of red and gold and pink. Here, the fiercest competition for light took place meters above the ground, and the forest floor was almost empty of vegetation. There was a carpet of sorts, like moss, but softer, almost liquid, and glowing the color of ripe grain in a New American field. Some growths were festooned with dripping masses of foam, which appeared to be a life-form in its own right rather than some analog of sap flowing from the trees . . . mildly disgusting until Katya remembered a tiny New American creature that churned small masses of froth to hide itself and its eggs. A particular insect on Earth did much the same.

That link in form carried with it a measure of familiarity. However alien the life, there were certain rules that would be obeyed, certain forms that would be repeated. Unless the DalRiss genengineers had twisted the natural system completely out of shape, predator and prey would establish the same relationships, and the formulas this world's life used to eat and grow and survive and reproduce would all have been familiar to Darwin, however strange the shape of the life itself.

Katya felt out of place here, moving her four-and-a-half–meter duralloy body through that pristine riot of alien vegetation. She'd had to cut out the input from her motion detectors as soon as she'd left the Imperial base, and in this heat her thermal sensors were all but useless. Still, she was aware of what had to be animal life as well. There were . . . things in the trees and plant-clusters around her, small and secretive for the most part, though once something crashed away through the brush in front of her with the noise of a small avalanche.

And there was other noise as well, bombarding her through her external sound pickups. The air around her was filled with a cacophony of high-frequency whistles, chirps, buzzes, and hissing static. She could not tell whether she was listening to the mindless calls of animals, the ranging chirps of sonar . . . or an invitation to stop and take part in some intelligent conversation.

It might also have been a challenge . . . or a warning. She tried not to think about that possibility.

Katya brought the Swiftstrider to a halt well inside the forest and scanned her surroundings carefully across a full 360 degrees. She was surrounded by life here. Save for a nearby outcropping of rock and for the duralloy shell of her warstrider, every visible surface was an organic one, even if some of the textures and surfaces looked like nothing she had ever seen before. This place would do well as a test site.

The experiment was an inherently simple one, concocted after she'd reviewed once more what she knew of the DalRiss.

The key to understanding the DalRiss seemed to be their reverence for life ... or was it simply their fascination? At the Imperial base, however, she'd been struck by the blatant confrontation between the duralloy and fabricrete of the human-built structures and the living ecology that surrounded it. She couldn't help but wonder if the DalRiss attack had somehow been the product of that confrontation, either an admonition to keep off the local equivalent of grass, or an expression of the fear that creatures capable of burying that grass under pavement must be capable of *anything*.

Evidently, the Imperials had been thinking along the same lines, though they hadn't yet dared to do anything about it. According to the personal journal he'd kept in the base computer net, Kosaka had been trapped in an agony of indecision after the DalRiss attack. Unwilling to demand an evacuation—fleeing after that one incident would have resulted in a considerable loss of face—he'd nonetheless feared doing anything that might trigger another assault. He'd not repaired the perimeter fence because some of the civilian scientists had speculated that the DalRiss might be sensitive to the flow of electric current, that they'd therefore deliberately knocked part of the fence down while inflicting only minor damage to other parts of the facility.

Katya was pretty sure now that it hadn't been the fence that had provoked the attack. Indeed, it was likely that the "attack" had been pure accident. The southeastern corner of the Dojinko base happened to lie directly between the former site of the nearby DalRiss city and the immense gathering known as the Migrant Camp a thousand kilometers to the southwest. The DalRiss were blind by human standards, lacking even vestigial eyes. They "saw" using a kind of sonar, like terrestrial bats or dolphins, and possibly through other senses for which humans had no referents.

Was it possible that they'd begun moving toward the Migrant Camp in pursuit of some logic or instinct unknown to the human observers ... and simply blundered into something they hadn't even seen? The mesh of that perimeter fence was composed of extremely fine conducting wires, wires so fine that they might well be below the resolving threshold of the DalRiss senses.

Katya had carried her reasoning farther. Brenda Ortiz had told her once that the DalRiss actually claimed to sense *life*, to be aware of it as humans were aware of light, that they thought of themselves as moving through a three-dimensional sea of interlocking, living systems, from the haze of bacteria adrift in the air to fellow DalRiss. Assuming that was literally true and not an artifact born of differences in language and culture, was it possible that the DalRiss sensed human structures, buildings, say, as dead space, as a kind of emptiness defined only by the life pressing in around it?

Was that how they perceived a warstrider . . . or a human encased in a plastic and ceramic E-suit?

Katya was determined to find out, and she'd come here to do it. Carefully, she studied her met and environmental readouts. The temperature outside was a sultry forty-two Celsius, the humidity stood at seventy percent. The concentration of sulfuric acid was running about eight hundred parts per million, enough to irritate unprotected eyes or mucus membranes over a period of time, but too weak, she was sure, to damage exposed skin. Being caught in the open by a sudden rainstorm would be bad, but she ought to have time to get to cover before she was burned. More dangerous by far, she thought, would be the ultraviolet from the sun. Exposure to Alya A's direct rays would burn unprotected human skin in minutes. This far into the shade of the forest, though, she should be safe enough.

Methodically, she ran through the Swiftstrider's checklists, shutting down systems and putting the machine into a stand-by doze. The communications center she left switched on and primed to relay any incoming messages. Then she broke linkage with it, waking inside the Ares-12's slot. Holding back the familiar, smothering feeling of claustrophobia, she jacked a compatch into her right T-socket. If a radio call came in while she was outside, she would hear it. Then, moving carefully in the padded near-darkness, she donned mask and PLSS pack, then opened the hatch.

Golden light filtered through the forest canopy, bathing her in sauna heat. Swiftly, before she could lose her nerve, she climbed down the rungs set against the strider's armored leg, then stepped off onto mossy ground. She stood there for another moment or two, watching the surrounding woods. Then, taking a deep breath, she began to strip off her clothing.

She left on her mask, of course, which included built-in goggles that protected her eyes both from sulfur compounds in the air and from the high levels of ultraviolet in the light. Her PLSS pack was small and light enough to be worn slung from her left shoulder. She also kept her boots on. She was willing to risk exposing bare skin to the ShraRish atmosphere, but the vegetation was something else. If it was anything like plants on New America or Earth, it would concentrate water in its tissues . . . and possibly other compounds as well, such as the sulfuric acid that tainted everything here. For now, at least, she would keep her feet modestly covered.

Katya draped the suit from one of the ladder rungs on the strider, then moved away from the looming machine. The ground vegetation—might as well call it moss, which it resembled more than not—didn't move and writhe the way some Alyan vegetation in the open did, probably because it received less light in the shade of the forest. Each step, however, launched surges of scarlet color against the gold that flowed out from her feet like ripples in a pond, fading with distance. The rock outcropping was dry and empty of native vegetation. She would wait there for a time and see what happened.

Nudity had never been a requirement for communicating with the DalRiss before, certainly. During previous meetings, she'd usually worn an E-suit with either an air mask or a helmet, and it hadn't seemed to pose any problem for communications, either perceptually or diplomatically.

But if her guess about the DalRiss and the way they perceived humans was right, they would be curious about beings that went about wrapped up in nonliving material. Possibly, humans were only visible as empty shapes against the background of DalRissan life, or as disembodied fragments of living skin when they actually dared to remove helmets or gloves. For their parts, DalRiss never wore clothing, though some had been seen to wear a kind of harness, which was itself a living, gene-crafted organism of some kind.

Given that the trouble with the Imperials almost certainly stemmed from their deliberate separation from the surrounding tapestry of life, they might interpret Katya's gesture as courtesy; at the very least they should be curious enough to initiate a conversation.

And the gesture served a second, conscious purpose, too, a means of showing the DalRiss that she was somehow different from the duralloy-shrouded strangers that had occupied the base before.

At least, that was the idea, but the longer Katya sat on the rock and waited, the more foolish she felt. She had no reason beyond a rather vague intuition to think that any DalRiss might be nearby and watching. Had they been humans, they certainly would have left scouts nearby to keep an eye on the—to them—alien base, but the DalRiss were not human, and what seemed reasonable to Katya might be utterly beyond their ken. Consulting her cephlink for the time, she decided to give them thirty minutes. After that, well, she would have to think of something else.

If she waited much longer than that, she might find herself having to explain what the hell she was doing to whoever came out here looking for her.

Minutes passed, with no response from the woods. The heat was overwhelming, sapping her reserves, draining her as sweat dripped around her mask and trickled down her bare back. She wondered about the ultraviolet here . . . and about the acid in the steamy atmosphere. After a while, the sensitive skin of her breasts began prickling, then itching, enough so that she wondered if the droplets of acid floating in the air were irritating her after all. The itching spread, to shoulders and throat, belly and thighs, and it was all she could do to keep from scratching . . . or giving up and fleeing for the shelter of the warstrider. When she glanced down at herself, though, she saw no redness or other sign of irritation.

In fact, the sheen of sweat covering her entire body was reassuring in a way. Any acidic droplets of water floating in the air would become so diluted when they mingled with the moisture coating her skin that she would never feel it. With that realization, much of the itching faded away, the product, she decided, of an overactive imagination.

When this was over, though, she was *definitely* going to enjoy a long and luxurious shower back at the base.

She'd almost decided it was time to give up when she became aware of the Alyan standing among the dancing shapes of light and shadow, some twenty meters to her right. How long had it been there? Seconds or hours, there was no way to tell. She recognized the usual incarnation of the DalRiss, however, a six-armed starfish body, measuring perhaps three meters from armtip to armtip, but standing on the ends of those arms in a most unstarfishlike way. Sprouting from the top of the body was the complicated cluster of body parts and tentacles that was the Riss portion of the symbiosis.

The joining was complete enough that it looked as though the two life forms were one. Katya was reminded of a download she'd taken once in Earth history describing the arrival on the American continent of European explorers and conquerors. The population of that continent had never seen horses and had imagined the alien soldiers on their strange mounts to be hybrid monsters combining the body parts of men and deer in one enormous creature.

The sheer strangeness of Alyan biology had fooled the first human researchers for some time. The Riss were all but helpless without their mounts, shriveled creatures, all tentacles and spines, bent beneath the weight of that massive, crescent shape of fat and bone. According to Brenda, they'd started off as arboreal parasites infesting various of the semimobile trees of ancient GhegnuRish. Eventually, perhaps two million years before, they'd learned to parasitize the forerunners of the Dal, huge, fully mobile, herd-grouped life forms that combined features of both plants and animals. The Dal had provided more than sources of food to the parasites. Their mobility had given the Riss a far greater range, while their herd instincts had created a sense of social order among creatures that had existed as strictly one-to-a-tree individualists before. Nor had the relationship proven one-sided. As Riss intelligence improved, they learned to guide their herds to good grazing areas and to protect them from a variety of nasty predators. With time, parasitism became true symbiosis.

So far as Katya was concerned, the being before her was a single individual, standing over two meters tall, the upper horn of its bony crescent reaching perhaps half a meter above her eyes. She thought of that crescent as the DalRiss's head, though, as she studied it, she realized it could as easily be the Riss-symbiont's main body, rising from the bristle of spines and tentacles that grew from the horny skin of the Dal-symbiont's back. Two appendages extended from either side of the crescent, like eye stalks . . . or like withered arms?

Analogies with more familiar creatures simply broke down. Those appendages, she knew, were closer to ears in function, serving to catch returning echoes from the creature's sonar broadcasts with the aural equivalent of binocular vision, and as organs of balance.

Katya watched the ungainly head angle toward her slightly, then shift up and down, and had the impression that it was staring at her hard. Despite the DalRiss's nonhuman form and the knowledge that she'd deliberately chosen to meet it this way, the fact was that she felt a brief, sharp pang of embarrassment. Katya was from a culture that did not consider casual nudity to be taboo, but there was something about sitting like that beneath the being's inhuman scrutiny that made her feel uncomfortably vulnerable. Suppressing the feeling, she rose from her perch on the rock and stood so that the DalRiss could scan her from head to toe and back again. For a moment, she imagined that she sensed a faint buzzing, something felt more than heard, like a tickling somewhere deep inside her body as it probed her with focused beams of sound generated within those bony horns, but, once again, that was almost certainly her imagination.

Abruptly, almost as though it had suddenly made up its mind, it started toward her.

The Dal moved with far more grace than such an ungainly-looking beast should have been able to muster, walking on armtips with delicate, lightly flickering steps that kept its spiny body a full meter off the ground. It stopped a short distance in front of her, and the rider leaned forward as if to inspect her more closely. The concave portion of the vertical crescent was lined with leathery folds of skin that reminded Katya vaguely of a face, though there were no eyes or evident facial features. A swelling at the back of the structure, she knew, was the braincase.

Katya remained motionless as it studied her, save to slowly move her arms out from her sides to show that her hands were empty. She didn't know enough about DalRiss protocol or society to know what gesture might be interpreted as friendly, and what might offend.

With surprising flexibility, the Riss-symbiont dipped one tentacle, one more massive than the others, into a kind of iridescently scaled pouch slung from the joint between Dal and

Riss. When it emerged again, something black and glistening hung from the partly coiled tip. Like the unfolding of a pocket telescope, the tentacle lengthened toward her.

Strangeness kept her from recognizing what it was holding at first, but then the shimmering gel moved in the tentacle's hold. A comel! The DalRiss was offering to communicate!

Excitement made Katya's heart leap, and she almost had to sit down again. Somehow, she kept her composure, though, extending her left arm until her fingertips touched the offered comel. The gel quivered at the contact, then rapidly flowed across her hand and up her arm, its touch like living ice. Tar black thinned to translucent gray as the comel, a living, gene-tailored organism, spread itself to paper thinness from her fingers to her elbow.

"You are not like the others." The voice, high-pitched, almost feminine, sounded in Katya's mind, just as if she were receiving a radio call through her jacked-in compatch.

"Thank you," she replied at once, and with considerably more confidence than she felt. "I was hoping you'd notice."

And the two of them began to talk.

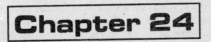

Chapter 24

We take for granted that alien life, when we encounter it, will be the product of a different evolutionary structure than our own. Their bodies, their means of manipulating their environment, even the way they perceive that environment through senses other than the five we take for granted, all will be different.

With different origins, different organs of perception, won't, too, the way they look at the world be different from the way we view it? What new view of the universe might we gain, what new insights into our own

*nature might arise from a free exchange of mutually
alien thoughts and philosophies?*

—*Life in the Universe*
Dr. Taylor Chung
C.E. 2470

Dev stepped off the ascraft's debarkation ramp and into the
steaming, late afternoon heat. Alya A shone low above the
bare-topped ridge to the west, a dazzling, shrunken disk
with the eye-aching brilliance of the flare from a laser
cutting torch. Swiftly, he walked across a narrow stretch
of the rooftop landing apron and into the base receiving
lock, which waited for him with open door. Moments later,
the lock cycled him through, and he was greeted by a small
coterie of Confederation military officers.

Katya was conspicuous by her absence. She was represented, however, by Vic Hagan, her number two, and several
of the Ranger platoon leaders.

"Welcome to ShraRish, Commodore," Hagan said, saluting.
"It's good to see you again."

"Thank you, Vic. Where's—"

"Ah, the colonel's waiting for you in her office, Commodore. She sends her regrets, but she's unable to receive you
formally just now."

"*Kuso!* Since when do I require a formal reception?"

Hagan gestured at the receiving area, where a number
of Rangers were at work unloading supplies brought down
aboard Dev's ascraft. "It's just that she felt it would be more
appropriate for her to see you in a less public area."

"I don't understand."

"I think you will when you see her. Would you like to talk
to her now, or meet with the members of the science team
first?"

"I think I'd better see Katya." It certainly wouldn't
do to have the expeditionary force's two senior people
feuding.

"Very well. If you'd care to come with me, sir?"

Dev hesitated, then nodded. He was still sensing the distance
between himself and people who'd once been close friends,
comrades. Worse, he had the feeling that he was the source of
that distance. How many times, recently, had he misunderstood

something one of his people was trying to tell him? The trouble wasn't with them, but with him.

And now, there was this argument with Katya.

During their last ViRcom exchange, he'd tried to catch some trace of sarcasm in her voice, or some hint of anger, but he'd detected only a neutral, slightly chilly formality, and he'd not expected her to give him an official snub upon his arrival. The ViRcom session before that had not been pleasant, a disagreement that had not degenerated into an out-and-out fight only because he'd ended up pulling rank.

Well, he thought ruefully, he'd been the one to start it by scolding her for what he'd called her "nullheaded, exhibitionist stunt" and telling her that she could have gotten herself killed. She'd bristled, then rather sharply reminded him that *she* was in command of ground operations, and that she had simply exercised her best judgment in arranging, as quickly as possible, direct communications with the DalRiss Collective.

The worst of it was, she was right. He'd gone into this project assuming that it might be weeks before they could arrange a meeting with the DalRiss, and that it might prove impossible to convince them that the Confederation was substantively different in their philosophy than the Empire.

And Katya had managed to do both within a few hours of her victory over the Imperial ground forces, simply by wandering off alone into the woods and stripping herself down. God, what had she been thinking of? There were still so many unknowns, so many complete blanks in the human understanding of this environment, this alien ecology. She could have been horribly burned . . . or killed by some quirk of the local ecosystem that no human yet even knew existed. Send an alien research team to Earth; put them down at some random point on the surface. How long would it take them to discover rattlesnakes or liver flukes, toxic decon dumps or the Uralsk meltdown site, high-speed maglev traffic or tidal surges during a storm in Florida? And Earth was a tame place compared to ShraRish. Most natural predators were extinct, most hazards man-made.

Come to think of it, the same could be said of ShraRish, since all of the local biology appeared to be more or less artificial. Besides, most native life wouldn't find a human appetizing, any more than a liver fluke would be able to parasitize an Alyan.

But still, there were so damned *many* unknowns. . . .

The farther Dev walked into the facility, the angrier he got. Who did Katya think she was, pulling a stunt like that . . . then grandstanding his arrival on base, sending her number two to meet him. She could be cold as an ammonia glacier when he saw her, but damn it, he was going to tell her what he thought. Let her be as cold or as officiously formal as she liked. He was going to give her one hell of a lecture. . . .

"She took over Kosaka's office," Hagan said as they walked into an outer work area, where several officers lay in open ViRcom modules, jacked into the base AI or to remotes in the field. He gestured toward an inner office door. "This is it, sir. She knows you're coming. I'll wait out here."

Dev walked up to the door, which dissolved as he approached.

"Hello, Dev," Katya said, smiling a bit ruefully as he stepped inside and the door sealed at his back. "No virtual reality to hide behind this time, huh?"

Dev tried to suppress his shock but didn't entirely succeed. Katya's naturist excursion had exacted a price, one that hadn't been visible during their ViRcom exchanges. Alya A radiated much of its energy in the ultraviolet, and the ShraRish atmosphere, though it did possess a substantial ozone layer, was only three-quarters as thick as Earth's. Even though she'd insisted that she'd been careful to find a well-shaded patch of deep woods for her meeting with the DalRiss, enough ultraviolet had been mixed with the visible sunlight scattering through the forest canopy to give her a savage sunburn.

She stood there naked. The skin that had been covered by her air mask, PLSS strap, and boots stood out startlingly white against the flaming, blistered scarlet of her burn, a color mottled in various places by the ugly white patches where dead skin was already peeling away.

"Lovely, huh?" she asked, spreading her arms and looking down at herself. She grinned as she looked up again, meeting his eyes. "Close your mouth, Dev. You'll inhale more floating shreds of charred epidermis than are good for you."

The lecture he'd been rehearsing was forgotten. "Good God, Katya! Are you all right?"

She gave a small grimace. "Nanomeds are taking care of it fine," she told him. "It doesn't hurt much at all now."

"That's sunburn?"

She nodded. "Exposure to the atmosphere didn't hurt me at all. It was just uncomfortable, mostly because of the heat. But there was enough UV in the light to fry me in, oh, less than an hour."

"Damn it, Katya. You could have—"

"First- and second-degree burns over ninety percent of my body, Dev. *Believe* me, I know. The somatechs told me in no uncertain terms that without the medical nano I would have been dead. As it was, I was in shock, only half conscious, by the time I got my strider back to the base. They had to come in and peel me out of the slot, and I think I left half of my skin on the couch. Anyway, I'll have a complete new skin in another couple of days." She plucked gingerly at a flaking bit of skin on her shoulder. "In the meantime, I'm shedding a lot . . . and it's damned irritating wearing clothes, especially those goking, snug-fitting skinsuits and shipsuits our nanofactories are programmed to turn out."

"And I was going to chew you out for not meeting me up at the receiving lock. What an idiot! . . ."

"Huh. I'd look mighty dignified greeting you up there like *this*."

"I had no idea. . . ."

"That," she said primly, "is why we have virtual communications. So you can look at my electronic analogue instead of at me. Well? Are you going to say it?"

"Say what?"

" 'I told you so.' "

He shook his head. "I don't think I'd better."

"Wise man." She picked up a filmy length of synthsilk draped over a chair and dropped it again. "I had this run off special, for when I absolutely have to go out in public and don't want to scandalize the sexual conservatives, but it's easier just to go around like this when I can. I hope you don't mind."

"Normally," he said with a half grin, "I'd be delighted, though I have to admit that I don't find overcooked meat all that appetizing. What worries me right now is what kind of precedent you've established. We can't burn ourselves raw every time we want to talk to the DalRiss!"

"Don't worry, we won't have to," she told him. "They've known all along that we need protection from their environment, just as they can't enter ours without becoming uncomfortably cold and sluggish."

"Ah. So we can talk to the DalRiss and still wear E-suits, at least?"

She laughed. "Of course!" She moved her hands, outlining the shape of her breasts and torso without touching the damaged skin. "This was just to get their attention."

"Well, I never thought it would affect other species," he said, grinning at her, "but it certainly gets mine. But since I'm sure you'd rather I didn't do anything about it, just now, I'll forgo any physical demonstrations."

She quirked a smile at him. "Good. I *really* appreciate that, at least until my skin grows back. And even my skin was a small enough price to pay for what we got."

"And that is? . . ."

"A fresh look at the DalRiss, things that the Imperials didn't learn in three years of working with them. Dr. Ozaki and the other Imperial scientists are still in shock, I think. And there's other stuff that the Imperials knew but haven't been sharing with the rest of us. Did you know the DalRiss have a government?"

"I assumed they must have but never heard what it was like."

"Don't make any assumptions about the DalRiss. Nine times out of ten you'll assume wrong. But they do have a social structure that combines government, what for lack of a better name we're calling religion, and music, of all things. They call it something that translates as the Collective."

"Communism?"

"Not quite. Or maybe it's what communism was supposed to be like, before Lenin and Mao and the other early dictators got through with it. There's certainly a sense of everybody working together toward a common good, and a common racial goal, though we haven't quite figured out what that is, yet. The Communists wanted to create the ideal Soviet Man through applied sociology and economics. The DalRiss are moving toward a perfect DalRiss. You've heard the old expression, 'better things through chemistry'?"

"In history sims."

"Well, for the Riss, it's better things through biology."

"Gene tailoring. Nothing new there. Humans have been arguing about the ethics of improving their own species for five hundred years at least."

"That's a very small part of it. The Collective part refers to all life on the planet. The DalRiss see themselves as the caretakers of that life."

"Um. Caretakers for who?"

"That we don't know yet. We're not even sure they have anything like a religion. Some of what they say sounds like belief in spirits or souls. If this was a human culture we were studying, I'd say they worshiped some kind of supreme principle or force of life. But they're not human, and we don't know enough yet to tell whether they're talking about mythology, religion, or a genuine understanding of the physical world that extends into what we would call metaphysics. I'll tell you this much, though. DalRiss biological sciences are going to transform what we think of as biology . . . and probably nanotechnology and our overall view of the physical world as well. Some of what they've been telling us about quantum mechanics, and how belief shapes the universe, rather than the other way around . . ."

Dev shook his head. "Sounds like I have a lot of catching up to do. You've done a great job, Katya. And . . ." He stopped, floundering for the right words.

"And?"

"And I've been the nullhead lately, not you. I'm just realizing that I came down here ready to chew your ass, like you were some shiny-socketed, newbie striderjack fresh out of recruit training. If we can build on what you've accomplished already with the DalRiss, get them to help us, then the Rebellion might actually have a chance. And it'll all be due to you."

Katya flushed at the compliment, her face coloring, her already reddened throat and breasts darkening slightly. "That's nice of you to say that, Dev. But it's been a group effort. You know that as well as I do. Or it *was*. You've been awfully distant lately."

Jerkily, he nodded, accepting the blame and the implied criticism. "You're right, of course. I'm beginning to realize that, too. But . . . it's like I don't fit anymore. I want to, but I simply don't."

"Because of the Xenolink?"

"I think so. It must be. I don't know what else could have . . . changed me so much. Changed the way I think and feel. I've always had some trouble getting close to people. Now, well, it's as though I have nothing in common with them at all."

Katya crossed the room to lay her hand on his shoulder. "Devis, if you can look at me the way I look right now, tatters and all, and still think of, um, that 'physical demonstration' you mentioned a moment ago, I'd say you're still human. And male. And very much a part of the human species."

"I suppose so. It doesn't say anything about my sanity, though."

She arched one eyebrow. "I'll assume that you're not talking about your sanity as it relates to your relationship with *me*. We do still have a relationship, don't we?"

"It's changed."

"I know. People change. It doesn't mean they're . . . turning into something else."

"I've felt like I've been drifting apart from you, too. But . . . well, out of everybody I've ever known, Katya, you're the one I want most to hold on to."

She leaned forward, offering her lips. He kissed her for a long, lingering moment. As he drew back, he found himself thinking that, despite everything, it was Katya who was most helping him cling to his humanity just now. The Xenolink had . . . not created, exactly, but unleashed something inside that vaguely shaped center of existence he thought of as self, something very much larger than he was, and far stronger. It . . . *wanted* things, things that he could not provide.

Katya was damned near his only reason for holding the thing, the monster, at bay.

"I'm glad your lips didn't burn," he told her.

"Let's hear it for Mark VII adjustable polynanoform, full-face breathing masks. We can try something a little closer in another day or two."

"I'm looking forward to it."

"Right now, come on. We have a staff meeting scheduled to fill you in on what's been going on down here. And tomorrow, at first light, a delegation of the DalRiss is going to be here. We all have to meet them."

He eyed her burned skin doubtfully. "That doesn't include you, too, I hope. You can't go out again like *that*."

"I'm afraid it does. But by tomorrow, I ought to be a lot less tender, enough so that I can slip into an E-suit, at least. I'll manage."

"Is this some sort of diplomatic get-together with the DalRiss?"

"More than that. We've told them you were coming. I was right, by the way. They *do* remember you, Dev. You specifically. They're coming tomorrow just to see you."

"Huh? Me? How come?"

"Because you are . . ." She paused, her eyes closed as she pulled an unfamiliar word from her RAM. "You're *Sh'vah*. And because of that, it just could be that you're the real key to their helping us."

"Sorry. That just went . . ." He gestured with his hand, a short, sharp stab past the top of his head. "What's 'shevah'?"

"*Sh'vah*," she corrected him, pronouncing the word with a short, hard glottal stop. "And maybe I'd better let one of them translate that. I'm not sure that I can."

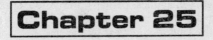

Chapter 25

Ancient Greece was not a single state, but a collection of dozens of tiny and fiercely independent city-states, separated one from the next by the rugged mountains and inlets that characterize that land. It was this very separation, and the resultant cross-fertilization of ideas as trade between alien cultures was established, that led to the flowering of science, art, and culture.

Indeed, some of the most shining examples of Greek scientific thought arose not in Greece proper, but in colonies such as Abdera, where Democritus pondered the atom, and Samos, where Anaximander suggested a scheme that sounds to modern ears startlingly like evolution. Mankind requires diversity, the freedom to experiment, if he is to achieve his full potential. It is natural to wonder if future ages will see similar leaps in the advancement of Mind when the cross-fertilization occurs, not between cities, but between the products of mutually alien evolutions.

—*On Human Freedom*
Travis Sinclair
C.E. 2538

The word *Sh'vah*, it turned out, was the closest pronounceable equivalent available to a three-level stack of hissing and clicking sounds that referred to a particular concept in the Alyan worldview. For the DalRiss, evolution was viewed as a complex and aeons-old dance; the *Sh'vah* was a particular, pivotal organism that evolved by chance or design at the right place and the right time in order to profoundly influence all future evolution. Examples in the evolution of life on Earth might have included the long-necked sauropods of the Jurassic, which had prompted the explosive increase in height of hardwood trees, a kind of evolutionary race between taller and taller dinosaurs, and the taller and taller trees upon which they fed. Better examples, perhaps, were those species of fish first able to use their swim bladders as lungs ... and which opened up the land to conquest by the sea.

By DalRiss standards, Man himself was *Sh'vah* in the Great Dance of Life, having reworked the face of his own world for both good and ill, then providing the technological means for vaulting to other worlds and seeding them with life. And the DalRiss, who'd left few of the life-forms on GhegnuRish as they'd found them, were perhaps the most accomplished dancers of all.

But Dev, it seemed, held a special place within the framework of the DalRiss concept. He had been the first, within the depths of GhegnuRish, to join the separate dances of Naga, DalRiss, and human. It was, Katya had pointed out, not only a singular mark of distinction for Dev. It was the key to the Confederation's hoped-for alliance with the DalRiss.

Dev stood with Katya, Brenda Ortiz, Vic Hagan, and a number of others, both military staffers and civilians, on a plant-covered slope nearly a kilometer from the former Imperial base. Dr. Ozaki, the chief of the Imperial civilian team, was there as well, along with several of his people. The *Nihonjin* scientists were working under Professor Ortiz's direction now, as the expedition tried frantically to catch up with three years of largely classified Imperial research. All of them wore lightweight E-suits and masks for protection from the heat and atmosphere but had bared their left arms to the chilly embrace of DalRiss comels.

The DalRiss, five of them, had met the human party as promised, bringing comels—Translators, as the name was rendered over the organic linkage—with them to the site. The DalRiss stood before them now a few meters away, silent, utterly enigmatic in their lack of readable emotions, face or body expressions, or gestures. Dev had seen DalRiss from close up many times during his first visit to the Alyan system, but each time he met with them he was surprised by their sheer alienness, each time noticing details that he'd missed before, each time having trouble putting the confused tangle of comparisons, thoughts, and impressions that was his perception of the DalRiss into a coherent and meaningful whole. Those slippery, leechlike creatures sliding in and out among the leathery folds of the Riss portion of the body ... he'd never noticed them before. Each the size of a dinner plate, they appeared to nest between the horns of the crescent, and among the wrinkles of loose skin connecting the "head" to the lower body. What were they, parasites on the skin of beings that were themselves parasites? A snatch of doggerel tugged at his memory, something about greater fleas with lesser fleas upon their backs to bite them.

With the DalRiss outlook on life, though, Dev doubted that those organisms were chance infestations of Alyan body lice. More likely they were young ... or, for all he knew, they were the DalRiss equivalent of the handkerchief or the comb.

"We welcome you back to this round of the Great Dance," a voice said in Dev's mind, jerking his attention from the small creatures to the alien symbiosis in its entirety. "It was *daltahng* that you return."

"*Daltahng?*" Involuntarily, he glanced down at the comel glistening on his arm. Was it working?

"The Translator cannot always find exact parallels in the concepts necessary for communication between your people and ours," the voice said. "*Daltahng . . .*" It hesitated, as though searching for another word. "What you call 'destiny' or, possibly, 'fate' is one part of it. What is necessary for the completion of a great task is another. That which is in harmony with the universe is a third."

"*Daltahng* might be easier to say at that," Dev said, smiling behind his mask. He wondered if the DalRiss were even aware of human facial expressions. Probably not, since sound waves couldn't provide detail enough to resolve the upward twitch of the corner of a mouth . . . and they wouldn't know what they were looking at anyway.

He also wondered at the word itself. Was the "dal" part of it a root word, related somehow to the word for the Dal-symbionts? Dev thought that likely, that it might have something to do both with the fact that the Dal gave both direction and power to the otherwise helpless Riss-symbionts, and that the Dal provided completion for the DalRiss organism as a whole. *Daltahng*, indeed. Power-direction-giver, he thought, might be the literal sense of the word, and there would be more and deeper meanings in the fully sounded, native-spoken version of the term.

"It's good to be back," Dev told them. "It's been a long time, and I wasn't sure you'd remember me."

"Longer for us than for you. But we remember. You are *Sh'vah* of our dance with what we once called Chaos."

Chaos was what the DalRiss had called the Naga, which they'd envisioned as a kind of embodiment of death, a reasonable enough view to a civilization that rejoiced in the order, art, and purpose of life. Somehow, Dev found he was able to sense a hidden unfolding of the meanings behind DalRiss terms and concepts, even those that were untranslatable. Was that facility derived somehow from the comel, or was it some new and developing sensibility or sensitivity within himself?

He couldn't tell. The comel itself was quite literally a translator and nothing more, a means of retrieving vocalized thoughts from one, then reshaping and transmitting them to the other. It was composed of little more than modified nervous tissue cloned from Riss brain cells, grown together with the microscopic components of an organic radio transceiver. From what he'd been told when he'd first encountered them three years before, they were grown already programmed for specific languages; those given to humans apparently contained the keys for both *Nihongo* and Inglic, for as the DalRiss spoke, Dev heard the words in Inglic, but with a faint echo in Japanese. Presumably, if he'd been *Nihonjin*, he would have heard the translation in that language instead.

Direct access to Dev's mind was established through his cephlink by way of the circuitry implanted in his left hand and arm, and as he used the comel, he occasionally could feel it drawing on his personal RAM for meanings and definitions. It communicated with the DalRiss over the radio circuit; they heard his vocalized replies through a natural and inborn radio sense, something apparently possessed by many forms of Alyan life. Dev wondered if the DalRiss talked to one another by radio in a kind of natural telepathy. Certainly, their radio links through an active comel gave them considerable information about humans . . . more, Dev was pretty sure, than humans had been able to learn about them.

By far the greatest wonder of the comels, though, had been realized in their use to achieve communication with the Nagas, a one-individual-to-a-world species that didn't even have a spoken language, which thought in terms of *communication* only as it related to wordless exchanges of information between different parts of its single, massive, far-flung body. Somehow, the DalRiss, who'd fought the Nagas on two worlds for millennia, had figured out how to program certain comels to translate Naga emotional content and memories into something humans could make at least fragmentary sense of . . . and human memories into something intelligible to the Naga. Comels had been the key to understanding the Xenophobes, to communicating with them, and to effectively ending what the Nagas had believed to be problems with natural phenomena, and what humans had thought was a forty-three-year-long war with xenophobic aliens.

The technology involved in that development seemed like sheer magic to Dev. Human computers, even the most sophisticated artificial intelligence systems, still needed to be specifically programmed for their tasks, and while they were tremendously flexible, it was a flexibility only within sharply delineated boundaries. Too, how was a comel able to interpret the flicker of electrochemical impulses through the human nervous system?

True, the DalRiss must be masters of deciphering alien neural impulses, learning how to attach meaning to them and even how to control them; somehow, they'd learned to do as much with the Dal millennia ago, when they'd taken the first steps in converting the Dal from food animals to symbiotic partners. Perhaps, for the Riss, reading the signals of an alien nervous system was no more difficult than was puzzling out the meaning of a foreign language for a human equipped with a translation sequence downloaded to his personal RAM. With the right tools, the most formidable language became a simple substitution code, easily deciphered.

The sequence of thoughts, about Nagas, comels, programming, and DalRiss bioengineering techniques, flickered through Dev's mind with bewildering rapidity. The comel, he was certain now, *was* affecting his thoughts, affecting them in ways he'd not experienced before, or, at least, it was affecting him in ways he'd never before noticed. The voice had mentioned that it had been longer for the DalRiss than for Dev since he'd been here, a simple statement of fact for beings who experienced life—metabolic rates, chemical reactions, *thoughts*—faster than was normal for living systems evolved beneath a cooler, less energetic sun. It was as if the pace of his thinking had increased, almost as though he were thinking now at the same speed and level as the DalRiss.

But that was impossible, wasn't it?

"Do you know why we came back?" Dev asked.

"Katya Alessandro told us something about your mission," the DalRiss voice replied. "You had evidence of fighting between us and the humans, the . . ." Again, Dev felt the touch of the comel searching his cephlink RAM. "The Empire," it concluded. "You hoped to gain our help in your war and felt that help might be forthcoming if we were at war with the Empire of *Dai Nihon* as well."

"A logical reasoning sequence," another DalRiss voice said. "In fact, however, we are not at war with them . . . if we understand what you mean by the concept 'war.' We never were."

"You fought a war with the Naga, both here, and on GhegnuRish."

"That was 'war'? We knew it as part of the Dance of Life. You might call it 'survival.' "

"The . . . the buildings of the city that used to be over there," Katya said, pointing back toward the empty field to the east of Dojinko. "They accidentally destroyed part of the Imperial base. That was it, wasn't it? An accident? They didn't even see that the base was standing in their way."

"You humans have the habit of shrouding yourselves in materials invisible to our *ri*-sense. We knew about the things you call buildings, of course. Great, hollow, immobile caves composed of various, artificial *ri*-empty substances. We could sense them as, as hollows within the *Yashra-ri* and avoid them."

Ri was what the DalRiss called life, though the word had so many additional connotations for the Alyans that it was rarely fully translated by the comels. The *Yashra-ri* might have translated as "the Ocean of Life" and referred to the three-dimensional sea of living emanations in which the DalRiss lived and moved. "Empty" things were dead or artificial objects—like man-made buildings, warstriders, or a person in a sealed E-suit.

"We sense your buildings that way," the first DalRiss added, "as we sense you humans when you . . . wear? Yes, wear those garments you call E-suits for protection from our atmosphere. But there was something around your base invisible to us, something charged with electricity. We broke through that barrier by accident and with considerable hurt to several of our own. We were then fired upon . . . without provocation, so far as we could tell."

"Still, that is no reason for us to involve ourselves in your war," a third DalRiss said. "The movement of that city had nothing to do with you or with the Imperials."

"We recognize now the need to employ our Perceivers when dealing with humans," the second voice said. Each voice was distinctive, but Dev was finding it difficult to determine which particular DalRiss was speaking at any given time. The sounds his comel was translating were generated deep within those crescent-shaped heads, and there was no external change in posture or gesture or in the arrangement of those leather folds to suggest which one was making them.

"A Perceiver was present when Katya Alessandro came to us three days ago. By shedding those *ri*-opaque garments, however, it allowed our Watchers, those left to watch the human settlement, to see it as more than emptiness within the *Yashra-ri*. We recognize the physical discomfort that act must have caused. It is why we are here, knowing that you humans wish to participate in our version of the Dance."

"These Perceivers," Brenda put in suddenly. "Are they here now?"

In answer, one of the DalRiss gestured with several of its smaller tentacles, slender threads that quivered and flickered with such energy that it took Dev a moment to realize that the being *was* gesturing, pointing to one of the "parasites" on its body.

There were several different species of smaller life-forms living on the larger, Dev realized now, and possibly some of them *were* combs or baby DalRiss. The particular creature the Riss was pointing to, however, was as wide as Dev's hand and half again longer. Superficially, it resembled an octopus, gray-green mottled skin glistening with some mucuslike secretion, but with five short tentacles instead of eight long ones. Nearly the whole of the upper surface of that body was taken up by a single, external organ very much like a fist-sized eye, one made of some glassy, yellow-translucent stuff and covered over by a clear membrane.

Within the translucence, varying numbers of inky holes opened, drifted, then closed over again, seemingly at random, though there were never fewer than two nor more than six. These, Dev realized, were the multiple pupils of a single eye, their mobility and separation providing excellent depth perception, their numbers permitting greater light-gathering power in low-light conditions. It joined the group, three pupils focusing on Dev as it braced itself on three splayed tentacles. One of the DalRiss stood behind it, a single black tentacle snaking down from atop the Dal-symbiont's back and attaching itself to the creature's head, somewhere behind the eye.

"This is one of our Perceivers," the voice told the humans.

"We first designed them when we realized there were radiations in the natural world that we could not sense directly, but which could potentially carry a great deal of information about the world around us."

"Is it . . . intelligent?" Its strange gaze certainly felt intelligent to Dev.

"Is it self-aware?" Katya added.

"Of course. It must be, to process information which we, the Riss, are not designed to sense. It is what you would call symbiosis, where they feed upon the Riss as the Riss feeds upon them."

"Feeds?" The word held a queasy fascination for Dev. Did the parasite-descended DalRiss see their relationships with all of their created creatures in terms of masters and . . . food?

There was a moment's hesitation, as though the being were reconsidering its words. "A holdover from our past," it said, finally. "You might say instead, 'as the Riss links to them.' "

"Ah."

Still he felt an unpleasant stirring. Man had only recently reached a crossroads of biological development that the Riss had passed millennia before by genengineering artificial intelligence. For a long time, research in this area had been restrained by certain ethical concerns, by the question of whether it was morally right to create a sentient and reasoning being for some particular purpose—as research animal or slave or even as *objet d'art*.

Eventually, though, the power to do a thing had found the will to do it, despite ethical considerations, and the genies had been the result. Mingling various animal and even artificial genes with the human genome had resulted in a number of species, subspecies, and types, from miners and heavy laborers to the startlingly beautiful *ningyo*, the delicate but fully human-looking sex toys that were a mark of distinction among Earth's elite. There were even rumors of sentient beings created as art, living sculptures unable to move, unable even to die, designed only to experience sensations programmed by their designers and to be self-aware. That, for Dev, represented perhaps the fullest possible horror of a technology used without ethical constraint.

Evidently, the DalRiss had passed that point in their technological evolution long ago, for now they incorporated intelligence into many of their biological tools with a casual nonchalance that Dev found chilling. He'd heard, for instance, that the comels were intelligent but not self-aware, a concept he'd found hard to imagine at first until he'd remembered certain human computer systems were designed within the same limitations, and probably for the same reasons.

Other Riss inventions, though, seemed to incorporate both intelligence and self-awareness. The creatures they called "Achievers," for instance, played a role in the DalRiss version of a faster-than-light drive. If what he'd heard was true, they died after completing the task for which they'd been engineered . . . "became empty," as their Riss masters put it. Presumably, the Achievers had also been designed to be content with their deliberately abbreviated lives; they wouldn't feel cheated or mistreated if they'd been made to anticipate the emptiness that ended their existence as the culmination of their lives. "I got us where we were going; now I can die content." Dev had navigated plenty of starships in his day, and the thought gave him a shudder of sympathy.

"The Perceivers opened the sky to the Great Dance," one of the DalRiss was saying. "Without them, the next step in the Dance would be the emptiness that will follow. Instead, we can become Sky Dancers."

"Sky Dancers?" Brenda repeated. She turned to Ozaki, who shrugged and shook his head.

"A few of us take the Great Dance to the stars," the radio voice explained. "Many have already left for our ancestral home. Others will be leaving soon, before emptiness claims our suns."

Several of the humans gasped surprise. "What?" Vic Hagan said sharply.

"Please." Brenda shook her head. "What do you mean, emptiness claims your suns?"

"Emptiness," Dev repeated. Somehow, he'd heard the connotations behind that single word and felt its full meaning. "They're leaving," he told the others. "They're moving their whole ecosystem off world, taking it to the stars."

"Of course," one of the DalRiss said, and its voice sounded almost cheerful. "We'd thought that you humans had remained here to help with this new part of the Dance. That was why the actions of those you call the Imperials seemed so bizarre, why we cut off all contact with them.

"But we still need your help. We've been wondering if that was why you came."

"But why are they leaving?" Ozaki wanted to know. "In three years of study, we'd thought this migration they were talking about had to do with their religion. Or with some obscure use of metaphor."

"It has nothing to do with religion," Dev said bluntly. Carefully, he glanced up toward the eastern sky, where Alya A was an intensely glaring point of light that caused his protective goggles to darken as his head turned that way. "Or with metaphor. They've simply decided to leave before the Alyan suns explode."

Chapter 26

Our G-class sun lies conveniently in the comfort of middle age, with mass enough to keep it on the Main Sequence for another five or six billion years at least. The orange Ks and red-dwarf Ms, less massive stars, are misers, hoarding their much smaller reserves against the cold of the Ultimate Night. Some may be burning unchanged ten or twenty billion years hence.

As for those stars more massive than Sol, the Fs and the still hotter and more spendthrift As, they are wastrels consuming their hydrogen capital at a rate that will leave them bankrupt in a fraction of the time left to Sol. For an A-5, for example, a measly billion years might be extreme old age.

—*The Stars: A Speculative Odyssey*
Dr. Sergei Ulyanov
C.E. 2025

"We do not expect it to happen anytime soon," one of the DalRiss told them, "even by your standards. But by the standards of the Great Dance, it is clear that our next step must be to the sky."

"Our understanding of the physics behind the stellar fusion process is still primitive compared to yours," another said. "We were not even aware of the danger until after our first contacts with humans."

The Alyan suns, younger by far than cooler stars like Sol, must have already reached the point where helium ash was concentrating in their cores. Soon—at least in cosmic terms—that accumulation of helium would force them off the main sequence. Briefly, they would burn hotter but grow so much larger that their surface temperature would drop, and for some millions of years they would shine as red giants before they began their final and inevitable collapse into white dwarfs.

By that time, of course, their respective planetary systems would have been absorbed or charred lifeless. Dev wondered how a race so life-centered as the DalRiss perceived such an ultimate and absolute extinction.

"The DalRiss were most interested in our understandings of physics and cosmology," Ozaki said. "We never stopped to consider that it had an, ah, a practical application for them."

"Evidently it did," Brenda said. "How long do they have?"

Numbers flickered through Dev's awareness, drawn from ephemeral data on the Alyan suns. "There's really no way to come up with an exact figure," he told the others. "Not unless they have more precise data on their stars' neutrino fluxes. It could happen any moment. On the other end of the scale, I'd say that fifty million years is a reasonable upper limit."

"Fifty million years is a long time," Hagan said, "at least for a civilization. And didn't you say these guys think and live faster than we do? Hell, for these guys, fifty million years is *forever*!"

Katya laughed. "I don't know. Hey, we're facing the heat death of the universe in just a hundred billion years or so. We'd better get busy now and figure out where we're going to go when *that* happens!"

"Cute, Katya," Dev said. "But remember that the DalRiss think in terms of the transfiguration of entire species." He hesitated, choosing his words. It was as though he could see DalRiss reasoning, plans tracing particular sets of genes and chromosomes across countless generations. The DalRiss did not have a technically based nanotechnology as the humans did; all of their research and manufacturing on any ultrasmall scale had to be carried out by the *original* nanotech—the biochemistry of cells and enzymes and living systems. With his newly found depth and speed of insight, Dev could see the monumental patience the Alyans needed to carry out even a simple nanotech-scale experiment using tools designed and bred from carefully controlled mutations, which themselves were the products of long, long lines of genetic experimentation, and he felt a surging rush of admiration, even wonder. *Kuso!* Why couldn't Katya and the others see the miracle of it?

"I suspect," he said slowly, "that the DalRiss have research programs extending tens of thousands of years into the future. They may have long-range plans, plans encompassing the creation of new species or the alterations of whole worlds, plans that won't see fruition for millions of years. These people take the long view. To suddenly be told that their suns could grow hot enough to cook them all at any time between tomorrow and a couple of geological ages from now and interrupt everything they've been working on would place a pretty rough strain on any long-range ideas they might have."

The other humans were staring at him. Presumably, the DalRiss were as well, though it was impossible to know for sure where their attentions were directed at any given moment. He spread his hands, pleading. "Good God, people, don't you understand? Don't you *see*? Over the past few million years or so, the Riss have taken over every aspect of their ecosystem, every detail. How many native species are there on New America, Katya? How many on Earth? Not just humans or horses or dogs, but insects, fish, grass, nematodes, plankton, amoeba, bacteria. Hell, even viruses, if for no better reason than that I suspect these people use tailored viruses to transmit genetic information when they're tinkering up a new species. If you assume that all life in a given biome is interdependent with all the rest, if you change even one species, you ultimately change them all. The one thing they can't control, though, is arguably the most important . . . the power plant that keeps the whole system running. If they think in terms of control of their environment, the fact that they can't control their own sun would be intolerable!"

Brenda was first to break the silence. "Frankly, Commodore, we haven't seen any evidence that they control their environment to the degree you suggest. If they were capable of doing what you claim, then surely the Naga wouldn't have posed the threat to them that they did."

"Sure," Hagan said. "They could have introduced a virus that reproduced within Xeno supracells and made them wipe themselves out. Biological warfare. But from what we learned in the first expedition, the DalRiss had been fighting the Xenos for thousands of years. They'd been pushed off GhegnuRish entirely and were on the verge of losing ShraRish too. They needed us to come along and give them a high-tech edge."

"Because," Dev explained, "the Naga live and work and experience on a nanotech scale. If the DalRiss are expert biologists, remember that the Naga are expert chemists ... and when you get down to molecular and submolecular scales, there's no difference whatsoever between the two. I'm guessing, but I would imagine that the DalRiss spent a lot of effort trying to create viral or bacterial weapons for use against the Nagas, and the Nagas just assimilated each weapon and made it harmless ... or else turned it on its creators."

"Dev Cameron shows remarkable intuition," the third DalRiss said, "and an excellent grasp of the nature of our struggle. Few of the weapons we were able to design had any significant effect on the Chaos. A few weakened the enemy, and on numerous occasions we were convinced that we had eradicated the threat. Each time, however, a small reserve of uninfected Naga tissue survived hidden somewhere within the recesses of the planet's crust. Within a few hundreds or thousands of your years, however, they would strike again and with an immunity to the weapons that had stopped them before."

"I submit, Vic," Dev said, "that you compare the scale of their Xeno war with ours. They fought the Nagas on two worlds to a standstill over the course of ... what was it? Ten thousand years? Something like that. At the end of that time, the Nagas had the upper hand on both worlds—they'd won on one and were coming damned close on the other—but that was after ten thousand years. In our case, we'd been fighting the Nagas on six worlds for forty-odd years. We'd lost completely on four of them, and two of those worlds, Herakles and Lung Chi, had significant planetary populations. In all four cases, we'd been smacked right off the planet within one year. *One year!* On Loki, we won . . . or, at least, we think we won. What do you want to bet, though, that there are still isolated bits of viable Xeno cells and nano hidden away 'way down deep, where the nuke penetrators couldn't reach them? The only place we *know* we won is Eridu, and that's because we made friends with the thing instead of trying to kill it!"

"Scary thought," Katya said. She stamped her boot on the ShraRish soil. "That also suggests we didn't win *here* like we thought, either. That the ShraRish Naga will be back someday."

"It is their nature to survive," the first DalRiss said. "And to expand their influence from world to world. Fortunately, we no longer have to fight with them for mastery of the *Yashra-ri.* Though we learned, through a very long process of trial and error, the key to direct communication with the Chaos, it was Dev Cameron who actually made that breakthrough. The . . . the *Naga* of GhegnuRish is now our ally. We will take part of it with us when we carry our Great Dance to the stars."

"I'd think the DalRiss and the Naga would have a lot to offer one another," Dev said.

It was curious. As they'd been talking, he found he was learning how to tell one of the beings from another. He wasn't sure how . . . but there was something about the manner of each as it stood in the semicircle of DalRiss before the human party that communicated itself to him as it spoke. It was like reading the body language of a human during an ordinary conversation, something normally automatic and even unnoticed.

To his considerable surprise, Dev was aware of this accelerated level of communication and understanding with the other humans in the party as well. The facility, he realized now, had been growing for some time but had remained unnoticed behind the churning wall of fear and stress that had occupied more and more of his thoughts over the past months.

He could tell by looking at her, for instance, that Katya was still struggling with the idea that humanity's long war with the Xenophobes had not been won after all. The friendly relations achieved with the Nagas of Eridu and Mu Herculis seemed to guarantee mutually useful cooperation between Man and Naga from now on, but no one who'd spent as many years as Katya had fighting the Xenophobes could shake the feeling that the Xenos still didn't really understand what people were, that human and Naga viewpoints were so mutually alien that a new misunderstanding—and war—were possible at any time. Dev noticed the look Katya exchanged with Hagan, and even through their air masks he could read the new fear that the two of them were sharing. As for Ortiz and Ozaki, they were lost in strangeness, more concerned with the new insights into DalRiss history and biotechnology than with any merely theoretical concern about the Naga.

"We are initiating a new symbiosis," the second DalRiss said. "We have been working closely with the Naga of GhegnuRish, the Naga you first made peaceful contact with, Dev Cameron. It has been induced to bud portions of itself, which we are learning to incorporate into the biological matrix of our space vessels. These buds will serve a wide variety of purposes within the new aspect of the Great Dance, as what you would call the computer network of our ships, as a means for storing and using data, as a means for repairing damage."

"It sounds like we could learn a hell of a lot from all this," Dev said. "I'd like to see how you blend Naga and DalRiss biologies."

"The sharing between two mutually alien *ri* is basic to our philosophy," the third DalRiss said. "The two together accomplish more than either apart." Dev felt the touch of his comel searching for data. "Yes," the DalRiss continued. "You humans call this synergy."

"There could be a tremendous synergy if there was a similar sharing of what you know and what we know," Dev said. "We *need* your help, but there may be much we could offer you in exchange."

"We see one point of philosophy that binds the DalRiss to you humans of the Confederation as opposed to those of the Empire," the first DalRiss said. "We respect diversity, in particular as it applies to the life of a world. But we could argue the need for cultural diversity as well. Just as a large number of interacting species are necessary for the viability and security of an ecosystem, a large number of interacting cultures is important for the life and health of a species."

" 'Interacting cultures,' " Ozaki put in. "Do you mean war?"

"Not at all. War is the attempt by one culture to suppress another, not to encourage its flowering. We refer to the interaction of ideas. Of philosophy. Of science and scientific discoveries. Of the products of research by one group shared with another to the improvement of both."

"Trade," Katya said.

"Trade does not occupy the place in our culture that it seems to hold in yours," the DalRiss told her. "But that, too, would be a factor."

A lot more study was needed on the DalRiss social structure and how it worked, Dev reflected. The Collective appeared to operate without such human social constructs as trade because each individual DalRiss provided for its own needs. Groups of DalRiss worked together on such projects as the creation of a new life-form, but the benefits of those life-forms were available to all.

Trade among humans had begun, it was believed, when agriculture had become so efficient that individual humans could specialize in their work, exchanging such skills as, say, pottery making for a share of the grain grown by the community's farmers. The DalRiss had never needed to specialize to that degree; each Riss fed off his Dal or from the living, mobile plant shell that was its home. The Dal ate the gene-tailored "moss" that covered so much of the open landscape, while DalRiss buildings drew nourishment from sunlight and directly from the ground. Cities were temporary groupings that dissolved when the mineral content of a given area was leached away. Since food and most other necessities were to all intents and purposes free for the taking, the concept of an individual performing work which it then sold to its neighbors appeared never to have taken hold among the DalRiss.

"You of the Confederation seem to share our interest in maintaining a diversity of cultures," the first DalRiss said. "From what we were able to understand in our exchanges with the representatives of the Empire, this is not a philosophy they share. If we were to provide aid to your Confederation in this war, it would be on this philosophical basis."

"After a while I'll recite the Declaration of Reason for you," Dev told them. "It's a statement of what we believe, what we're fighting for. You might be interested in hearing it."

Dev wondered if, when he was crafting that document, Travis Sinclair had known that it would be used to persuade alien listeners of the rightness of the Confederation cause as well as humans. The theme at which that document hammered again and again and again was that humanity, in the variety of the peoples and cultures, races and religions living on the far-scattered worlds of the Hegemony, was too diverse to be ruled by a single government located on far-off Earth. Under Japan's Imperial rule, the very characters of those hundreds of separate peoples were stifled at best, and at worst were twisted into a mocking imitation of the shallow and elitist *Shakai*, the upper-class society of *Dai Nihon*.

If there was any one aspect of Japanese life and culture that singled it out as different among all of the other cultures born of Earth, Dev thought, it was the outward need for conformity. That was not to say that other human cultures didn't from time to time view difference as a disruption of the natural order; Jews, blacks, and the unusually bright or gifted, among many others, all had had reason to fear whatever it was that set them apart from their neighbors at one point or another in the long and often bloody history of Civilization.

But the need to be different, the need to express one's individuality, had long ago become a luxury that the crowded Japanese islands could ill afford.

Each *Nihonjin* thought of him- or herself as an individual, of course—indeed, they were often frustrated by the realization that *gaijin* didn't seem to understand that—but social pressures served to embarrass any Japanese person who stood out within the crowd, especially anybody perceived as unwilling to work for the common good of company, of community, of nation, of race. It was a social emphasis radically different from that of the West, where voluntary cooperation for the common good tended to come behind the needs of the individual.

"Any information on Confederation beliefs would be welcome," the third DalRiss told him. The Perceivers on the Riss-symbiont's body all appeared to have their pupils focused on Dev.

"Then I propose a trade," Dev said. "An exchange of information. I would like to learn more about what you're doing with the GhegnuRish Naga, and these spacecraft you mentioned. Both could have a very direct application in our war with the Imperium. In exchange, one of us will read and explain our Declaration of Reason and answer any questions you may have about why we're fighting to be free of the Empire."

"That seems reasonable, though we don't understand why you expressed it that way. We would have answered your questions without this exchange."

"Perhaps. Consider this another means of learning about us, about how we think."

"For you to learn about the Fleet of the Great Dance," the DalRiss said slowly, "it will be necessary for you to come with us to GhegnuRish. Does this interest you?"

"It certainly does," Katya put in. She glanced at Dev, then looked back to one of the DalRiss . . . not the one that had been speaking, Dev noticed. "We'd like that a lot."

"We certainly would," Dev added. "And we'd like to see how your stardrive works, if that's possible."

"Of course. We will arrange for you to see one of our ships in the company of an expert in directing the Achievers. Also, we will arrange for you to commune with the planetary Naga, which can give you details of our control and communications systems. Perhaps you could make use of some of these ships in your war to good advantage."

Dev started to reply, then stopped, unable to speak, afraid that he was going to reveal the surge of emotion he was feeling. It looked as if everything Farstar had been designed to do was about to be handed him.

Despite that, though, he was anticipating a trip to GhegnuRish with mingled joy and dread. The secret of the DalRiss instantaneous drive might well be the weapon that would make the Confederation victorious.

But at GhegnuRish, he knew, too, he would be facing another planetary Naga. A capricious fate, it seemed, was pressing him hard toward a second Xenolink.

Fate . . . or was it *daltahng*?

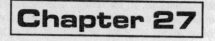

Chapter 27

It has been well established for at least three centuries that humans possess the equivalent of two brains apiece, the left and right hemispheres of their cerebrum. In general, the left side of the brain appears more closely associated with mathematical and analytical abilities, while the right side directs those applications requiring visual-spatial and artistic skills. One possible explanation for differences in individual intelligence, incidentally, involves the number of cross connections within the corpus callosum between these two brains, with a greater degree of cross connectivity being associated both with a smoother overall processing of information and with that curious something-from-nothing spark of creativity known as intuition.

In line with this is a curious datum of comparative anatomy: women, by and large, tend to have a greater number of connections between the two halves of their brain, explaining, possibly, that largely anecdotal phenomenon known as "woman's intuition."

—*The Science of Mind*
Dr. Harvey Carpenter
C.E. 2285

The system of Alya B was much like that of Alya A, a young retinue of worlds circling through a dust- and meteor-choked volume of space centered upon a dazzling, type A star. The fifth world out closely resembled ShraRish in most respects, its land surfaces showing more vacant stretches of lifeless dun and ocher, but tinted here and there with the mottled shades of pink and orange that marked emergent Alyan life. Its seas shone violet and copper-sulfate blue in the hard white light of its sun, just as they did on ShraRish, and the clouds dazzled the electronic eye in swirls of white highlighted in blues and purples.

Eagle had dropped out of K-T space several hundred million kilometers out and approached cautiously. Their informants on ShraRish had indicated that there were no Imperial forces at GhegnuRish, not so much as an orbiting observer station, but Dev still wasn't sure how sophisticated DalRiss technology was, especially in the—to them—new medium of space.

As they neared GhegnuRish, however, his doubts were fading. There were no Imperial ships or stations in the Alya B system, but the region close to the DalRiss homeworld was thick with objects, with *ships*. Over a thousand had been counted by *Eagle*'s AI through the ship's sensor suite, and there were more yet masked by the bulk of the planet.

DalRiss vessels tended to be large, measuring anywhere from five hundred meters—twenty percent longer than *Eagle* herself—to monsters like the starfish shape at the Migrant Camp, two kilometers or more across and massing many millions of tons. Perhaps half were starfish shaped, flat and round, with varying numbers of thick arms; Dev was struck by their outward similarity to the Dal, until he realized— again, that unexpected flash of intuition—that he was looking at genetically altered Dal, enormous life forms grown from the tissues of creatures normally no more than three or four meters across.

The rest were, Dev supposed, descended from the ambulatory house-organisms of the DalRiss, albeit grown enormous. They tended to assume cylindrical, spherical, or flat-headed mushroom shapes, and some, as Dev watched them through *Eagle*'s navsim link, appeared to change shape slowly from one form to another. Though any comparison with human technology was dangerous, he knew, he couldn't help but think of the starfish shapes as the DalRiss equivalent of human military vessels, uniform in appearance, faster, more maneuverable than the others, while the ships grown from buildings were the freighters, the tankers, the heavy-hauler logistical arm of the Alyan fleet.

"Our new friends have been busy," Katya said, linked into the net with Dev. "Do they really intend to abandon both their worlds?"

"I don't think so," Dev told her. "The impression I get when I'm talking to them is that individual death doesn't matter that much to them, that even if they knew precisely when their suns were going to explode, any one of them would just as soon stay and take notes as leave. But they do value, oh, call it experience. Knowledge. Viewpoint, even. They try to save that . . . the way life saves particular combinations of DNA, I suppose."

"You know, Dev, I get the feeling that you get a lot more out of your conversations with them than the rest of us do."

Dev hesitated before answering. Katya had just touched that part of his new self he'd most been questioning during the past few hours.

"I guess I do. But I seem to be getting a lot more out of everything lately."

"It's the Xenolink, isn't it?"

"I . . . I think so. I think it must be." Absently, he reached for a bit of planetary data he knew to be stored in an ephemeris stored in his personal RAM, then realized with a small start that the data was already there in his mind . . . without his having had to frame a coded search request. That sort of thing had been happening more and more lately, as though subprograms were running in his implanted hardware that had been placed there by some unconscious part of himself.

"When I linked with the Naga on Herakles," he went on, thoughtfully, "part of it, about a kilogram of its tissue, entered me, mingled itself with my body. Most of that tissue, I'm pretty sure, was Naga nanotech. Molecule-sized living machines that interact with each other like tiny computers in a very, very large network."

"That's how you shared minds, right?"

"I suppose so, though I'm still not quite sure what 'mind' really is. If you can picture 'mind' as a series of computer programs overlapping one another, running in parallel, yeah. The Naga's programs were definitely mixed up with mine, and I could sense what it was thinking. Well, some of it, anyway. Remember, a planetary Naga masses as much as a small moon. But for a while there, the part that I was relating to and I were . . . joined. Part of the same organism. Or set of nested programs. While I was . . . changed, I sensed, I don't know. A quickening. My thoughts were faster. My time sense was accelerated . . . I think I was processing data as quickly as the Naga. At least, when we shared thoughts, there was no sense of it having to wait for me to catch up. There was no sense of difference at all. We weren't just linked. We were one."

There'd been more besides, things that he still didn't quite dare tell anyone. He'd sensed an actual increase in his intelligence, or possibly it had simply been that the speed and the certainty of . . . call it his *intuition* had increased. The somatic technicians and monitor AIs that had checked him out afterward had speculated that, at least temporarily, there'd been an increase in the number of connections between the left and right hemispheres of his cerebrum through his corpus callosum.

Now, though, Dev was beginning to suspect that the increase had not been temporary. It had taken him this long to arrive at that conclusion, possibly because the connections had been growing throughout these past months, possibly because it had taken him this long to learn—all unconsciously—how the new equipment worked. Had the Naga made permanent, physical changes to his brain during its brief tenancy? Or, after he'd ordered it to withdraw, had it left some small part of itself, perhaps a few million molecule-sized nanobiomachines to continue the work begun by the planetary Naga as a whole?

He was pretty sure that a physical scan of his brain now would reveal what had not been there eight months ago: a host of new connections between the left side and the right. He knew of no other way to account for the leaps of reason and insight, the speed and accuracy of thought, the sudden flashes of information that seemed to drop out of nowhere. In many ways, it was like being constantly linked to an AI, with information available for the asking, though it was not as dependable, and the information it provided was limited to that available to his ordinary human senses.

"At first," he told Katya, "I suspected the comel, thought that it was doing something to me, because it wasn't until I put one on that things started to fall in place for me. Now, though, I'm pretty sure that it was just that the change in me became clearer . . . came into sharper focus, let's say, while I was talking to the DalRiss." The increased level of intuition that allowed him to pick up more of the meaning behind the Alyans' many-leveled speech than was possible for other people had only been revealed when he'd been speaking with them . . . and intuition or no intuition, he still needed a comel to communicate with the Alyans.

"It'll be okay, Dev. I know it will. You must've retained, somehow, that flash of genius you said you experienced during the Xenolink. Maybe it's only now getting to the point where you can control it."

Through the cephlinkage, Dev could sense Katya's concern, a warm, soft stirring, a reaching out. A detached part of his mind noted that this, too, was a new ability, for the cephlink wasn't supposed to transmit emotions the way a direct link with a Naga did, for instance. He suspected that what he was feeling was a highly increased sensitivity to Katya's moods, expressed by subtle inflections in her mental voice.

"I think you're right. The question is whether I can handle the additional information."

"What additional information?"

"Let's say I'm just processing the same information, the same input more completely than I was before. It's a lot like being linked, but without having much control on what's coming through on a download. My vision is sharper, and my hearing and sense of touch. What I'm getting is overtones, secondary meanings, special insight on the same input my senses have always been giving me. That's how I can, oh, hear a DalRiss word and guess at more of the meaning behind it than you can . . . and *know* that I'm right."

"It must be . . . a little frightening."

"And by that," Dev said gently, "you mean that you're wondering whether I can handle it, wondering if I might not, in fact, be insane . . . or at least just a little unbalanced."

"No!"

"And now you're wondering if you should relieve me of command, since there's no way of anticipating how I'll react under pressure. Oh, yes. I can pick up more from human speech than I could before too, especially if I can see your face and body. I think I must be capable of processing very subtle clues from, oh, lots of things. Posture. Subtle movements of muscles in face and hands and body. I feel . . . I feel much the same way that I did in the Xenolink. Not as complete, not as whole. I still feel . . . incomplete. *Empty*, in the way the DalRiss mean the word. It's not as bad as it was when the Naga withdrew from me. Maybe I'm just learning how to handle it. Or maybe I'm still . . . changing."

"I don't want to have you relieved," Katya said. "Dev, you've always been a tactical genius, especially in space combat. It's, I don't know. A gift. A talent. If your brain is working at a higher level now, faster, more smoothly, with greater insight, well, that could be a real advantage for us, couldn't it?"

"You're trying to talk yourself into believing that." Dev gave a mental sigh. What *was* best . . . for the mission? And for the people under his command? "I think we're going to have to work closely together, you and I."

"With me as your keeper?"

He heard the flash of anger in her voice. "If you like. Or as my human judgment and reason."

"You're as human as I am, damn it!"

"Maybe. I hope so."

But he was surprised to note that he didn't really care, one way or the other, about his humanity anymore.

And that change in his thinking was perhaps the most disturbing of all.

Eagle had made the passage from Alya A to Alya B in a single, short hop through K-T space. The mean separation between the two suns was nine hundred astronomical units, about five light days, and the passage lasted only a few minutes. The DalRiss Dev had been talking with at Dojinko, however, had made the trip instantaneously and were waiting for the Confederation destroyer as it approached.

DalRiss starships employed a means of overcoming the limitations of the speed of light totally different from that employed by Man. Just as they grew the bodies of their ships, they bred and grew the means of shifting from point to point in space, semi-intelligent creatures known to the DalRiss as *Achievers*. Human researchers still didn't understand how Achievers did what they did; the best explanation suggested that they somehow tapped into the half-magical potential of quantum theory, literally *imagining* the ship and its contents to be in a distant place, and transporting it there instantly by sheer force of will. Magic . . . yet no more magical, perhaps, than the K-T drive that allowed human starships to skim along the interface between the Quantum Sea and normal fourspace.

The biggest problem was that in three years of study, the *Nihonjin* researchers at ShraRish had been unable to even come up with a testable hypothesis as to how the Achievers accomplished their space-bending trick, much less find a way to apply it to human spacecraft designs.

As *Eagle* slipped into orbit around GhegnuRish, one of the smaller DalRiss ships took up station close alongside. Longer than *Eagle* by nearly two hundred meters, the four-armed starfish shape appeared to be maneuvered not by plasma jets, as with human spacecraft, but by manipulating the local stellar and planetary magnetic fields. The alien ship glowed brightly in Dev's navsim view, a representation of the magnetic forces bathing the vessel as it matched course and speed.

"Commodore?" the voice of *Eagle*'s communications officer sounded in his mind. "We're picking up a transmission from the Alyan ship. Standard radio."

With neither computer systems or transmission codes in common with those employed by human ships, the DalRiss could not talk to *Eagle* through the usual ViRcommunication links. They did employ radio, however, and with comels aboard both vessels tied into the comnet, the two could speak with one another, using audio alone.

"Patch it through."

"Dev Cameron. This is the DalRiss." Again, that odd lack of individual identification. Dev wondered if the DalRiss even had names for each other. "We thought you would appreciate a chance to see our fleet at close range."

"I'm . . . astonished," Dev replied, "to say the least." And he was. The Alyans must have been growing and launching ships constantly for the past three years.

Katya still linked in, spoke into the momentary silence. "Is this one of the DalRiss we were speaking with on the surface of ShraRish?"

"It is," the voice said, "though that scarcely matters. So long as the information is the same."

"I understand," Katya said. "But I'm curious. These starships we're seeing . . . they're identical to shapes we observed on ShraRish from orbit. Do your Achievers jump them straight from the surface of the planet into space? Or do you use the magnetic drive we're observing in your vessel now?"

"We can enter space either way. In our case, this ship was on the ground near where we talked with you. We entered it before your ground-to-orbit shuttle had reached orbit, and our Achiever brought us here to await your arrival."

If the Confederation could master that trick! . . .

"How are you generating the magnetic fields to drive your ships?" Dev asked.

"That is one of the things we have the Naga to thank for. As you must know well, they are masters at creating and manipulating magnetic fields."

Dev suppressed a start of surprise. For all of his improved powers of intuition and observation, he'd not seen that one coming. It made splendid sense, however. The Naga could directly sense magnetic fields, and they used them extensively for moving about the surface of their planet, even for flinging bits of themselves into the void at velocities of up to thirty percent of the speed of light. That was how they seeded other worlds across the cosmos; that was how the Naga he'd been Xenolinked with had destroyed the ships of the Imperial battlefleet at Herakles.

He was about to ask about their power source but decided not to. There would be time later, and he didn't want to irritate his hosts with what might be annoying or imbecilic questions.

"You have a Naga fragment aboard your ship?" Katya asked.

"Aboard every one of the ships you now perceive, yes. They provide each with its ability to maneuver, to fight, to repair itself. They are also quite useful for helping to maintain the necessary environment."

They would be, at that. Dev turned his gaze briefly on the planet turning slowly below. Birthworld of DalRissan life, GhegnuRish had been abandoned by them after centuries of near-incessant war with the Xenophobe lurking beneath the planet's crust. At some time after the last DalRiss evacuated the world, the Xenophobe had undergone a transition natural for that species, from what human researchers called its acquisitive phase to its contemplative phase. By that time, much of the planet's surface had already been altered by the dark interloper. Whole DalRissan cities had been assimilated within the Naga's plastic embrace, and the atmosphere itself was slowly being changed, not, it turned out, in any deliberate attempt to render the world uninhabitable, but simply as the vast Naga in its subsurface tunnels and caverns had drawn on cities, on rock, on the atmosphere itself as building materials for its own use.

After Dev had established contact with the Xeno, however, a dialogue between the Naga and the DalRiss had begun. Even before the First Expeditionary Force had departed for Earth, DalRiss had returned to the surface of their homeworld and had begun guiding the planetary Naga in reconstructing the demolished environment. For three years, the Naga had been absorbing air from the GhegnuRish atmosphere, converting it to the standard gas mix favored by the DalRiss, and releasing it again. DalRiss biologists had even been using the Naga's ability to pattern living forms absorbed by it and piece together replicas literally atom by atom to begin repopulating the planet's surface with the plant and animal species that long before had been driven to extinction by the original war.

Oh, yes. If the Naga could do all of that, they would be real wizards at creating and maintaining specific environments!

"Could you modify your ships to carry humans?" Katya wanted to know.

"Creating an area within a ship that supplied your range of temperature and gas mix would present no problem," the DalRiss replied after a moment. "There would be difficulties, though, in control."

"I imagine," Dev added, "that you, the Riss part of you, anyway, tap into the ship's nervous system directly."

"That is essentially correct. We receive input directly from the ship's senses. Our thoughts guide the ship just as they guide our Dal. With this new construction, there is actually a three-way linkage between the ship, the Riss piloting it, and the Naga fragment that makes up part of the ship's nervous system."

"It sounds very much like the way we do things," Dev said. "Humans are linked electronically to the artificial intelligence, the computer network that serves as a kind of nervous system for our ship. We do electronically what you do through some very advanced biology."

"We had surmised as much, from our studies with the Japanese observers. Your electronic systems, the implants you call cephlinks, would not be directly compatible with our biological systems. Some sort of direct connection would be necessary, too, in order for you to pass on navigational commands to the ship's Achiever. The Achiever, you see, must visualize the desired destination. That is simple if the Achiever has been at the target destination before. It can be accomplished if the target can simply be seen, by picking out a particular star, say. That is how we first made contact with your species, as you may know. We'd been receiving radio signals from that volume of space occupied by humans for some time. We were aware of a particular star quite similar in age and mass to our own, the star you humans call Altair. Basically, we pointed out Altair to an Achiever and told it to go there.

"The system works best, however, if the pilot has been to the destination and can pass on his impressions to the Achiever first. It allows a much finer focus and more accuracy when you emerge on the other side."

"Jumping blind, you could end up inside your target sun," Dev said. "Or so far away you might have to make several more small jumps to zero in on your target. I can see that."

"Precisely."

"You know," Dev said slowly, the hesitation dragging at his mental voice, "a comel is nothing but a translator and not always a completely accurate one at that. It doesn't provide enough of a bridge between humans and DalRiss for the level of linkage required for this type of navigation."

"It is not fast enough, either."

"Right. But a human could link directly with the Naga aboard one of your ships. The Naga would then be linked to the ship and to the Achiever. In that way, humans could pilot your vessels."

There was a long silence over the radio link, as though the DalRiss were considering this. "That could well be. Would you consider participating in the experiment?"

"Dev," Katya said, alarmed. "I don't—"

"I would," Dev told the DalRiss, interrupting her. He then sent her a private message over the navlink. "Don't worry, Kat. I know what I'm doing."

"You're thinking about doing another Xenolink!"

"Not quite. This won't be the same thing. The Nagas in these ships are buds off a planetary Naga, fragments massing a few tons . . . well, a few thousand tons, maybe, in the case of their biggest ships. Still, it won't be like tapping into that monster on Herakles."

"Then let someone else do it, damn it!"

"Why? I'm the one with the experience. If it works for me, maybe we could expand on the idea. But I'm the one with the experience linking with Xenos. *And* I can navigate a starship."

"So can I! And I've linked with Xenos, too!"

"Not the way I have, you haven't. I . . . let's just say I have an idea of what's possible."

"*Kuso*, Dev. I don't know if you should do this! If I should *let* you do this."

"I have to, Kat, and you have to let me. We've got to find out if humans can work DalRiss ships. If they can, oh, God! We've got the Rebellion won. Think of it! One battle, with ships that can travel instantly from point A to point B. The Empire would know they would never stand a chance. Katya, they'll give us everything we want!"

"But at what cost?"

"They don't seem to be into trade, much, Kat."

"That wasn't the cost I was talking about, Dev. And I think you're smart enough now to realize that."

Katya, too, possessed a keen intuition and knew that Dev had chosen to deliberately misunderstand her.

"You're right, Katya. Of course. But if Travis Sinclair were here, wouldn't he say that winning the war against the Empire, winning it without losing millions of lives in the process, was worth almost any price you could name?"

"No, he wouldn't, Dev. He'd say that victory wasn't worth it if it made us like the Imperials. Or if we had to give up being human. Damn it, Dev, what is it we're fighting for? Isn't it the right to be our own crazy brand of human?"

"And if only one human risks giving up his humanity? So that the whole Confederacy, the whole Frontier, maybe, can be free?"

"I . . . don't know, Dev."

"Neither do I. But we're going to explore the possibilities."

It didn't take much longer to arrange things with the DalRiss. The experiment, which the DalRiss were as interested in as the humans, could take place almost immediately.

And so far as Dev was concerned, the sooner, the better.

Chapter 28

Remember this maxim of space warfare. Ultimately, all weapons rely one way or another on mass and energy. A nuclear detonation yields tremendous energy in a single devastating burst. Know, however, that an asteroid, a rock, a single loose bolt, given sufficient velocity to yield kinetic energy according to the time-honored formula of $E = mc^2$, can yield more raw, destructive energy than the largest thermonuclear warhead.

—*Strategy and Tactics of Space Warfare*
Imperial Naval War College
Kyoto, Nihon
C.E. 2530

The DalRiss had provided Dev with a tiny compartment buried deep within the heart of the Alyan ship, a place where the atmosphere was identical to that provided by *Eagle*'s life support systems, where the temperature hovered at a warm and somewhat humid thirty-five degrees, where light came from no identifiable source but seemed to bathe every surface of the room in a diffuse and gentle glow.

That room was like no room aboard any human-built starship. With no corners, no sharp angles, with every surface like every other in the disorienting no-way-is-up of zero gravity, Dev found himself momentarily lost. He was a pro at handling himself in zero-G, of course, but the trick in free fall was to identify some arbitrary direction as "down" and keep convincing your brain that it was. With a little practice and some stubborn make-believe, the body adapted, and the mind could ignore the confusing loss of orientation.

Here, though, every surface was disturbingly like the inside of a huge, soft, glowing pink stomach . . . no, it was more like a living womb, with fleshy, muscular walls. It wasn't very large, either, and Dev was glad that he'd insisted on overruling Katya when she'd volunteered to come instead. With her claustrophobia, floating in a chamber so narrow that he could touch any two opposite walls with his outstretched arms and could never fully extend his legs . . . well, maybe he was the best one for this test after all. Despite what he'd told her, he'd had his doubts.

He'd floated across from *Eagle* wearing a full-body E-suit and been admitted through something disturbingly like a toothless mouth opening in the side of the DalRiss ship. Successive doors had opened before him, guiding him through the lumen of a glowing, slick-surfaced tube that brought to mind other anatomical comparisons that he'd much rather have ignored. A radio voice through the compatch jacked into his left T-socket told him when the atmosphere was right for him; he'd peeled off the E-suit and PLSS unit and left them in one room; now, naked except for the comel he wore on his left arm, he floated with knees curled almost to chest within the warm embrace of his quarters aboard the DalRiss ship.

"How am I supposed to link from here?" he asked aloud. The air had a faint odor, mildly unpleasant, somewhat sulfurous. He wondered if his hosts were listening to him over the comel or whether the room could pick up his speech and translate it directly. Not that it mattered, but he was interested in the way these people did things.

In reply, an irregular section of the wall directly in front of him and measuring a full meter across went dark. Slowly, a deeper darkness, inky absence of all light and color began diffusing through the living surface. Shapes swam in the blackness, tarry lumps, ranging in size from the length of his outstretched hand to the size of his head. He'd seen it before more than once and knew immediately what it was.

Somehow, the ship's Naga had extruded this portion of itself into his cell. Quickly, before he could lose his nerve, he stretched out his left hand and let the comel sink into the blackness. . . .

Completeness. . . .

. . . of being . . . of perception . . .

Well-being. . . .

Memories . . . of linking with the Naga of GhegnuRish . . . and again on Eridu . . . and still again on Herakles. Information, rich torrents of it . . . and the certain knowledge that I am not alone. . . .

Loneliness. I/we share that incompleteness.

Together . . .

. . . we share . . .

. . . completeness. . . .

For Dev, it was as though he'd just jacked in aboard the *Eagle*. The uterine, claustrophobic room, the black, tarry patch on the wall, the falling sensation of zero-G all were gone. Instead, he felt as though he were hanging alone in space.

No . . . it was not quite the same as *Eagle* in one critical respect. He was receiving visual input from every direction at once, viewing a full 360 degrees across two axes. When linked to ship or warstrider, data from all directions could be fed to the jacker, but his own cephlink program filtered out all but the area he was focused on. It was too disorienting otherwise, for beings that had never evolved eyes in the backs of their heads.

Strange . . . he found he could handle the input, as easily as he could override his own cephlink's programming. Was that part of the change within his own brain? It was difficult, even painful, like stretching muscles long unused, but Dev stretched . . . and found he was making sense of the jumbled cascade of incoming data.

Half the sky was occupied by GhegnuRish, a vast blur of white clouds and violet seas, of ocher deserts and the flecks of pink and orange that marked the return of life to the long-barren DalRiss homeworld. Opposite, backlit by the searing glare of Alya B, *Eagle* hung in space like a complex and crisply detailed gray-and-black toy, its hab modules rotating steadily about its long axis just aft of the bow, its strobing anticollision lights pulsing against the blackness of the shadows across its hull. Elsewhere, the host of DalRiss ships gleamed like snowflakes, each pursuing its own orbit about the world.

With a moment's practice, Dev found that he could voluntarily limit the information flooding through his brain, in effect blocking out the view in all but one direction. But he could also work with that data, and he decided not to exclude anything, at least until he had a better idea of the potentials of this linkage.

. . . this taste of the universe . . .

. . . is strange. . . .

. . . different from any tasted before. . . .

The Naga's thoughts were an alien turmoil of senses that Dev had experienced before, but only during linkages with other Nagas. He could taste the magnetic field around the ship, for instance, as a kind of smoky, pungent sharpness that brought to mind sensations of a tickle at the back of his throat. He sensed radio as well, pulses felt rather than seen or heard, but bearing with each brush information about direction and strength, with frequency distinguished by a kind of thrumming vibration sensed behind his ears, high-pitched or low, like the unheard trembling of sounds just beyond the range of human hearing.

Strangest, though, were the changes to his own human senses. His visual field, besides extending across the surface of a complete sphere, seemed distorted, as though he were viewing his surroundings through the light-bending transparency of water and a curved glass surface. *Eagle*, for instance, was distinctly bowed, as though seen through a fish-eye lens. There were sounds, too, the radio voices of the DalRiss aboard the ship, but they were distorted, hollow and echoing, as though he was hearing them in a dream.

"Are you in any discomfort?" a DalRiss voice asked. It was feminine but low-pitched, the intonation almost sultry. Other voices droned and murmured in the background, chance-caught snatches of conversation about temperature and pressure, about other ships and orbital paths.

"I . . . no. I'm not. Things just seem a little strange."

"For us, too. We have not before shared a human perspective. You were correct in your assessment. The Naga offers a unique bridge between your species and ours, like the comel, but far more complete. The way you see things seems distorted to us and filled with information that is very difficult for us to interpret."

Well, considering the fact that the DalRiss "saw" reflected sound waves and the *ri*-glow given off by living creatures rather than light, that was to be expected. The distortions in his surroundings that he was seeing probably had to do with the way his brain was processing the Alyan input to the Alyan-Naga-human symbiosis.

Or maybe it was because the array of organic visual receptors that was giving him his view of the outside universe had been designed by people who'd never closely examined a human eye and who had only the fuzziest notion of how the human brain put visual signals together into a meaningful whole.

Considering all that, they were doing very well indeed.

"We are ready to move the ship, Dev Cameron. Would you care to suggest a destination?"

That was part of the purpose of this experiment, to see if humans could control DalRiss ship technology. He hesitated before speaking, however, uncertain of the accuracy of what he was seeing.

With a moment's practice, though, he'd focused his full attention in *that* direction . . . blocking out input from every other source. With his cephlink, he opened a secondary window, calling up a three-dimensional display of the stars of human space as they would appear when viewed from over one hundred light-years out.

Once he blocked out all but the brightest stars of the near-space display, identification was almost automatic. *That* was Altair, the blue-white beacon that had first attracted DalRiss attention over three years before. And over there was Sirius, and that was Vega, two beacons even brighter and hotter than Altair.

Once he'd identified Vega, finding Mu Herculis, a yellow spark a handful of light years distant, was simple.

There . . .

Dev felt the brush of something moving behind his thoughts, of DalRiss and the far stranger node of twisted perceptions and alien half thoughts that must be the ship's Achiever. Information on the Mu Herculis system downloaded itself into the alien network. He could picture golden Mu Herculis in his mind as he'd seen it last, circled at a distance by the close pair of M4 red dwarfs. The third planet turned beneath the subgiant's brassy, yellow glare; close by, the slender thread of the cast-off sky-el turned end over end in majestic wheelings. He could feel the Achiever absorbing the information, absorbing his memories of being there, the feel of that particular point in space and time.

Somewhere, deep in the ship, inexplicable energies were gathering. Dev could sense that they were drawn from Quantum Space, but he could not sense the micro–black hole pair of a quantum power tap and could not understand how the ship was accessing energies that, liberated uncontrolled, might have vaporized a fair-sized world. The power was building. . . .

And then, without fanfare, without fuss, with no more than the unsettling flash of one starscape giving way to another, the Alyan vessel hung in a new space.

Excitement drummed in every part of Dev's being. He wanted to shout . . . to scream, not with fear but with the sheer, unbridled release of pent-up emotions he'd not even known he possessed. Mu Herculis! There was no mistaking the light of that star, bathing one side of the DalRiss ship now in its warm and glorious breath. And in the other direction, there was Herakles . . . *oh, God, no!*

Herakles . . . for one terrifying instant, Dev thought that they'd come out in the wrong star system after all, and then he wondered if possibly they'd emerged, somehow, at the wrong *time*, arriving over Mu Herculis III in some long-vanished aeon when the world was still under construction.

For the planet he was looking down on was decidedly *not* the world he'd left three months ago. It was cloud-swathed, yes, but in black clouds rather than white, and an angry scar glared out of those clouds like a baleful red eye. God of heaven, he could feel its heat through the senses of the DalRiss ship. Around that eye, clouds swirled clockwise in a whirlpool that embraced half a world. Even as he struggled to comprehend what had happened here, Dev's mind supplied the physics: a column of rapidly rising heat was energizing a storm that might have been more appropriate to the atmosphere of Jupiter or some other gas giant. Centered in the world's southern hemisphere, the storm was given its clockwise twist by Coriolus force. That impact scar—the glowing red eye could be nothing else—had punched through the planet's thin crust like an ice pick into fruit. The central eye, he could easily see, was surrounded by a host of red sparks gleaming through the cloud cover.

Confusion . . .

"Dev Cameron, we sense confusion and fear in your thoughts."

"Damn right you do. Somebody's dropped a rock on the planet, and a goking big one."

. . . or, the detached voice of his own thoughts told him, *they gave a small rock a very great deal of speed.*

He stared at Herakles with a hypnotized fascination for endless seconds, then, almost reluctantly, tore his attention away. The DalRiss sensors were picking up ships, displaying them before his mind's eye as golden sparks of light, some slowly circling the stricken world, others scattered across the sky, on extended patrol. Fifteen . . . sixteen . . . eighteen . . . and more, likely, hidden behind the bulk of Herakles.

Five of those points of light in orbit pulsed brightly, and Dev sensed the power suddenly energizing them.

"Dev Cameron," a DalRiss voice said, "we have almost certainly been detected."

Yes, he could feel that too, the throbbing tingle of radar pulses painting the DalRiss ship. He wasn't sure whether the vessel gave off bursts of neutrinos on their emergence into fourspace the way human-manufactured ships did, but the magnetic field would certainly set scanners warbling at considerable distances. Several of the stars marking orbiting Imperial ships were moving. Dev's visual display did not include the conventional graphics of a human-built warship's nav or combat sims, but he didn't need computer-drawn extrapolations of course changes and outbound orbits to know that a sizable number of ships had just broken orbit and was heading toward the lone DalRiss ship.

"Can we get a closer picture of these ships?" he asked.

For answer, part of his view of space shimmered, then opened like a flower, revealing a second view of space all but filled by an almost bow-on image of a warship . . . a *big* warship, built long and flat, tapering somewhat toward the bow and thicker at the stern, with a virtual landscape of towers and gun turrets bristling from nearly every heavily armored surface.

He recognized the class of vessel almost at once. A kilometer long, massing millions of tons, it was a spacefaring monster, an armed and armored city housing something like five thousand Imperials. The Imperials called them *Ryu*, or dragonships, and named them after dragons and great birds out of Japanese mythology. With firepower enough to subjugate a world from orbit, with a full wing of eighty or more fighters stored in her hangar bays, a Ryu-ship was the most formidable of all spacefaring warships. Only nine had ever been launched, and one of those, *Donryu*, the Storm Dragon, had been destroyed during the Imperial assault on Herakles.

Swiftly, Dev paged through Imperial ship identification files stored in his personal RAM. Each Ryu-class ship was unique in design, with a slightly different silhouette and arrangement of laser and particle gun turrets from its sisters. *There!* One of eight entries matched perfectly. The vessel bearing down on them now was *Karyu*, the Fire Dragon. The warbook entry listed her commander as an Admiral Miyagi, though that could have changed. Miyagi was known to the Confederation as a stuffy, somewhat unimaginative officer of the formal school of Imperial naval tactics.

With firepower like that, though, Miyagi wouldn't need much in the way of imagination. And those other vessels would be *Karyu*'s escorts, a collection of cruisers light and heavy, a number of destroyers and escorts, a section or two of patrolling fighters, plus a contingent of support and logistics vessels . . . perhaps eight or ten vessels all together, and more if this was an invasion fleet.

Without access to Confederation scanning techniques or AI-assisted identification schemes, Dev couldn't be sure how many ships there were in the Imperial battlefleet. Some of those moving stars—please, God, let it be so!—might be Confederation ships scattered by the Imperial attack. Dev couldn't count on that, though, and he didn't want to think about the alternative.

But he did notice that there was no sign of Rogue. According to his RAM ephemeris, the free-orbiting sky-el should be visible right *there* . . . just past the limb of Herakles and on the far side of the world, but he couldn't see it. Was that because they were in the wrong place? Because the DalRiss scanners simply weren't picking it up?

Or because it wasn't there anymore?

Dev felt a shuddering, mental chill, like a death-certain premonition of disaster. Rogue had been destroyed. Had Sinclair and the rest of the Confederation government escaped? "DalRiss!" he called suddenly. "Can you listen in on laser and radar emanations from the planet? Can we eavesdrop on them, get a picture of what's going on down there?"

"Laser, no," the DalRiss said. "We do not have the appropriate receptors, or the mechanism necessary for deciphering the light wave modulation. With the cloud cover, however, we doubt that lasers are being used for communication."

"That makes sense. What about radio?"

"There is considerable radio traffic on the surface. Little of it makes sense."

"Let me hear."

Noise exploded around him, most of it an eerie and singsong medley of piercing electronic squeals, chirps, and tones. Most of the Imperial traffic—and Confederation communications as well—would be coded and, again, the DalRiss had neither the equipment nor the programs to decipher them.

There were some voices, though, transmitting in the clear.

"Susume! Susume! Isoge!"

"San-ni-roku-hachi-roku-san! Chotto matte! Chotto matte! Moichido itte kudasai!"

"Dare ka? Mibun shomeisho o misero!"

"Kageni haire! Utsu! Utsu!"

Dev willed the voices to fade away. The babble of *Nihongo* had been so fast and furious he'd not been able to get all of it. Most of the phrases had been various military commands, though, orders to advance, to present identification, to hurry up, and even strings of numbers, probably referring to map coordinates or radio frequencies.

That last phrase, though, was revealing. *Kageni haire* was a command to take cover. And it had sounded like the speaker had then been giving the order to fire.

It sounded as though some Confederation personnel at least were still on the surface of Herakles, fighting on in what must be a last-ditch fight inside a literal hell.

"Dev Cameron, we should leave. Our sensors are detecting a different type of radar now, possibly associated with that large vessel's weapons-targeting systems."

"You're right." Dev felt lost, too, since he couldn't translate what he was seeing into tactically useful information. How distant was that Ryu-ship, anyway? "Can the Achiever take us back to Alya B?"

"The first Achiever is empty," the voice told him. Dev had forgotten that the creatures, for reasons yet unknown, died after a single use. "The second is ready, however, to effect a return."

Missiles were spewing from the *Karyu* now, the flashes of their launchings rippling across that enormous hull like twinkling sparks. That must mean they were within missile range . . . perhaps eighty thousand kilometers.

"Get us the hell out of here!"

With a silent shimmer of stars, the DalRiss vessel winked into emptiness.

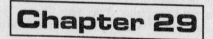

Chapter 29

Always seek to master the unexpected in warfare. Surprise over an enemy on the battlefield is worth any number of armored divisions.

—Strategy and Tactics of Space Warfare
Imperial Naval War College
Kyoto, Nihon
C.E. 2530

"How many Imperial ships were there?" Lisa Canady wanted to know.

"Yeah," Vic Hagan added. "And was there any sign of an invasion fleet?"

They were gathered in the main building of the captured

base on ShraRish, Dev and Katya, Hagan and Ortiz, and some thirty other senior expedition members, including both Katya's platoon and section leaders and the captain of each Confederation ship. The return from Mu Herculis had been carried out with almost deceptive ease, as the DalRiss ship materialized once again in the same orbit from which it had set out, moments before. *Eagle* had hailed them then, inquiring whether something had gone wrong. The alien ship had only been gone for a few moments, after all. It was still hard to imagine a space transport system that could cross interstellar gulfs in the blink of an eye.

Though the DalRiss had offered to transport Dev directly back to the surface of ShraRish, he'd elected instead to return aboard the *Eagle*, then take an ascraft from orbit to the roof of the ex-Imperial base. First, though, he'd had a long discussion with the DalRiss who'd been with him to Herakles and back. The delay of a few hours gave the department heads and platoon commanders back at Alya A time to assemble.

Besides, he'd needed time to digest what he'd seen and to think about the future. The discussion with the Alyans, and what he'd experienced aboard their ship, had given him a number of ideas, and there was a very great deal to consider.

He was also going to need time to sell some of those ideas to his people, and he had to think about how best to do it.

"I don't know," Dev told the assembled command staff. "I'm sorry, but I wasn't much more than an observer, and I didn't have an AI downloading enhanced imagery, IDs, or cephlink-level control through the data feeds. There were at least twenty ships in orbit around Herakles, but I couldn't tell whether they were Imperial or Confederation. There was no sign of Rogue, though it could have been behind the planet. It should have been visible, according to the ephemeris data I was using, but it's also possible we emerged into fourspace far enough off course that it was hidden. And I had no way to check the navigational feeds."

"The DalRiss," Katya said softly, "do not impress me as people who would make that kind of mistake. If they said they brought you out at a particular point in space, I'd guess that they were right."

"That's the feed I get on them too," Dev told her. "In any case, there was no mistaking that carrier. It was *Karyu*, and that means that at least half of the ships I saw were the other members of her battle group."

Dev pulled his gaze from Katya, and studied each of the others in the room in turn. They were seated about a large table set up in what had been a recreation room. Not for the first time, he was struck by how young nearly everyone present was. It was an unsettling feeling, knowing that Sinclair, General Darwin Smith, all of the leaders of both the Confederation government and its military might well now be dead, that *this*, these men and women, could well be the last vestige of the Rebellion.

"There's no hope then, is there?" Commander Robern Strong was captain of the *Mirach*, and his long face mirrored the emotional content of his words. "I mean, all we've got is this little expeditionary force against a Ryu battle group. And we don't even know if there's a Confederation left to go back to."

"Sinclair and the others might have made it out," Katya said. There was duralloy in her voice. "They were getting ready to leave. But even if they didn't, the Rebellion is still being fought. On Eridu. On New America. The Frontier worlds that signed the Declaration aren't going to simply give up just because Sinclair and Morton and a few hundred other people were caught or killed on Herakles. And we *can't* let them down."

"Katya's right," Dev said. "The Rebel Network still exists. The army we left on New America must still be fighting, even if it's a guerrilla action in the mountain outback. Liberty and Rainbow and Juanyekundu and half a dozen others haven't even been bothered yet."

"They will be, Commodore," Hagan said. "At the very least, their governors will be replaced by hard-liners sent out from Earth, and an Imperial garrison will replace the local militia and Hegemony forces. If they resist, well . . ." He spread his hands. "Bombardment from orbit might change some minds."

"Orbital bombardment is useless against guerrillas hiding out in a city," Dev said, "unless, of course, the government is willing to wipe out the whole city to get them. And actually finding them in rugged terrain and under nanoscreened shelters is a lot harder than giving the order."

"You think the Rebel Network will keep fighting then?" one of the Ranger platoon commanders asked.

"Hell, yes. The war hasn't ended," Dev insisted. "It's just entered a new phase."

"Aw, *kuso*, Commodore!" Lisa Canady said. Her fists were clenched on the tabletop before her, the tendons showing white against the backs of her hands. "What's the point? There's nothing we can *do*, no way we can make any impression at all against that battle group you saw, let alone against the whole goddamned Imperial fleet!"

"Lisa's right, Commodore," *Tarazed*'s skipper, Captain Jase Curtis, added. He jerked his thumb back over his shoulder. "We'd be better off heading out into the unknown, find ourselves a planet where the Empire can't find us!"

Mirach's skipper nodded. "Commodore, I have to agree with Captain Curtis. We should run, and there's no shame in it. We're a handful of ships and six or eight thousand-odd people, not much more than the complement of a single *Ryu*-carrier. We could start a new colony somewhere, a light century or two away. Then, maybe someday . . ."

Commander Ann Petruccio, captain of the *Vindemiatrix*, shook her head. "Gok that, Rob. I'm no settler. And I'm not going to sit around waiting for the Empire to come arrest me! I say we hit the bastards!"

"May I point out," Hagan said, "that it's a three-month passage back to Herakles? By the time we get back, any survivors there will be dead or standing trial back in the Palace of Heaven."

"If any of our ships got away," Petruccio pointed out, "they'll be seeking refuge with other Declaration worlds. We have the codes to slip in and find out where they'll be."

"Damn it," Hagan said. "How do we even know if Sinclair or President Morton or any of the rest of them are still alive? The Commodore heard scraps of radio conversation that could have been a battle, but that could have been the last of a mopping-up operation."

Lisa leaned back in her chair, her arms folded belligerently across her chest. "We could ask the Imperials, of course. They'll be here any day now!"

"That is *enough*!" Dev brought the flat of his right hand down on the tabletop, the crack as sharp as gunfire. "We are not going to abandon the DalRiss to the enemy, and we're not going to assume that our people are all dead or captured! We're going to *fight*!"

"How?" Katya asked him. "If it takes us three months to get back—"

"Damn it, don't you people understand? We don't have to take the long way back. With the DalRiss to help, we can be in orbit over Herakles within a few hours after we decide to go!"

A stunned silence descended over the table. Dev stared hard at the people who'd been opposing him one after the other, at Hagan and Strong and Curtis. He used the pause to get his own emotions back under control.

Katya had been right. He did need a keeper. His momentary link with the Naga aboard the DalRiss starship had been like the injection of some powerful and addictive drug, one that had fed the endless craving he'd been feeling for these past months. *Kuso!* Once you'd tasted that kind of power, how could you possibly refuse to drink of it again? To drink until that terrible thirst was quenched, until you drowned in its sweet, glorious torrents . . .

He shook himself, breaking the thing's grip on his mind, at least for the moment.

"Dev," Katya said, speaking into the silence, "are you saying, I mean, do you really think we can use the DalRiss fleet?"

"I thought you said the Alyan ships didn't give you the control you needed," Hagan said. "They couldn't even feed you appropriate data."

"Details," Dev said, dismissing the protest. "If we tell them what we need in the way of special equipment, they'll provide it for us. They can grow almost anything to spec, and faster than you would think possible."

"We still might not be in time," Canady pointed out. "Jumping back in an instant is great . . . but it's going to take time to get ready, to make plans. Even if we could leap right now, this instant, we might be too late."

"And the alternative is what? To do nothing?" Dev spread his hands. "Either Morton and the rest were able to escape in the Confederation fleet. Or they're hiding out on Herakles's surface. Or they're already dead or captured. We can't affect any of that, one way or the other. But we can try. If we don't, failure is guaranteed."

"There's still the question of whether or not the DalRiss will even help us," Katya pointed out. "They don't want to get mixed up in our war."

"They aren't looking at this as getting mixed up in our war," Dev said. "The way they hear it, they share some common philosophical ground with us, and they're willing to give us just about anything we ask for."

"What, just like that?" Lisa Canady asked. "Give us a fleet? What do they want in return?"

"That's just it," Dev said. "They don't think in terms of trade. Keep in mind that they don't make decisions, they don't *think* the way we do. Three years ago, we showed up here and stopped the Xenos from wiping them out. They are grateful—"

"There you are, then," Hagan said, interrupting. "You're the, what is it? The *Sh'vah*. And now you're calling the account due."

"Not quite. The way they look at it, we helped them because we happen to share an aspect of the way they looked at things. We didn't want the Xenos to annihilate their civilization, and neither did they. So we helped them.

"Now, we, the Confederation, I mean, we're fighting a war because, as they see it, we want greater diversity within our own culture, rather than allowing ourselves to be melted down and recast in the Imperial mold. So they're going to help us."

"It still looks like *quid pro quo* to me," Robern Strong said. "You fight my war, I'll fight yours."

Dev shrugged. "If you want to look at it that way, fine. It doesn't make much difference. The point is, they told me that they would let us use as many of their ships as we needed for this."

"What, and pilots too?" Canady said.

"And pilots too."

"And when an Imperial battle group comes out of K-T space over ShraRish?" Katya asked. "I don't care what the Alyan point of view is; Tokyo has to see this as an alliance between us and the DalRiss."

"Then they may end up cooperating even more closely

with us. I don't know. Point is, this is what we came for. Isn't it?"

"I don't see that DalRiss troops are going to be much help," Hagan said. "Their ground forces, during the Xeno War, well, they wouldn't stand up long against a company of warstriders."

"No, but there are some significant ways they can help. Most important, I think, they can provide transport. *Fast* transport. You've seen their ships. Their smallest is bigger than *Eagle*, and their largest is twice the size of a dragonship. I discussed the idea at length with them before I returned to the *Eagle*. They assure me that, yes, each of our ships could be taken aboard a big DalRiss vessel, probably a transport, since those have a lot of room inside. Jumping back to Herakles with one of our ships in its stomach would be no different, in principle, at least, than jumping there and back carrying me. When we emerge, they drop us off and we go to work."

Hagan leaned forward, his hands clasped together on top of the table. His eyes were wide, wondering. "You're saying, Commodore, that we can have the DalRiss ships carry our whole fleet back to Mu Herculis? That they can drop us off where we could launch a sneak attack against the Impies, before they even knew we were back in-system?"

Dev nodded. "We might even be able to arrange things so that they provide us with tactical mobility too, jumping in, letting us look around, then making another short jump that would put us right alongside the bad guys." Dev looked at Captain Jothan Bailey, the commander of *Tarazed*'s warflyer wing. "Jo? How would you like to have your flyers deposited a few meters off the *Karyu*'s port side, inside the reach of her point defense batteries?"

"Interesting thought. . . ." Bailey was clearly churning through the possibilities.

Dev turned to Katya. "And our ground troops could be placed directly on the ground, right where we wanted them, without having to take them down aboard ascraft."

Katya looked startled. "No orbit-to-ground assault?"

"Don't need it. Those starfish of theirs can materialize anywhere that can be visualized. They can appear right on the ground, or just above it, just as easily as in space. All they need is one of us, someone who's been there, linked through the ship's Naga to give directions. We can land troops. We could zip in and pick up our people on the ground. We could drop ships or fighters off right next to the Imperial ships, before they even knew we were there. Remember, people. In combat, surprise can be everything. And this new alliance could give us an overwhelming advantage, just in its sheer shock value."

"It's like having a whole arsenal of new toys," Hagan said. "My God . . ."

"It gets a whole lot better than that." Dev stopped, tugging at his chin with one hand as his thoughts raced. How was he going to spring *this* one on them? "It's occurred to me that with the DalRiss offer, we could use the GhegnuRish Naga in, um, a rather creative way. As a weapon. And as an ally."

"You're going to start throwing rocks again?" Katya asked. The words sounded light enough, but Dev saw the shadow behind her gaze.

"No. Or at least, not entirely. You all remember Xenozombies?"

Heads around the table nodded. Several of those present scowled, and Dev knew what they must be thinking. It was bad enough working with the Nagas. To be reminded again of the war . . .

The Xenophobe War had confronted Man with nightmares in the form of an alien foe no one truly understood. For forty-some years, human defenders had battled a bewildering array of what were assumed to be the enemy equivalent of warstriders, snakelike constructs that could tunnel beneath the earth, emerge, then transform themselves into hovering combat-mode shapes that fought with nano-disassemblers and magnetically hurled bits of themselves. Only when Dev had made contact with the GhegnuRish Naga was it learned that the Xenos, with their nanotech-based cellular structure, had learned the trick as a survival mechanism. All of the strange and alien shapes encountered on the battlefield were in fact combat forms faced by the Nagas aeons ago on other worlds, patterned by the victors and incorporated into the group-memory of future Naga generations.

Frequently, though, human warriors would encounter human-built warstriders that had been only partly absorbed . . . and changed, somehow, by the Xenophobes, their pilots dead, their weapons and armor turned against their former owners. Frequently, the legs would be gone, while the torsos and heads drifted eerily across the battlefield on the blue-glowing halos of the Xeno's magnetic field, hideous parodies of their original forms. It was as though the Xenos were battlefield scavengers, picking up anything that might be useful and incorporating it into their nightmarish arsenal.

Xenozombies was the name given to these hybrids.

"Okay," Dev said. "Hear me out on this one.

"First, our primary target. If we're going to carry this one off, it's going to have to be the Ryu. We could annihilate every other ship in the Imperial battlefleet and still lose if the *Karyu* was still able to fight. We could land Katya and her whole regiment of Rangers on the ground, and *Karyu* could wipe them out from orbit. On the other hand, if we can kill or cripple the *Karyu*, the other ships might break and run, and the Imperial ground troops will be ours for the asking."

"That's a big 'might,' Commodore," Captain Curtis said.

"Not so big, Jase," Katya told him. "The *Karyu* will be the flagship for the whole squadron. With their senior officers and battle staff out of the fight, the rest will be uncoordinated."

"*Kuso*," Ann Petruccio said. "Uncoordinated? They'll be blundering around in the goking dark!"

Dev could sense the doubt in the minds of some of the people at the table, the excitement in others. He grabbed at the excitement, shaped it with his words, rode it.

"That will be our strategy, people. Cut off their head, and the rest of their deployment is going to die. At the same time, we will employ a new measure of coordination and control within our own force, one that should give us an edge even against a Ryu-carrier."

"What new coordination?" Hagan asked. "What are you talking about?"

"I'll be directing the fleet," Dev said. "But not from the *Eagle*. Instead, I'll be in *Daghar*."

"*Daghar*?" Hagan asked. "What the hell's that?"

"It's one of the DalRiss ships. Their newest one, actually, just about full-grown and ready to go." He looked at their faces, gauging the feelings behind expressions that ran from interest to bemusement to shock. He smiled. "It's also the place we call 'Migrant Camp.' I'm told the name means 'Joining.' Actually, 'Moving toward a joining' might be a better translation. I was told that that ship, people, is going to be the flagship of the entire DalRiss exodus fleet.

"But first, the DalRiss are going to use her to help us."

"You, you'll be coordinating the Confederation fleet from there?" Katya asked.

"That's the idea. It'll be like the Xenolink on Herakles again, only this time, I'll be directing a warfleet."

"But how does that help us with the coordination?" Curtis asked. "Okay, you're in a DalRiss ship. Fine. How do you talk to the rest of us? I thought you said the DalRiss couldn't even handle lasercom transmissions."

"I'm coming to that," Dev said. "Now, warstriders are self-contained combat machines, capable of fighting in any environment, right? Miniature space ships, warflyers, if you like, but with legs instead of propulsion units and reaction mass."

Bailey grinned. "Hell, Commodore. I always thought of warflyers as warstriders with plasma jets instead of legs." Several at the table laughed nervously.

"Either way," Dev said. "The point is, we have one wing of warflyers, eighty-odd ships. Captain Bailey? What're our chances of taking out the *Karyu* with eighty flyers?"

Bailey shook his head, frowning. "Not good, sir. Not good at goking all. If you could work the big ships in close enough to take out most of their PDLs first, well, maybe. But we'd lose a lot of good boys and girls in the process. And you'd probably lose *Eagle* and *Constellation* and the rest."

"That was my feeling, too. Now, what if we take, say, two battalions of Katya's warstriders. Two, maybe three hundred machines. We bring them aboard a DalRiss ship, one of the big ones, like *Daghar*, where a fragment of the GhegnuRish Naga is waiting for them. Each warstrider accepts a fragment of that Naga, after we tell it what we want, of course. We then use the DalRiss ship to deposit those warstriders where we want them in space, as close to the *Karyu* as we can get them."

There was a sudden rush of noise around the table, sharp intakes of breath, the bump of chairs against floor or table, several shouts.

"Christ, Commodore!"

"That's *nuts*!"

"Is he crazy?"

Katya's eyes met Dev's and held them, burning. "Dev, you want my people to link with *Xenos*?"

"Symbionts," Dev told them. He grinned. "A three-way combination of Naga fragments, DalRiss comels, and humans. And here's the way it's going to work. . . ."

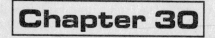

Chapter 30

". . . so there I was, comin' in like this, see, and he pulls a wing-over hard to the left but I seen it comin' and I just slide in on his six, sweet and slick as your lover's ass. He started jinkin' of course, but I locked on, got tone, and cut loose. Sweet Jesus, you shoulda' seen the goker burn!"

—Lieutenant Harriman Douglass
In the ViRdocumentary *Spacefighter*
C.E. 2375

Nearly thirty hours later, Katya met Dev in the cargo hold of an ascraft slung from *Eagle*'s belly, the same ascraft, in fact, that they'd made love in once before, just before the expeditionary fleet had departed Mu Herculis. The canisters of organic precursors were gone, now, used up during the passage to Alya or transferred to other storage compartments aboard the *Eagle* as space had become available. The nightmare that had ended that last rendezvous was forgotten now, replaced by the excitement of discovery, and by an urgent, almost frantic passion that acknowledged, tacitly, that this could be the last time.

Certainly, it would be the last opportunity they had to be alone together for some time to come. Ever since Dev had given the final set of orders, both of them had been working furiously to prepare for the return to Herakles, an operation that Jothan Bailey had dubbed "Changeling." Katya's troops and Bailey's flyers all had been briefed, their plans drawn up, communications protocols worked out with the DalRiss.

Next, the First and Second Battalions of the 1st Rangers had been flown to the *Daghar*, where, one by one, they'd met smaller pieces of the huge ship's controlling Naga fragment. Each small fragment, measuring two or three meters across and massing a couple of tons, had flowed out from the ten-thousand–ton mass of the big fragment at the heart of the grounded DalRiss ship-city and encased a warstrider's legs and lower torso. Slender extrusions had grown their way along sensor and power conduits and infiltrated the entire internal system of each warstrider; a physical link with the pilot provided communications—and the new means of coordination Dev had been looking for.

At the same time, the DalRiss city that the humans had known as Migrant Camp was breaking up, the thousands of mobile buildings and their DalRiss parasite-occupants moving well back from the starfish-shaped mountain of the city-ship. When the last warstrider was finally aboard and the city completely evacuated, the DalRiss had expended a single Achiever. There was a thunderclap, an explosion of sky-rending noise as the vacuum remaining when the huge ship vanished was suddenly and catastrophically filled. *Daghar* had reappeared in orbit over ShraRish, in company with the human squadron and the growing fleet of smaller DalRiss ships. On the ground, the Migrant Camp DalRiss had begun moving once more, crawling toward a new site, where they would begin growing a new city-ship for their eventual exodus from their world.

Katya, after seeing to her troops aboard the *Daghar*, had crawled through one of the winding tunnels of the DalRiss ship and into *Eagle*, which was being held to *Daghar*'s flank by an extrusion of the Naga. Soon, after completing some necessary planning with the human squadron's senior officers, both she and Dev would return to the DalRiss ship.

First, though, they found these minutes for each other. As before, the two of them clung to one another in free fall, linked at the waist by the slender tether of the *tsunagi nawa*. Katya had needed this time. Even more, she'd needed to talk to Dev in privacy.

"Something's changed in you," she told him, holding him close. "Again."

"Oh? How have I changed?"

"I'm not sure. You're more certain of yourself. And more committed to, to the cause, I think. More than you've ever been before. But I'm scared."

"What about?"

"You're going to be Xenolinking again."

"A lot of us are going to be Xenolinking, you included."

She shook her head. "That's not the same thing, and you know it. The rest of us, we'll just be touching a small Naga fragment, the one we have on our striders. You'll be tied in with a big fragment, bigger than the one that took you to Herakles and back. It's the difference between having a compatch jacked into your socket, and being in full linkage."

She'd tried to tell herself that this wouldn't be the same as when Dev linked with the planetary Naga on Herakles. These two-ton fragments she and the rest of her people would be linking with would be nothing like the incredible repository of knowledge and power and memory of a full planetary Naga.

She also knew, deep down, that mass wasn't the issue. Dev was being transformed by this damned physical and mental communion with the Xenophobes, and each experience seemed to take him farther from her.

He smiled at her, but his eyes were cold and a little distant. "That's no reason for you to be scared, Kat."

"I think it is. Not my Xenolink, that I can handle. Maybe not even yours, though I feel like you've . . . surrendered to that addiction you told me about once. No, Dev, I'm afraid I'm losing *you*. These past few days you've been, well, *growing*. In ways I don't understand. Once you were afraid you weren't human anymore. Now I'm beginning to wonder if you're not more than human, somehow. The way you know things without being told . . ."

" . . . is fundamentally no different from the artificial enhancements provided by our cephlinks," he finished for her. "Through our links, we have direct access to AI-controlled hardware, to information, to instant communications that we take for granted, but that our ancestors would think was pure magic."

"You didn't want to Xenolink again."

"Hmm. Yeah, I was scared of linking again. But I feel differently about that now. When I linked with the DalRiss ship, with the Naga fragment in that ship, I mean, I was in control. I was *me*. If anything, the larger fragment in *Daghar* ought to give me even more control. Over my surroundings, and over me. And I'll need it, too, if we're going to pull this off."

Daghar's Naga fragment was still only a tiny, tiny fraction of the mass of the Heraklean Naga. Still . . . would linking with it sweep Dev up in the madness that had embraced him on Herakles, that storm- and lightning-torn day when the sky had gone black and a man-become-god had hurled rocks into the heavens, challenging an Imperial battle group to single combat?

Just the name of the DalRiss bio-construct—*Daghar*—filled Katya with unease. She'd learned from Brenda Ortiz that the DalRiss did not have distinctive names for their ships as human vessels did, and their cities were given temporary and changeable names that apparently reflected some aspect of their creation. The human contingent of the fleet, however, had taken to calling the ship by the name of the city. "Moving Toward Joining" indeed! Dev was going to join with that monster, and she was terrified that she would never see him again.

"You know," Dev said, interrupting bleak thoughts, "we ought to get back. I want to talk to the DalRiss about how many Achievers they're going to have along in storage."

He started to fumble for the *tsunagi nawa*, trying to release the catch. Reaching down, she took his hand, moving it away. "Not yet," she whispered. "Please . . . once more . . . once more now . . ."

She felt a flush of embarrassment as she said it, knowing what the words sounded like. She knew, though, that it was not lust that was driving her as she coupled once more with Dev Cameron, but rather a deeper, a more fundamental need untouched by the passion that had brought them together in the first place.

Inwardly, she directed a coded thought checking one part of her implant, a molecule-thick plating of silver, silicon, and gold physically entwined with the cells of her hypothalamus. It was still switched off.

Good. . . .

She gasped as Dev's touch sent a burning shudder pulsing through her body.

Chujo Takeshi Miyagi had been sleeping when an aide called him.

Three days earlier, a mysterious vessel shaped like a *hitode*, a giant starfish, had winked briefly into existence a few tens of thousands of kilometers from Herakles. The vessel had been closely examined by teleoperated probes orbiting in the region, which had relayed detailed images back to *Karyu*, and he was certain that the visitor had been a DalRiss ship. He'd read reports filed by the Imperial Alyan Mission released by Earth and Japanese Military Intelligence, and he knew that Alyan ships could be starfish-shaped, and he knew they could materialize anywhere, just as the first had appeared near Altair three . . . no, four years ago, now.

He'd also read the reports that indicated the Alyans were hostile, having attacked the Imperial Mission.

He'd certainly not expected an Alyan ship to appear *here*, however, and the incident had left him uneasy. Assuming the vessel to be hostile, he'd first ordered *Karyu* and several of her escorts to break orbit and close with the intruder; when it had ignored his repeated lasercom demands for identification and communication, he'd ordered *Karyu*'s missile batteries to fire.

For three days, now, he'd wondered if he'd done the right thing, wondered if, possibly, there'd been some kind of breakdown in communications that had led to some dreadful mistake. For a time, he'd half expected the stranger to appear again, this time with a fleet behind it, and weapons impossible even to imagine. Against that possibility, he'd loosed more teleoperated probes, and he'd put all of *Otori* Squadron on special alert, extending patrols of frigates and corvettes farther out from Mu Herculis A and ordering meticulous and continuous scanning sweeps of all surrounding space with radar, ladar, and infrared searches.

As the hours had passed, however, Miyagi had begun to allow himself to relax. The DalRiss vessel, if that was what it had been, had been in sight for only a few minutes, and it had vanished within seconds of *Karyu*'s missile launch. Possibly, he reasoned, he'd glimpsed a refugee from Alya;

he'd heard rumors, passed on by one of his destroyer captains newly arrived from Earth, that an Imperial fleet was on its way to the Theta Serpentis suns to deal with the DalRiss for their unprovoked attack on the Imperial Mission. The stranger might have been fleeing that battle . . . though Miyagi could not understand why they'd chosen *this* system as a refuge. True, they were aliens, and like all *gaijin* they did not reason in logical ways. Still . . .

After nearly three full days, however, Miyagi was exhausted. He'd remained linked in the tacnet for nearly that entire time, relying on the link module hardware to feed him and care for his body's physical needs, on brief, private periods of alpha stimulation to keep him refreshed and alert.

But the strain was beginning to tell. He'd told himself that he was serving no cause, fulfilling no duty with the exhausting mental stress of continual linkage. The campaign on Herakles was going well, the victory over the Confederation fleet had been as complete as any in history. Finally, he'd broken the link in order to get a real meal and some real sleep.

He'd gone to bed, as was his habit, in a small compartment in *Karyu*'s zero-gravity habitat, strapped to a bulkhead with Velcro fasteners to keep him from drifting with the currents from the air circulation ducts. Fifty-one minutes after strapping himself in, by the time function in his cephlink, his aide was shaking him awake. "*Chujosama! Chujosama!*" The man's normally impassive face was creased with worry. "Please, sir, wake up!"

"Eh? I'm awake. I'm awake. What is it, *Fukkansan*?"

"The Alyan strangers, sir. They're back!"

"Strangers . . . what? When?"

"Minutes ago, *Chujosama*. But they are close! Less than ten thousand kilometers!"

"*Chikusho!*" He groped for the straps, tugging them free. His aide began helping him with his uniform. "Is it just the one again?"

"I am sorry to say, no, *Chujosama*. We have counted at least ten Alyan craft, ranging in size from approximately that of a large destroyer, to one vessel that is at least twice the size of *Karyu*."

"*Baka-ni suruna-yo!*" Miyagi snapped. "Don't think I'm stupid!"

"Sir!" Somehow, the aide managed an abject bow in zero gravity, no mean feat when he was adrift in the middle of the room. "Please, sir! It is the complete truth!"

"We will see."

And Miyagi saw, moments later, as he jacked into *Karyu*'s tactical simulation. The Alyan craft—damn it, they *had* to be Alyans, for nothing of human manufacture looked remotely like those bizarre, bump-surfaced shapes with their stubby arms and hulls like rusted iron—the Alyans were grouped in a ragged, spherical shape with their largest vessel hanging toward the rear, and they were accelerating toward the *Otori* flagship at an estimated four gravities. There was no sign of plasma flare, no ion trails, not even a neutrino flux to give clues to the weird-looking vessels' power plants. There was an unusual magnetic flux encasing each ship, a pulsing, rippling flow of power that might be propulsion, or it might be some kind of weapon.

Seconds after he linked into the net, eight more Alyan ships appeared . . . or were they? The first ten were starfish shapes, differing one from another in numbers of arms and in overall size, but all essentially of the same design. These newcomers were different, lumpy, organic shapes that looked more like dark-skinned escapees from some giant's vegetable garden than starfaring vessels. And these ships were spilling neutrinos . . . not to mention radar and ladar signatures that identified them as human-built and human-manned ships.

"Battle stations," Miyagi said softly. The order was picked up by the tactical net and broadcast throughout all the ships of the Imperial battlefleet, though most of the warships were already on full alert. "*Shosho* Kima? Are you on the net?"

"*Hai, Chujosan!*"

"Bring all weapons to full power. This looks like an attack formation of some kind."

"I agree, *Chujosan*. All weapons are at full power and standing by. We are tracking the targets."

"Excellent. Has there been any attempt at communication?"

"We have been querying them for identification since they appeared. There has been no reply."

"Ah." Miyagi watched the approaching vessels, suddenly uncertain. The hell of a battlefleet command was that there was no higher authority to appeal to . . . save for that of the

Imperial Staff Command back at Earth. A wrong guess, a wrong move, a misstep in diplomacy or a stupid underestimation of a military foe, and at best his naval career would be ruined. At worst, well, even the modern and enlightened *Dai Nihon* still expected those of its servants bearing the greatest responsibilities to apologize for their mistakes with their lives. It was, Miyagi had always thought, an excellent system, one that wonderfully focused an officer's attention on his duty.

The enemy ships were well within range and still approaching. "Stand by to fire."

"*Hai, Chujosan!*"

Miyagi sensed the awesome power of the *Karyu* gathering about him. . . .

The Alyans approached the core of the Imperial battle group in two formations. In the lead were ten Alyan "warships," the starfish shapes, including the enormous bulk of *Daghar*. Trailing by a thousand kilometers came eight DalRiss transports, each carrying a Confederation vessel in its bowels.

The Imperials, Dev thought with a barely suppressed quiver of anticipation, must be beside themselves by now. The incoming ships would be unlike anything the Imperials had ever tracked; the transports would look bizarrely alien, yet their electronic signatures would include spills from the human-built ships in their bellies, neutrinos from powered-up fusion plants, and the questing fingers of weapons radars and laser ranging devices peeking through the Alyan ships' flexible and immensely adaptable hulls.

Linked into the Naga that was *Daghar*'s brain and nerves and senses, Dev felt the prick and tingle of Imperial track and search radar, and he knew that gigawatts of raw energy were about to be released. He'd been counting seconds, steadily and automatically, since the first DalRiss ships had broken into fourspace. He was estimating four minutes from the time the Alyan fleet was first sighted to their decision to open fire.

At two hundred seconds, some part of his hyperawareness overrode his intent to count out another forty. The Imperial commander must be steeling himself *now* to give the order to fire.

"Group Two!" he called out over his link. "Leapfrog, *now*!"

During the planning sessions back at ShraRish, Dev never had been able to explain to the DalRiss what leapfrog was, but the concept was clear enough, in any case. The trailing squadron vanished from normal space . . .

. . . and reappeared instantly ten thousand kilometers closer to their goal, inside the core of the Imperial battlefleet and less than half a thousand kilometers from the *Karyu* herself.

"Group One! Shift *now!*"

The ten starfish winked out, dropping back into fourspace well behind Group Two, and angling in toward the planet, a feint designed to draw the fire of other Imperial ships. *Karyu* launched a salvo of missiles in the same heartbeat, followed, two beats later, by the flicker of lasers and accelerated particle beams.

Dev felt the familiar drumbeat of excitement thundering in his linkage, the godlike thrill of destiny and power and martial glory. "Niner-niner!" he cried over the radio linkage, a code phrase meaning the call was for all spacecraft. "This is Sword. *Commence fire!*"

"Targeting systems."

"Go."

"Life-support."

"And go."

"Communications. Switch off ship ICS. Going to squadron tactical."

"Switching to squadron taccom, and testing: alfa, bravo, charlie . . ."

"Reading you on taccom, Three-five. Comtest is go."

Van's mind wandered as Commander Cole went on to check the comm circuits of the rest of the squadron's warflyers. Fighter pilots had a certain reputation, one reputedly going back centuries to the very first men to risk their lives in fragile, aerial combat machines, a reputation for being hard-living, hard-loving, hard-fighting bundles of testosterone and machismo. More often than not, the female members of the squadron came across as harder than the males, as though they had to work harder to prove that they were part of the fighter pilot fraternity.

Still, that image had always been more for public consumption than a reality shared among the pilots themselves. A good pilot was part of an intricate and smooth-running machine, an intimate part of a team and not the lone wolf of popular ViRdrama. In many ways, he was more engineer than warrior, and jacking fighter or warflyer in combat more often than not required ice-cold focus and concentration, not fire-and-blood bravado.

Sublieutenant Vandis had nonetheless done his best to live up to the image, a responsibility always encouraged by the other members of his squadron, men and women alike, whether they were drinking with yujies in a public bar, or sharing there-I-was war stories with fellow pilots. It had been a long, long time, though, since he'd mingled in what the fraternity called "the real world," so long that Vandis was beginning to think there was no world but the tight, close camaraderie of the junior officers' mess and the squadron ready room.

Kuso, the last time he'd been in a dirtside bar had been back on New America, just before the Impie invasion, hell, almost a year ago, now. He and Marlo had jacked the tails of those three militia leggers. The last time he'd had real sex, the sweating, dirty, skin-on-skin kind with a willing stranger, instead of the canned fantasies of ViRsex . . . yeah, the same night as the bar episode. Memories of that sweet little *ningyo* could still trigger erotic dreams.

For nearly an entire year, then, he'd been living aboard the *Zed*, enclosed by gray walls, rarely seeing anyone but shipboard technicians and maintenance personnel, his yujies in Gold Squadron, and the other pilots of 1st Wing. He'd recjacked a lot, of course, including some fun and enthusiastic jackin'Jill three-ways with Lynn Kosta and Carey Graham, Gold Squadron's two female pilots, but Van had always preferred the real thing to electronic feeds, and gok the jackers who claimed you couldn't tell the difference.

He was sick of shipboard life. He wanted to walk dirt again . . . civilized dirt, not a vacant desert like Herakles or an alien jumble of surrealist art and jack-feed hallucinations like ShraRish.

Van recognized that at least part of the frustration was this endless waiting in the dark, figurative and real, waiting for the order to launch. He was used to watching the battle unfold in his tac feed; even if he was a helpless spectator, at least he knew what the hell was going on!

But *Tarazed* had been engulfed hours ago by one of those monster DalRiss transports. Since there were no electronic feeds from the Alyan ship to its cargo, the *Zed* was riding along in the darkness too, unable to present a tactical feed to the warflyers resting in the converted tanker's bays and launch tubes. The only word Van had about the outside universe were periodic verbal updates by either Commander Cole or the Wing CO, Captain Bailey.

"Right, everybody," Cole's voice said. "Twelve for twelve, checked and ready. Gold Eagle set for launch." The Skipper sounded taut and hard, maybe a bit worried. Well, who the hell in their right mind wouldn't be worried right now? He tried to picture Gold Eagle's principal target, the Ryu-carrier, stretching across the heavens like a mobile fortress, then gave it up. He was nervous enough without deliberately conjuring up nightmares.

"Wish they'd get a move on out there," Sublieutenant Carey Graham said, her voice as sharp-edged as a monofilament blade.

"Watch," Cal Schmidt said with a chuckle. "They'll wait until things are in a goking mess, then send us in to—"

"Damp it down, Gold!" Cole's voice snapped. "Fleet feed coming through!"

"Warflyer wing! This is Sword!"

The new voice came in through his cephlink by way of *Van'sGuard*'s new DalRiss radio circuit. Van recognized the voice—none other than Deadly Dev himself.

"Your transport has just made a tactical shift and is less than eight hundred kilometers from your primary target. The larger ships will move in first and try to hammer down the Imperials' PDLs and close defenses. I'll give you the word to launch in about thirty more seconds."

Thirty more seconds. Van felt a quiver at the back of his thoughts, what his body might have felt as an anticipatory shudder rising from the hollow in the pit of his stomach. Strange. Commodore Cameron's voice, his voiced thoughts, rather, had sounded fast-paced, almost racing. There'd been all kinds of who-was spreading through the *Tarazed* for the past few months, rumors that Cameron had mutated into some kind of Naga-human hybrid, rumors that he'd developed strange new mental powers, rumors that he'd formed a symbiotic link with the DalRiss. Van had discounted all of those stories as the mental short-circuitings of men and women cooped up too long without outside input. A fighter squadron was like any other close-knit group of people; deprive them of outside stimulus and they began creating their own.

Time . . . time . . . God, it had been twenty seconds already. When were they going to get the word?

"Warflyers! This is Sword!" Static swirled and spat. "Stand by!"

Come *on*! Come *on*!

"Launch warflyers!"

"Gold Squadron, launch!"

Stars exploded around Van's head.

Chapter 31

The entire concept of space fighters needs a serious review by experts unbiased by the wilder and more romantic notions of this type of combat. After all, the exploits of fighter pilots have been the staple of the cheaper sort of fiction and ViRdrama for so long, it is necessary to examine the problem with a cold and skeptical eye. Consider! A space fighter, massing fifteen, maybe twenty tons, armed with a few lasers and some ship-to-ship missiles . . . how is such a toy going to fare against a behemoth massing a million times more? How is the pilot to get close enough to employ his weapons, how can he hope to survive even a near miss by a particle beam powerful enough to burn through meter-thick duralloy sheath?

—*Shosho* Nobuo Fujiwara
Testimony before the Imperial Staff Command
during hearings on military research appropriations
C.E. 2439

Dev's order loosed the warflyers from *Tarazed*'s launch tubes, minnows to *Karyu*'s whale flung into the darkness four at a time. An instant after the DalRiss transports shifted in close to the Imperial squadron, the carrier had opened fire. Most of the shots missed completely, the ranging and targeting locks broken by the sudden spatial shifts of the Alyan ships. One DalRiss vessel, though, the one carrying the *Constellation*, glowed a dazzling white for an instant as megawatt lasers seared across its hull.

Now the other Alyan transports were already opening up, however, unfolding like bizarre flowers, disgorging their cargoes, then flickering away into nothingness like fleeting wraiths. *Constellation* had to break free of the kilometer-wide starfish that had carried it this far, accelerating sharply on glowing starbursts of blue-white plasma; the Alyan ship, jolted by the release, began tumbling slowly through space, a hazy fog of crystallizing water vapor and air slowly englobing it.

No human mind could have followed the rapid pace of events. Dev, his perceptions working at superhuman speed, could scarcely keep up.

"*Rebel!* Move in close, toward the bow," Dev ordered. "Suppress the main laser batteries there and keep them from sniping at the fighters!" His thoughts, picked up by the Naga aboard *Daghar*, were relayed through DalRiss organic radios to comel-equipped communications personnel aboard each Confederation vessel. "*Tarazed!* Start launching your wing, and keep launching, no matter what! *Constellation*, focus on the Ryu's big guns, but keep an eye on those escorts! They're coming up fast astern! *Intrepid! Daring!* Missiles! Use your missiles!"

The Xenolink fed a steady chatter of voices back to Dev, scraps and snatches of conversations between ships, between pilots and gunners, even—as high-pitched electronic warbles that meant nothing to Dev—between the guiding AIs of the Confederation vessels.

"This is *Audacious!* We've got a heavy concentration of fire coming up from three-five-niner. Charlie . . . see if you can give us some support there. . . ."

" . . . launching fighters! . . ."

" . . . One-two, this is One-five. Damn it, Gold, where are you?"

"Niner-niner, this is *Eagle*. We have two Imperial frigates coming up the Ryu's stern. *Constellation*, how about giving us some support here? . . ."

"Watch it! Watch it! We're taking fire from those bow guns!"

"We're hit! *Rebel*'s hit! Oh Jesus God *Jesus!* . . ."

Rebel, cutting close past the *Karyu* less than one hundred meters above the monster ship's prow, was speared by twin lances of coherent light that slashed her open from hab modules to stern, spilling slush hydrogen into space in a vast, sparkling, amoebic cloud.

To Dev's mind's eye, he seemed to be adrift in space, aware of his entire surroundings, though he'd narrowed the focus of his newly enlarged vision to that three-dimensional area of space where the battle was rapidly unfolding. At such impossibly close quarters and at relatively low speeds, things were happening with bewildering rapidity. He winced as he heard *Rebel*'s death scream, winced again as a short-range missile sank into the frigate's hull and detonated with a silent, piercing strobe of blue-white light. He'd hoped to get the Confederation ships in so close that only a fraction of *Karyu*'s batteries could bear, but so heavily armed and armored was the Ryu-ship that a fraction of her firepower could still be devastating to relatively small and thin-skinned craft like a frigate.

Seconds later, however, two spreads of missiles launched by *Eagle* and *Constellation* slammed into *Karyu*'s dorsal surface. High-explosive warheads detonated in rippling, silently popping flashes that peeled open the big ship's duralloy skin in gaping, black-edged blotches, smashed weapons turrets, crumpled communications and fire control towers, and penetrated far enough to explode within deeply buried spaces. *Karyu* fired back; *Eagle* was struck in her port fairing by a laser beam that momentarily overloaded her power feeds to every weapons turret on that flank. With her portside PDLs off-line, a missile penetrated her ventral surface and detonated with a savage concussion. Air shrieked through ruptured bulkheads on decks three and four, and two ascraft cradled in their transport racks were transformed into twisted, half-molten wrecks.

"*Eagle!*" Dev called. "Get closer! Get closer!" Safety—relative safety—for the Confederation squadron lay in moving so close to the Imperial giant that other Japanese vessels didn't dare fire for fear of hitting their flagship, while *Karyu* herself could not bring her full firepower to bear on any one target.

"Damn it, Commodore, I'm as close as I can goddamn get!" Lisa Canady's voice snapped back. "Any closer and I'll be goking the bastard!"

But *Eagle* did begin moving closer, her 395-meter length sliding into the ink black shadow of the far larger *Karyu*. Huge patches on both warships were alive now with sullen red and orange heat, twisted, fiercely radiating scars where warheads had turned duralloy into glowing slag. Canady was cleverly maneuvering the Confederation destroyer into a dead zone behind and beneath the *Karyu*, where most of the larger vessel's turrets had been smashed by *Constellation*'s missile barrage a moment before. The two Imperial frigates, however, were moving in fast, angling so close to *Karyu*'s hull that they could open fire on the Confederation ships without danger of hitting their larger consort.

Throughout the battle, the ten DalRiss ships of Group One had attracted little attention at all, though some missiles were inbound from a pair of enemy destroyers just coming over the Heraklean horizon. Using the DalRiss vessels to decoy Imperial fire, it appeared, had been less than successful; the Imperial fire control officers were ignoring the unknown quantities represented by the Alyan ships and were concentrating instead on targets with well-known potentials. Fighters were beginning to spill belatedly from the *Karyu*, as her wing scrambled and launched.

Military starships, whether corvettes or Ryu-carriers, were not designed for combat at ranges measured in meters rather than kilometers. Dev was shocked to realize that less than ten seconds had passed since the opening volleys had been fired, and the Confederation fleet had already been savaged.

At this rate, they wouldn't be able to keep fighting for very much longer.

"*Whee-ooo!*" Sublieutenant Vandis screamed into his linkage as his Warhawk blasted from the launch tube in *Tarazed*'s ventral hull, a yell of sheer exultation. The convoluted, black-gray complexity of *Zed*'s hull flashed past his awareness; for an instant, golden sunlight bathed him in warm light, and then he was plunging once more into shadow. The immense bulk of *Karyu* loomed above and ahead, blocking the sun as Vandis triggered his thrusters and lunged ahead at a thundering 5 Gs.

"This is Three-five, in the clear!"

"And Three-seven," Marlo's voice chimed in. "Right behind you!"

"Goddamn, that thing's big!" Lynn Kosta said over the link. "I'm pulling right, looking for a soft spot."

"That'll be like looking for a soft spot on a goking nickel-iron asteroid," Lieutenant Alfred Horst, Three-six, added. "Skipper, we're taking fire from up forward."

"Never mind the fire," a new voice said, cutting in. "Come on, get in closer! *Closer!*"

"Who the gok is that?"

"This is Wing Six-zero-zero. Now cut the chatter and odie in close, or you're all walking home!"

Vandis felt an electric thrill surge through him. Wing 600 was the code identifier for the 1st Wing's skipper, Captain Bailey. Bailey himself had launched with the squadron! "Damn, next thing you know, we'll have Deadly Dev out here lending a hand! Three-two! This is Three-five! I'm sliding in under your ass!"

His link-fed visual field was a complex dance of realtime objects and computer graphics, filled now by the growing bulk of the Imperial carrier. He cut acceleration, falling now toward the target as he readied his missiles for launch.

Then the rapidly growing bulk of the Imperial carrier exploded with light, the rapid-fire twinkle of a thousand point defense batteries, and things started to go very badly wrong.

Strangeness . . . and loneliness, >>self<< surrounded by hordes of not-Self, voices in the darkness of the Void of the Universe. . . .

Katya tried to shut out the eldritch ripple of black thoughts seeping through her linkage with the Naga, tried instead to imagine what must be happening out beyond the blackness surrounding *Assassin's Blade.*

This was, she thought, a strange way to go to war, three-hundred–odd warstriders sealed into the belly of a living starship, hidden away inside several million tons of alien, gene-tailored flesh. Dev, she knew, was elsewhere within the *Daghar*, waiting and watching for the proper moment to unleash the Naga-enhanced—she tried hard not to think the term *Xenozombie*—warstriders. The rest of the Confederation squadron, including the fighter wing aboard *Tarazed*, would be hitting the *Karyu* right now with everything they had, trying to batter down her defenses . . . and even more, to turn the Imperial battle staff's full attention to the attack. At the right moment, *Daghar* would jump in close, releasing Katya and the two battalions of Naga-warstrider hybrids, then jump back to safety once more. Three hundred warstriders, able to maneuver and fight in space and linked together by Naga and comel to each other and to Dev back aboard the *Daghar*, should prove to be a devastating and totally unexpected surprise for the Imperials.

Warflyers had been used lots of times in actions against ships or orbital stations—at Eridu, in the capture of an Imperial destroyer later renamed *Eagle*, at an Imperial shipyard at Athena . . . but in all the history of warstrider warfare, there was no case that she had ever heard of of *warstriders* being used to board and storm an enemy ship.

She felt . . . alone.

Loneliness . . . >>self<< severed from the far vaster reserves and knowledge that was Self, lost in the agony of budding that had given birth to this new and sharply limited awareness . . .

But she wasn't alone, not really. She was linked in with Ryan Green and Kurt Allen aboard *Assassin's Blade*, and the Naga fragments provided instant communication along DalRiss-engineered organic radio circuits with every other warstrider in the group, but no one, *no one* out of all those hundreds of striderjacks was talking now. Oh, there'd been some chatter, some nervous banter and gallows humor earlier, before they'd made the jump from ShraRish to Herakles, mostly comments about being Xenozombies now.

At this point, however, every person in the assault group was alone with his or her thoughts, feeling the strangeness . . . and the fear.

Perhaps the strangest aspect for Katya was a change she'd discovered in herself. She was riding in darkness, literally in the bowels of the beast, unable to move, unable to see anything at all with her Warlord's sensors blocked by the embrace of the creature-ship around her. Always before, darkness and the inability to move had all but shut her mind down as she battled the gibbering terror of her claustrophobia. It would have been wrong to say she felt nothing. The darkness was unpleasant, almost painful, and even worse was the nerve-grating helplessness, knowing that a battle was raging somewhere out there, beyond these walls of alien flesh, and she could do nothing to fight, to run, to hide, or even to know.

But there was no panic . . . only a cold, sure knowledge that this was what she had to do. For the Rebellion. For Dev. For herself.

She was pretty sure that the claustrophobia hadn't kicked in because, for so long now, her attention had been so completely focused on Dev, on what was happening to him. This strange mix-and-match of human and nonhuman minds was the stuff of nightmares.

Katya shuddered. It wasn't her own Xenolink; she'd linked with them before without any particular problem. She could feel the Naga fragment embracing her Warlord's legs and hip joints now and knew that she only had to open a particular communications circuit and its strangeness, sensed now as that rippling undercurrent of alien thought about Self and >>self<<, would fill her mind.

No, it was Dev and what he'd become, remote and godlike in the embrace of *Daghar*'s Naga. She wondered how he was handling his role, coordinating the entire battle from the womblike embrace of *Daghar*'s human-conditioned inner sanctum.

She listened to the murmuring silence, watching the enfolding darkness . . . and like the warriors of ten thousand years of battles, waited for the orders that would send her from the twilight world of waiting and into the blaze of combat.

It was like being God.

Dev could feel the power surging around him, *through* him, felt the challenge and the pounding bloodlust of single combat on a scale no mere human had ever known. He was completely unaware of the *Daghar*, save through a kinesthetic sense. He stood in space, motionless relative to the mountain-sized mass of the *Karyu* . . . and through the Xenolink the other ships, DalRiss and human as well, all felt like parts of that body, reaching out as he would stretch out his hand.

Sometimes he spoke, his words link-transmitted to the appropriate ship or ships through the DalRiss communications net. In a sense, Dev's mind was no longer wholly within the *Daghar*, but scattered across the entire combined fleet. He could feel the flutter of probing, targeting radar, feel the prick and stab and sting of beams and missiles, hear the steady, background roar of thousands of voices speaking, ordering, acknowledging, shouting, pleading, praying at once.

He felt the waiting hundreds of warstriders still huddled inside *Daghar*'s belly. *Soon . . .*

Sublieutenant Vandis tried to concentrate on targeting the monster ship that filled his forward view, but ships, warflyers, his friends were dying in the sky all around him. Lynn Kosta's ship brushed the deadly, invisible flame of a particle beam, and then her warflyer, half molten and half crumpled hull and internal wiring spilling like a disembowelment, was spinning end over end over end as glowing fragments scattered across the night. "I've got lock!" Al Horst screamed. "Target lock! I'm—" and then he was gone too, his Warhawk vaporized by a laser pulse that chopped through the warflyer like a white-hot iron through plastic.

Marlo . . . where was Marlo? "Three-seven! Three-seven! Where the gok are you, Ger?"

"On your five and low. *Jesus*, Van, it's a firestorm!"

"Watch the PDLs and pull in tight! I'm targeting amidships, where there should be a cryo-H tank as big as the gokin' *Eagle*. You with me?"

"With you! Punch it!"

Acceleration . . . and the two Warhawks leaped side by side toward the monster.

"Van! I got targeting radar lock! Watch it! Watch—"

Vandis flinched as white flame blossomed off his starboard side and aft. Gerard Marlo's Warhawk flared like a tiny sun, duralloy and steel and plastic and flesh and blood all boiling away in a puff of star-hot vapor.

Oh, *kuso, kuso*! . . .

No time. *Karyu* was a mountain . . . a world looming ahead and below. A target . . . he needed a target . . . that crater! Vandis put his Warhawk into a slow spin, the movement crafted to keep tracking as the hurtling warflyer streaked across the carrier's hull at a range of less than five hundred meters. The warflyer's AI gave him the precise tick when range, speed, and vector all were perfect; he downloaded the command code and the Warhawk fired, sending two auto-linked Starhawk missiles streaking into the glowing ruin of a crater that gaped in *Karyu*'s side like the imprint of some angry giant's fist.

Hit! . . .

Red-glowing duralloy flared white, blossoming outward in a cloud of million-degree plasma. The crater floor dissolved in light, then gaped open, spilling molten gobbets of metal and burning hydrogen that washed across *Van'sGuard* like a white-hot sea.

Then he was through the cloud and into the open. Stabilizing his ship's spin, he angled his stern toward his line of flight and triggered his drive, full power. The Warhawk bucked and shuddered as he piled on the Gs.

He'd managed to slip in and deliver his punch, but the battle was still going all wrong, so far as he could tell. The main ships in the Confederation squadron were taking a hellacious pounding. God, *Constellation* looked like she was nearly done . . . and *Rebel* was dead and Christ, where were Cameron and his damned, Naga-jinxed warstriders?

Vandis had expended his missiles, but he still had his lasers. He would make another pass. At the very least, some of those gunners jacked into *Karyu*'s fire control might fire at him, instead of at one of his buddies.

Its velocity in one direction killed, *Van'sGuard* began accelerating on a new vector, angling back toward the flame-wracked mountain of *Karyu*.

Some of Dev's confidence had deserted him. The battle had been raging for almost two minutes now, and while *Karyu* had been hit dozens of times, her firepower was unslackened, while his own squadron was dwindling away like a snowball steaming on a hot skillet. If he was going to do it, it had to be now.

One part of him persisted in wondering if there couldn't have been another way to do this thing. If *Daghar* had simply materialized alongside the *Karyu*, with no initial attack, spilling its payload of Naga-enhanced warstriders, maybe they could have fought their way into the Ryu-carrier without this, this *slaughter*.

But the DalRiss ship could not possibly have leaped clear from Alya A to appear alongside the target. They'd had to make the first jump into the system, to a point where Dev could spot *Karyu* and order the next DalRiss Achiever in line . . . "jump *there*." And with the Imperials warned by that first jump and already going to battle stations, he'd had to use the Confederation squadron to blunt their defensive fire.

Hadn't he?

Hadn't he?

The problem with that line of thinking was the realization that ordering *Eagle* and the human squadron into that hellfire had taken precisely the same commitment of will and discipline and judgment as had the order to invest the life, the "soul" of another Achiever.

He was using ships and people the way he would use a tool. The way the DalRiss used their gene-tailored biotechnology, Perceivers, Achievers, and all the rest.

Now he was about to send Katya into that hell, and he didn't even know whether the scheme of piggybacking Nagas to warstriders would work.

He'd thought all along that Xenolinking was like being a god in the scope of new vision, the control, the sheer, vast power of control over mind and matter. The problem was, godlike power conferred godlike responsibility . . . in this case over the lives of his people.

Over Katya's life.

God, what's happened to me? . . .

Chapter 32

No other art is so founded on uncertainties as is the art of war. A lifetime must be put into its preparation, where its exercise takes but a brief while. Experience cannot be gained at any time, or from the study of any

*age, and experience once gained may be put out of date
tomorrow.*

—*The Art of Modern War*
Colonel Hermann Foertsch
C.E. 1940

"*Now!*" Dev's mind screamed. "*Jump!*"

Daghar vanished from one point in space as an Achiever
stretched forth its imagination and will, grasped reality for
the first time in its short life . . . and died. The DalRiss ship
reappeared in the same instant it had disappeared, a vast,
star-shaped mountain that swallowed the warring *Karyu* in its
shadow. Beyond, the blue-black swirl of storm clouds masking
the face of Herakles added the reflection of an eerie, twilight
glow to the shadowed Imperial warship.

A cavern gaped in *Daghar*'s belly, at a wrinkled twist in its
hide where, hours earlier, it had been attached to ShraRish by
what could only be described as a tree root, one as thick and
as massive as any sequoia. Motes spilled from the cavern, tiny,
glittering things that wafted toward *Karyu* on blue-glowing
flickers of magnetic flame, riding the intermeshed lines of
force encircling Herakles and the Heraklean sun itself like the
currents of a solar wind.

Guided by Dev and his link through *Daghar*'s Naga, the
motes hurtled toward the *Karyu*.

"*Go! Go! Go!*"

Katya felt herself falling through the night, suspended,
momentarily, between the vast, outstretched arms of the
Daghar and the elongated, patchwork clutter of armor and
turrets and glowing craters that was an Imperial Ryu-carrier.
In another instant, the last of the warstriders was clear and
Daghar vanished, reappearing as a star in another part of the
sky, the span of a fair-sized continent distant.

Point defense lasers whirled and canted, as fire control
officers noted this new threat and downloaded targeting data
and calculations from the carrier's AI. One battery fired . . .
then another, then a dozen more. To left and to right, above and
below, Warlords and Fastriders, Swiftstriders and Ghostriders,
warstriders by the dozen flared dazzlingly white as outer layers of armor boiled away into space, as the Naga fragments

propelling them first charred, then exploded, unable to handle the megawatt torrents of energy slashing through their mix of natural and artificial cells.

Katya returned fire. Neither Kurt Allen nor Ryan Green had much to do for the fall across to the Imperial ship, so each took a different weapon and began blazing away, aiming for PDL turrets, targeting radars and fire control towers.

Halfway across, the Nagas propelling them reversed polarity and began decelerating.

And warstriders continued to die.

There they were.

Vandis had seen the DalRiss ship swim into visibility a kilometer above *Karyu*'s dorsal surface, blotting out the sun. A moment later, he'd seen the sparkle of the warstriders catching the reflected glare of Herakles as they fell, as they died in the fusillade of defensive fire from the carrier's dorsal hull mounts.

Flashing scant meters above *Karyu*'s armored skin, Van downloaded the commands readying both of his EWC-167 payloads. He'd hung on to them during his first pass since he'd needed to see the target to hit it, and he was damned glad now that he had. A cloudscreen, detonated there, might shield the incoming warstriders for a critical few moments. *Steady . . .*

His Warhawk lurched hard to the left, wobbling out of alignment. *Gok! I'm hit!*

A spacecraft flashed past at the edge of Van's field of vision; his AI captured the image, enhanced it, identified it: an Se-280 Soritaka, one of the best of the Imperial's frontline interceptors. It was slewing around as it passed, lining up for another shot. . . .

. . . and then it exploded in an eye-searing burst of light and radiant fragments.

"Nailed him!" Jothan Bailey's voice cried. "Three-five! See if you can slip a cloudscreen in—"

"Already on the way!" He delivered the firing command, and a missile bearing an EWC-167 warhead streaked across the convoluted gray landscape, following the targeting guidance he'd fed to its gnat-sized brain moments before.

The warload detonated an instant later, a silent flowering of silver between *Karyu*'s hull and the flame-streaked night.

*   *   *

The flash caught Katya by complete surprise, and for a horrible moment she thought she'd been hit.

Then she recognized the burst for what it was, a cloudscreen detonated between the surviving warstriders and the *Karyu*. They were moving fast enough that they would be through the screen in seconds, but in combat seconds routinely measured the fleeting interval between life and death. For a handful of heartbeats, the deadly point defense fire was blocked, the beams scattered and reflected by the silver, mirror's sheen of the expanding cloud. Elsewhere in the sky, ships were dying, but for that critical instant nearly two hundred warstriders sheltered behind that screen . . . and lived.

Then she was through the dispersing cloud of motes. The sensation was almost exactly like that of a warstrider air assault, punching through the cloud layer on flaring jetbacks, dropping toward the surface of a planet. The "ground" was rushing up at Katya, filling her view, as her Naga dragged at the invisible fabric of magnetism in surrounding space, slowing her . . . slowing her . . .

Impact!

Katya's Warlord, weightless, but still packing the inertia of a falling, sixty-ton mass, slammed into *Karyu*'s hull with a concussion that jolted Katya and her crew even through their links.

Through the link with her Xeno, Katya gave it orders. That way. Her Warlord skimmed low across the surface beneath a silver sky. She'd seen something that way during her descent, a crater, a gap in the *Karyu*'s armor, a possible gateway to the spacefaring fortress's inner works.

Other warstriders were falling out of the silver canopy on every side. "With me, Rangers!" Katya cried. "*Charge!*"

Dev could feel himself losing control.

The earlier exhilaration of controlling ten warships and eighty flyers and hundreds of warstriders like extensions of his own body had dwindled away, had vanished, at last, like a half-remembered dream as he'd watched the point defense lasers sweeping Katya's Rangers out of the sky. It had been akin to a juggler with too many balls in the air losing control, watching the balls fall one by one. The relief he'd felt when a fighter's cloudscreen had burst, sheltering the assault group the rest of the way, had been almost overwhelming . . . but it had brought with it an emotion-laden jolt: *I should have thought of that!* Somehow, he'd neglected to have them supplied for the warstrider assault on the Ryu-carrier. For *Katya's* assault, and the oversight could have killed her and every striderjack in her team.

No, that wasn't quite correct. He couldn't forget about cloudscreens, not having used them in his spaceborne assault that had taken *Eagle* from her Japanese masters, and again in his raid at the Imperial shipyard at Athena. They were a basic part of modern space combat tactics, as elementary as radar, and he'd given orders to use them liberally during the approach, to screen the fighters.

What had failed, he feared, was his identification with the men and women occupying the ships and fighters swarming now around the embattled mountain that was *Karyu*. He'd been thinking of Katya's striders, directed through the Naga link of his symbiosis, as a part of him, something that didn't need protection.

Technomegalomania . . . a feeling that he was invulnerable within the aura of high-tech magic that linked him with organic minds and electronic systems distributed across a thousand kilometers of space. What he'd forgotten was that those motes drifting toward the *Karyu* were humans. People. Friends.

Damn! He could have *killed* her! . . .

Elsewhere, the enemy escorts were moving in closer now, and the tide of battle appeared to be swinging around, turning against the Confederation assault force. *Rebel* was dead. So was the corvette *Daring*, savaged by repeated hits by lasers, particle beams, and rounds from the carrier's hivel cannons. *Constellation* was adrift, her engines shut down, her maneuvering system shot to bits, though she continued to blaze away at *Karyu* and the other Imperial ships with as many batteries as she could bring to bear. *Eagle* was practically touching the Ryu-carrier, still fighting and moving but with half of her turrets out of action and a portion of her starboard flank glowing red-hot.

In bloody exchange, one Imperial frigate had been destroyed by a missile salvo launched by *Eagle*, and a light destroyer had been badly damaged. A light cruiser had tried to come up astern of the *Eagle*, but a sudden, unexpected barrage from *Constellation* loosed past the looming, black-and-gray barricade of *Karyu*'s flank had punctured the larger ship's armor in a dozen places and left her powerless, at least for the moment.

And Dev watched over the carnage like a bloody-handed colossus, like a god of war, hurling his people into that sacrificial altar. Enemy fighters were swarming around the beleaguered *Karyu* now, hunting down the warstriders clinging to her back.

God . . . Katya! . . .

Had his own people become such . . . such faceless tools that he no longer thought of them as flesh and blood? . . .

A Soritaka fighter angled down out of a silver sky rapidly tattering away to star-filled black. Soundlessly, gouts of white fire erupted from the hull-metal ground twenty meters away. "Kurt!" Katya screamed over the strider's ICS. "Nail him!"

"Tracking!"

The Warlord's dorsal hivel cannon pivoted, and Katya sensed the vibration of its buzz saw fire . . .

. . . and then the fighter was past them, its wings aglow in sunlight. A missile detonated, and shrapnel slapped off the hull of Katya's warstrider. A second fighter flashed in the sunlight . . . a third . . . a fourth.

"Damn it, they're too fast!" Kurt yelled. "And there's too many of them. Here comes another! . . ."

God, *Karyu*'s whole damned fighter wing must be out here, picking off the warstriders like vermin. Another silent explosion, and Hari Sebree was screaming wildly in her mind's ear, a rasping wail of sheer agony . . . and then his stricken Scoutstrider ruptured in a glowing sphere of hot gas and fragments.

The gap in *Karyu*'s hull yawned a hundred meters ahead, a tunnel, a cavern yawning into the carrier's vitals. Katya exerted her will through the Naga and streaked across broken and flame-streaked metal toward its shelter.

Shaken by the slaughter, shaken worse by his new insight into the bloody workings of his own mind, Dev extended his will, reaching out to the other DalRiss ships. He'd hoped to keep the other DalRiss vessels out of it. Maybe, he thought, he was still thinking like a human after all: *I can't ask that of them.*

And neither could he watch the slaughter of his people and do nothing.

In lightning pulses of thought, he relayed his last orders to the far-flung network of DalRiss ships. The DalRiss ships themselves were unarmed, but extrusions of the Naga fragment nested within each provided a weapon as devastating as any in the Confederation or Imperial arsenals. Drawing on the Dal-ships for power, the Nagas generated intense, tightly focused magnetic fields, using them to accelerate kilogram-sized chunks of themselves to speeds of hundreds of kilometers per second.

An Imperial light cruiser overhauling *Karyu* from astern took a chain of five hard-flung projectiles in rapid-fire succession, the impacts flaring white-hot in searing explosions of vaporized armor and escaping gases. The bow section of the cruiser shattered, the rest of the vessel's length crumpling and folding and splitting wide open beneath that storm of high-velocity death. A corvette took three rounds and vanished in a dazzling nova-flash of light.

Daghar, meanwhile, was moving again, gathering its energies for yet another short-range leap. Dev, his thoughts flickering from vessel to vessel, momentarily sought the bright node of familiar warmth that was Katya. Was she even still alive after descending through that wall of fire?

Yes! He sensed her through her Naga's touch. Briefly, he glimpsed her surroundings through her Warlord's sensors . . . a storm of laser and particle beam fire as she led twenty or thirty of her warstriders toward a gaping, flame-shot maw opening in the side of the Imperial carrier.

But enemy fighters wheeled toward her. She wasn't going to make it. . . .

"Niner-niner," Dev said. "This is Changeling. Get ready, everybody! I'm going to provide a diversion with the *Daghar*! You're all on your own! When you see your chance, take it and go!"

Goodbye, Katya. . . .

"Good luck, all of you. . . ."

Jump! . . .

* * *

So far, the entire battle had been taking place in Herakles's orbit, with all of the vessels involved moving at more or less the same velocity and, except for the back-and-forth slashes of the highly maneuverable fighters, in more or less the same direction.

Now, though, the small suns tucked away within the cavernous overhangs of *Karyu*'s stern flashed on. Cones of charged particles, as hot as the wind sweeping from the face of the sun, blasted astern, driving the monster carrier's ponderous bulk slowly forward, and when by chance they swept across *Daring*'s riddled and dying hulk, they turned armor incandescent and killed instantly every man and woman still alive aboard the crippled corvette.

Faster and faster. Under one gravity of acceleration, the carrier broke orbit, angling out and away from the storm-wracked planet. Those ships that could still move and maneuver followed, Imperial and Confederation both. The hulks—*Rebel* and *Daring* and the dead Imperial escorts—the cripples— *Constellation* and the powerless light cruiser—remained in Heraklean orbit, falling farther and farther behind.

"They're moving!" Katya cried over the tacnet. "The bastards are moving out!" The side of the crater lunged toward her, slammed against her Warlord's hull . . . and then suddenly there was gravity again as acceleration dragged at the strider's frame. Katya's orientation swung wildly for a moment, bringing with it a stab of vertigo. Down was *that* way, toward *Karyu*'s stern, and she was balanced on the lip of a giant crater, together with a handful of other warstriders as the carrier drove "upward" into space.

For a moment, she wondered if the Imperials were running, but immediately she discarded the idea. No, damn it, the Impies were winning . . . *winning*! By breaking orbit, they could lose the *Constellation*, which was continuing to snipe at the Imperial ships even though her main drive was down, and they might well shake some of the other ships that were snapping at her fire-torn flanks like hunting dogs. So far, the only thing keeping the Confederation ships alive was the fact the *Karyu* herself offered pretty good cover.

The enemy fighters had momentarily vanished from the sky,

but they would be back, matching accelerations with the *Karyu* and continuing to blast the warstriders from their toeholds on her hull.

Then *Daghar* was back, two kilometers away and so huge it filled that half of the sky, making Katya feel as though she was clinging to the side of a cliff in a steep-sided valley, with canyon walls extending above and below her for as far as she could see.

She'd heard Dev's transmission, but she'd been too busy at the moment for its meaning to seep through to awareness. *Kuso*, what was the damned fool doing now? . . .

At a range of two kilometers, Dev was throwing rocks again . . . kilogram-sized chunks of the Naga itself, accelerated to high speed and hurled across the narrow gap into *Karyu*'s stern section, just forward of the ravening blast of her flaring plasma drives.

In a ship as large and as massive as the *Karyu*, the vast majority of the ship's hull is armor, or fuel tankage, or skyscraper-sized masses of circuits and power feeds, fusorpacks and sensor leads, all of them multiply redundant and with remarkably few vulnerable points. Ryu-class carriers were designed to *survive*, which meant there were no isolated places that could be precisely targeted for a kill . . . or simply taken out by a stray, lucky shot.

At point-blank range, though, Dev could target the general area directly ahead of *Karyu*'s huge drive venturis. Somewhere beneath meter upon meter of duralloy and fabricrete plating would be the fusion chambers that fed those flaming suns astern . . . and the pumps that fed them with cryo-H, the lasers that flashed the hydrogen to fusion heat, the fusorpack-driven generators that powered the magnetic bottles and containment fields.

A stream of pellets slammed into *Karyu*'s dorsal hull with an impact felt throughout the ship like the blasting of a jackhammer against a tin roof. Cubic meters of duralloy and steel vaporized; a crater yawned; inner circuitry and power feeds and tubing flashed and vanished like cotton in the blast of a blowtorch.

For a fraction of a second, the fusion reaction in *Karyu*'s drive chamber threatened to run wild. As magnetic grids failed, though, the ship's AI recognized the danger of imminent containment field failure and scrammed the entire network. The ship's driving suns winked out. . . .

"Fire control!" Admiral Miyagi screamed over the combat net. "Concentrate on that damned alien!" The ship's drive had just cut out, and they were in free-fall once more. In another moment, that *gaijin* starfish would peel the mighty *Karyu* open from stern to bow. "*Kill it! Kill it!*"

Karyu's remaining weapons swung about, tracking the Alyan monster. The fighters shifted aim too, loosing the first of a swarm of missiles against the huge DalRiss ship's hull.

Zero-G again. Katya drifted above the gaping crater in *Karyu*'s side. The other warstriders that had been trapped with her and been freed when the carrier stopped accelerating were flashing past her and into the cavern. Others, those that had been caught by surprise when the Ryu began accelerating, were catching up now, flashing in from astern on hard-driven Naga mag fields. It was almost eerily peaceful in her small part of the battlefield. The fighters were gone, the PDL fire was concentrating on another target.

Katya was unable to move, however, unable to will the Warlord into the yawning darkness of that cave. Her full attention was focused on the *Daghar*, drifting now a little way astern of the *Karyu*. Imperial fire was tearing into the Alyan city-ship; its organic hide was not nearly so tough or so resilient as duralloy, or the other artificial, nano-layered materials of human technology. Missiles slammed home, each one burying deep beneath the ship-creature's hide before detonating, each detonation flinging huge, fiercely radiating chunks of tissue into space.

It looked as though the entire, star-shaped mass was burning with a radiant, white-glaring flame.

"God!" she screamed. "God! No! *Dev!*"

The DalRiss ship's explosion lit the blackness of space like the utterly silent, eye-searing flash of a supernova.

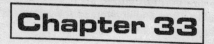

Chapter 33

We pay a high price for being intelligent. Wisdom hurts.

—*Elektra*
Euripides
413 B.C.E.

Once the Confederation warstriders smashed their way on
board the Imperial Ryu-carrier, the outcome of the battle was
a foregone conclusion. There were Imperial Marines aboard
the *Karyu*, and several thousand surviving crewmen, despite
heavy losses during the battle, but Imperial naval vessels did
not routinely carry the sort of weapons, as shipboard sidearms,
that would make any impression at all against a warstrider.

Katya learned later that teams of warstriders, too large and
bulky and clumsy to move or stand upright within the thousands of kilometers of passageways filling that city-sized ship,
had dragged themselves along with weapon-heavy arms gouging and clawing into centimeter-thick bulkheads, or propelled
themselves with the magnetic push of their Nagas, burrowing
headfirst like enormous, duralloy-sheathed moles, tearing up
decks, smashing down partitions, plowing through every barrier in their path. Each time they burned or smashed their way
through interior bulkheads into a new section, they were met
by storms of escaping atmosphere that shrieked out through the
opening in whirling snowstorms of freezing water vapor and
air. As assault teams moved ahead, the ship's damage control
systems sealed off breaches behind them and repressurized
those areas of the ship that had been depressurized, but those
systems could only take so much punishment before they
started to fail. More and more Confederation strider teams
blasted their way aboard, some through air locks, some through
shattered gun turrets and external hardpoints, and most, like

those with Katya, through the breaches blasted open by naval gunfire and warflyer assault and missiles, and soon whole sections of the ship were closing down as cold, hard vacuum claimed their passageways and compartments, and severed power feeds plunged them into darkness.

In all, 265 Rangers made it aboard the *Karyu* and began fighting their way forward, one passageway at a time. Imperial Marines, many in heavy armor, fought back, but the only casualty was the pilot of a Scoutstrider that had already suffered heavy damage from laser fire during the approach. The hand laser fire from a team of Imperial Marines blew an already weakened access panel; when the circuit boards beyond vaporized, a bolt of high-amp current downloaded through the unfortunate pilot's brain, killing him instantly.

Marines or crew personnel who tried to make stands at critical corridor junctions were fried by blasts from lasers or particle guns, or cut down by blasts from hivel cannons or machine guns. Few of the defenders cared to stand in place and fight back when the corridor-filling bulk of a Ghostrider or Swiftstrider dragged itself into view. As a result, many of the ship's larger compartments—recreation decks and barracks, supply vaults and hangar bays—grew more and more crowded with ship's personnel who'd given up the fight and were simply looking for a place, anyplace, to escape the crawling, armored behemoths. Those who could reach *Karyu*'s escape pods and lifeboats abandoned ship, filling circumambient space with the drifting sparkle of strobing emergency beacons.

Miyagi broadcast a general call to all personnel to fight to the death. Few in his crew had radios or compatches, however, and most intercom channels were off-line by that time, so the only ones to get the order were the marines. These retreated when they could and fought to the death when they had to. Soon it was clear that even the most valiant efforts—headlong, zero-G charges down fire-filled corridors dragging satchels of explosives—could avail nothing against warstriders, which could spot such teams as soon as they came into view and sweep them with laser or projectile fire.

Twenty-eight minutes after the first warstriders smashed their way through blast-charred bulkheads and into the still-pressurized portion of the ship, the first warstriders reached the bridge, buried at the ship's core some two hundred meters from the first entry point. At that point, a pale and shaking Admiral Miyagi emerged from the link module from which he'd been directing the battle, then brought the muzzle of his own laser pistol to his head and pulled the trigger.

His second-in-command broadcast the call for surrender.

Katya saw little of this at the time. Dev was dead . . . *dead.* The agony of that realization filled her mind, blocking her thoughts, blinding her to the battle that was continuing to flash and stab across the heavens. She knew that she ought to join the fight. Damn it all . . . this amounted to dereliction of duty, hanging here in space watching men die.

She opened her link to the Naga, urging it to move.

She failed.

Oh, *kuso.* She ran a diagnostic, found nothing wrong, and tried again. Still nothing. "Kurt? Ryan?"

"We're here, Colonel."

"I . . . I'm having some trouble."

Kurt's voice sounded a bit distant. "I think there's a fault. Maybe in the interface with the Naga. I'm working on it."

"We'll hold position here okay," Ryan told her. "Don't think they'll be needing us, though. Everything looks pretty much in hand."

"I'm . . . I'm sorry about the commodore, Colonel," Kurt Allen said. "I know you two were pretty close."

"Yeah. We were . . . close."

"Can we do anything?"

"Sign off. Let me . . . deal with it. Okay?"

"Sure, Colonel," Ryan said. "We'll be on sentry, and jacked in if you need us."

"And let me know as soon as you have the problem fixed. We should . . . should be moving."

The rest of the battle was clearly almost over. Though the human ships had been badly handled, the surviving DalRiss vessels, most still fresh and relatively untouched by the storm thus far, were continuing to hurl their high-velocity projectiles, slamming them one after another into the Imperial ships. Even before *Karyu* gave up, several of the smaller Imperial ships were drawing off at high speed. When *Karyu*'s XO broadcast his surrender, the rest of the Imperial battlefleet was already more than willing to break off the fight and begin accelerating for open space. One after another, they arrowed out into the night beyond Herakles's orbit, then vanished into K-T space.

The Confederation ships, content to hold what they'd won in orbit, did not pursue.

Against all odds, the Confederation—and their DalRiss allies—were victorious.

But at what cost?

Katya stared at the fuzzy, glowing cloud that was keeping pace with the *Karyu* on its outbound orbit—*Daghar*'s funeral pyre, still radiating the fierce heat of its brief, furious ignition. The debris from that explosion continued to drift out from the center of the blast, retaining the velocity it had had before the explosion. Since they'd already achieved escape velocity from Herakles, it would no doubt fall into an extended and highly elliptical orbit around Mu Herculis.

Katya had already probed that cloud with her Warlord's radar. The largest piece she'd been able to find measured perhaps a meter across . . . one meter, out of a structure that once had been two *thousand* meters across.

"Oh, Dev!" She cried out, suddenly overcome by a devastating loneliness. "*Dev!*"

"I'm . . . here, Katya."

The jolt nearly knocked her off-line. She said nothing, but stared wildly into the glowing mist left from the explosion, here thoughts racing. *Oh, God oh God I'm going mad he's dead I must've brain-burned oh dear God he's dead oh God—*

"Please, Katya. You're not crazy. And . . . I don't think I am, either."

"Dev . . . Dev . . ." She stopped, groping for feelings that were whipcracking through her brain. *Dev you goker don't do this to me you can't possibly be alive!*

But she ran a quick systems check, looking for the source of the feed that was carrying that voice, so eerily like Dev's on-line speech.

It was coming through the Naga.

"You know how we've speculated about the Naga?" Dev's voice asked her. "About how their subcellular makeup is an awful lot like networks of human neurons . . . but it's also like a computer network, in a way, with lots and lots of separate processors. That's how they can encode memories that, that go back billions of years, in matrices of nanotechnic subcells."

You're dead I saw you die oh Dev, Dev, Dev I miss you so much!

"I miss you too, love. And I guess I am dead, in a way. My body certainly died in that explosion."

That jolted her too, but the shock smashed the chain of uncontrollable thoughts racing through her brain, made her stop and pull her thinking back into some semblance of rational cause and effect, stimulus and response.

"Dev?"

"Yes, Katya."

"Where are you?"

"I . . . I think I'm in the network of Naga fragments in the DalRiss fleet. I find . . . yes. I find I can shift from ship to ship. I'm in your warstrider now. With you. At least a part of me is."

The thought was at once bizarre, almost horrible . . . and reassuring.

"We've known for a long time that Nagas are very good at patterning things. And they can think . . . very quickly. Faster than the DalRiss. Somehow, I'm still not sure how, they, they patterned my thoughts. Made a replica of me, I guess, but as an electronic pattern, stored within the matrix of their organic computers."

"Are you . . . are you real? Or a copy?" The questions hurt, brutally direct.

"Kat, that question is meaningless. I remember myself as Dev Cameron. I remember my whole life . . . better, I think, than I ever could with a brain of flesh and blood. I remember . . . oh, God. Things from when I was little. My mother. My father . . ."

"Dev . . ."

"I remember making love with you in that ascraft." She *felt* him smile. "Twice."

"I saw *Daghar* explode."

"Yes."

"Your body was destroyed."

"Yes. But, well . . . where is your mind, Katya?"

"*Mind* is the interaction of all of the patterns of neural stimuli in the active brain, Dev. There's no such thing as a mind apart from body. There's no such thing as a *soul*."

"I used to believe that. I'm not so sure now. The DalRiss know a hell of a lot more about how brain and body work than we do, and I think, I *think* that they believe in souls. Spirits, if you like.

"Maybe all we need to know at this point, though, is that mind, whatever it is, must work over teleoperational distances, somehow. Look, it doesn't matter whether you see over optic nerves a few centimeters long, or by way of optic sensors and a lasercom link a few million kilometers long, right?"

"Of course. That's the whole point behind teleoperation. Or warstriders, for that matter."

"Okay. While I was linked through the Nagas in the DalRiss fleet, I was . . . I was touching the other ships. At one point, I looked for you. I could feel you over the link. Was that, that sensation traveling to my mind aboard *Daghar*? Or was my mind traveling to you, here aboard your warstrider?"

"I think the question is meaningless."

"Don't be so sure, Kat. When someone says his mind is elsewhere . . ." He stopped, and she heard his chuckle. She shivered. It was as though he really was right there beside her. "Anyway, the Naga on one of the other ships must have picked up the pattern of my mind when the *Daghar* exploded."

"Dev, you're not a pattern. *People* aren't patterns!"

"Maybe not. But if you can call mind a set of programs run in parallel . . ." The voice stopped, pausing for a moment. "Here's one way to think of it, Kat. We've talked before about the Nagas being like an enormous computer network. Each fragment is a node, itself a collection of some trillions or quadrillions of molecule-sized computers. Organic nanotechnics."

"Yes . . . ."

"The whole could be considered to be a massively parallel networked system, a widely distributed processing network with one hell of a lot of redundancy. I, the important part of 'I,' anyway, was distributed throughout a large part of the whole system when *Daghar* blew. It patterned my mental software, copied everything that I was . . . or saved it, or whatever term you want to use. Think of it . . ." and she'd felt him grin. "Think of it as having me permanently jacked in. The important thing is, I'm *alive* . . . sort of, anyway. And that's enough for me right now."

"Are you, Dev?" *Dev I want to see you want to hold you be held oh Dev I want you inside me again oh please—*

"I'm afraid I can't, my love. Not anymore. But I'm here. With you. For as long as you want me."

Her thoughts were crumbling again, veering into chaotic nonsense. She battled for control. She felt as though she was going to cry . . . she *wanted* to cry, and yet, linked into the Warlord's AI, she couldn't.

Warstriders, she found, couldn't cry.

Epilogue

Many wonders there be, but none more wondrous than man.

—*Antigone*
Sophocles
Fifth century B.C.E.

Travis Sinclair, it turned out, had made it safely to Liberty. It wasn't necessary, though, for the Confederation fleet to track him from system to system, as planned. Ten hours after the battle, a Confederation frigate, the *Freedom*, jumped back into the outskirts of the Heraklean system in order to check on what the Imperial fleet was doing. When Darlene Vonnegut, *Freedom*'s skipper, found Miyagi's battlefleet scattered and fled, his flagship still broadcasting its surrender call, she jumped back to Liberty to summon a task force, scraped together from those ships that had managed to flee the debacle at Herakles.

And a good thing, too, Katya thought, for the only ships able to enter K-T space in the entire Confederation fleet were *Tarazed*, *Mirach*, and *Vindemiatrix*, and sending those lightly armed starships hopping from system to system in search of the missing Confederation fleet would have verged on foolhardiness. *Eagle* and the other Confederation survivors of Second Herakles might be jump-capable again someday, depending on how the repairs went . . . but it wouldn't be soon.

"I was damned sorry to hear about Dev," Sinclair told her. It was nearly three months after the battle. They were on Liberty, in the new Confederation headquarters in the capital city of Lincoln. They sat alone together, in Sinclair's office. A viewall looked out over the city, and the sullen, ember-bright glow of Liberty's sun, 70 Ophiuchi A.

She nodded and managed a smile. "Thanks, General."

"Are you all right?"

Again, she nodded.

"That's the Katya I know. There's a hell of a lot to do yet, even now. I'm going to miss Dev. I would miss you, if we lost you as well."

"I'm not sure what you need me for now. The war, well, the war's over, isn't it?"

"If the truce holds. If the Emperor ratifies the new agreement. If hotheads on one of the occupied Confederation worlds don't launch an attack on the Imperials during the next few weeks. A lot of ifs . . . but yes, I think the war is over."

"Thank God."

"Yes. And thank the people who bought that victory for us. People like Dev."

Clearly, the Empire, the entire Hegemony, had been shaken from Frontier to Core Worlds to Earth herself by the Battle of Second Herakles. The knowledge that the Confederation had allied with the DalRiss had proven to be at least as critical for this revolution as an alliance with the nation of France had been in another revolution, over 760 years before. A cease-fire had gone into effect almost at once, and so far it had lasted, even on New America, where armed guerrillas continued to share the world with Imperial occupation forces. Negotiations were under way, both on Earth and on Liberty. Imperial recognition of the Confederation was widely accepted as fact; all that remained was to map out the actual extent of their victory. Rebel worlds currently unoccupied by Imperials, like Liberty and Rainbow, would certainly receive full independence. Occupied planets, those like New America and Eridu, would probably be allowed to go, or the question might be put to a vote ratifying the decision on each world. Other worlds that had indicated their desire to be free by signing the Declaration of Reason, but which had not joined in the fighting, planets like Loki and Juanyekundu and Deseret . . . well, their fates still had to be worked out.

But *peacefully*.

Both sides were sick of war.

As for the DalRiss, they would be all right as well. She'd heard later that the long-expected Imperial fleet had, indeed, arrived at ShraRish some weeks after the fight at Herakles. They'd dropped out of K-T space, taken up orbit . . . and vanished.

Could Achievers make other things go away? Or bend space in unexpected ways? Gods, so little was known yet about these beings, able to bend reality with a thought. It was a dreadful mistake to underestimate them.

"Actually, General, I think what I need most right now is work."

"That's the spirit. I'm sure Dev would approve."

She almost laughed out loud. No one but her knew of Dev's curious survival.

They'd talked about it a long time, after she'd been picked up and returned to the *Eagle*. When she'd jacked in to ViRcom a message to *Freedom* and the other Confederation reinforcements, he'd been there.

She'd seen him . . . *touched* him. And they'd made love together on a nameless, deserted beach with the ocean surf crashing nearby. All of the myriad and intricate programming that had been Dev, it seemed, had been saved, and that included the far cruder programs that had once been resident in his now vaporized RAM. What was a program but saved information? The information was still there, distributed through the DalRiss fleet.

They made love, and she tried not to think about the fact that his touch, the feel of him on her and around her and inside of her, was not real.

What was "real," anyway? She closed her eyes and downloaded the scene to her biological memory once again.

"They want me to go with them," Dev told her afterward, as they lay together on the wet sand. "I'll be gone a long time."

"What? Who?" She'd been wondering about Dev's body.

It was just information, after all, and the Naga might have preserved a pattern of that as well. . . .

"The DalRiss, of course."

"Can't you . . . stay? We could talk with Sinclair, maybe see about having the DalRiss migrate to human space. . . ."

"Uh-uh, Kat. They sacrificed a lot to help us here. And I sure as hell don't want anyone trying to lay claim to their fleet just because the . . . call it the *soul* of one human striderjack is somehow trapped inside their communications network."

"What . . . so you're going with the DalRiss exodus? Where are they going?"

Again, she felt the warmth of his infectious smile. He couldn't be dead, he *couldn't.* She couldn't be imagining his warmth, his humor, his smell, his *presence* in this much detail, and it had none of the hollow emptiness of a recorded encounter. He, everything about him, was too real. Somehow, the Naga link had preserved so very much more of his personality than words and thoughts alone.

"You know what the DalRiss think about life," he said. "It's damned near a religion for them."

"Yes."

"We're going . . . out there. Beyond human space. Jumping from star to star, looking for life. They believe—and I believe with them—that the galaxy, the whole universe is chock brim full to overflowing with life . . . and tidal theories and prebiotic matrices be damned. They want me to navigate for them."

"But you haven't been out there. I thought you had to have been to a place, to pass its feel on to the Achiever."

"Maybe what they really want is a human viewpoint. A human outlook on the universe. Remember, both the DalRiss and the Naga are blind to the visible spectrum. They've both learned to see, in the same way that we've learned to 'hear' radio with artificial receivers, but we have a clearer perspective on the universe than they do, the way it's made, the way it really is . . . at least in some ways. I can help them."

Katya sighed. "I find it hard to believe that humans can see *anything* clearly."

"I know what you mean. But, well, the perspective of seeing things from someone else's vantage point, that always makes things clearer in the end. Don't you think?"

"Dev, I don't want to lose you. Not again."

"I'll be back. But I think you need some time on your own. Time to get used to . . ."

"To you being a ghost? Maybe so. And maybe those DalRiss biological wizards can do something about a body for you, someday."

"Maybe. Right now, I don't want to even think about it. Katya, I *want* this. You know, since my memories have been coming back, from my childhood, I . . . I'd forgotten how much I wanted the wonder of it all. The stars. Katya, the *stars* . . ."

"You always wanted to be a shipjacker, didn't you? Until you got sidetracked into the warstriders."

"It was a good sidetrack. I met you there, right? I wouldn't have missed that for anything."

"I'm glad I knew you, Dev."

"Me too. And . . . I *will* be back."

She'd not told him, even then, that when she'd last seen a DalRiss, aboard one of their ships, the being had "looked" at her with the curiously scanning crescent of its head . . . and mentioned the new life growing deep in her belly.

Katya had deliberately kept a piece of Dev for herself, that last time aboard the ascraft, by switching off the part of her cephlink that regulated her sexual rhythms.

"I love you, Dev," she'd told him.

And, through the Xenolink, she'd felt his lips brush hers, as warm and as sweet as reality.

Terminology and Glossary

AI: Artificial Intelligence. Since the Sentient Status Act of 2204, higher-model networking systems have been recognized as "self-aware but of restricted purview," a legal formula that precludes enfranchisement of machine intelligences.

Alya: Naked-eye star Theta Serpentis (63 Serpentis) 130 light-years from Sol. A double star system, home to the DalRiss.

Analogue: Computer-generated "double" of a person, used to handle routine business and communications through ViRcom linkage.

Ascraft: Aerospace craft. Vehicles that can fly both in space and in atmosphere, including various transports, fighters, and shuttles.

Cephlink: Implant within the human brain allowing direct interface with computer-operated systems. It contains its own microcomputer and RAM storage and is accessed through sockets, usually located in the subject's temporal bones above and behind each ear. Limited (non-ViR) control and interface is possible through neural implants in the skin, usually in the palm of one hand.

Cephlink RAM: Also RAM. Random Access Memory, part of the microcircuitry within the cephlink assembly. Used for memory storage, message transfer, linguistics programming, and the storage of complex digital codes used in cephlinkage access. An artificial extension of human intelligence.

Compatch: Small radio transceiver worn on the skin and jacked into a T-socket. Allows cephlink-to-link radio communications.

Cryo-H: Liquid hydrogen cooled to a few degrees absolute, used as fuel for fusion power plants aboard striders, ascraft, and other vehicles. Sometimes called "slush hydrogen."

C-socket: Cervical socket, located in subject's cervical spine, near the base of his neck. Directs neural impulses to jacked equipment, warstriders, construction gear, heavy lifters, etc.

DalRiss: Nonhuman intelligence first contacted in 2540. Native to Alya B-V (GhegnuRish), they are highly advanced in biological sciences, relatively backward in engineering and metallurgical sciences. Compound name reflects use of Dal, a gene-engineered organism as "mount" by Riss ("Master").

Durasheath: Armor grown as composite layers of diamond, duralloy, and ceramics; light, flexible, and very strong.

Embedded Interface: Network of wires and neural feeds embedded in the skin—usually in the palm near the base of the thumb—used to access and control simple computer hardware. Provides control and datafeed functions only, not full-sensory input. Used to activate T- and C-socket jacks, to pass authorization and credit data, and to retrieve printed or vocal data "played" inside the user's mind. Also called 'face or skin implant.

Genegineering, bionangineering: Use of nanotechnology to restructure life-forms for medical or ornamental reasons.

Genie: Gene-engineered human. On some worlds they have full rights of ordinary humans. On others they are property. Appearing in many different forms, they are used for a variety of purposes, from mining to heavy labor to companionship to entertainment to sex.

Gun tower: Unmanned sentry outpost armed with various energy or projectile weapons. May be automated, remote-controlled, or directed by an on-site, low-level AI.

Hegemony: Also Terran Hegemony. World government representing fifty-seven nations on Earth, plus the Colonial Authorities of the seventy-eight colonized worlds. Technically sovereign, it is dominated by Imperial Japan, which has a veto in its legislative assembly.

Herakles: Mu Herculis III. Former colony world 26.2 light-years from Sol overrun by Xenos in 2515. Later occupied by Confederation forces.

Hivel Cannon: A turret-mounted rotary cannon (the term *hivel* comes from "high velocity"). Similar to twentieth-century CIWS systems, it fires bursts of depleted uranium slugs with a rate of fire as high as fifty per second. Usually controlled by an onboard AI, its primary function is antimissile defense. It can also be voluntarily controlled and used against other targets.

Jacker: Slang for anyone with implanted jacks for neural interface with computers, machinery, or communications networks. Specifically applied to individuals who jack-in for a living, as opposed to recreational jackers, or "recjacks."

Kansei no Otoko: "The Men of Completion." *Nihonjin* faction at Court and within the Imperial Staff dedicated to cleansing upper levels of Imperial civilian and military organizations of *gaijin* influence.

Kokorodo: Literally "Way of the Mind." A mental discipline practiced by Imperial military jackers to achieve full mental and physical coordination through AI linkage.

K-T Plenum: Extraspacial realm at the hyperdimensional interface between normal fourspace and the Quantum Sea. From Nihongo *Kamisama no Taiyo*, literally "Ocean of God." Starships navigate through the K-T plenum.

Liberty: 70 Ophiuchi A III. Colony world 16.7 light-years from Sol.

Loki: 36 Ophiuchi C II. Colony world 17.8 light-years from Sol. Xenophobe incursion here defeated in 2540.

Lung Chi: DM+32° 2896 (Chien) IV. World terraformed by colonists of Manchurian descent. Overrun by Xenophobes in 2538.

Nangineering: Nanotechnic engineering. Use of nanotechnic devices in building or in medicine.

Nano-Ds: Nano-disassemblers. Weapon delivered by mag-accelerated projectile consisting of billions of submicroscopic machines programmed to disassemble molecular bonds. A high concentration of nano-Ds can cause several kilos of mass to disintegrate into its component molecules within seconds.

Nanoflage: Nanofilm on military vehicles designed to transmit colors and textures of vehicle's immediate surroundings. Selectively reflective, it does not reflect bright light or motion.

Navsim: ViRsimulation used in ship navigation.

New America: 26 Draconis IV. Frontier colony 48.6 light years from Sol.

Null: Person possessing no cephlink hardware and unable to engage in financial transactions, interface with computers, or engage in useful work. Large numbers of nulls on Frontier worlds and even in some areas on Earth constitute a growing and problematical lower class.

Prebiotic: A world similar to Earth in the distant past, before the evolution of life. Possessing primitive atmospheres of CO_2, water, methane, and ammonia, they can be tailored through terraforming techniques to eventually develop Earthlike environments.

Quantum Sea: Energy continuum reflected in "vacuum fluctuation," the constant appearance and reabsorption of vast quantities of energy on a subatomic scale. Tapped by starships operating within the K-T plenum.

Rainbow: 36 Ophiuchi A-II. Colony world 17.8 light-years from Sol.

Rank: Terran Hegemony ranks are based on the Imperial Japanese rank structure, though the English terminology is preferred in common usage. A rough comparison of rank in the Hegemony military, as compared to late twentieth-century America, is given below:

Enlisted Ranks

	U.S. Army/Marines	Imperial Military
	Private 2nd class/(no equivalent)	*Nitto hei*
E-2	Private/PFC	*Itto hei*
	Superior Private/(no equivalent)	*Jotto hei*
E-3	PFC/Lance Corporal	*Heicho*
E-4	Corporal/Corporal	*Gocho*
E-5	Sergeant/Sergeant	*Gunso*
E-9	Sgt. Major/Sgt. Major	*Socho*
WO	Warrant Officers (CWO)	*Jun-i*

Commissioned Ranks

	U.S. Army/Navy	Imperial Military
O-0	Cadet	*Seito*
O-1	2nd Lieutenant/Ensign	*Sho-i*
O-2	Lieutenant/Lieutenant (jg)	*Chu-i*
O-3	Captain/Lieutenant	*Tai-i*
O-4	Major/Lieutenant Commander	*Shosa*
O-5	Lieutenant Colonel/Commander	*Chusa*
O-6	Colonel/Captain	*Taisa*
O-8	Major General/Rear Admiral	*Shosho*
O-9	Lieutenant General/Vice Admiral	*Chujo*
O-10	General/Admiral	*Taisho*
O-11	General of the Army/Fleet Admiral	*Gensui*

Rank within the Confederation forces was initially based on the Hegemony model, but later changed to the pre-Imperial form once used in North America.

Recjack: Using implants for recreational purposes. These range from participation in ViRdramas to shared multiple sensual stimulation to direct stimulation of the hypothalmic pleasure centers (PC-jacking).

Riderslot: Opening in an ascraft or other transport's hull designed to receive striders. Usually equipped with grippers, magnetic locks, and autoplug ICS and datafeed connectors.

Sekkodan: The Imperial Scout Service, tasked with exploring and cataloging new worlds, as well as operating high-speed courier ships between the worlds of the *Shichiju.*

Shakai: "Society." The elitist, upper-class culture of Imperial Earth.

Shichiju: Literally "The Seventy." Japanese term for the seventy-eight worlds in seventy-two systems so far colonized by Man.

Sky-el: Elevator used to travel between a planetary ring and the surface of the planet. A cheap and efficient way of moving people and cargo back and forth from surface to orbit.

Slang, profanity:
  brain-burned: Someone addicted to direct stimulation of the hypothalmic pleasure center (PC-jacking). Also jolted or jolt-rider.
  easy feed: Slang expression for "No problem," or "That's okay."
  gok, goking: Sexual obscenity. From Japanese *goku,* "rape."
  iceworld: Military slang. "Stay cool. I'm cool."
  I'm linked: "I'm with you." "I'll go along with that."
  jackin' Jill: Girlfriend, especially as a casual RJ sex partner.
  null, nullhead: Stupid. Empty-headed. By association, crazy. Also, people without jacks, unable to interact in technic society.
  odie: Let's odie = "Let's do it." "Let's move." From Japanese *odori,* "dance."
  yuji: From Japanese *yujo.* Comrades-in-arms. People sharing a warrior's bond.

Slot: 1) Linkage module for human controller. Warstriders have one, two, or three slots; a three-slotter strider has places for a commander, pilot, and weapons tech.

2) Space for equipment aboard transport. Ascraft have "slots" to carry four or six warstriders. (Slang) By popular usage, a place for a person in an organization, e.g., a "slot in the infantry."

Synchorbit: That point, different for each world, at which a satellite has an orbital period exactly matching the planet's rotation. Planetary sky-els rise from a world's equator to extensive constructions—factories, habitats, and other orbital facilities—in synchorbit.

Synchorbital: Facilities built at synchorbit.

Tacsim: ViRsimulation used to plan or coordinate combat.

Tacsit: Military slang for "tactical situation."

Teikokuno Heiwa: "The Imperial Peace." The Pax Japonica.

Teikokuno Hoshi: "Star of the Empire." Imperial medal for supreme service to the Emperor.

Tenno Kyuden: "Palace of Heaven." Seat of Imperial government, located at Singapore Orbital.

Terraform: Also T-form. Converting an existing planetary atmosphere and environment to one that supports humans.

T-socket: Temporal socket. Usually paired, one on each side of subject's skull, in temporal bone above and behind the ear. Used for full-sensory, full-feedback jacking in conjunction with an AI system, including experiencing ViR, full-sensory communications, and computer control of ships or vehicles.

ViR, Virtual Reality: Made possible by cephalic implants, virtual reality is the "artificial reality" of computer interfaces that allows, for example, a human pilot to "become" the strider or missile he is piloting, to "live" a simplay, or to "see" things that do not really exist save as sophisticated computer software. An artificial world existing within the human mind that, through AI technology, can be shared with others.

ViRcom: Full-sensory linked communication. Linker enters a chamber and plugs into communications net. He can then engage in conversation with one or more other humans or their computer analogues as though all were present together.

ViRdrama: Recreational jacking allowing full-sensory experience through cephlinkage. Linker can participate in elaborate canned shows or AI-monitored games. Two or more linkers can share a single scenario, allowing them to interact with one another.

ViRlinked: Connected mind-to-mind through interface software, cephlinks, and an AI.

ViRpersona: The image of self projected in virtual reality dramas or communications. Clothing styles and even personal appearance can be purchased as a cephlink program, much as someone would buy new clothes.

Warstrider: Also strider. Battlefield armor on two or four legs, giving it high mobility over rough terrain. Generally consists of a fuselage slung between two legs, and equipped either with two arms mounting weapons or with interchangeable weapons pods. Sizes include single-slotters (eight to twelve tons), dual-slotters (ten to thirty tons), three-slotters (twenty-five to seventy tons), and special vehicles such as Armored Personnel Walkers that carry large numbers of troops.

Who-was: Rumor, scuttlebutt. Corruption of Japanese *uwasa*.

Xeno, Xenophobe: Human name for the life-form that first attacked the human colony on An-Nur II in 2498. So-called because of their apparent hatred or fear of other life-forms.

Investigations within the Alya system in 2541 proved Xeno-phobes are machine-organic hybrids evolved from fairly simple organisms billions of years ago. Later referred to as "Naga" from a Hindu serpent deity.

AVONOVA PRESENTS
AWARD-WINNING NOVELS
FROM MASTERS OF SCIENCE FICTION

WULFSYARN
by Phillip Mann 71717-4/ $4.99 US

MIRROR TO THE SKY
by Mark S. Geston 71703-4/ $4.99 US/ $5.99 Can

THE DESTINY MAKERS
by George Turner 71887-1/ $4.99 US/ $5.99 Can

A DEEPER SEA
by Alexander Jablokov 71709-3/ $4.99 US/ $5.99 Can

BEGGARS IN SPAIN
by Nancy Kress 71877-4/ $4.99 US/ $5.99 Can

FLYING TO VALHALLA
by Charles Pellegrino 71881-2/ $4.99 US/ $5.99 Can

ETERNAL LIGHT
by Paul J. McAuley 76623-X/ $4.99 US/ $5.99 Can

THE FANTASTIC ROBOT SERIES

ISAAC ASIMOV'S
ROBOTS
IN TIME

by Hugo and Nebula Award Nominee
William F. Wu

EMPEROR
76515-1/ $4.99 US/ $5.99 Can

PREDATOR
76510-1/ $4.99 US/ $5.99 Can

MARAUDER
76511-X/ $4.99 US/ $5.99 Can

WARRIOR
76512-8/ $4.99 US/ $5.99 Can

DICTATOR
76514-4/ $4.99 US/ $5.99 Can